KREWE'S KNIGHT

KREWE'S
KNIGHT

GERALDINE GRAEBEL

TATE PUBLISHING
AND ENTERPRISES, LLC

Published by Tate Publishing & Enterprises, LLC
127 E. Trade Center Terrace | Mustang, Oklahoma 73064 USA
1.888.361.9473 | www.tatepublishing.com

Tate Publishing is committed to excellence in the publishing industry. The company reflects the philosophy established by the founders, based on Psalm 68:11,
"The Lord gave the word and great was the company of those who published it."

Book design copyright © 2013 by Tate Publishing, LLC. All rights reserved.
Cover design by Rtor Maghuyop
Interior design by Stephanie Mora

Published in the United States of America

ISBN: 978-1-62854-841-9
1. Fiction / Romance
2. Fiction / Mystery
13.11.04

CAST OF CHARACTERS

ALEXIS ROCHELLE TALBOT
A graduating college senior seeking adventure and a new future.

LUCIAN ALBERT DEVEREAUX
President of Devereaux International.

JANET WINSLOW
Friend and classmate to Alex at the University of Victoria, B.C., Canada. A best friend.

AIMEE' DEVEREAUX
Aunt to Lucian, Sister to Jean-Claude Devereaux. The keeper of the secrets.

LANGLEY ALLAN DEVEREAUX
Younger brother to Lucian, A ne're-do-well, the Black Sheep of the family???

CHARLES HENRY DELACOURT
Old friend and school chum to Lucian. Old family that lost fortune to gambling

COURTNEY ANDERSON
Ex-Executive Secretary to Lucian Devereaux. One angry lady.

GENEVIEVE DUPREE
Antique Shoppe Proprietress and landlady to Alex.

JEAN-CLAUDE DEVEREAUX
Patriarch/Founder of Devereaux International. Uneasy in retirement.

LUCINDA CASEY DEVEREAUX	Youngest child and only daughter to JeanClaude. Little Cindy, the newest debutante to the Mardi Gras Balls!
JOSEPH CHARLES THORNDYKE	Older brother of Jonathon Preston Thorndyke. Alex's father's brother? Alex's uncle?
JONATHON PRESTON THORNDYKE	A.K.A. Joe Talbot???
SARA BILLINGSLY TALBOT SAMANTHA BILLINGSLY	Alex's deceased mother. Samantha Billingsly?? A.K.A. Sara Billingsly Talbot???
JUDD CONKLIN	a young hoodlum, a bank robber, gunned down by police in an out-of-town bank job.
SIMONE' SORREL & PATRICIA LACOMBE	Seamstresses and dressmakers.
ANNE LOUISE	Charles full-time nurse.
CANDIDA (CANDY) Y DE LA GONZALEZ DE CHAVEZ	Secretary/Assistant for Alex.

CHAPTER ONE

Alex Talbot clutched her ticket tightly, scanning the train terminal with interest. She watched the ever-changing arrival and departure schedules flashing overhead on a wall-mounted unit, traveling at dizzying speed. The hustle and bustle, rattling and chugging of trains moving into and leaving the station was fascinating, if not deafening. The constant flow of traffic entering, then pulling out of the terminal, trains and passengers alike, never ceased to amaze her and only relieved her to be clutching her own ticket so tightly. It was hard to believe she was really here at the Seattle Amtrak Terminal waiting for her train to New Orleans gripping a one-way ticket to a great new job, an exciting new life, a new city, and adventure. Such a change from little Briscombe Bay, Washington. A place where nothing ever happened, nothing exciting for sure. This was so exciting, but frightening, too. Ticket in one hand, her mother's precious shoebox tucked safely up under her other arm, with a handful of New Orleans brochures balanced on top, Alex sat back calming herself. She needed reading material to keep her mind occupied on this trip. She did not want to think on this trip taking her so far from home and the only life she could remember.

So much had happened, so quickly, she still felt a little shell-shocked, as if her head were still spinning. End-of-term reports, papers, and tests had given way to the excitement of commencement ceremonies, then thoughts and dreams of an exciting and glamorous future. This jubilant and exhilarating period was marred only by a niggling, insistent worry over her mother's nagging, persistent cough. The persistent cough that had so rapidly deteriorated into a chronic, then critical, and finally into the symptoms of a life-threatening and terminal condition.

Alex was relieved her mother's death had come so mercifully fast, though not as painlessly as she would have liked. Only s hand-written note awaited her when she finally reached her mother's hospital room after competing her last shift at the University Book Store. The note had directed her to this shoebox with mysterious and cryptic clues. This shoe box with small bits of her past. This shoebox that was evidently so important to her mother, but vaguely disturbing and frightening to Alex. An uneasy feeling settled into the pit of her stomach, moreover, she could not bring herself to examine the contents of the box right at that moment. The intense and urgent tone hidden in her mother's note only heightened Alex's fears and uneasiness in addition, tightening her arm around the shoebox pulling it closer to her side.

*All Aboard! All Aboard! Leaving for
Portland**Las Vegas**Salt Lake City**Riverton**Grand Island
Des Moines Chicago**Springfield**St. Louis**
Little Rock**Shreveport**New Orleans**
and All Points Southeast**All Aboard!*

The conductor's litany droned on over the PA as the train pulled into the station and at the gate just behind Alex. She jumped to her feet, spilling the brochures and shoebox onto the floor in front of her. Seeing her dismay, a porter offered his assistance along with a luggage dolly. The train had pulled to a stop only a short distance behind her, as the porter gently pried the crumpled ticket from her hand, noting the date, destination, and compartment number assigned by the agent. The porter loaded her luggage onto his dolly and said, "Please follow me and allow me to drop off your luggage in your compartment. Stay close, there may be many passengers filling the narrow passageways, at least until we leave the station." Alex was impressed by the way, he expedited her travel and forms to get her quickly checked in and safely aboard the train. Finally, rousing herself into action Alex stood and followed the porter down the gangplank and toward the train compartments. Her porter deposited her ticket with the ticketing agent who punched the ticket and waved them on through to the compartments. Following the porter down the long corridor until arriving at one marked "This is a private compartment," the porter said depositing her luggage inside the compartment. "Just let me check out the compartment to make sure it has been cleaned and readied for you," the porter replied checking doors and opening windows and airing out the compartment. "Can I help in any other way?" he asked backing toward the door. "I almost forgot, here are your keycards, just follow the corridor to the left if you would like to see the observation car or the dining car to the right," the porter said backing out of the room. "I will be just fine, I just want to sit awhile, maybe unpack a little, get organized, then explore the train a bit.

The bathroom is tiny, if you could call it a bathroom, thought Alex as she moved around her compartment, organizing her things into the bathroom and drawers around the room, the main compartment. Compartment? A stateroom is what the ticket agent called it! It sounds like first class to me, she continued thinking. Is this the way Lucian Devereaux travels? Always first class? I really like this, I could get used to this! I like my privacy, the quiet, the promise of leisure for the next 1 or 1½ days. This is so soothing and restful to my frazzled nerves, no jostling, no crying, fighting, overtired, or vexed adults or children, nor drunks to manhandle or bump into me. The perfect way to travel! Lex thought collapsing onto the open berth, pulling the shoebox and brochures closer to her. At this point, Lex pulled a pillow down after opening the upper berth. She half heartedly slid the shoebox tightly against the back pillow and shoved the forward pillow tightly up and over the box against the back pillow. She slid down onto her own berth thinking back to her long trip down from Briscombe Bay, WA slipping into a semi-conscious state and falling into an exhausted sleep.

Beginning the 140 mile journey from Briscombe Bay to Seattle on Washington State's northern Route 112, Alex mentally said fare-well to her earlier life, the life she had known, and started putting her memories on hold for a time. Skimming the Strait of Juan de Fuca on the left and sliding under the shadow of the Olympic Mountain Range on her right, Alex's mood had become increasingly dark, somber, even melancholy. Alex's best friend, Janet Winslow, sat behind the wheel of her newly purchased fifteen-year-old Chevy. The Chevy she had bought from Alex's mom's estate, only to take it off Lex's hands. But she had needed a car and this one was in such wonderful shape! Lex was attempting to settle her mom's estate and raise some traveling money anyway, it was a win-win situation. Worried about her friends prolonged silence, she reached over and grabbed her old friend's hand. "This car is in wonderful shape for its age and only 80,000 miles to boot! I know the care you and your mother put into this car, it is like brand new, off the lot!" Janet gushed excitedly, nearly shouting in her enthusiasm. She was thrilled to get this old car so cheaply, for a song, as they say, and just after college graduation too. "Cheer up, will you, Lex. It's not like there are no telephone lines or post offices between Briscombe Bay and New Orleans….you're not leaving the planet, you will just be a phone call away, and besides I, for one, is looking forward to my vacation time visit to New Orleans later this year! I will want the grand tour you know!" she said trying to draw Lex out of her doldrums. Lex snapped out of her reverie, realizing her friend was being deliberately upbeat and encouraging for her benefit. She sat up little straighter, put smiles on her face, and started taking notice and an active interest in the scenery passing by her window. Thinking back, Alex realized there had been positive aspects within the bleakest clouds these last few weeks.

Executive Administrative Assistant to Mr. Lucian Devereaux, President of Devereaux International in New Orleans no less, the thought just blew her mind away, it left her head in a fog! The offer of employment, even paid her transportation and moving expenses to New Orleans! Transportation and in particular transportation costs, had been a sticking point in the negotiations, but this had been quickly solved by Lucian Devereaux and unbeknownst to Alex, her own mother! It became one less worry for Alex. The funeral costs had been covered by her mother's life insurance policy at work, but there were so many hospital bills left to pay!

The little apartment Alex had shared with her mother since her father's fishing boat accident, had to be cleared and cleaned before taking the new job in New Orleans and moving so far away. There had been so much to do, so many things to accomplish, and so frustratingly little time to do anything as thoroughly and completely as she would have liked. Admittedly, the position with Devereaux International was unexpected, but it offered such a good salary, benefits, even temporary lodging, it would have been foolish not to take it, to jump at it actually. Automatically, Lex reached down to the floor at her feet and grasped the handles of her purse, and rummaged through it, seeking the letter she had received from Lucian Devereaux. This letter from the President of Devereaux International had personally made the employment offer, shortly after her mother's death. It was a bit unusual, but Alex had not had time to think to about it, to analyze it. Lucian Devereaux had even enclosed a liberal travel allowance, and even authorized a substantial period off to mourn the loss of her mother before assuming her new duties at the Devereaux offices in downtown New Orleans! It was this letter and the funds in this envelope that validated her initial desire to accept Lucian Devereaux' generous offer. But why so generous? Even the offer of a company VIP apartment temporarily, until she found something for herself. How great was that ?! She had thought at the time.

Coming to, Alex responded to her friend, "We're fine Jan. We just stay on 101 till we are a few miles south of Gardner, then we pick up 104 south until we reach Bremerton. At Bremerton, we will catch the ferry across Puget Sound into Seattle. And thanks for taking the time off to take me to the train station in Seattle. I am so nervous and apprehensive about this move!" Alex said in gratitude, refolding the map across her lap providing a few more minutes of distraction from her melancholy thoughts that had suddenly engulfed her senses on this trip. Her thoughts played on her mother's illness, then her death. and finally, the funeral had left Alex adrift, bereft of family and with little money. Her mother had been her last link to her world, since her father's death when she was only nine. She knew of no other family members, no aunts, no uncles, no grandparents. She had wondered for a long time, since childhood, about this, had even been teased at school about this. That was nothing compared to this, she thought, but this move is another thing altogether. She was scared, really scared!

"I really like this car, Lex! It handles beautifully, hugs the road, and is absolutely perfect for me!" Janet enthused relentlessly. "It is wonderful and priced right, too!" she continued. The Ferry ride soon provided yet another interesting diversion and adventure of its own. The Ferry sliced a path through a plethora of pleasure craft, fishing boats, and other harbor and channel traffic in Puget Sound before docking in Seattle. The view of the Kingdome and the Seattle Center had certainly been quite impressive, magnificent in fact, especially for someone who had lived so close and had never even seen it before. The Ferry eventually docked in the Washington Street terminal near the Seattle Aquarium. Then it had been only a short ride, a very short ride, from the waterfront to the train terminal for her Amtrak Train. Here the two old friends decided to say 'goodbye', amidst a flurry of hugs, kisses, tears, more hugs, kisses, and even more tears with promises to call and write often made by each of them sealed with one final last big hug! Then, Alex was alone in the Seattle Amtrak Terminal clutching her tickets to New Orleans.

Alex pushed and pulled her luggage over to the seating provided in the terminal, with the shoebox still tightly tucked up under her arm. Grabbing her purse, she continued watching, but left her luggage beside an end seat. She needed to pick up some brochures on New Orleans, then wandered over to the Newsstand and Concession area to pick up reading material before returning to her seat beside her luggage. Still squeezing the shoebox tightly under her arm, she wondered if she could juggle a newspaper and a soda while getting more change out of her wallet. In the end, she decided a newspaper would be good, but still her thoughts dwelled on the shoebox! This was the question that plagued her thoughts day and night since getting the note in the first place. Alex dedicated her to studying her brochures. It's like a dream…

Alex suddenly found herself looking around her compartment in a daze. Had she asked her porter about the dining car? club car? the observation car? She thought she had, but it could have been a dream. I must have fallen asleep very hard, very fast. I wonder what time it is now. Then it started coming back to her. I have to start getting organized, I have to face whatever is in that shoebox. She had not remembered closing the upper berth before falling asleep, but she opened it again to remove the shoebox. Reaching up and pushing aside pillows to get at the shoebox, she pulled it out of its hiding place. It was so snug up there, like nestled in a tree. I have to take a look before going out to explore the train! Collapsing onto her own berth, she dragged the shoebox with her into her lap. Slowly, removing each rubber band wrapped around the box, she grasped diagonal corners on the lid and pulled. Nothing happened! It would not budge! The rubber bands dangled from her fingers, as she picked up the shoebox to inspect the lid and the bottom half of the box itself. Taped! Her mother had been determined to keep her secrets. What could be in here anyway?, Lex wondered. I cannot believe mom kept any secrets from me, we shared everything! What could this secret be? Her soul cried out for answers and the fear and anxiety were rapidly being replaced by curiosity, tinged with a little indignation!

Looking around her compartment for something sharp to cut the tape, she finally gave up and rang for the porter. Explaining her dilemma, the porter supplied her with a scissors and a letter opener. Thanking the porter profusely for his kindness and ingenuity, Alex let the porter out into the passageway, then continued her single-minded attack on that blasted box! The task of getting inside the box had only been delayed. Approaching the shoebox with determination, she made a small slit in the cellophane tape, then masking tape, and then duct tape? Really, mom! Whew! Grasping one end tightly, she gave the tape a yank. Alex was forced to rotate the shoebox continuously to remove all the tape. This is like the proverbial 'mission from God" she thought quoting an old line from a movie, she liked 'The Blues Brothers', then tried to lift the lid again. It was still not lifting off as easily as it should, the determination and frustration were growing in equal proportions. Now what is up with this thing anyway? she asked herself. The curiosity gripped her whole being as she vowed to get inside. She examined the edges of the lid again and found faint traces of dried …Glue?!? What could her mother have been thinking? It was infuriating and frustrating at the same time

She sat on the berth pondering her next move on getting inside the box now. The last resort, of course, would be to rip open the box completely, something she did not want to do. I wonder if a little dab of finger nail polish remover on a q-tip would work on the glue as well as it does on the on the nail polish? She located her Q-tip travel pack in the smaller travel bag she carried. She removed several single q-tips and the finger nail polish remover she brought with her, then dipped one end of a single q-tip into the polish remover. With this q-tip firmly in hand, Lex ran it under the lid on two sides, repeating the practice using the other tip on the other two sides. Just to make sure, she again tried to lift the lid, It 's coming! Then she looked around the compartment at the scattered debris her notions and schemes had left behind. What a mess! nothing could be worth this, mom, she said to herself picking up the last shred of evidence on the floor. She lifted the lid at last. A gentle tug was all that was needed to remove the stuck lid now! OPEN AT LAST! She exhaled with great relief, finally!

Inside the shoebox, lying on top of the contents, was a closed and sealed envelope, a large Manila envelope. "Not again!" she exclaimed, the words forced out in exasperation. Examining the envelope, she noticed the licked seal was already lifting with age. Old secrets, sighed Lex, dismissing some of the urgency in her mother's note, and dug deeper into the box. She found several old photographs, some old report cards, a few of her old class projects, and many old memories were revived and stored in this old box. Nothing important in here, Alex thought to herself, certainly nothing to be worried or frightened about. Then she reached for the envelope, and using her thumbnail, flicked open the flap. Gently taking hold of the assorted stack of delicate papers inside, she gently coaxed and finessed the papers from their hiding place. Alex picked up each document one at a time, studied it tried to comprehend its meeting and set it aside. Papers clipped together from some old news stories, she did not recognize. Not the paper, not the names listed, and certainly not the people identified. She set these news articles aside and checked the other documents hidden inside this envelope. She found birth certificates, marriage certificates, and even death certificates! Slowly examining each document thoroughly and carefully, she sorted them into separate piles, one for birth certificates, another for marriage certificates, and another for death certificates. Taking more time to scrutinize them more closely, Alex was dumbfounded by what they revealed, or rather what they hinted at. A wide-eyed dazed look fell across her face, matching the chaos taking over her mind!

Horrified, Alex tried to digest what she was reading. Or had she just read it? The first birth certificate had to be her own, or so she believed, it contained the correct date and time of her birth-- but not the correct name! According to these documents, her name was really Alexis Rochelle Thorndyke, how could that be? I do not even know who I really am!?! She gathered up the other documents and began sorting them chronologically, by name, by gender, and the name listed under parent. The dates, times, and names of herself, and her parents, were the same -- or were they? It seems she and her parents each had two different sets of birth certificates, each with other names. Was she Alexis Rochelle Talbot or Alexis Rochelle Thorndyke? Her mother was either Samantha Billingsly or Samantha Billingsly Conklin, or Sara Billingsly Talbot? Did she even know her mother? After all this time, did she really know her parents? Her father was either Jonathon Preston Thorndyke or just plain old Joe Talbot, fishing captain? Or rather Joseph James Talbot. WHY??? Where did these names come from, and are they real? This is astonishing! Picking up the manila envelope, she plucked another small sealed envelope from it and carefully pulled the new seal open so as not to damage or tear the contents. This new envelope provided a wealth of confusing, conflicting, and contradictory information: confusing, but morbidly fascinating! She could not leave it alone! Arranging the contents again on a time-line basis as simply and logically as she could, she found what she thought might be her mother's true birth certificate. It was a birth certificate for one Samantha Laine Billingsly! Also attached to the envelope were some old newspaper clippings. These newspaper clippings narrated a convenience store robbery nearly thirty years ago. Later clippings covered the search for, arrest of, then trial and conviction of one

Judd Conklin. The sentencing of Judd Conklin followed another, an engagement/marriage announcement announcing the marriage of Samantha Laine Billingsly to Judd Alan Conklin!?! What? Underneath these top copies it appeared Samantha Billingsly was seeking a divorce from Judd Conklin. The next news clipping enlightened her to the reasoning behind the abrupt wedding, and the equally sudden divorce of these two young people. The clipping was an item from the Baton Rouge Gazette concerning the shooting of Judd Conklin in a shootout with police outside a local bank, he had just robbed. Finally, hidden away under the rest was another birth certificate: for a Judd Conklin, Jr., just after the death of his father. The article again focused on the aborted bank robbery and capture of his father, Judd Conklin. JUDD CONKLIN, JR !!! This was two maybe three years before I was born!?! No wonder this was hidden away for so long, was this mother, how could she have left her baby? What happened to the baby? Did this mean she had a brother, or more accurately a half-brother? This was almost more than she could digest. Now she would have to find a better hiding place for the contents of her shoebox, just in case she wanted to leave this compartment, and her mother really did have compelling reasons to keep this information secret for all these years.

Raking her eyes over the entire compartment, she sought out a hidey-hole for her secret stash. Where could it go? Somewhere no one would think of looking? Where? Where? Then she noticed it, a hollow bottom under an ashtray built into the armrest attached to the side or actually the end or corner of her berth. She wiggled the papers, documents and clippings into the hollow. Then placed the shoebox back up in the upper berth amidst the pillows. A decoy, perfect! She tried to conceal any disturbances around the compartment, not having to do with stowing her clothes. 'I need time to digest all of this information I discovered today. Who am I really? What name should I really be using? Do I have a brother... a half-brother? Is this what mom really wanted me to find out? What she tried to tell me? It sounds as if he may still be in the New Orleans area. Where do I belong? So many questions. I need some time to sort things out a bit more'. She scanned the compartment quickly before leaving in search of the club car and dining car should her appetite ever return. Picking up her purse, she suddenly needed to check out the letter she had gotten from Lucian Devereaux after her mother's funeral again. "Here it is!" She exclaimed triumphantly. "I thought I had read something about a loaner apartment. I will just need it long enough to find a place of my own!" 'Now I just need time to think, to digest all of this new information. It all has to fit together somewhere, somehow, she thought feeling a bit shell-shocked.'

CHAPTER TWO

Wandering down the passageway, she eventually found her way into the club car. Alex sat back into a chair and ordered her first legal drink and nursed it slowly, deep in thought. She knew it was a good stiff drink, her eyes watered, her throat felt like sandpaper, and the fiery liquid burned her throat raw! She felt like it was battery acid as she coughed and sputtered. She felt numb, totally disconnected from her old life in Briscombe Bay. Rising from her chair, she made her way to the door of the club car still nursing her drink looking for the dining car. 'I have to get something into my stomach, she thought, realizing she really should not be drinking on an empty stomach. A light dinner, soup or a sandwich, then try to sort this all out. Tea or coffee, even milk would be better for me than this drink. Maybe a dinner salad with a roll on the side? That's it!' she thought 'I am not all that hungry, but that BLT Salad, sure sounds good, and with a dinner roll, too.'

She sat down at a table hoping to trade her drink in for a simple glass of water. Catching a waiter's eye, she successfully traded her drink for a glass of water and ordered her BLT salad, with a glass of milk on the side. Waiting for her order, Alex had the chance to study her fellow travelers and diners for the first time. She studied their faces, some strange mannerisms, their body language, even the way they moved. It was an old habit of hers, a hobby really, and it was so much more fun to do with so many new strangers! Briscombe Bay was a small town, fishing village really, so small everyone was on a first name basis. People watching was no fun at all, until she started classes at the University of Victoria in British Columbia, Canada! University towns traditionally grew so much faster than non-University towns. So, Alex did most of her people - watching on campus. It was a safe, harmless hobby, a schoolgirl joke, an amusing game, an innocent amusement, a diversion. Giving herself a mental shake, she focused on the waiter rolling a dinner cart toward her table. Dinner was laid out in an array in front of her: the BLT Salad, buttered rolls and biscuits, water, and milk. Taking a quick gulp of her water, she noticed an elderly woman seated at an adjoining table having tea and another kind of biscuit, one with jam or preserves, a woman smiling cautiously at her. Alex thought her smile a little unnerving, though she looked so refined and gentle. But they always look innocent, don't they? She could be hiding something sinister behind that smile, then immediately felt ashamed and guilty for having such thoughts. Alex now focused her attention on her dinner and scrutinizing her remaining passengers, except the elderly woman seated at the adjoining table. The remaining dinner guests were scattered around the dining car: the middle-aged couple sitting just behind the elderly lady, who had obviously had too much to drink, then there were several middle-aged men scattered about the room, most too intoxicated and quite obnoxious, even trying to hit on Alex. Others boasted of being on a sales junket of one kind or another, then a number of vacationers heading for New Orleans on holiday. It was a little intimidating to have such a variety of people to watch or more truthfully, to observe, such a mostly drunk bunch of people. in their most vulnerable situations. She began categorizing them into classes and sub-classes according to the classifications described in her Psychology textbook. These textbooks were for Psychology courses taken in conjunction with her business major degree courses, became very helpful and practiced in her hobby, and assisted in gaining insight into some very bizarre and outlandish behavior in this group.

Alex finally began nibbling on her BLT salad, and buttered a biscuit. She sipped her milk then picked up her fork to attack her salad. This should fill up the hollows, she thought lying her fork aside, and took a long drink of water. Meanwhile, the elderly lady finished her tea and biscuits, leaving payment and a tip on her bill.

She stood looking down at Alex, a look filled with anxiety and some fear, too. She then asked if she could sit for a moment and talk with Alex.

Alex hesitated momentarily, then invited the well-groomed, very nicely dressed woman to take the seat opposite her. "Hello, my name is Aimee', please forgive me for being so forward, but you seem to be such a refined young lady, so quiet and nice compared to some of these other young ruffians and hellions. I could not help but notice. I may need to ask an important favor of you! Unfortunately, I booked my reservation too late to get a through ticket to New Orleans reserving a private compartment for myself aboard this train. I was called back to New Orleans just this very morning because of a family emergency. Now I need to get or share a compartment on this train to get back to New Orleans comfortably and on time. But there is nothing left aboard this train, the entire train is filled. The entire train is filled with partying conventioneers, or whole families traveling to New Orleans on holiday! Of course Mardi Gras' is also quickly approaching. There is not a single compartment available on this entire train! I had just resigned myself to sitting in one of the train seats reserved for day travelers, but I believe I am just too old to do any traveling in such a cavalier way anymore. I do not have a sleeping compartment, and I am trying to make other arrangements, but I was just wondering if I could share your compartment for the afternoon and evening, just until I hear of any possible changes in accommodations and routing. This has been an incredible day, has it not?" Aimee' excused herself, displaying a kind of remorse for this intrusion.

Alex was startled, to say the least. "I do not even know you, but I doubt my compartment will accommodate two easily," Alex responded uneasily. "Oh dear, I am so sorry. Not only have I startled you, but I may have alienated you now, too. Besides being unforgivably forward andshamefully frank, but I just did not know what way to turn!" Aimee' apologized effusively. "It is the height of effrontery, is it not?" she asked. "I am not normally so brazen, so audacious, but extreme need seems to have trumped the niceties, and calls for action, "Aimee' ventured apologetically. Alex just stared, to stunned by the interchange. But after a few minutes to think about the situation, she decided a little peaceful conversation would not be too bad, given the other options at the moment, and she really liked Aimee' soft southern drawl. "I am sure we can just slip back to my compartment quietly and chat privately for a few moments. You may just want to shower, wash up, and brush your teeth, whatever before returning to your seat. Or perhaps you will want to store some of your more personal items inside my compartment for security reasons. "Why don't we find out what we can actually do in the first place?" Alex queried. "Yes, we should," Aimee' responded enthusiastically. They gathered up the purses, settled the charges, then made their way back to No. 19. Opening the door to the compartment, Alex led Aimee' inside. "This is really one of the larger suites on the train, at least of the available compartments I have seen!" Aimee' acknowledged. Aimee' then pointed to the upper berth above Alex's own berth. "You see you do have another sleeping berth, we can just pull it down for anther sleeping space." "Now why did I not see that extra space up there? Dunce, I cannot believe I did not remember noticing or registering or even associating the space for extra sleeping," Alex was mortified to be caught in her little deception, though she had forgotten with everything else going on in her life today. "Why not sit here for awhile and chat while watching the scenery passing by the window," Alex almost apologetically suggested. They began exchanging some family information, life and career goal information, and so on in the relative privacy of compartment

For Aimee' it was also almost like getting the daughter she had never had, and for Alex it felt like actually getting a surrogate mother to give her advice. In general, it could be called a win-win situation, mutually beneficial to both of them, though leaving Alex a bit uneasy with the entire situation. It provided each of them with exactly what they needed at this point in their lives. 'BUT WHY?'

Eventually, they buzzed for the porter and two cups of tea, and a tea service of biscuits or cakes. Neither wanted to ruin their dinners, so they settled for tea and scones. It was Alex's first experience with a scone, interesting she thought but not a true delicacy, she thought not wanting to make an issue of it. Interesting texture, but I do not know if I would ever like another. They continued to sip and chat, talked and sipped for at least another hour. Calling the porter to remove the tea service and empty biscuit plate, Alex inquired about the train's exact location and it's ETA in New Orleans's. They were informed they would be arriving in Salt Lake City for a brief stopover, before moving on to Denver after the dinner hour. However, New Orleans was another 1 ½ to 1 ½ days off. Aimee' seemed pleased with the progress they had made so far today, so a look of bewilderment crossed Lex's face when Aimee' said, "I will be getting off in Denver to make a flight connection to New Orleans. I am traveling back to New Orleans, called back by a medical emergency, a family health problem. A crisis has developed and I need to be back there as quickly as possible, to straighten out some problems that has been developing over the course of the last few weeks. Will you please notify me as we are approaching Denver?" Aimee' inquired anxiously. The porter answered in kind, "Yes ma'am, but you should be able to have a brief dinner with us, before making your connecting flight to New Orleans from the Denver airport. Would you be wanting an early menu of soups and sandwiches first? Would you just be waiting until the dining car opens up again, in oh fifteen minutes, checking his wristwatch." "I believe I will look at an early menu, before getting my things together. Thank You kindly," Aimee' answered. "And you miss ?" The porter asked directing the question to Lex. "I do not think I will need anything but a nice cup of herbal tea, Mint I think. I will just be keeping Aimee company this evening until she leaves the train. Then I will get a late dinner in the dining car later. Thank you, anyway," Alex answered still more than a bit surprised by Aimee's unexpected request and comments. Interesting, very interesting she thought perplexed by this unexpected revelation. They both se back into their seats gazing out at the bleak countryside streaming past the window. "Not much to look at right now, is it?" Aimee' commented gazing at the endless sand.

Alex took out her brochures and leafed through them, stopping occasionally for verification of items she did not understand. "What is the 'Vioux Carre'?" she asked Aimee'. "Just Our most famous sights and the location of our world famous 'Mardi Gras' parade. It is really quite extraordinary, it is 'the old French Quarter, some very historic, very unique architectures, the Old Farmers Market, many antique Shoppes', very narrow streets, an eclectic combination of cultural styles, colors, and historic buildings. It is something you must experience to understand fully," Aimee' explained emphatically. "Each year The Mardi Gras Parades wind their way through the 'Vioux Carre' in anticipation of the Lenten sacrifices that will be made. It is the ' Let the Good Times Roll' feeling that overtakes the entire city from the Epiphany until Ash Wednesday. It precedes the Lenten Season on the Church Calendar, leading into the celebration of Easter Sunday," Aimee' elaborated. "It is the most exciting, intoxicating, fascinating and festive time of the year!' Aimee' finished. Alex restarted paging through her wad of travel brochures, "Look, I have more brochures on a Lake Ponchartrain, which looks lovely in this brochure photograph, In addition, another on the Garden District. Everything looks so beautiful, I cannot wait to see the city myself. I know there has been a lot of damage done by 'Katrina', but I want to be part of the rebuilding, a part of the city and what looks like it's vibrant life!" Alex stated with enthusiasm despite the sudden yawn, that over took her. "I know it may be hard, but I really look forward to the challenges, to the demands that will be necessary to finish the rebuilding," Alex answered rising to answer the knock on the compartment door. The porter had returned with Aimee's Soup and Sandwich, and also Alex's herbal tea. "I think you had better drink your tea, you look all in!" Aimee pointed out quietly. "Wake Up! Come on now," Aimee said patting and rubbing her hand solicitously. "I have become so drowsy all of a sudden. Whew!!" Alex slurred rubbing her eyes. Alex tilted sideways, falling onto her berth, the brochures slipping through her fingers and fluttering to the floor.

CHAPTER THREE

Alex awoke to the shaking of the porter. She had missed the stopovers in Salt Lake City and Denver. Aimee' had disembarked, having gotten off the train to make her connection with the airline. The porter seemed genuinely surprised she did not seem to know her friend had left the train.! Did not even register that she had missed the first and second settings in the dining car?! he had cleaned up the tea service, taken Aimee's order for a light lunch, even brought the lunch back while she napped. Everything seemed to be in order and he had not given it a second thought. She had difficulty wrapping her mind around this, difficulty thinking at all. The fog was so thick. waving the porter away, she asked for a cold or wet washcloth. She just needed time to clear her head, to pull herself together. "The last setting for dinner will be coming up soon, in a half an hour really, miss. Will you be coming down?" he inquired. "Let me clear my head a little longer, However, I believe I will be coming along for a light dinner, and I think I need some very strong coffee. My head feels like a block of concrete, I will be along in just a minute. Thank you for waking me," Alex replied gratefully.

Alex groped around her berth, gathering up her brochures. Then she staggered to the tiny bathroom, to splash water on her face trying desperately to clear her head. She was so groggy, she began to suspect a drug-induce sleep! Aimee' would not do this to me, would she? What is going on? She began feeling so helpless and alone, so abandoned. She immediately went to her little stash point. She looked around the compartment skeptically. The ashtray was still securely set into the armrest at the end of her berth.

She lifted the ashtray out of the armrest and gently pulled out her documents. Nothing was missing, but as she retrieved each piece of information they were out of order? So maybe she did take a look at her documents, so what? But why? Why would anyone else even be interested? This is so unnerving, so confusing really-- but why, what was happening here? She locked her compartment after stashing her papers back into their hiding place, tucking her purse into her tote bag, and strode down the corridor to the dining room.

The dining car had a limited number of diners still in 19e car, so she had her choice of tables to claim. First coffee, strong coffee, then something to eat, food, something high in protein to give her energy and dispel the remaining fog and lethargy, and focus her befuddled brain. She chose a western omelet with extra cheese on it. A lot of eggs for the protein, with sausage links, and an English muffin with jam on the side, and of course coffee, more coffee! When the coffee was brought to the table, she sat back enjoying a long, slow swallow welcoming the new alert feeling that began clearing the remaining fog in her brain. While waiting for her omelet and the English muffin, she observed the rest of her dining companions. A few were rowdy, but a couple dined in an elegant fashion, a late dinner as in Europe, or a sophisticated city anywhere in the world. It was nice to watch them enjoying their late romantic dinner. Then her omelet arrived and she concentrated on her own dinner for a time. She ate in silence, keeping an eye on her fellow diners. She nibbled, pushing her food around her plate, slowly eating her omelet and crunching her English muffin. Surprisingly, the other patrons did not hold their previous fascination for her, she was tired again, exhausted after her possible sedation, wary of the strangers around her. She quietly ate her late dinner, paid her bill, and then made her way back to her sleeping compartment. I need a good night's sleep tonight, then maybe spend some time in the observation car sorting things out. I need to understand everything that has happened to me today, seeing a little of the countryside, observing the people that came around her, and what she expected her new position to be in Devereaux Industries. Alex stumbled back to her compartment.

But for now, she showered, changed, and brushed her teeth. She checked her locks again, then collapsed on her berth after leaving a 7:00 a.m. wake -up call. Lex was fast asleep within minutes. The train rolled on, closing in on New Orleans with each passing hour.

She fell soundly asleep, not waking until her 7:00 a.m. wake-up call nudged her from sleep moving around her private compartment, she went through her normal morning routine. She washed, dressed, even applied some make-up lightly. She sauntered down to the dining car for her breakfast. She had an entire day to explore the train and the observation car. The observation car promised to show her more of the country she had only read about. She was always a bit shocked by discovering her rather sheltered upbringing. She looked forward to this adventure. She only had 1 day and 1/2 of another before she completed this part of her adventure, and she wanted to make the most of it She slipped down to the observation car to have a look see at the rest of the country side. She asked the conductor for the trains location in conjunction with the New Orleans arrival. He told her the train was right on time, maybe even a little ahead of schedule. I think we left Wyoming about 25 miles ago, now we are crossing South Dakota. The conductor explained they had to cross South Dakota to get into Minnesota and then cross into Wisconsin to follow the rails down to the Chicago switching yards. Now she would get to see a lot of dairy farms and grain and vegetable producers in the Midwest. At Chicago we will be chugging due south into Missouri and Arkansas right into Louisiana. We should be pulling into the New Orleans station by mid morning tomorrow.

Thanking the conductor profusely, she sat back musing about all the farmland she was seeing for seemed they were going along quickly as the scene outside this windows flashed briefly before her It was not long before they were already crossing into Minnesota. Minnesota looked just like the South Dakota farmlands, and appeared Minnesota would be the same as Wisconsin farmland. Gazing out the windows of the observation car she observed very little difference in the farm terrain or the products it produced. At lunchtime she stood to make her way back to the dining car. Ordering a modest lunch, she again glanced around to see any recognized fellow travelers. That rowdy, drunken bunch from last night sat holding their heads today. That lovely couple was not present in today's diners. But the families' with small children the booths to her right. She was amused by some of the little ones antics, and continued her observations through the ordering and serving of her lunch. By the time she returned to the observation car, they were already in Southern Wisconsin awaiting the Chicago switching station.

She stayed in the observation car eager to observe the actual switching of cars in the train yard. It seemed like they were flying south through all these fields. It was not long before Missouri border approached. She rose to return to her own compartment. Now she would be able to watch privately from her own window. Lush farmland all looked alike to her. Now just dinner and a good night's sleep. She would be in good shape for her arrival in New Orleans.

CHAPTER FOUR

The impending arrival in New Orleans jumpstarted her heart. The adrenalin was pumping through her as she hurriedly cancelled her order and scurried back to her compartment. Opening the door, she found her luggage missing from the end of her berth. The porter seemingly had gotten her luggage out of the compartment and delivered it to the train platform. Dashing to the window she verified her bags were out there waiting for her pick-up. She nearly jumped off the three or four little steps getting off the train. She quickly took stock of all her bags sitting on the platform and gathered them around her. She pushed and pulled them all into a tight formation around her, lining them up at the end of a central platform bench. She looked down to the end of the platform to the end of the gangway. The porter was down there, helping another couple into a taxi. Was that the romantic couple she had seen having a private, quiet moment in the dining car the other night? I think so. Could be? At that moment, the porter noticed her sitting on the bench with her luggage all around her and hastened toward her with the luggage trolley, or was that a dolly? "Would you be needing a taxi, a bus, or we even have a street car or two in the city. Where are you going, I will suggest the quickest way to get there," the porter inquired. Alex looked at the address in the letter she was holding, "it says I should go to an antique Shoppe at 115 Royal Street."

"I will get you a taxi; you are heading into the 'Vioux Carre'. You will like living in the 'Vioux Carre'!" the porter announced. "What is the 'Vioux Carre'? I remember seeing that term in one of the brochures I was reading on the train," Alex asked the porter while following him down the platform to the gangway and the taxi stand. "Oh, the 'Vioux Carre' is the Old French Quarter. You will be able to view all of the Mardi Gras parades and festivities from your balcony, besides enjoying the eclectic architecture and old-world feel to this city. I am surprised you have a place to stay in the city at this time of year," the porter chatted amiably. "Why is that?" Alex asked innocently. "This is 'Mardi Gras', not a single room left unsold in the city!" he answered. "That is very interesting, but I need to know a couple of other things about the city first. I need to know about churches, banks, groceries, where I will be working, the name of my new landlady' etc., etc., etc.," Alex spurted out. "I know this address. It is the Antique Shoppe of Genevieve Dupree, a very hospitable and gracious woman here in the Quarter. I am sure your taxi ride to the Shoppe will a very pleasant one. It must be your apartment that sits above the Shoppe. I did not know the remodeling was all finished yet. Enjoy it!" The porter continued stopping at the Taxi stand waiting at the curb. He brought the dolly to the rear of the taxi, to toss the luggage into the trunk of the cab. Conferring with the driver, he supplied the name of the Antique Shoppe, the name of the Proprietor, and the address of the apartment. "Good Bye, Have a great day, and enjoy the sights!" the porter said enthusiastically. The porter slammed the trunk lid down, while the cab driver opened the back door for Alex to get in. She settled into the back seat for the short trip to the 'Vioux Carre'.

Alex was wide-eyed, so excited, wanting to see everything, and yet so very tired at the same time. The cab driver chatted freely about his city. He talked about the Mardi Gras parades going on in the Quarter, the ones that had started with the Epiphany and would end at Ash Wednesday. This will all come to an end on Easter Sunday! I hope all the revelry won't be disturbing you in the final coming days," he said pulling up in front of a two-story building on a narrow street beyond a gated park-like area in the back of the building. The cab driver deposited her bags on the sidewalk in front of the Antique Shoppe. Alex pulled her bags together and rang the buzzer beside the door. Alex looked up from her traveling bags, and noticed a small woman coming to the front door of the Shoppe. "You must be my new tenant, Alexis Talbot! I am Genevieve Dupree! I hope my customers and I will not be too much of a disturbance for you, and I hope you will like the changes I have made to the apartment's décor. Lucian Devereaux pays no attention to the amenities and ambiance necessary to make an apartment livable, comfortable as they say. I hope you like all of my new ideas and will consider this your new home for as long as you need it," Genevieve Dupree went on. "Lucian said you would be arriving today or tomorrow, so I hurried to finish the remodeling and the decorating this afternoon!" she said breathlessly. "I must say I am a little taken aback by your informal and casual reference to my boss. Lucian is his given name, I am still at Mr. Devereaux. I really do not know him all that well. Only the hiring and duties dealing with my hiring!" Alex responded to a surprised Genevieve Dupree.

Lucian Devereaux and I have been friends for many years now. He owns this building and others in the Quarter. We are just cleaning out here after the devastation of Hurricane Katrina. I was out most of the morning putting the final touches on your apartment". Do you have a back door into the garden area from the store? The cab driver said most stores and Shoppe's had them along with a large, locked gate just down the street?" Alex inquired.

"I should have realized, I thought I saw Reynaldo drop you off out front. He drives by here a couple of times a day usually. But fares have been light around here recently. The neighborhood is just beginning to come back to normal. Lucian still seeks my advice on colors, fabrics, and styles so I do hope you will like my simple style upstairs. And, yes I do have rear access to the gardens and courtyard out back. Follow me to the back of the shop and I will show you how to get out there, I do need to get your keys for the apartment. Can you get your luggage out to this door ?" she asked in afterthought. Alex was distracted by the reverie going on outside the front windows of the Shoppe. "Another parade seems to be headed this way again, let's hurry up to the apartment so you can get your first glimpse of a Mardi Gras parade from your own balcony!" Genevieve said excitedly. "We will just be following the path to the left once we leave the back door. Then we take a quick right at the stairs up to the second floor. The balcony encircles this side of the building, the front of the building overlooking the street, and halfway down the other side of the building. Your door is just up ahead, there is a light to help you along just hit the little button alongside the key on the keychain. There are several keys here on the keychain, a small one for the apartment door, a larger one for the deadlock, and a very large one for the front gate! She dangled the keychain in front of Alex, as Alex stumbled up the staircase pushing and pulling her suitcases along with her. "I am so sorry, I did not even realize you were having such a problem, let me take one or two of your cases."

Alex dropped the two medium suitcases she held, up on the floor of the balcony deck. Genevieve turned and picked up both cases, turned and led Alex a few feet down the balcony before coming to a stop in front of an unobtrusive door, partially hidden because of an architectural design, was it a flaw or a preferred structural design of interest? Hard to tell. Unsuspectingly, Genevieve placed the apartment key in the lock. The door opened, no deadbolt engaged. They pushed the door open further, the apartment was dark, but there was a spoiled odor wafting out to greet them. "Oh my," Genevieve exclaimed. "Should we even go inside?" "No, drop everything right here, they might still be inside!" Alex said softly, trying not to alert the vandals. "Let's get back to the antique Shoppe and call the police," Alex suggested. "And then I will call Lucian Devereaux, he is the owner of this building and most of the block after all," Genevieve tossed in. "OK, but let's hurry! It might be important! Alex whispered harshly, more raspy than she thought. They clambered down the stairs as quietly as they could, but it sounded thunderous to both women. Running to the back door of the shop, they crossed the threshold and slammed the door behind them. The beating of their hearts pounded in their ears as they listened for any unknown sound around them-inside or outside. Genevieve placed a shaky hand on the telephone on her desk, another hand over her heart. "Wait, let me calm myself a little, before I make these two calls. It has been quite a shock. I heard nothing! How could they have gotten in without my knowing? I just put in some supplies for you this morning. A few items to tide you over until you can find your way to the farmer's market. Some coffee, some baguettes, some fresh fruits nothing really special, a little milk, a little butter," Genevieve sputtered showing some early signs of shock." Alex took the telephone receiver from Genevieve's hand and dialed 9-1-1 to report the break-in. Genevieve roused herself from the shock of finding the apartment upstairs in what looked to be a shambles. "We must put in a call to Lucian. This is his building, after all. He needs to see and know what has happened here. All the money, time, and remodeling costs he has spent here in the Quarter since the hurricane. All for nothing!" she said collapsing back down into her chair, head-in-hands. Alex patted Genevieve's shoulder and walked toward the front of the Shoppe to wait for the police and actually watched some of the revelry out in the street. 'Not a particularly auspicious arrival in New Orleans', she thought, No boss to meet the train, and now this, a trashed apartment! Now what do I do?' Alex's thoughts raced around her head until the knock at the door ended her reverie. The police had arrived1 She opened the door to two police detectives and led them to the back office. The detectives busied themselves opening small notebooks and retrieving pens and pencils, now the questions started. They all joined Genevieve in the back office for a question and answer session in earnest. Opening questions identified the two women, the relationship to each other, the reason for the complaint, and access to the apartment earlier today. Was anyone scheduled to be in the apartment at all today, workers, remodelers, redecorators, plumbers, air conditioning people, anyone at all? "We need to see the apartment, inventory the damages, take stock of anything that needs to have codes met." "I have the keys right here, I was showing the apartment to Alex just moments ago when we discovered the break-in," Genevieve informed them. At that moment Lucian Devereaux walked into the office, he identified himself to the police detectives and said "I will go up with you and see the damage for myself, hopefully the damage will not be as significant as you all believe. I just finished paying the final bills on the remodeling and redecorating," Lucian told the officers. "Let's go up and take a look," the officers said to Lucian, "we have not taken a look and gone over all the damages yet, it will help you catalogue everything for us and the insurance company, too." With that they all trooped out the back door and wound around to the left and climbed the stairs. Genevieve took her natural place at the head of this little procession the keys jangling from their rings. Reaching the door, she looked over her shoulder for reassurance before fitting the key into the lock again. The entry lights had been switched off, as had the kitchen lights, lights she knew she had switched on the first time they had been there but the odor was still here, then a tremendous crash came from the front bedroom overlooking the street. Everyone rushed forward, only to find smashed balcony windows and dangling ropes hanging from the wrought iron balcony walkway. Rushing to look out into the crowd below, only dashing figures could be seen parting the assembled throng scurrying into the distance and the dark.

Now that they had all made it back to the bedroom, they began to register the damages done to the apartment in their mad rush back toward the sound of the crash. The furniture had been upended, cushions slashed, contents of the bathroom cabinets tossed onto the floor. Now they could go back to the kitchen and take a look at the damages there. Alex and Genevieve did not notice Lucian and the police officers had stopped to poke around the bedroom and the bathroom on their return to the front room of the apartment. Instead Genevieve took Alex into the small bedroom and bath off the kitchen and dining area up front in the apartment. These two rooms seemed to be relatively untouched. The bed in this back bedroom was a double bed, maybe she could sleep here temporarily, it did have a second ¾ bath off the bedroom she could use? Alex tried to assemble this new information into a useful database, when the police came forward to ask more questions of her and Genevieve. The officers had become ill between the front bedroom and the larger bathroom toward the front street.

The officers, even Lucian were acting in an agitated fashion. They moved in a frenzied, maniacal manner, asking crazy questions about drug use and the time of her arrival in New Orleans. Genevieve was shocked and frightened when the officers accused her of selling and providing drugs out of her Antique Shoppe on the main level. What were they talking about? Why was everyone talking about drugs all of a sudden? Even Lucian was a little strange, very aggressive, with complaints of stomach pains, numbness, and spasms. The officers had dilated pupils, irregular respiration, fast heartbeats, and nausea. He grabbed Alex's arm, saying "These are all symptoms of cocaine poisoning, what have you gotten into?" "I just got here. I came directly from the train station. The cab just pulled out from the curb. We were just taking our first tour of the apartment. I have not had time to go out and buy drugs of any kind, much less cocaine, who would want to anyway? Cocaine kills! I learned about it in school," Alex shouted back. Lucian slowly sat back into a ladder-back dining chair in the office, "call 911 and get some medical help for me and the officers, someone seems to have left a very dangerous and unwelcome gift for your new apartment, a house-warming gift so to speak," Lucian rasped.

CHAPTER FIVE

lex dialed 9-1-1 quickly. She turned to Genevieve and whispered urgently for her to watch the patrol officers or detectives, actually, that had answered her burglary call. She explained what Lucian had said about cocaine poisoning. Genevieve's hand flew to cover her mouth- cocaine? "Is that what this is all about? Have they been poisoned, the police detectives?" Alex faced the Shoppe proprietor, reached out and patted her shoulder turning her back to the other room, "Watch the two detectives out here on the sofa, while I telephone for an ambulance. They think someone left it as a housewarming gift!" "Gift!" shouted Genevieve. "What kind of monster leaves this kind of gift?" Alex phoned for an ambulance and more police detectives, while making her way back to the front of the store. Looking out into the street, she watched the festivities and the merriment and the cavorting going on out in the street. She called back to Genevieve, she waited for the police and the ambulance.

Staring out the front windows, Lex hoped to connect her thoughts into some sort of logical thinking, logical and reasoned thought. She remembered staring into the widening opening of the door that first time, both women stood in shocked silence accessing the evidence of the violent, fanatical, destruction facing them. She remembered Genevieve murmuring over and over again 'When could this have happened, I just finished the apartment this morning!? How, when, why?' The room looked torn apart, furniture slashed, chair and sofa cushions torn apart and slashed mercilessly, before hearing the arrival of the sirens out front. The sirens and lights of the police cars and ambulances came to a halt in front of the shop. She called out to Genevieve to let her know the police and paramedics had arrived. She slowly and deliberately went to the door and unlocked it for the officers and medical technicians before locking it again to keep out the rabblerousing thongs out in the street.

The paramedics rushed toward the back of the store, shouting questions, then seeking Genevieve and her police charges and Lucian, leaving Alex to deal with the newest police officers and detectives. The detectives began the questioning immediately, wanting to know the details of the original complaint and the necessity of this latest complaint. Alex had very few answers for them, only the few words Lucian had imparted to her. Here the two original detectives were brought through from the rear office and taken out into the first ambulance, now suffering with muscular spasms and convulsions. Alex's worried face showed some signs of relief when the last paramedic walked through leading Lucian slowly through the front office. Lucian was obviously feeling somewhat better, though not his old strong and perky self. A bit grouchy and put out with the entire situation, he turned to the new detectives interviewing Alex in the Antique Shoppe. He interrupted insistently as the owner of the building, the whole block for that matter. Alex was just a new employee that had just come into New Orleans from northern Washington state to fill a space on his staff to ferret out some of the corruption in his organization, even more of the corruption in the Port Authority post he had just accepted from the governor. Alex had not even settled into her job at Devereaux International yet and she already seemed to be a target of the culprits he was after. "By the way, each of you will need to wear a face(breathing) mask if you go upstairs to inspect the damages done upstairs. It got very bad just walking through the apartment, unfortunately the other detectives kicked up most of what I suspect was some kind of cocaine dust dumped onto the floors, counters, cabinets, and solid surfaces in the apartment. Though I do not know how anyone could have found out about the apartment Alex and Genevieve will have to see most of the devastation up there to catalogue the damages and repairs necessary," Lucian told the detectives, diverting their attention away from Alex and Genevieve.

This was a new and very frightening development to both Alex and Genevieve. Could they should they stay in the Shoppe and apartment, were they targets of some mysterious and dangerous drug lords? It is very scary not to know what or who is targeting you! The two new detectives went out to their car and came back with new facemasks for the trip upstairs. Though they were gentler, calmer, and a more soft spoken on their return they still had a certain insistence and focus since talking with Lucian. It seems Lucian had a great deal of pull with the local authorities. They all donned masks and followed the path up to the second floor apartment. The devastation was complete. Genevieve was horrified that so much destruction had occurred in such a short period of time while she was just downstairs in the Shoppe. Well most of the time she was down here in the Shoppe she had to admit. She admitted she ran out to the market for a few minutes to pick up a few supplies for the new tenant expected to arrive tonight. Genevieve also admitted taking possession of a few final accessories for the apartment. Now everything had been destroyed, slashed, stomped, broken, and smashed!

As they made their way through the apartment, Genevieve jotted down item after item that had to be replaced or repaired for the insurance and decorators. She was very thorough and efficient in her duties as the manager of the apartment. The shock was slowly receding from her face and brow as a new determination set into her countenance, a stiffer, hardened attitude, as an outrage filled her. She jotted and checked, checked and jotted until she had quite a list prepared for both the insurance company, the remodelers, and upon reaching the back bedroom overlooking the street, the builders. Replacing the windows, or more accurately the sliding glass balcony doors, would require more security measures. Stopping at the master bathroom near the front bedroom, she began jotting and scribbling again in earnest. This was a larger bathroom than the one at the front or rear of the apartment, depending on the way one looked at it, near the kitchen, dining area. This master bath was nicely appointed with a Jacuzzi tub prominently displayed, cabinets and countertops. Some cabinets had been yanked off the walls, the countertops and Jacuzzi showed signs of attempted scratching and damage due to breakage. Genevieve scribbled feverishly, trying to note all the damage done. Coming back into the kitchen, Genevieve noted the luscious Italian sweets just purchased from the Carrollton Confectionary tossed onto the floor, kicked and trampled underfoot. Most of the cushions from the new furniture were thrown on the floor, sliced with a knife or scissors, stuffing pulled out. What a mess!

Bathroom towels littered the floor in the bath, everything splashed with mud and dirt. "A good boot print here in the bath on the towel!" one of the detectives called out. "Bring it with, put it in an evidence bag," the other detective called back. "Any blood evidence in the front bedroom, where everyone jumped out the window up front?" the second detective asked the first. "Nothing I could see, but there could be fingerprint evidence, we will need a forensic team to come in to dust and spray. The renter will not be able to move into her apartment for awhile., at least not until after the forensic team and other officers finish in the apartment!" The officers led the two women out of the apartment and back into the office of the Shoppe. Genevieve and Alex, quietly spoke with the officers explaining events and timelines for the day until a call came into the office from Lucian and the precinct captain telling the four of them to get back to the station. Genevieve locked up both the Shoppe and the upstairs apartment, and left with the officers for the station.

Meanwhile, down the street, four pairs of eyes were trained on the view at the front of the Shoppe. They chuckled as Alex and Genevieve were led out of the antique Shoppe into a waiting squad car. However, no handcuffs were visible. That could be a problem. Why no handcuffs? They certainly had sprinkled enough of their product around to warrant the use of them.

Alex grappled with feelings of helplessness, of being exposed, violated, defenselessness, and finally outrage. She snuggled into the back seat of the squad car wanting to talk things over with her old college friend, Janet Winslow. Janet always made everything look better. The squad turned into the precinct parking lot, the detectives opening doors for themselves, and then for both women, saying the night was still young, and there was much paperwork to be completed. At that precise moment Alex's stomach growled loudly. It was noticed. Startled out of her lethargy Alex wound her arms around her empty and complaining middle. Genevieve was mumbling vacantly, "of course, we'll have to mount new doors and new deadbolts right away too.! And of course, newly strengthened patio doors overlooking the street, new bedroom paint and furniture. What a mess these vandals have made, especially of all the pretty and cozy colors and fabrics I chose for this apartment." The mumbling and grumbling got louder as her anger rose. "What petty, miserable people these must be. So full of hate and mischief. It is hard to comprehend!" Genevieve said at last.

CHAPTER SIX

Genevieve and Alex sank into stunned, incredulous silence for the brief ride to the precinct recalling the despicable and flagrant destruction found in the apartment. It had been unbelievable. It was so monstrous, so villainous, so wanton, so wicked and heinous. Alex was overwhelmed by the excessive and fierce violence wrought on her new apartment, by who or is it whom? I always did have trouble with that one, Alex thought to herself. The squad car pulled into the precinct parking spaces provided for the public, the detectives, and the beat officers. The two detectives got out and opened both rear doors for Lucian and the two women. It looked like it was going to be a long night, and a fierce night with one on New Orleans most prominent family sons. They would have to mind their P's and Q's.

Thankfully, Lucian answered most questions on the technical, and mechanical aspects of Alex's new position with Devereaux International. It was a good thing because Alex knew so little about what would be expected of her. Mostly straight accounting, with a touch of investigative auditing. Checking, re-checking, re-checking, and checking again.

Meanwhile, three sets of eyes stared intently at the front door of the Dupree Antique Shoppe before making their way back to the fine old hotel Charles managed. It was a good thing The French Quarter had so few blocks to traverse. The Fairmont beckoned as Charles, Langley, and Courtney moved swiftly and stealthily toward it. It was rapidly approaching one a.m. as they crept into a back door, and up to an already reserved suite under an assumed name. The suite had been put in reserve by Charles himself for an emergency situation as this one was. Charles checked Courtney in personally, and dropped the two key cards into his suit jacket pocket. Reasonably sure the desk, audit, and housekeeping staffs were either engrossed in their own tasks or sufficiently busy not to notice the arrival of his visitors, he ushered them up to the clandestine suite.

"Langley, check the hallway behind us, make sure no one is watching our arrival! What were thinking, Courtney? I know you have better sense than you have been exhibiting tonight. You could have, and probably did jeopardize all our plans already!" Charles said angrily. He was beyond angry, he was livid! The signs of stress apparent in his face. "I did not appreciate having to rescue you from this fiasco!" Charles shouted irritably.

Langley sat back quietly, listening, trying to remain calm, to determine their next move. "Stop arguing, the damage is already done. Now, we have to figure out where we go next, determine what our next move will be, where do we go from here?" he asked. Courtney and Charles sat back in the sitting room loveseat, alternately gloomily and obstinately. They faced Langley seated in the opposing upholstered chair. Charles sat back glumly, frowning, and mumbling under his breath. "Since Courtney will be unable to gain access to Luke's schedule....and we must have that information on this 'special project' too...and Alex Talbot mat be our only source for the information we need now, and because she knows no one here, she may be on guard now, the possibility remains to get that information from her," Charles thought aloud.

Charles lifted his head and spoke directly to Langley trying to formulate a new plan. "We will have to undertake the responsibility of gaining the trust and friendship of Ms. Alexis Talbot. We must gain our information through deception and misdirection... or perhaps if Courtney still has her keys and access codes we may be able to stage a break-in at the corporation offices to get information on Luke's thinking, Ms. Talbot's 'new project', what they suspect about our operation, and how much time we may have to complete this operation," Charles said disguising his dissatisfaction with the entire situation and with Courtney in particular. "It appears dubious the police fell for our obvious and desperate attempt to plant a false trail. It was too soon. She just got off the train tonight, for pities sake, you could have waited a little longer. Now they will know she is being set up. It complicates things on our end. This little deception, this contrived falsehood has put them all on their guard now. We cannot allow Ms. Talbot to become suspicious of us now Langley," Charles began formulating aloud again. "Hey, wait a minute, Lucian could not have changed any keys or access codes at headquarters while he has been traveling out of state, we could get into the offices this weekend and look around. Really shake thing up a bit," Courtney spoke up, not the least contrite. Langley's devastating charms will be lost to us after Lucian's not so glowing descriptions of him sink into Alexis Talbot's psyche. I know it won't be pretty, he always thinks the worst of you Langley, why is that?" Charles continued.

Langley closed his eyes momentarily, thinking and mumbling; "Courtney, did you say Alex was supposedly going to be Lucian's hostess for this year's Mardi Gras Ball?" "She will be, from what I overheard. The other office cows were simply cackling about my implied termination!" Courtney hissed. "That would be the only reason Luke would even consider firing me! I had him right where I wanted him before she came along! There must be an appropriate way for disposing of Ms. Alexis Talbot." "Calm down, Courtney. I had the impression you might be overreacting to Alex's role in this entire fiasco. Yes, I think I might be right, Charles. My brother rarely does anything he has not thought through carefully, if not actually planned outright," Langley mused reflectively. "What really disturbs me, is Lucian neglected to inform the family of his imminent return to New Orleans, and then did not return directly to the house when he arrived at the airport! That is very unusual behavior for my solid, steadfast brother. If I had not accidentally spotted him in the airport terminal, we might never have known he was back. Even then, I had to rush our friend out of the terminal before anyone saw us together. He might be suspicious already. He was very tight-lipped around the house before he left on this most recent trip."

"Let's try to keep our minds on the business at hand. I think the first item on our agenda should be to discover just what Lucian and Ms. Talbot are up to, Charles inquired softly. "Are they even in town anymore?" especially after today's fiasco. Where would they go, what would they tell the police? Are they alerting the police at this very moment?" Langley sounded worried. Courtney silently listened to Charles and Langley's comments and seethed.

"Langley, I believe it would be a good idea to go home tonight. Just inform Courtney here at the hotel if Lucian is already at home, or if he returns by morning. Try to pick up some information on this 'special project' too. You may overhear your father or brother discussing it accidentally, they may not be so guarded in the privacy of their own home. I will keep watch at the corporate apartment for any new developments there," Charles concluded.

Lucian dropped off Genevieve at her small home just outside the French Quarter. It was a small one-story, cottage almost to the Lakeview district north of the Vioux Carre.

As they left, Courtney opened the overnight bag she had quickly thrown together at her apartment. Every minute she had spent packing, she expected Lucian to burst through her door. But, Courtney was angry, it was inexcusable of Lucian to fire her with-out even stating a reason. 'I did my best work for him, it should not matter about our little side business, besides he did not even know about it, we hid it so well. It has to have something to do with that little snit that just finished school in Washington State. Why get rid of me? Why eliminate my position at headquarters? Why doesn't he trust me anymore? This was so sudden, I have not even removed my personal property from my office at work! This was all her doing!' Courtney worked herself up more and more, until she made another error in judgment. She snuck out of her room and down the hall, tiptoeing past all the rooms until reaching the fire stairs at the end of the hall. Courtney was hell-bent to teach that little slip of a girl a sound lesson in not crossing Ms. Courtney Anderson! It was her job and she wanted it back!!! She made her way out to the street and back into the heart of the Vioux Carre to her parked car hidden in an out of the way garage not far from Alexis Talbot's apartment. She located Charles watching the apartment and sat in her darkened watching both Charles and the damaged apartment face.

She did not have to wait very long before a local squad car slowly made its way around the back of the Antique Shoppe to the garage behind the back gardens. She watched as Charles quickly sat up straight, then shifted to the side trying to remain unseen and unnoticed on the narrow thoroughfare just down the street from the Antique Shoppe. Courtney watched intently from her hidey-hole just around the corner from the antique shop nestled into the black recesses of an adjacent garage across the street from the back alley to Alex's apartment. From her vantage point, Courtney could see much more than Charles could sitting just down the street in front of the antique shop facing the shop. She noticed a light switch on in the interior of apartment's garage. 'Now, what are they doing back here?, she asked herself' She sat back quietly looking for the slightest movements to cross the courtyard in the blackness. She listened for any rustling or shuffling sounds emanating from that direction. Courtney was distracted by Charles slowly coming toward her down Royal Street, instinctively, she ducked down into her own seat in the dark garage not wanting to raise Charles' ire again today.

The shopping activities of the last few days were the final preparations Genevieve had completed for Lucian's renovation of the corporate business apartment. This preparation activities had been made for Alex's arrival in New Orleans though not for her sole benefit. It also corrected some damage done by the hurricane and its aftermath along with updating and freshening the apartment in general. Lucian, Genevieve, and Alex had spent over an hour repeating their information to the police officers before the police supervisor had arrived to take charge of the investigation. Lucian was a prominent and well-known member of New Orleans society, something of a financial wizard. He was the face behind the historical and well established Krewe in the city. The Mardi Gras Parades are put on by the old and wealthy, supporters of each Krewe. I believe Lucian was elected King of this year's parade, each of the old families has their own Krewe and supplies their own floats with party favors as well as hosting one of the many Mardi Gras parties around town between the Epiphany and Ash Wednesday. As a well-known resident of New Orleans Lucian had been offered an oxygen mask by the first responders at the shop and had kept it with him all through the interviews and statements. Lucian and the police Watch Commander whispered quietly in a corner off the office, Lucian puffing into the oxygen mask periodically while Genevieve and Alex signed their statements. "I have gotten the Commander's permission here to start the clean-up and repairs on the apartment as soon as possible," Lucian spoke softly to the two women as he gently led them toward the door. He also let Genevieve and Alex in on necessary security measures that needed improving and correcting at the apartment starting tonight. "Genevieve, I will get you back to the Antique Shoppe so you can pick up your notes and lists before locking everything down again securely, very securely!" Lucian reiterated, "Then, I will get you back to your cottage, all right?" "I am so tired this evening, it has been such a long day, such a busy day!" Genevieve exclaimed feebly. "I know, I know, and a night at a police station brought the day to such a ceremonious ending. But I still need all those lists and repairs started tomorrow. Can you make the calls from your home? You could come in late tomorrow," Lucian asked solicitously. "You should not be in this building until repairs are started anyway" Lucian said smoothly. Turning to Alex, he said "You obviously cannot stay in your apartment for awhile, so you have the choice of a hotel/motel in the city, at least until a more secure alternative can be supplied. I am quite sure my family would be most pleased to offer you one of our guest rooms for the duration or as long as needed. Lucian was saying distractedly. In the meantime we will return Genevieve to her cottage for some calls, some well earned sleep, and some genuine rest and recovery from this day. "he spoke softly and thoughtfully. "We have a number of guest rooms, and only one is occupied at the moment." "It really is quiet, comfortable, secluded even, and very protected. It is in the 'garden district' a rather exclusive area of New Orleans, you may have read something about it in one of your brochures or heard about from your cab driver? Lucian probed.

They spilled out of the squad car and hurried into the back garage entrance of the Antique Shoppe. Genevieve picked up her notes, addresses, and telephone number from her desk and hurried back to Lucian and Alex. Courtney went rigid, first Lucian stepped out of the squad car followed by a dragging Genevieve, and then a new one. A young, nicely dressed inexperienced woman. Not glamorous, but comely, tall (maybe 5'6" or so), long, lush dark auburn hair, and eyes that flashed amber and green under the streetlights. 'So this is the person he hired to replace me, we will just see about that!' Courtney smoldered inside her late model Ford Explorer. 'Very attractive Lucian, I have to admit, very attractive, but not any more attractive than I am. Why were you in such a hurry to be rid of me?' she fumed.

Lucian led the two women through the garden gate directing Genevieve and Alexis toward the back door of the Antique Shoppe while jogging in the opposite direction toward the garage. Once inside the shop, Alex followed Genevieve's instructions for locating the notes and lists and numbers necessary to start and complete her restoration tasks. Lucian entered the garage and found his beautiful black Jaguar snuggled safely inside. He hurriedly examined the auto for any damage like that wreaked in the apartment, not noticing any severe damage he backed out of the garage and into the narrow alley behind Royal Street and pulled up to the front door of the shop to pick up both women. He drove Genevieve out to the Lakeview district, just NNE of the French Quarter, dropping her at her front door reminding her to get a little sleep before starting those calls, no one liked getting up in the middle of the night to this kind of news. "Finish the calls from home before even showing up at the shop, start with the new security measures, and then proceed with repairs, refurnishing, and the like. At least you will not be alone there and you can even verify the companies and workmen that show up.

Alex was drawn by his confidence, his strength, his self-assured manner, and his quiet authority. "I realize there are no vacant rooms to be rented in New Orleans at this time of the year, but I did not expect to be put up by your family. Do you have a large family waiting for you at home?" His mysterious nature only added to the aura he had built around himself. "I met a woman on the train, an elderly woman. Do you know Aimee' Devereaux? She shared a compartment with me for almost a day. She was very nice, and very inquisitive, too" Alex gently probed. "It is a family house. My father is the head of the house, and yes, I do have an Aimee' Devereaux, also residing there, a sister, Lucinda Devereaux, younger and just coming out this Year at the Debutante Ball, and there is one other who may or may not be there, my younger miscreant brother, Langley. You will not be alone there, besides family there are an assortment of maids, cooks, gardeners, and handymen around the estate. Safer there than at any hotel/motel in the city. Not a large family, but a very protected and protective one," Lucian answered her question. Leaving the Lakeview district he headed toward the Superdome, with the Garden District just beyond, and sandwiched between Tulane University and the Superdome before noticing a pair of headlights behind him.

CHAPTER SEVEN

"I think we may have some company, I 'll try to lose them with a couple of quick turns just to check," Lucian said turning a corner very sharply, skidding the tires. The pursuer followed closely, matching Lucian's quick movements, nearly flipping the explorer onto its side. "The car is definitely following us, he said as he more slowly rounded the next street corner, then sped up to put more distance between him and his pursuer. He continued this strategy until he had enough time to spin around and come face-to-face with the pursuer. Caught in his headlights unexpectedly, Courtney panicked momentarily, tried to stop, then flee the explorer as fast as she could, hoping Lucian had not identified her, but knowing that was not true. Courtney terrified when she saw the look of thunder on Lucian's face, shoved the explorer into gear, came head- to-head with Lucian, stomped on the brake, spun around and fled the area. Lucian verified the person in his headlights was actually Courtney Anderson, his trusted and Private Confidential Secretary, the person he had confided in for so many years. The Governor was right all along, I cannot believe it! Unbelievable. She had my complete trust!! Lucian slowly turned around and drove deeper into the Garden District finally pulling into a long circular driveway leading up to a large, white, antebellum mansion surrounded by long lush green lawns and vibrant flowers. The front door swung open flooding the entryway with light and an inviting glow. He stopped, turned off the engine and opened Alex's door. He introduced Alex, first to the butler, then meeting his Father at the bottom of the stairs, introduced them. Lucian began explaining the events of the evening to Jean-Claude explaining Alex's arrival at the family home.

Alex nodded her greetings to Jean-Claude Devereaux, her eyes involuntarily rising up the stairs to a lovely railed second floor. This beautiful old house actually had a third floor she could not see look-ing up from the ground floor. 'Wow!' she thought. "Alex dear, There is someone here I think you should meet. But hearing about all your escapades today leads me to believe you need sleep more than any-thing else. Everything else can wait till tomorrow morning," Jean-Claude said sympathetically, "I want you to be fresh and alert when I introduce you to your real family. It is too complicated to under-stand this late in the day!" he finished. "Maude, would you please take Ms. Talbot up to the third floor guest suite? Make sure she is up and fresh at 9:00a.m. tomorrow morning". Maude, the maid, led Alex up to the Third floor and opened the door to the most beauti-ful suite of rooms Alex had ever seen. The colors of pale lavender and yellow accented everything in the bedroom and sitting room. 'I just want to crawl up into this big bed and sleep! she thought taking the nightgown Maude handed her. In the nightgown were a toothbrush and toothpaste and even slippers for her feet. "You come on down here at 9:30 tomorrow morning for breakfast, I'll wake you at 9:00 a.m.," she said leaving Alex on her own. Alex looked into the bedroom, spying the door to what most certainly had to be a bathroom and hurried in setting the dental items on the edge of the sink.

Alex brushed her teeth quickly, rinsed and left the bathroom faster than she could ever have imagined. She looked longingly at the nightgown she half tossed on the bed. Pulling the comforter down away from the pillows, she crawled up in to the soft, warm, and deliciously scented bed and she fell asleep almost instantly. She lay across the bed, fully clothed, and deep in slumber.

At 9:00 a.m. precisely Maudie knocked on Alex's door, rous-ing her from a deep sleep. It was such a momentous day yesterday, first the move, then meeting the landlady of a new and completely furnished apartment, the break-in, and then hours in the police station; It was both wonderful and exhausting at the same time, quite disorienting. She came to groggy, sleepy, and unwilling to open her eyes. Then she remembered the way her evening ended, being followed from the antique shop to the Garden District, and probably from the Lakeview District too! Confronting a possible assailant who had invaded her new apartment Fleeing aggressors that were barbarously evil and wicked, and unidentified! Her eyes sprung open with the insistent banging on the door. Springing out of bed, she hurried to open a door she could not remember locking the night before, meeting Maudie halfway into the sitting room. Maude had let herself in finally, not expecting to find Alex awake yet, especially after the pounding the door had just taken. "You had best hurry, everyone is in the dining room waiting to meet you," she chirped. "Everyone? Who, everyone?" Alex asked stunned. "Why, the family, of course! Mr. Lucian, Mr. Devereaux, Mr. Langley, Miss Lucinda, Miss Devereaux, and even the Doctor for Mr. Thorndyke has come down to make an appearance. He may wish to speak with you later," Maude said enigmatically. Her face was inscrutable, it showed nothing. Alex looked down at her wrinkled travel suit. She sighed audibly hoping no one would notice her travel weary wardrobe, when Maude brought in a lovely dress in mint green! "It is beautiful! But will it fit?" Alex wanted to know. "It should fit nicely, I can estimate sizes fairly quickly, as I make most of the dresses around here anyway," Maude stated proudly and confidently. "But this is just a store bought one, Mr. Lucian called for it this morning" she continued. Alex scurried into the new dress as fast as she could, hoping to get downstairs briskly.

Alex hustled down the stairs to meet Lucian and his family, maybe get some questions answered, then more questions asked. 'Was Aimee' family? Was she a plant on the train to keep an eye her, to acquire some kind of information from her, or about her? Am I becoming paranoid? Buck up kid, face it head on!' she told herself. Restoring some of her confidence, or at least some bravado, she raised her chin and marched into the dining room. She met Lucian, his father, his brother Langley, sister Lucinda, then the doctor. The doctor for someone named Joseph Henry Thorndyke. What is his connection to me.

"Joseph Thorndyke, is probably your father's brother!" the doctor said. "Lucian and Jean-Claude can tell you more about tracking your father and mother down over the years. Even Aimee' Devereaux knows a great deal about that sorry period of time!" he finished. "An Aimee' Devereaux was on the train with me for a short time day before yesterday, Is that the same Aimee' Devereaux? Alex asked joining all the pieces together. "Just what was she trying to learn about me?" a bewildered and exasperated Alex called out. Aimee' Devereaux rose from the chair beside Jean-Claude, "Dearest Alex, I am so sorry to have deceived you. I just had to make sure you were the one we were looking for all this time! When I saw the look of surprise and pain on your face reading that letter from your mother on the train, I knew you were shocked by her revelations and truly lost. I could not bring myself to say more than you were ready to hear," Aimee' said softly. "It will not be any easier to tell you things you do not want to hear now! Your father was my god-child; Jonathon Preston Thorndyke, the younger brother of Joseph Thorndyke in the bedroom upstairs. Joseph Thorndyke is a very ill man today, unlike the strong, vibrant man he once was. Many years ago, there was a falling out between Joseph, his father, and Jonathon about the marriage between your father and mother. Jonathon was insistent on marrying your mother, even vowing to run off and elope, which they eventually did." Before that happened, circumstances occurred that sent them fleeing before Joseph Charles Thorndyke, decided to claim Samantha and Judd's baby boy was an illegitimate bastard. I took steps myself to sidetrack Joseph' from making that final, regrettable mistake," Aimee' said in a hushed whisper for Alex's ears only. "I really am so sorry I was so deceitful on the train. Broaching such a sensitive subject was unbelievably difficult, even more difficult that I imagined. I could see the shock and strain showing up on your face. It became too hard for me to continue hurting you. I just could not do it! Leaning forward, Aimee' Devereaux gracefully lifted the silver cover server "Let me refresh your cup, dear, or would you enjoy a glass of iced tea or lemonade now instead?" Aimee' inquired softly. Lucian entered the dining room through the French doors from the patio and took his seat at the dining room table directly across from his father, Jean-Claude. Alex was already sitting on the edge of her seat. She looked into the many strange faces around the table. "Actually dear, there is more I must say to you, later this morning. But eat first, it will give you the strength to hear the rest," Aimee' said confidentially.

The doctor entered the dining room and selected a chair near Alex intent on discussing something with her, or so it seemed. "You are the last blood relative of Henri' Joseph Thorndyke?" he asked solicitously. "Alex was flummoxed! "I really do not know. These are names I have never heard before. I am the daughter of Joe and Sara Billingsly Talbot. What do these other people have to do with me?" Alex asked, starting to feel the paranoia beginning to creep into her soul. Voices all around the table began at once, a cacophony of sounds, asking, shouting, explaining, and retelling the stories of so long ago. So much noise, Alex finally pressed her hands firmly over her ears trying to block out the sounds that assailed her ears. Alex sat back from the table, a mask hiding her features. She began picking at the food on the plate in front of her not tasting anything, but deep in thought instead. She was quietly pondering her thoughts, feelings and turbulent emotions when a new voice broke through the foggy mist of her new life. Lucian was introducing his brother Langley and sister Lucinda to Alex. Alex came around just in time to politely acknowledge their greetings. Now for the first time she truly glanced around the table seeing this family for the first time. She would need time to adjust, were to put her trust and faith and belief. So far no one had really told her the complete truth. Now she was really alone in a sea of sharks.

Lucian broke into her thoughts following the introduction, a little more insistently this time, "I do believe we should go on a couple of excursions today, the first back to your new apartment to check on the restorations, the repairs, the renovations, and the construction. Then I need to take you to our offices and show you around, then I need to get you to a dress designer for measurements on your Mardi Gras ball, and finally if we have time we might be able to see some of the sights." But Alex was in a daze. She heard, but did not hear anything spoken to her. The cacophony had become a din of clattering noises, hard to hear clearly. It was the doctor who who noticed Alex's obvious distress and unhappiness. He sat down beside her, rubbing her arm and squeezing her shoulder in comfort, talking in a low, soft voice. The calming sound helped to calm her, and bring a sense of peace and quiet back to her. She began to respond. The doctor had begun describing Joseph Thorndyke's many and debilitating illnesses to Alex encouraging her to come back to reality. Aimee' joined the doctor revealing much to Alex in the same quiet, empathic tones the doctor used in speaking to her. Alex roused herself slowly as the information seeped into her brain. She learned of her parent's flight from New Orleans into oblivion and the reasons for their flight. At this point, Lucian broke into the explanations apologizing for his inconsiderate way of handling things so far. "The shock must have been terrifying for you in these last few days, and then the events of last night besides, -Horrific! I am so sorry to have put you through all of this," Lucian spoke softly to her. "I will not push you into doing much of anything today anymore, if you are not up to it. Do you feel well enough to go up to see Joseph a little later this morning? It will mean a lot to him," he said compassionately with just a hint of coercion and insistence in his voice. Langley, Lucinda, and Jean-Claude sat back quietly watching these things play out before them. Everyone looked directly at her, expecting an objection. "I believe I will go up and speak with Joseph Thorndyke this morning, maybe ask a question or two. Depending on the answers, I guess I would like to see where I will be working. And if time does not become a problem, we could do some of the other things on your list," Alex responded softly. Following the doctor up the stairs and down a short corridor they entered the sick room set aside for Joseph Thorndyke. Joseph Thorndyke lay not quite sleeping on a massive bed. He did not look intimidating or impressive lying here just a little small and poignant. It was heart-rending, and moving, sad and touching at the same time. He roused briefly and extended a hand out to her, saying "You look just like your mother, the last time I saw her," with this he fell back into unconsciousness. She was bustled out of the room.

Lucian had followed her into the room and then out again. "I really was quite fine this morning after the great sleep I finally got last night," Alex commented off-handedly. "But all this new information has taken me quite by surprise! It seems I did not know my mother, nor my father as well as I thought I did. It makes sense with my father, because he died when I was nine, but my mother and I were so close, even closer after my father's fishing accident years ago. Why didn't she say anything to me, especially after I received my scholarship to the University of Victoria in British Columbia? I was certainly old enough by then. It is taking me a long time to wrap my mind around all of this! It was very unexpected, astonishing really. When I read my mother's letter on the train I could not believe what I was reading. I thought it was a mistake, I could not believe it. I was trying to mesh what I knew of my mother with the person revealed in the letter."

"It must have been a very horrible, traumatic time in my mother's life. I remember reading, reading about another marriage, a divorce, and even about a son being born. But was that woman really my mother, or just someone she may have known? It is so confusing and so hard to believe! Lucian placed a comforting hand on her shoulder and gave it a light squeeze "I have heard most of the story from Joseph through the years and I know he sided with his brother against their father in that disagreement, but to no avail. Henri' Thorndyke was quite a cantankerous, obstinate fellow in his later years. I was too young to have seen or understood what was going on at the time, but I agreed to help Joseph find his brother and his wife after the death of his father several years ago. The detectives I hired followed a very circuitous route these many years before picking up a trail that finally lead me to a news article covering your father's fishing boat accident years ago. From there I simply asked and verified the clues to your mother, first in the apartment and later in the hospital to know I found the right woman. In conversations with your mother, while you were at school, and my confirmations about Henri' Thorndyke had indeed died nearly eight years ago, your mother finally confirmed the detectives and my suspicions about her true identity, and that of her husband, and you, of course. I know how great a shock this has been to you, and I am sorry I could not have told you about any of this before. I promised your mother I would wait to tell you about this until I got you back to New Orleans and safely to your uncle Joseph. Well, here we are, in New Orleans, but now your uncle Joseph is very ill. We moved him into the house to watch over him and care for him while he waited to see you, to meet you after all these years!" Lucian spoke softly weighing her responses and feelings. Alex's eyes were blank. She was on overload. "My uncle, as you say, is now unconscious. I will not be able to confirm any of these allegations until he wakes again. Just where did you plan to go exploring today?" Alex asked tremulously.

"I had wanted to take you by the corporate offices and show you around, introduce you to the staff. I had also wanted to introduce you to the best seamstress and costume designer in New Orleans. We could also go by your apartment and check out how the repairs, remodeling, and security upgrades are coming along. They were working most of the night and should have accomplished quite a lot by now. Genevieve has been calling, hiring, and directing workmen all through the night. I did not want her to be in that building alone until people and security systems could protect her. But only if you are up to this. It will be quite exhausting, and the exertion will be quite fatiguing., especially after last night's events. The person driving the vehicle chasing us last night was unbelievably my executive secretary, Courtney Anderson! I saw her quite clearly when I spun the car around to confront her. I caught her full face in my headlights, and I had to admit grudgingly the governor was right. I feel so betrayed, this is the woman I was going to ask to marry me at the end of this year's Mardi Gras. She had access to everything in my office, most especially the shipping and receiving records in the Port of New Orleans. Now that the Governor has appointed me the new head of the Port Authority, he has given me the assignment of cleaning up the Port, finding and closing any alleged drug trafficking outlets and prosecuting the felons involved. That is why your apartment was targeted. For some reason they wanted to somehow discredit you by planting some cocaine in your apartment, only they planted it too soon. I cannot understand how Courtney got involved in this, and who the other players are," Lucian mumbled, thinking out loud. "I do have some very important questions to ask Mr. Joseph Thorndyke when he wakes. Questions that have been stalking my thoughts for a couple of days now. But, until he wakes, I will be free to join you in your excursions. Although, I am surprised to hear about any work taking place at my apartment, how did you get anyone working on it so fast?" Alex asked doubtfully. "It was not very difficult, with all of the unemployed workers in the city now. I am paying double and triple overtime on this job now. I relied on my best contractors to run the security screens on their new hires, especially the new security features," Lucian impressed on her. "Maybe we should head over there first, I still cannot believe anything could have been accomplished so quickly," Alex said in singular admiration. "Well, we can just go take a quick look and see how things are progressing, before moving on to the dressmaker and costume shop just off Lafayette Square. Then if we do have enough time we can cruise up to the new office building in New Orleans Center," we will on push it too hard today anymore. "You will want to be back to talk to you uncle when he wakes in any case. All right?" Lucian asked.

"I find it difficult to believe any work could have been finished at all in so short a time," Alex responded quizzically. "I am sure Genevieve called the cleaning services people first thing after we dropped her off last night, then the security service people, and then finally the construction and refurbishing/remodeling people. I want to see what they have accomplished since late last night," Lucian said distractedly. "Then she should have gone to sleep and gotten a good rest after all that upheaval last night. And I know she showed up this morning to check up on all the work crews showing up against our approved list of workers. She will be so very careful after last night, she will not want any more destruction of her handiwork. I certainly do not want to pay for any more remodeling and refurbishing than I have to," Lucian added.

Dr. Ingram adjusted his coat and tightened his grip on his medical bag, looking directly at both Alex and Lucian standing overlooking the front entry hall while Jean-Claude Devereaux and Aimee' Devereaux joined them outside Joseph Thorndyke's room. Dr. Ingram spoke softly to the group "I have left my number with the nurse. She will notify me of any changes in Mr. Thorndyke's condition and she has my instructions for his care. I will drop around again to check on Joseph's current condition later this afternoon after my rounds at the hospital. Lucian spoke next commenting "We have some errands to run today but we will return this afternoon to get an update on Joseph's condition upon your return." With that everyone cleared out of the hall, leaving the hallway quiet outside the sickroom.

Pulling up in front of the Antique Shoppe, Lucian watched Alex's face pass from startled to amazement. It seemed the work crews had indeed accomplished quite a lot overnight. The cleaning crew had gotten all the demolished furniture and smashed debris out of the apartment and the security crew was installing new sliding glass doors leading out to her balcony off the bedroom. They were installing new locks and deadbolts in her apartment too. "I cannot believe they have accomplished so much overnight!" Alex's astonishment was evident. "I just want to check with Genevieve on the companies that have shown up this morning and the names of the workmen in the building now. I am paying premium prices to accomplish this feat. I do have to get you the dressmakers shop to start your costume today too. We will have keep a steady pace to keep our appointments today. And I did want to introduce you to some of your co-workers quickly today, too. "Let us get inside to talk with Genevieve, so we can get started on the rest of our day!" Lucian said in exasperation. He chafed under the pressure of his time constraints plus this repeated remodeling of the apartment that was already finished for the second time. "Let me check with Genevieve and get lists of the companies and workmen that have shown up, I can send payment vouchers through at company headquarters," Lucian articulated. He opened the door quietly and exited the car saying, "I will return in just a few minutes after talking with Genevieve and collecting her lists and estimates for job costs, stay here or run upstairs to peek into the apartment," he said with finality and hurried inside the Antique Shoppe. Alex took him up on checking the apartment with a quick peek. It was definitely cleared out but all the locks were drilled out, and the doors left open. Alex hurried back down the stairway to reach the car before Lucian finishe with Genevieve. She settled herself in the passenger seat just before Lucian strode out of the the shop. "Well let's get to the Trade Center offices right after measurements at the costume maker's shop downtown. We have to make up some time to get back to the house to talk with the doctor this afternoon," Lucian informed her settling into the driver's seat, laying a file folder on the center console between the seats. "We can pass Mardi Gras World on our way to the costume maker's shop. You might get a glimpse of some of the props and giant figures from past Mardi Gras parades, catch the excitement running through the city," he said. "Why do I need a costume?" Alex asked. "Will you be my hostess for my Krewe's Mardi Gras Ball? I certainly cannot ask Courtney to be my hostess in light of everything that has happened.?" Lucian appealed sheepishly. "Really, what if I cannot do it? I know nothing about this Mardi Gras, besides what I have been reading. I do not know your friends, your family, who to invite, what to wear, how to act or respond. What is a Krewe?" Alex implored. "The costume maker is right up here around the corner. We can stop in and quickly get measurements and chose styles and colors that flatter you. We can talk it through, argue fiercely, but in the end we will have the basics chosen just in case. Then we can continue on to Corporate Headquarters. I wanted to show you some of the innovations I am trying to incorporate into the building to update and streamline office procedures. This being a weekend, I won't be introducing you to co-workers, but you will get a feel for the layout of the building and its location with regards to the location of the apartment. We still have to return to the house in time to intercept Dr. Ingram. So let us not waste time today trying to settle disputes or gloss-over injured feelings," Lucian spoke hurriedly as if pursued. He turned his car toward Canal Street turning off at the foot of Canal Street near the Algiers Ferry and pulling onto Convention Center BL. As they passed Harrah's on the edge of the Vieux Carre she saw the Creole Queen pulling up to the ferry dock. "This is not so very different from living in Washington State. We also have ferries that dock to carry passengers across Puget Sound daily," Alex commented. "I see we are now on Convention Center BL. This must be the area we are headed for-- Company headquarters?" "Our company is one of many in the World Trade Center, not the company itself but the corporate offices. I need to pull some information together and segregate it from all the rest of the documents in our records. I must get hold of the records before Courtney has a chance to alter any more information!" Lucian uttered with some irritation. "Here we are at the costume makers shop. Let's get those measurements taken, select the style you are comfortable with among the many dresses she has to offer. Then we can move on along down Convention Center BL to the World Trade Center offices. Let's go and get this done!" Lucian continued.

Alex stepped inside the dressmakers shop with some trepidation. From the rear of the shop a disembodied voice called out a greeting and welcome. Moments later, Simone Sorelle burst into the room with a flourish, tape measure wrapped around her neck and scissors in hand with extra pins in a cushion wrapped around her wrist. "What can I create for you today mademoiselle?" she asked as Lucian strode through the door. "Messieurs Devereaux, you must be here to see about Mademoiselle Anderson's Mardi Gras finery, she has chosen three that I have started. I only hope I will be permitted to finish them before the balls continue! I will be requiring a down payment on the cost of the finery she has chosen," Madame Sorelle stated. "I am so sorry Madame, but I will not be escorting Courtney Anderson to any more balls this year, I will be escorting Mademoiselle Thorndyke to the remainder of the balls and she will be my hostess for King Neptune's Mardi Gras Krewe ball at my family's home this year!" Lucian replied apologetically introducing Alex to Madame Sorelle. "Oh no! This could be a disaster! Let us begin with some measurements immediately! She said quickly, pushing Alex into a side fitting room. "I do not know how we can accomplish this miracle in so short a time, unless……… maybe yes, maybe no depending on your taste in style and your measurements for the gowns I have already begun for Mademoiselle Anderson?" Simone Sorel's thoughts raced on. With that, she brought out three gowns she had almost finished for Courtney Anderson and placed them on a rolling dress cart for Alex's scrutiny. "How beautiful they are!" Alex exclaimed. "I have never in my life seen such beautiful dresses and such fine work. Not even in the bridal ware in Briscombe Bay! Unbelievable!" she called out. "Try one on, check the fit, how does it feel? Do you like the style, how about the color?" Simone Sorelle entreated. "Patty will be so exasperated with this sudden change in our work schedule! Patti LaCombe and I are the joint owners and dressmakers in this Shop. We do all of the work together. I will try to explain to her these changes. Your measurements are slightly slimmer than Mademoiselle Anderson, but you are nearly the same height, with a few tucks we should be able to pull this off!" Simone rattled off, her thoughts straying wildly. "Let us show Messieurs Devereaux how this looks on you!" Simone said quietly. "Is this supposed to look like this? I seem to be popping out of my dress!" Alex exclaimed.

"The proprietress/head seamstress is Patricia Lynn LaCombe or just Patti LaCombe as she calls herself. She does not stand on formalities and is quite relaxed and self composed most times of the year." Lucian filled in some of the background for Alex. Rushing out to greet her guests upon entering, Patti LaCombe extended a hand, then turned unexpectedly to hug Lucian instead. "O Cheri', I have been trying to reach you for so long. Your secretary, Courtney has been in three times in the last two weeks to see about her ball dresses. We took measurements but I have been waiting for authorization from you to make these dresses, they are not cheap, as you know!" she explained anxiously. "I must apologize for my oversights Patti. Courtney Anderson will not be my hostess for the balls this year. This is Alexis Thorndyke, she has graciously consented to be my hostess for the family's King Neptune Krewe Mardi Gras Ball. She will also be attending the rest of the balls with me." With those ad bits of news still swirling around in her head, Alex stopped short and dug in her heals. "I am Alexis Rochelle Talbot, not Alexis Thorndyke and I have not consented to be your hostess for any King Neptune Krewe Mardi Gras Ball or date, consort, or partner at the rest of the balls. I have no knowledge of Mardi Gras Balls, what to do, what to say, who to invite, or how to act! This is a potential disaster!" Alex exclaimed. Now Lucian tried to quiet Alex and get Patti started with measurements. He spoke soothingly to Alex, reminding her of the abbreviated time schedule they were under. Argue and fight later he implied, we must stay on track now. Patti LaCombe began her measurements for Alex's ball gown, then sat to discuss the measurements and ideas Simone had brought to Alex on first arrival. A sigh of relief. "A tuck or two here and there and she is nearly the same size as Courtney Anderson! Is this not wonderful? It is very good, yes? The dresses I started for Ms. Anderson, I can rework for Mademoiselle Thorndyke and the dresses can be finished on time!" Patti said triumphantly. "I have never not completed an assignment on time. But time is short now and I will need to take a shortcut or two to complete this assignment. I do have two, maybe three of the ball gowns near completion now, not the special one for the King Neptune Krewe Mardi Gras Ball. But maybe we can get a look at the other two gowns and check the fit and style of the gowns," with that she ushered Alex to a back dressing room chattering all the way. In less than an hour, both gowns were fitted to her slightly smaller frame, at which time her face flamed at what the dress revealed of her shape and side profiles. "Too revealing," she cried emphatically. "Do women really wear such revealing costumes for these balls? They are not even decent! Alex cried out. She glanced pleadingly at Lucian, who just smiled at her reflection. "Make some modesty adjustments and changes and send the dresses on to the house," Lucian said with finality.

"Let's move on to the Trade Center and check out the offices. We need to get back to the house in an hour or so. Two hours at most," Lucian expanded, opening the car door for her to get in. Quickly, they bid good-bye to Patti and Simone who were already putting their heads together excitedly to salvage this big sale, waving good-bye from the open door of the shop.

Once inside the car, they moved into traffic along Convention Center Blvd. "There is under ground parking below our offices, we can take an elevator up to our main offices. We may even be able to catch some of your co-workers before they leave for the day," Lucian said carefully checking his side and rear-view mirrors, still looking for any sign of Courtney Anderson or any other familiar face in the crowds along the street. He took a right onto Napoleon Avenue around the Trade Center and then another quick right to access the underground garage using his key card pass raising the long gate arm to the garage. They narrowly missed a truck and a van hastily leaving the garage speedily. "What was that all about? Did you recognize anyone in either vehicle? Lucian shouted to the Gate Guard? He then followed the arrows painted on floor down to the underground parking areas. Three full floors of underground parking facilities available to the residents of the Trade Center. Still skittish about recent attacks on his business properties, employees, and new and old friends he claimed a parking space near the elevator doors listening for amplified sounds in the garage. He heard the low rumble of a car idling somewhere in the darkened garage in the distance, but could not identify the direction it came from. The sound seemed to come from everywhere ! He urged Alex to hurry from the car to the elevator, move quickly and call the elevator as soon as possible. "Do not stay out in the open for too long. We don't want to be targets!" explaining while closing the car door and hurrying after Alex toward the elevator. He heard the engine revving up and the squealing of tires as the SUV careened around the corners coming at them. The lights on the SUV came into sight, neither had reached the elevator doors yet as the SUV bore down on them. With a superhuman burst of speed he dove into Alex hurling her toward the elevator. The SUV came right at them, swerving at the last minute to avoid colliding with a parked car jutting out into drive lane narrowly missing Lucian and the girl he was trying to protect. "Alexis Talbot, the lucky tart! What makes her so hot?" Courtney's brain shouted. He brought her to her feet gingerly as she limped toward the elevator clutching his arm. Courtney thought briefly about making a U-turn and taking another pass at them, but quickly vetoed the idea. She saw them reaching the elevator and safety in her rear-view mirror.

CHAPTER EIGHT

"Are you all right, did you sprain an ankle? Is anything broken? I really didn't plan on tackling you so hard, but the headlights were coming straight at us. I reacted instinctively relying on old football tactics. Unfortunately, I never played with girls! Lucian sputtered hesitantly. "We can relax a moment now, away from harm and more possible attacks. We go up to the ninth floor offices to see if anyone is still in the office. I especially wanted to introduce you to Candace Chavez. Or, more accurately Candida Rodriguez y de la Gonzalez de Chavez as she has informed me since her marriage last month repeatedly. She will be your secretary and aide in getting through the labyrinth of offices, customs, and etiquette, and people in these offices. Now if you are able, we can get out of this elevator under our own power and meet and greet the employees of Devereaux International!" They exited the elevator to a rush of female devotees or enthusiasts all wishing him well after his unexpectedly long absence. The secretaries and aides all over the office inquired after his health, the new business acquisitions, the long trip, and this new executive secretary/consultant they had heard so little about in his brief calls and notes sent back to the office. "Hold on a minute, ladies. First of all, I my health is great, as usual. Negotiations went well in the acquisition of the fisheries, and this is my new Executive Secretary/Business Consultant, Ms. Alexis Rochelle Talbot late of the University of Vancouver, Accounting and Business School. Is my introduction to your liking, ladies. Get acquainted with your new co-worker on your own time. We have to take care of a lot of minor things to see while we are here. I will need to look at our business records in connection with the Port of New Orleans immediately," Lucian said rapidly. "And we have very little time. We need to get back to the house to speak with the doctor. How has the remodeling gone in the offices while I was gone?" Lucian asked the office secretaries. Candy Chavez spoke up from the back of the crowd "It was going well until this past weekend when Courtney Anderson arrived with her cohorts. First thing we noticed was Mr. Lucian's office and then Miss Talbot's office. Come take a look…" and she lead them down a short corridor into a door with PRESIDENT neatly labeled on the door. "The office next door is labeled ASSISTANT EXECUTIVE SECRETARY for Ms. Talbot. The rooms have been trashed pretty much. Thoroughly I should say, Sorry!" Candy Chavez murmured apologetically. "Give us an hour to sift through the debris. You and my secretary, wait a minute, one of the other secretaries, I forgot Courtney Anderson no longer works in this building momentarily, locate all the records we have for the Port of New Orleans and deposit them on the table outside my office. We can see if we can save anything in these two offices. Do not let us stay here any longer than an hour and a half. Call us then," Lucian said emphatically. Candy Chavez volunteered eagerly, both her assistance and her time. "Will you be needing any help in the sorting, organizing, or filing? I am great at tabulating and organizing. That's how I got hired!" Candy said excitedly. "Yes, I know how good your skills are. We could use those skills out here pulling together the information I asked for on the Port Authority," Lucian agreed with her. "Just file the information in some file boxes that we can collect and take home with us. We will salvage what we can from the offices. We will leave the clean-up for you, the other secretaries, and finally the cleaning crew. Sorry" Lucian explained. Alex wandered into her office expecting to see the carnage she had seen in her apartment earlier yesterday. It was a mess, papers strewn everywhere. It looked like knick-knacks from the bookshelves, desk accessories, and a lot of office paraphernalia mixed with blank copies littered the floor. She gingerly crossed the floor to the door directly across the office behind her desk. She opened the door, and entered the chaos of what was once Lucian's private office. That means my office must have been Courtney's old office, Alex thought blankly. What kind of person destroys her office just because someone else is taking over her position? Somehow she doesn't appear well balanced, what is wrong with her? She finally took a studied look around Lucian's devastated executive office. The room was annihilated, it was obliterated. How could just one lone woman inflict so much damage by herself? She must have had accomplices. How many?

Lucian entered his office quietly, shocked by what he was seeing. He stooped down picking up a pile of debris from the floor, sifting through each piece methodically. "She could not have done this by herself, she had to have had help. Did she do this while the rest of the staff was out here in the lobby, or did she and her cohorts show up here after trashing your apartment over the weekend? Thinking out loud, he mumbled "could it have been those vehicles that tore out of the parking garage when we arrived? Remind me to ask the gate guard some very pointed questions when we leave today," Lucian speculated. Lucian scooped up and set aside some personal items that had missed shredding. "How is your office?" he asked hopefully. "Trashed, but it is mostly blank paper and desk items tossed to the floor, and bookcases pushed over onto the floor. I cannot say if anything is missing since I have never been in the office before," Alex replied softly. "We have to see what the ladies have collected outside the office on the end table. Check your drawers to see if anything can be salvaged, and I will do the same. We can put everything into one large file box and carry it out to the trunk of the car," Lucian carefully clarified his thoughts and expressed resentment and fury over the destruction. "Let's look over the lobby end table and grab a dolly to get the boxes downstairs and out to the car," Lucian stated. "I hope we can get all of this into the trunk. I should have bought a van instead of this little Mercedes 350. Maybe I should have asked one of the secretaries with a station wagon or van to drive them over to the house? Seeing Candy leaving for the day, Lucian called and motioned her over and asked some very pertinent questions about her ride home. Candy Chavez graciously agreed to drive the boxes to the Devereaux Mansion in the Garden District. Lucian loaded all the boxes into the waiting pick-up carefully stacking so as not to interfere with Candy's rear-view of traffic. She followed him out of the parking garage and watched as he pulled over to the gate-keepers box to ask some questions and checked the logbook waving himself and Candy then out into the Garden District. She followed him into the front drive of the mansion and waited patiently while several servants unloaded the boxes. She waved enthusiastically and shouted her good-byes to her boss and new co-worker.

Walking up the stairway to the house, Alex headed toward the entrance door to check on Joseph Thorndyke and get some answers from the doctor, while Lucian parked the car. As she hurried up the the stairs to the sick room she met Dr. Ingram leaving the sick room and began questioning him. "Why are you so convinced I am related to Joseph Thorndyke? Why is he so determined to establish me as a relative? I just do not understand any of this. Can I speak to Joseph Thorndyke now, maybe he has some answers for me. He did say something quite provocative before he lapsed into sleep when I was here earlier," she said to Dr. Ingram. "Yes, he is awake, and quite alert now. I have not sedated him, so he is in a moderate amount of pain, but should be able to answer your questions and clarify things for you," the doctor replied. "Is he ready to see me now?" Alex asked breathlessly. "Go right on in, Mr. Thorndyke has been asking for you since waking after lunch earlier this afternoon." With that, Alex turned the knob and entered the sickroom tentatively. A nurse was sitting in a comfortable chair facing the bed quietly talking to a man, presumably Mr. Joseph Thorndyke. In a hushed manner, she carefully let herself into the room fully, greeting both Joseph Thorndyke and his nurse simultaneously. "How are you feeling this afternoon, Mr. Thorndyke? You are certainly looking much better this afternoon, some color has come back into your face," Alex softly commented on the apparent improvement in his health. The nurse slowly rose from the comfortable easy chair and gathered her knitting project to assist in passing long periods of time. "I'll just get out of your way here, and give you some privacy. Do not get him too excited now. I will be back to give him his medications in 45 minutes or so," Anna said introducing herself to Alex. "It is good to meet you," Alex answered distractedly.

"Hello, Mr. Thorndyke, I just spoke to Dr. Ingram, he said you have been asking to see me. I tried to hurry back to speak with you, I have many questions to ask you. My day with Lucian was filled by a myriad of fascinating, and wondrous, and yet frightening things. It seems my new position at Devereaux International may be filled with some scary, if not actually dangerous moments. It was definitely exciting," Alex babbled. "As I mentioned to you this morning, I am your Uncle. Really, it is true, Lucian was my Emissary to Briscombe Bay, Washington. My private detectives finally traced my brother and his new wife to Washington State, but it was too late. My brother was already dead, killed in a fishing boat accident, and his wife was already in the hospital, dying. She did confirm this information to Lucian from her hospital bed, before her death. Lucian faxed this information to me before leaving Briscombe Bay's Community Hospital. He mentioned planning to attend Samantha's funeral, and intended to offer you a position at Devereaux International here in New Orleans. It is giving me this chance to meet you, my last living relative," Charles Thorndyke said softly. "My mother confirmed all this? I am shocked! She finally started disclosing some of this information to me in an off-handed sort of way, by introducing me to her private shoebox filled with old news clips, birth certificates, even death certificates. It has been a confusing, and alarming time. Quite unbelievable, really. Does this mean I do have an older brother? She did leave a copy of a birth certificate for a Judd Conklin, Jr.? Do you know anything about that? I just cannot believe my mother would have left her child, put him up for adoption, or left him in an orphanage. I simply cannot understand it," Alex stated boldly. "As I am trying to convince you, your mother and father had few choices years ago. My father was dead set against their marriage, and it would have been difficult traveling with an infant under the best of circumstances, but our father promised to make it impossible. But Aimee' Devereaux helped ease the way for your mother especially to adopt her child to another prominent New Orleans family. And that is all I know. Have a long and detailed conversation with Aimee' Devereaux. She will clarify anything I have said that you do not understand fully. She has been a dear friend. Now, if you do not mind, I am in need of a nap. This long explanation has drained me of my earlier vitality, you can also verify much of this information with Lucian, too By the way where has he gone off to. You did say you spent much of the day with him?" and then as if on cue, Lucian entered the sickroom. "I hope you had enough time for explanations and clarifications? I was parking the car in the garage to give you some kind of privacy. I know what kind of a surprise this has been for you. You needed time to take it all in and absorb it all. Your mother was certainly surprised to see me, too. I must have startled her into providing you with that shoe box. Sorry. Though I tried to reassure her the problems created by old Henri' Thorndyke were over, and that Joseph was very interested in finding his little brother's family," Lucian continued with the saga of the Thorndyke family. "Uncle Joseph, I will leave alone now to rest and take your medications, But I will talk to you later, when you are more rested," Alex said gently, shooing Lucian out of the room before her. In the hallway, Alex and Lucian joined the doctor while the nurse reentered the sickroom with a tray of medications. They spoke in lowered, hushed voices to avoid alarming Joseph Thorndyke and disturbing his nap. "Today has been a very big for Charles Thorndyke. He is a very ill man, and I need to discuss some very real and difficult treatment options with you, Ms. Thorndyke. I realize these decisions might be hard for you to make considering everything you have gone through with your own mother so recently. But, as I understand this situation, you are Mr. Thorndyke's closest living relative and decisions must be made," Dr. Ingram continued weighing his words. "Perhaps, we could use one of these vacant guest rooms to talk in private," he urged. "I could join you to provide Alex with some support. It has been a very strenuous day, already," Lucian said instinctively. "I will want to continue our discussion about this Mardi Gras Ball situation later, but I do want to hear what the doctor has to tell me in a quiet, sequestered place, Lucian I will come for you if this truly distresses me, scouts honor," Alex said holding up the common three fingers salute of the boy and girl scouts of her youth. Jean-Philippe ascended the stairs then intent on drawing Lucian away for a surreptitious conversation about some troubling business matters. Alex then led Dr Ingram to an unused bedroom adjacent to Joseph's room, and quietly opened the door to the suite. They sat quietly talking on the settee in the outer room of the suite in a guest room not unlike her own. As the doctor started to explain Joseph Thorndyke's condition, Alex leaned in attempting to hear every word, not that she understood every illness or condition. "I was conversing with Jean-Claude after an initial examination of Charles after completing my rounds earlier. I gave him my diagnosis, but I will yours and Charles' authorization to implement my suggestions. At least while Charles is still cognizant with the ability to understand and make decisions on his own medical needs. As I explained to Jean-Claude, Charles condition is serious, but can be treated with medications and complete bed rest. I have found a private Sanitarium not far from here, but Jean-Claude suggests Charles stay here. He can afford to hire a private duty nurse, and he definitely has the space to put up his very good friend. What are your thoughts on this situation?" Dr. Ingram finished explaining. "It is a lot to think about, but if they are indeed old friends, and Jean-Claude can indeed provide all the benefits and comforts of a Sanitarium, then our only consideration should

be Joseph's comfort and to alleviate any fears or diminish any wran-
gling or frustration such a move might generate," Alex answered
the doctor. "I am pleased your only thoughts are for Joseph's' well-
being, very commendable," the doctor responded. "I will inform
Jean-Claude of your thoughts and decisions concerning his care.
You seem to have had quite an exciting day of your own, maybe
you should clean up before going in to see your uncle. Your clothing is disheveled and torn, and could potentially alarm your uncle
if you see him in this state, I suggest a hot bath and a little primp-
ing beforehand."

Alex was letting herself and Dr. Ingram out of the empty suite
when she ran into the nurse she had met in Joseph's room this
morning. The nurse was moving her things into the same suite they
were just vacating. "Mr. Devereaux has just hired me to be a private-
duty nurse, or at least one of them to care for Mr. Thorndyke in the
coming weeks," she hurriedly uttered. "I will be the full-time nurse
with another part-time nurse to cover me in my time-off," she continued. "Great! I need to bathe and clean-up before going in to see
Joseph this afternoon. Is he awake and rested now?" Alex inquired
rapidly, striding up to her own room. "Dinner will be served in an
hour down in the dining room. Dress for dinner, please," she heard
climbing up the stairs. 'Of course I dress for dinner. I always put
clothes on, except when I am at home alone', she thought. Then
hurrying into her room, she found a gorgeous gown laid out on her
bed, 'This is really dressing for dinner! Now I understand what they
meant,' she confirmed scampering into the bathroom. She drew a
hot bath, added some scented oils lying on the sink, and dropped
her clothes outside the tub. In the sink mirror, she glimpsed her
reflection. The bruising was just beginning to appear. It was stunning to say the least. It was Technicolor, spectacular even. How
will I wear a gown? She carefully climbed into the tub and slowly
sank into the depths of the steaming, inviting bath. She languished
in this hot, spa-like environment complete with oil and scent to

heighten the experience. She could not say how long she soaked in this idyllic place, but she finally dragged herself out of the bathroom at the sound of voices in the hall. She toweled off her body, winding the towel around her body. A second towel on the bar, was used to wrap her shoulder-length tresses tightly around her head. She stepped out into the bedroom, only to find Maddie waiting to assist her in dressing. She moved toward the bed, lightly fingering the soft, silky feel of the dress and the even softer feel of the lingerie placed next to the dress on the bed.

"Oh my, where did all these bruises come from?" Maddie asked, concerned with the bruising showing under the gown. Alex was stepping into the first of the lingerie pieces. It felt so luxurious, so incredibly sinful, she felt decadent. Maddie hooked her bra, examining the bruises on her arms and shoulders. "We will be needing some coverage for these. Let me mix up something to cover them all," Maddie spoke reaching into her bag of concoctions. "It's just some healing, soothing things mixed with light make-up substances to cover and blend over these darkened splotches. Now just lean forward, and I will try to pull the dress over your head and shoulders. I will pull up the zipper and fluff out the skirt around you too," she continued, stepping back to take in the view. "Beautiful!" they both exclaimed in unison. But Alex was more concerned about the bust line of her new dress. "Do all the dresses made in New Orleans show so much cleavage, so much skin?" she inquired trepetitiously. "Can't you put something in here to cover this just a little?" "Simone and Jackie only delivered the dress this afternoon. And yes, this is a Mardi Gras Style Ball gown, and you do look fabulous in this dress. But I can contact the dress shop and ask them to put in a small tuft of modesty lace up front for you if you like," Maddie was uttering absently. "But you go out and get your uncle's reaction as well as Mr. Lucian's before making a final decision. Well, suck in your breath, and draw on your courage, and go out and face the world!" she said pushing Alex toward the hallway door. She grabbed the high-heeled shoes matching her dress and completing the outfit, and literally jumped into them while going out the door.

Alex stepped awkwardly across the hall trying to regain some form of grace and skilled proficiency in these fancy new shoes. Turning at the rail, Maddie looked impressed, both by her appearance and the athletic, adroit way she regained her balance. From here, she looked beyond Maddie to see Lucian entering the hallway. Lucian's costume had also been delivered. He was now, Jean Lafitte, the legendary pirate and patriot of the revolutionary war and the war of 1812. He cut a dashing and handsome figure from where she stood. With his black eyes and hair, and his mysterious, raven-haired, good looks, he was quite a handsome and dashing figure. He took her arm and escorted her to the stairway and walked her down one floor, first to greet her uncle, and then another floor down to the main floor dining room. "You are absolutely gorgeous. You look dazzling, smashing, and magnificent! We are the King and Queen of the King Neptune Mardi Gras Ball here in this house. I cannot wait to show you off to everyone!" Lucian exclaimed loudly. "Lucian, isn't this dress too revealing? Maybe a little bit of lace or other fabric up here for an attempt at modesty ? I cannot think my uncle will approve of this at all." "Alex, this is the style for ball gowns during Mardi Gras. Let us see what your uncle thinks before we go on down to dinner!" he cajoled in an attempt to quiet her nerves.

"No, Lucian, how can I seriously consider hosting this Mardi Gras Ball? It's not that I am not flattered you asked me to be your hostess, but I really do not think I am qualified. I know nothing of the customs, people, friends, clients that this may entail. I am just a college student from up north. A fish out of water," Alex tried to demur. "Well we are almost to your uncle's room, let's run it by him first. I can work with you and give you a crash course in all things Mardi Gras, just stick close and keep your eyes and ears open. You pick things up fast, or at least you seem to. I will attempt to find out what I can about modifications to your gown's bodice.

No, Lucian, how can I seriously consider acting as you hostess for this Mardi Gras Ball of yours? It's not that I am not enticed by your invitation, but I really do not believe I am qualified to act as your hostess. I know nothing about a Mardi Gras Ball, family friends, the guests to invite, color schemes, nothing. I have given this a considerable amount of thought since you first mentioned it, and it is not just a case of nerves! I really do not feel comfortable with this at all," Alex uttered nervously. "Here we are, outside your uncle's room, let us go see just what he thinks of this!" Lucian cajoled her, taking her arm and aiming her through the sickroom door. "Come in Lucian, and Alex unless my eyes deceive me, hiding there behind Lucian. Come out where I can see you." And then, as Alex stepped out of Lucian's shadow "Oh my, you are stunning, absolutely astonishing! You are truly lovely," her uncle expounded. "Alex has some reservations about this gown, Joseph, she thinks it too revealing, what is your opinion? Besides being absolutely beautiful!" Lucian goaded Alex with his compliments.

With a soft knock on the door, Maddie and the nurse entered carrying a dinner tray for her uncle. Maddie was visibly upset, saying "This is none of my doing or the cook's for that matter. This must be laid strictly at the feet of this nurse and her doctor's orders. With a skimpy, green rabbit food, DISGUSTING, and with soup that looks like water and nothing in it either." Setting the tray on the rolling hospital table by Joseph's bed. Maddie left in a huff, while the nurse entered the bath to count out and verify tonight's medications. Alex volunteered to sit with her uncle while he ate his dinner and talk, hoping to hide out here in Joseph's peaceful and private room. "No, No, you go on down with Lucian and wow them with your beauty, poise, and grace under fire. You make a handsome couple! Make a grand entrance downstairs and do me proud!" Joseph said, dashing her hopes of hiding out in his room.

Alex and Lucian stepped out into the hall overlooking the main entrance and followed the railing to the staircase. They descended the stairs regally, with poise and grace for Alex, confidence and boldness in Lucian's step. "Just hold on tight, we will handle this with aplomb," Lucian whispered as they stepped out into the main entry hall. "You represent Jean Lafitte's many female friends and lovers. Not only one of the many, but his favorite,… Marie Claire!" Lucian whispered into her ear. It made the movement seem so private and intimate as they entered the dining room to meet the family. Dr. Ingram separated himself from the rest of the family, adjusting his coat and tightening his grip on his medical bag. "Lucian, I am about to leave, but I have already given my instructions to the nurse and talked over Charles treatment and medications with your father. Ms. Talbot, you are stunning! You both make such a comely couple, you'll be the talk of the ball and of the town. A perfect pairing. The nurse and your father both have my emergency and home numbers, call immediately if there are any changes in his medical condition any time. Again, you are an impeccably dressed and handsome couple, striking, breathtaking really," lavishing praise on the couple. Exiting the dining room the doctor opened the way for family members, and Jean-Claude strode over and clasped his son's hand in a firm manner, throwing his arm around his shoulder and pulling him in close. "It is Jean Lafitte and his beautiful companion Marie Claire. You are the king and queen of this year's King Neptune Mardi Gras Ball, it is official! The votes are in and have been counted!" his father introduced them to the others standing around the table. Aimee' and Lucinda hurried over congratulating and complimenting them on their choice of costumes for the ball next weekend. Then another handsome young man sat at the table, taking in the scene with interest. Jean-Claude called his other son, Langley over, obliging Langley to be both appreciative and agreeable. Langley offered his hand to his brother, commenting on the cut of his costume and the beauty of his companion, giving Alex a hug and a squeeze of her own. Alex flinched involuntarily at the painful contact. Langley noticed the slight pullback, and turned to

Lucian, "You must be a bit more careful with your lady-love Jean Lafitte, she appears to be bruised, though the signs have been skillfully concealed., almost erased," Langley taunted his brother. "We had a little traffic mishap earlier this afternoon, I am afraid my efforts to get Alex out of the way may have caused her present injuries and discomfort," Lucian replied turning back to Alex, noticing for the first time the faint proof of Maddie's skillful ministrations. Charles Henri Delacourt rose from his seat at the table notably, appreciative of his old friends choices in attire and in his ladies. He pumped Lucian's hand enthusiastically. Such a striking couple!" Charles Delacourt added fervently.

"Dinner is served" Maddie announced in a commanding and authoritative manner. The entire room began shuffling toward the table, idly delighting in the way things were working out, not knowing at least one, maybe more of these amiable companions were not what they seemed. Jean-Claude took his place at the head of the table, Aimee' took her place to Jean-Claude's left, Lucian urged Alex to follow him to the chairs facing Jean-Claude at the other end of the table. Langley, Lucinda, and Charles Delacourt seated themselves around the table facing each other and conversing lightly. The table itself already boasted an assortment of delicacies, waiting for the main entree's to be brought out to the table. Once everyone was seated, Maddie placed herself at the kitchen door and buzzed the cook to start the proceedings. It was a sumptuous seafood feast served with parsley, and seasoned rice and potatoes along with complimentary vegetables and candied Sweet potatoes. "It all looks good, let's eat!" Langley proposed intently absorbed in the food before him. Everyone became immediately attuned with digging into the delectable array laid out on the table in front of them.

The conversation remained light, friendly, and companionable through dinner and into the early evening when Lucian and Alex had to excuse themselves because of early morning meetings, appointments, and of a generally busy and exhausting day as today had been. "This is a weekend, big brother, what could be keeping you so busy?" Langley pressed his brother. "I agree, Lucian old friend, what could weight so heavily on your conscious mind in importance," Charles Delacourt concurred. "Ms. Talbot is obviously a very beautiful, and vibrant young woman. She is in need of some fun, you know, relaxation, sight-seeing, definitely not some work related time, down time, she just graduated from the university after all!" Charles ventured. "Well, as I was just about to explain to Alex, that call I took during dinner concerned the repairs and refitting ordered and done on Alex's new apartment, we have to go and inspect the work that has been accomplished and also get the new keys for the apartment, plus try to learn the new security codes and routines, suggested by the new security company. We also have a final fitting on these costumes and on replica costumes just in case. Just little nips and tucks for final adjustments, then we also need to get back to the Trade center offices, first to see how the cleanup is coming along, and then put our heads together in looking over the books for the port!" Lucian answered. "Wait a minute! What happened at the apartment and at the offices in the Trade center?" Langley and Charles inquired in complete innocence. Jean-Claude responded to the questions, "Both the apartment and the offices were horribly vandalized by unknown vandals. Lucian paid excessive fees to get the apartment, first cleaned up and then repaired. I am not sure about the business offices, though Lucian put some of the secretaries to work on the problem while he was there. "Your apartment was vandalized? This is the company apartment we keep for traveling V.I.P.'s? The one that was just completed after the flooding?" Langley asked unbelievably, or so it seemed.

"I will be going up to spend some time with my uncle, too" Alex revealed. "What? Uncle Joseph? When did this happen?" Langley demanded. Jean-Claude clarified immediately, "You well know Joseph Thorndyke has been looking for his younger brother for some years now. He enlisted Lucian's help in following the investigator's leads. Unfortunately, the leads received by the private investigators were a little late in coming. Joseph's brother died in a fishing boat accident nine years ago, but Lucian did get the necessary confirmations from Sara Talbot in the hospital up in Briscombe Bay, Washington. Sara Talbot confirmed she really was Samantha Billingsly Talbot after acknowledging the truth behind the investigators findings and assurances from Lucian that old Henri' Thorndyke had indeed passed on leaving Charles free to search for his younger brother," Jean-Claude concluded. "Then she really is Jonathon Thorndyke's daughter?" Charles Delacourt questioned unaware of Joseph Thorndyke's search "Yes. she is. They have been getting acquainted in small snatches throughout the day. Probably want to do a little more of it now, too! Alex does seem to have many questions," Jean-Claude answered forthrightly.

Lucian escorted Alex back up to her uncle's sickroom for that brief visit. She did have many questions still swirled around inside her head, but by the time they entered Joseph suite, they found him asleep, with the nurse reading in another lounge chair beside his bed. I was reading to him from his novel and he just dozed off," the nurse commented apologetically. "He has had quite an exciting day, hasn't he?" she inquired hesitantly. "I suppose we all have," Alex answered. "If you need a few minutes to do catch up on something, I will sit here quietly with my uncle, while you do it," Alex queried. "I will be back in just a moment. Watch for any signs of distress, and I will return before you miss me," the nurse answered.

Lucian stuck his head in the sickroom, first to bid Alex good night and let her know to set her clock for 8a.m. so they could have breakfast before heading out. "Alex rose from the side chair beside Charles' bed, met Lucian at the door, whispering her assent saying she would be going right up to bed in a few minutes after bidding her uncle goodnight if he woke up again momentarily. "He just drifted off to sleep a few minutes ago, but the nurse will be coming back after a brief absence taken to attend to some personal items!"

Alex elucidated. "See you in the morning, Alex," Lucian murmured softly keeping his voice low to avoid waking Charles.

Alex sat down quietly, picking up what seemed to be Charles bedside reading material and scanned the pages, returning it to the table near Charles bed. Hearing the voices of a few of her dinner companions out in the hall, Alex burrowed into the plush wing chair across from the bedroom door and listened silently. She identified the voices as belonging to Lucinda, Langley, and finally Aimee'. They were wishing a good night to Charles Delacourt down in the entryway. The greetings were robust and congenial, sounding friendly, intimate even. But Charles Delacourt made her uneasy, no reason, no justification, just uneasy. She couldn't put her finger on it, but something did not seem quite right. Something was going on between Langley and Charles too! Am I the only one who can pick up on that? Their conversations often held double meanings. The first one she heard, brought her up short, making her doubt what she had heard, then she heard more bits of their conversations and became convinced she might be right after all. Maybe Lucian and the rest of his family were too close to the situation? Could it be? Something's wrong with this.

Anne Louise slipped back into the room quietly, bringing her chart and Charles medications with her. The nurse did not really like her name, but it seemed to fit her. Anne Louise did not gossip about any of her charges, but did discuss doctor's orders with the families. They conversed quietly, then heard the voices out in the hall of family members finally arriving here on the second floor after dinner. They continued to sit in silence until they heard doors start closing farther down the hall. The nurse counted and organized her trays' medications while Alex tidied up the room and picked up magazines and books around the room placing them near Charles bedside end table. Alex thought she had made some tangled, yet tantalizing discoveries on her own, but did not know if any were accurate yet. Alex crept out into the darkened hallway and found her way up to her third floor room. Alex found her way through the sitting room into the bedroom, undressing slowly on her way to the bed. The shoes were discarded near the inside door of the sitting room. She fumbled and contorted reaching for the fastenings on her back. 'It was so much easier with Maddie's help', she cried in frustration. Did thinking it make it happen, because here she gliding through the door. "Let me help you with that! It is hard, out-of -reach. I 'll take it from you and put it back on the hanger for tomorrow. I think I need to get it back into the dressmaker's bag before sending it on for final alterations. Will you be requesting a bit of lace, a modesty shield of some kind?" Maddie questioned. "I am not sure at this point. Uncle Charles and Lucian feel my objections are prudish. I don't think I am a prude, but I have never worn anything so revealing before. I am most comfortable in jeans and big shirts and old tennis. At least I can move freely in these old, comfortable clothes, not these new restrictive 'ball gowns'. My work clothes will never be so stiff and formal, not as easy as this leisure clothes, but not as formal as these gowns, "Alex responded testily, tired after her long day and exhausting schedule. "Just leave some leisure things out for me tomorrow. It will probably be another long, trying, exciting, and exhausting day! I do not know what Lucian has in store for me tomorrow, but I had better be ready for anything," Alex groused. Alex slipped into her nightshirt and succumbed to her weariness. She laid back against her pillows and drifted into a heavy and sound sleep. Maddie turned the lights off, laid some leisure clothes out beside the dressmaker's bag, let herself out of the bedroom, then crossed out of the sitting room and locked the door as had been requested. Langley and Lucian were in the hall arguing. They stopped their verbal sparring immediately as soon as she came into sight. The behavior was strange, bizarre even, but Maddie moved past them with an objective in mind,... Bed and Sleep! The last words that drifted to her ears were penalize... preemptory ...

imperious…immoral…illegal…. Laying her head on her pillow the words troubled her, but not enough to keep her awake after this day!

CHAPTER NINE

Alex woke at nearly her regular wake-up hour, 6:30 a.m. She had gotten up at this hour all through her college years. It seemed normal, although a little more tiring than usual and this magnificent room is certainly different than my room at home! Then it hit her; graduation from the University, her mother's death, the new job offer, and the wonderful train ride to New Orleans! My 8:00a.m. breakfast with my new boss downstairs before starting our busy day. What is on our agenda today? Lucian had hinted at a few of the items; checking on the apartment, cracking the books, double-checking the port figures, dropping off the costumes at the dressmaker's for alterations. All work and no play? I thought I would be getting a week or two off for grief counseling and leave. Shower time. A leisurely start to what could be a formidable day. I would prefer a little tourism time for a day or two, but we will have to take it as it comes. A lazy, shameful time away from what promises to be a hectic, frenzied pace at the new job. Just a week or so, that's all I will need to get my feet back on the ground. She jumped off the bed and headed for the shower and Alex came out in her towels attire, drying her hair. She picked up her heap of relaxed, easy-going, and comfortable clothes and deck shoes, sat down on a footstool at the bottom of the bed. She checked the time on her alarm clock at the head of the bed and unwound when she read 7:15 a.m. Plenty of time to get the gown out in the hall and start down for breakfast. Maddie came in at 7:30 to make sure Alex was up and ready and to collect the gown and add it to Lucian's costume. "Jamie is beginning to set out breakfast in the dining room. Lucian requested some specialties be on the menu for you this morning, Lucky girl!" Maddie said knowingly.

She went down the stairs, skipping lightly and ran right into Lucian, who took her hand, leading her into the dining room pointing to the buffet being assembled on the sidebar. "Smells wonderful," Alex said. "Yes it does smell good," Lucian agreed. He looked a bit haggard, unraveling a bit around the edges. "I was up most of the night trying to decipher the discrepancies in the port authority books, so I am looking a little rough this morning. I will not be at peak performance today by any means. When we visit the apartment this morning. I do not believe I will be able to concentrate very long on the difficult things today, I am exhausted. Maybe a little sight-seeing, some quiet, easy time. Your eyes will be better than mine looking at the books. We will be stopping at the apartment first this morning, they say the apartment is ready, the garbage has been cleared out and the apartment has been cleaned and Genevieve is already looking at new furniture for you. They said they will be there this morning to explain the security updates and transfer the new keys and/or key cards to you There are new grills and gates surrounding the property to deter break-ins in the future. We will hear the rest when we arrive. A quick stop at the dressmaker's, another stop at work, and then pure recreation time; a visit to Audubon Park? We can enter at the St. Charles entrance downtown. There are also some of the old plantation tours not far from here too! Tomorrow, I need to be in Baton Rouge for a governor's conference on drugs. You will definitely have some free time for yourself while I am away. Maybe visit some of the sights close to the apartment, The Aquarium of the America's at the foot of Canal Street, the Children's museum on Magazine Street or the Bead Shop uptown. Then there are the old stand-bys: the St Louis Cathedral, the Cabildo, Jackson Square, The Pontalba Buildings, the Old French Quarter Market all close to the apartment if you want to stay close to home. But first, let us partake of this feast here on the sideboard. This should pick me up a little! Jean-Claude entered the room, followed by Aimee', then Langley and Lucinda coming in last., Dr. Ingram decided to sit in on breakfast this morning, too. Everything looks and smells wonderful, let's get started! They all took their same seats from last night after filling their plates at the sideboard. Maddie and the cook filled coffee, tea, and juice cups after everyone was seated, and starting to eat. The conversations were lively, even exuberant from Lucinda and Langley. They all had big plans for the day, but Langley managed to get in a few brotherly digs into Lucian. Dr. Ingram pulled a chair out opposite Aimee' to carry on a private conversation with Jean-Claude. Something about Charles, no doubt, Alex observed mindfully, "Is there anything about Charles I should know about this morning, Dr. Ingram?" she asked with troubled concern. "Actually, Charles is in a better frame of mind this morning. I take it things are working out better than he expected. Or maybe you have calmed his fears. The dread and apprehension he has lived with these last two decades have taken their toll on him. But this morning, he seems to have taken at least five years off that toll! Check in on him after breakfast this morning, and see the difference yourself. He is not out of the woods yet, but he is improving!" Dr. Ingram pronounced confidently. "I will do that before we leave this morning," Alex answered softly. No one at the table was paying particular attention, or so it seemed, but the thrum of voices had softened and faded into the background. Lucian noticed, paying attention unobtrusively observing those at the table for any signs of change in intensity or concentration. The governor must be wrong! He thought, hoping the imperceptible cringe he saw in Langley was just that -a minor cringe, the nearly imperceptible twinges of innocent discourse. "Eat up, so we can check on Charles before we spend our day with our assorted projects," Lucian muttered absently.

They talked little avoiding joining in on the conversations around them after the initial greetings. They ate with determination, dispensing their breakfasts with alacrity. Langley watched with interest, vaguely asking about sight-seeing, the new hostess for the Mardi Gras Ball, security on the apartment and any tidbit of information he could extract nonchalantly and effortlessly with raising suspicions. "Maybe, we will get around to some sight-seeing later today, Langley," Lucian responded to Langley's rambling inquiries. 'We just do not know how things will stack up today," Lucian replied. Lucian rose from the table, offering his hand and arm to Alex. Alex rose swiftly, eager to check on her newfound uncle. Uncle Charles was sitting up conversing with Dr. Ingram and his nurse. He was looking better, he had color in his Cheeks, though he already appeared to be tiring. "Well we are off on another busy day Uncle Charles. We will be going by my apartment to see the repairs and new security improvements added because of the break-in, a stop at the dressmaker's, and even something I was hoping for before stepping into the shower this morning ... a little sightseeing, a visit to a park and some recreation and quiet time!" Alex said excitedly. I'll tell you all about the apartment when I return later. I hope it will be near completion when we arrive. I would like to spend my first night in my own apartment, not that staying here has been so difficult," she said. "I love the location of the apartment, it is surrounded not only by fragrant flowers, but also some historic and beautiful sites. I am interested in looking around my new neighborhood as soon as I possibly can." Alex and Lucian chatted quietly with Joseph and Dr. Ingram concerning his current prognosis and health condition. This conference only lasted roughly fifteen to twenty minutes, then they wished him a cheery good-bye, telling him they would see him again soon. "Rest now, I will see you again on my return Uncle Joseph, Alex bent forward to kiss her Uncle's cheek". Alex promised. "You cannot understand how good that sounds to my ears, Alex. I have worried about this moment for so long now, it feels so unbelievably wonderful to hear you call me uncle Charles!" his eyes misted as he said this.

Lucian led Alex to the door and they slipped out into the hall. "Did you want to walk with me out to the garage or wait to get picked up in front of the house?" Lucian inquired hastily, briskly speeding down the stairs toward the front door. "I need the exercise," she called over to Lucian, attempting to keep up with his frantic pace. Lucian looked over in admiration, remembering the bruised arms and shoulders from last night. "We need to pick up the costumes to deliver them for alterations, I forgot to bring them down to place them into this car for the trip to the dressmaker's this morning. I locked up my suite with the files I was looking at last night. I studied them intensely most of the night and have developed an idea or two. Your eyes may help verify my conclusions. I cannot believe the sneaky, suppressed, disguised, even obvious changes in the books. It is undeniably coming out of my office! It was so hard for me to accept my own secretary was involved with these illegal activities. At least I think they are illegal. You take a look! First, we stop in front of the house and have the costumes loaded into the car, and then on to the apartment!" Lucian was thinking aloud. "I am anxious to get started, but I am even more interested in getting back into my own place!" Alex resolved absently. He pulled up in front of the house, were the house staff were already assembling the costumes for the car's trunk. The costume boxes safely stowed in the trunk, Lucian and Alex headed to the dressmaker's shop, before moving on to the apartment. Lex was beginning to relax in Lucian's company. They were developing an easy, relaxed fellowship sitting side-by-side in the warm, gentle breeze. She could not believe this had happened so quickly A new uncle she hadn't even known she had, this beautiful city she was just now learning about, a new and very handsome boss to work for and with- unbelievable! She threw back her head, relishing the warm sun on her hair, head, and arms. This was a new experience for her, and she loved this new sense freedom that strangely warmed her soul. She sank back in contentment watching Lucian carry the boxes from the trunk and carry them into dressmaker's shop. She heard him tell Patti to make some minor adjustments to his costume and then even some modesty adjustments for her. Now they were set to make an appearance at the apartment. "I hope we have not kept the workers and security people waiting this morning," Alex remarked in anticipation. "Don't worry, they want to get paid! They will wait. Besides, they want to sign off on a much more sophisticated security system. It is now directly wired into the police station! It will keep you safe now!" Lucian acknowledged with some emphasis.

The French Quarter was only six or seven block away, so it did not take long for the sleek, powerful car to cover the distance. Rounding the corner onto Canal Street, Alex vaguely remembered seeing some of the historical sites that came into view, Harrah's, U.S. Customs House, and finally markings for the St. Charles Ave. Streetcar. "Isn't it only a block or two down to Royale Street?" Lex inquired in anticipation. Then they were turning onto Royale and he could sense her excitement. As they closed in on the apartment, she could not see much of a difference, where were the bars across the front windows on the balcony? She looked disappointed. Lucian stopped in front of Genevieve's Antique Shoppe. He exited the car and went around to open and hold the door for Alex. He stuck his head inside the shop and called out to Genevieve asking about the workers and the new security team. Genevieve came to the front door explaining she would call up to the apartment and ask the security team to come down to the garden entrance. Alex and Lucian strolled down toward the street gate into the side gardens. They were met at the gate by a man wearing a jumpsuit bearing the security companies logo on the lapel. "I do have some innovations for you here. There are no keys! Only these key cards and retinal scans to allow you into the secure grounds and the apartment upstairs. Come in to this side of wall, so I can set up your retinal scan now. We do not need the public's scrutiny. Then we match the retinal scan to your fingerprints. We can only do this for up to five people before resetting. We now will have three people with access to the gardens and the apartment: Lucian, the building owner, Genevieve, the building manager, and Alexis, the apartment resident. Upstairs, you will find some other amazing extras hidden from the outside world, invisible to the naked eye, but they are there. I will show them to you now, no one will be breaking in on you now," the security man clarified.

The three climbed the back stairs to the upper apartment. Alex had been surprised by the ease and complexity used in accessing the street gate. The front gate had looked formidable from the street, now the security consultant pledged it was truly formidable, unbreakable. Now the front door to the apartment faced them. "You know of course, the entire building is wired directly into both the local precinct and the main offices downtown to provide complete police protection to building residents and property. Even, Ms. Dupree's Shoppe, offices, and the rear gardens are motion and heat sensitive and trigger search and spotlights to frighten and intimidate any would-be burglars and vandals. There are cameras attached to the motion and light detectors, too. They will be caught! Now, the front door is a two-step process, which will require a little coordination. Your keycard goes in this slot on the right side of the door, the keycard has an imprint of your thumbprint on it, then, align your right eye with the peephole in the door." He handed Alex and Lucian keycards, and let them practice. The door was opened twice by each, just like the gate entrance. "Come on in and take a look at what we've come up with in here! Notice the doors and windows are barred and wired, the bars are secured in the bases of the windows and doors. Most of the improvements are invisible to the human eye, unless someone specifically looks for them, and then they will not be easily found. Let's get down to the bedroom and look over those improvements. It appears normal from the outside just like it used to. But the glass is now bulletproof, brick-proof, and mostly cutting-tool resistant. It would take a lot of time to get in, enough time to be caught! And there is no access to the balcony from the street anymore. Access to the balcony is now inside the garden area on the other side of the garden wall, hidden in the flower beds behind false walls," the security tech announced proudly.

"Let me show you some of the improvements we added in the front bedroom overlooking Royale. We also added some of these improvements all around the apartment, especially around the balcony, just to make this building into a fortress. The doors and locks cannot be picked or jimmied or even shot to open them, the same with the patio doors onto the balcony out front. I am sure someone on this busy street would notice. You can now work and relax here in safety and comfort. With all the building reinforcements made and now in place, it will most likely withstand most explosive charges today, barring a nuclear explosion or other catastrophic detonation. We made the reinforcements with as little change or problems for Genevieve, her customers, and the public as was possible. I did not think anyone even suspected what was happening in this building, we worked mainly at night, even completed the heavy and technical work after closure of the Shoppe," the young tech announced with pride. Lucian was definitely impressed with the work and security measures taken, "This almost rivals the pentagon or other government buildings and corporate offices around the country. Now I can transfer some of the Port Authority boxes from my suite to the second bedroom here in the apartment. I have worried about storing them in my room in the house," Lucian remarked whispering the governor's suspicions about the identities of the drug conspirators. "Would you mind if I transfer a few of the most sensitive files and boxes to your back bedroom. We can work on them from here. It is now safe, secure, and private," Lucian asked carefully wording his question.

Now armed with the new keys and security instructions, they passed through the now relatively unfurnished apartment to reach the outside door. "I have some of the sensitive files, folders, and boxes in my trunk. I did not want to leave them alone in my room for any length of time, so I brought them with me. Do you mind if I bring them up here right away?" ? He asked almost penitently. "Go ahead and bring them up, but be careful about who is watching though," Alex answered almost conspiratorially. "I will wait here and settle them into the back bedroom and start some form of filing and stacking in the bedroom. Lucian carried up the first of three boxes from his trunk and set them down on the floor in the vacant room, then left to get another as quickly as possible. "I want to get this done as fast as possible, because I cannot leave the trunk open at all! Prying eyes, you know. There is so much deceit and trickery going on here now, we do not know who the enemies are, it could be anyone. The drugs must be coming into the Port. But, I refuse to believe it is anyone I know or care about. It cannot be, and he left to bring up the last box from the car's boot. Alex thanked the security technician for the alterations and work done on the apartment while leaving him out the door." Are there any plans on file for all this work that could come back to bite us? She asked. "The original plans and files are in the closet in the second bedroom, but plans had to filed with the city engineers office downtown. It is a public record after all," the young man told her. Lucian arrived just as the security man was bounding down the stairs.

Carefully placing the file box beside the other two in the otherwise empty room, he left the bedroom. "Let's head out for a little of that recreation I promised you, and later a little lunch at one of our many French Quarter restaurants. The Audubon Zoo, The Café' Du Monde inside the French Market for beignets and dark roasted coffee and a snack, then The Court of Two Sisters or maybe 'Jimmy Buffett's Margaritaville Café of New Orleans'. Does any of this sound good to you?" Lucian inquired. "It all sounds wonderful. It is what I was hoping for just this morning!" Alex confided. "There are a few sights I have heard about just since arriving in town. There is a Brennan's Restaurant and the Riverwalk Marketplace, so many wonderful sights to see, Haunted History Tours and then a nature walk in a place called the Northlake Nature Center. So much to see in so little time! Then we can buckle down searching the files."

Alex gathered up her new key card, and the new electric bar key to open the exterior gate. "Do we need to stop at the trade center for anything before we begin our sightseeing excursions today?" She asked. "I would like to stop very briefly at the trade center, and retrieve one secret dossier from my locked desk. The Governor provided a very secure package to me when he asked me to take over the Chief Port Authority Post a couple of days ago, on my way home from Washington State. My father does not even know about the appointment yet. My desk drawer is locked, but Courtney may have found a way to obtain a duplicate key for the drawer. I still have a problem accepting everything the Governor told me," Lucian stated flatly. Alex agreed to the slight delay, wondering how they would keep the dossier safe while out gallivanting on these sightseeing excursions. "Let's go to the trade center then and I will remove the envelope, and drop it off in your new secure apartment. Then we can start our excursions, all right?" Lucian responded showing some signs of relief. They turned down St. Peter Street on the back side of the Trade Center and located the entrance to the underground garage. But a few pair of eyes watched as they made their way back to the home offices. Lucian felt much more confident about many things now that Courtney had lost her access to the office, but another subterfuge could be on its way. What if she tried to enter later tonight after the guards went home for the night? Or has she tried in the light of day? Get that dossier now and read and secure the documents in the safe house. It would be such a relief to get the dossier out of harms reach.

They took a parking space on level three, then made their way to the elevator. Almost instantly, Lucian alerted to something amiss in the garage. "What is it?" Alex quizzed. "I don't know, but something doesn't feel right. It is awfully quiet, but look at these tires treads and skid marks, they are all over this center aisle! Something went on here. We have to try to get up to the offices, but let's take a gander at the first floor entrance. We have to see if anyone registered to enter the building this weekend." They took the elevator up to the main entrance of the Trade Center. The doors opened onto the main floor entrance, again to silence. "There should be a greeter at the reception desk, a security guard on each floor, if nothing else. If we go around the reception desk, we can find out if Grace turned on the automatic answering system for the weekend yet. "But moving around the backside of the desk, Lucian came upon a sight he was not prepared to see. Stuffed under the desk overhang were a middle-aged woman and an older man. It's Grace and Frank Longoni, our receptionist and the first-floor guard. Something or someone has come into this building and it was not good. I have to check out the phone system. We need to contact the police, they may still be in the building. It's not a pleasant thought, but it's still possible. They may be taking out all of the other security guards upstairs. If the phone system is out, did you bring a cell phone along? I think I left mine at home," Lucian remarked, frowning heavily. "This is not the ideal way to start the recreational plans we made earlier this morning," Alex commented sadly. Yes, I do have a little Nokia, I purchased minutes for not long ago. One of those untraceable cells," Alex answered. "Good! That could be even better than I hoped for. We cannot light up the board lights on any of the receptionist's boards in the building, so we cannot go through the switchboard. We do need to contact the police, we do have at least two dead bodies here already." The stairways alongside the elevator will have to be ascended with some care. Listen for voices and footsteps, and any unusual noises in each stairwell. Open door stealthily, no noise, listen, and silently close the door. It was exciting, scary but exciting. She moved along silently in her old Tennis, more quietly than Lucian in his loafers.

Lucian took the little Nokia from Alex, and dialed his friend at the local precinct in the Vieux Carre. He informed the captain of the dead receptionist and security guard found in the Trade Center Building. He then made his way to the main entrance doors to the Trade Center making sure they remained unlocked for the arrival of the police. The doors had been opened, locked open by Grace, but then relocked pressing the deadbolt button. Certainly not something Grace would do until she punched out in the afternoon, and it did not appear Grace and old Frank would be doing that this afternoon. He released the deadbolt, and quietly made his way back to Alex. "We will have to use the stairs, but the doors will look the same if anyone comes down to check on them. Remember, one floor at a time. Stealth and silence!" he reiterated for emphasis. They climbed the stairs, single-file, stopping on the first floor landing to inch the door open slightly, listening intently for any sounds. The door seemed to be blocked, by something on the other side. Lucian shoved hard against the door, driving his shoulder into the door as quietly as possible. He wedged the door open a fraction, only seeing a blue security guard sleeve on the floor. On to the next floor! They crept up another flight avoiding the creaks and squeaks of the stairs, as they rose another flight. They passed a small broom closet, finding an elderly security guard hidden inside.

"Some young whippersnappers forced their way into the building about an hour ago, and began rounding up anyone they could find in the building. Maybe it was two hours ago now. It is hard to say," George answered hesitantly. "Me and Jake on the floor below heard some shots in the main entrance, Jake was going down to check it out. He told me to find a place to hide until he came back. That is the last I heard from him. Did you see anything coming up?" He asked quickly. "I do not believe Jake will be punching out with you later today. Is that gun in you holster loaded?" Lucian inquired impatiently. "It only holds two or three bullets," George answered slowly. "It is all the chief of guards allows us to load," he responded shakily.

Lucian was thinking very fast, he hurriedly enlisted George into the little band of rag-tag rescuers. The police are already on their way, we made a 9-1-1 call in the entrance hall downstairs. I released the deadbolt lock to give access to the police. I hope they will arrive soon. I fear we may be out gunned, let's continue on to the next floor, silently as before. If we just crack the door at each floor, and listen intently, we should be able to lock in on their location. We have to move as quietly as ghosts- silent and invisible." Lucian urged them upward.

They moved in unison, one floor after another, until the sounds of police squads and emergency equipment arrived out front. Then they heard shouts and scrambling footsteps descending on another set of stairs. A second set of stairs on the other side of the building. They were escaping! Lucian briskly now made his way up to his offices. George and Alex followed as quickly as possible. They panted breathlessly arriving in Lucian's office finally. "We heard a lot of shouting and scuffling downstairs just as we were running up the stairs," Alex gasped. "I think help has arrived!" George said trying to regain his breath. The first of the officers arrived on the floor demanding to know their business in these offices. "These are my offices! Did you manage to capture any of the vandals that did this to my business?" Lucian fumed indignantly. He carefully made his way over to his desk, extracting a key to the bottom drawer of his desk. The desk had been damaged, some drawers even pried open. Agog thing they had not made it down to the bottom drawer yet. Lucian clicked open the key lock and pulled out the drawer, grasping a file folder from the bottom, and clutching it to his chest. "Still here!" he said triumphantly.

The precinct Captain pushed forward probing for facts in today's 9-1-1 call. "You found the dead bodies of the receptionist and security guard when you arrived here on a visit to your office? How about the second security on the first floor? The live guard was found in the broom closet on the second floor? There are two more surviving guards that we have found, but they are more than a little shaken up," the Captain curiously studied the facts he had gathered. Lucian invited the captain to sit down and have a chat. "Did you happen to capture any of the vandals, the perpetrators? We heard them thundering down the other stairs as we were arriving up here in the office. Alex and George were especially disturbed by everything they saw and heard this morning." An officer entered advising the captain they had captured a single vandal before others escaped through a hidden tunnel to the outside world. The tunnel is difficult to traverse and the winding, twisting and zigzagging route is a hindrance to apprehension of these criminals. The precinct commander ordered his officers to make their way through this tunnel in an attempt to find stragglers' and to find out where it led. "Did you know anything about this tunnel at all? Who would have known?" the captain inquired of each of the witnesses. George acknowledged he had rumors at the time the building was going up, but had never asked anyone about it when he was hired. Another guard just nodded in agreement. Alex and Lucian just shook their heads in dissent. The commander asked about the file, Lucian had taken from his lower, locked desk drawer. "It is just a file I received from the Governor about sales and retail information on this year's economic conditions. I am now on one of the Governor's new economic support councils. I was just coming in today to retrieve it. I can look at it in my leisure." Lucian responded to the officer's questions. The Chief and his officers finished taking the statements of all the witnesses, and then departed for the precinct house.

"How will you get the file out of the building? They may be watching! We have not discovered the location of the exit of the tunnel. Will they be trying to get what is in that folder? Will it be safe in my apartment? How do we get it there, and will it be safe to leave it there?" Alex's questions became annoying, even irritating. "Just hold on a minute. Slow down. You heard what the security people said about the apartment. It sounds like a refuge to me. Hopefully, we will be able to relax, actually sleep, for a while before getting down to business. And yes, I do think we can go out on that sightseeing excursion. The apartment is now some kind of safe house," Lucian resolved.

CHAPTER TEN

Langley mused, apprehension disturbing his thoughts. "What really worries me, is Lucian's true motives. Lucian did not even bother to inform the family he was coming back to New Orleans, and then did not return home directly upon his arrival at the airport. That is truly unusual behavior for my solid, steadfast brother. If I had not accidentally spotted him in the airport terminal, we might not have known he was even back in town! Even then, I had to rush our friend out of the terminal before he saw us together. Still, he might be suspicious already. He has been incredibly tight-lipped around the house lately." "Maybe we are all overreacting to this situation. Maybe Lucian really has fallen for this girl, she is beautiful, and giving her a job gave him time to break down her defenses. That sounds more like Lucian Devereaux! From conversations with Lucian, and even passing conversations with Alex at your house last night and observations I have been making since he introduced her to his father a couple of nights ago, I believe they have only been together once or twice in the last week or two. Lucian seems quite taken with this girl he has had only a passing acquaintance with. It makes me wonder…" Charles rambled aimlessly.

Langley interrupted again. "She is a beautiful young woman, no doubt, Charles. I can understand why Lucian finds her so appealing. But I suspect the appeal may rest in the fact that Lucian has not gotten to first base with her yet," Langley interjected contemplatively. "But if Alex is as resistant as you seem to think, it would be quite a new experience for Lucian…a real challenge, the one thing he cannot seem to acquire or to ignore," Charles grinned thoughtfully.

"Let's try to keep our minds on the business at hand. I think the first item on our agenda should be to find out what Lucian and Alex are up to now. What is this 'Special Project' and where are they now? Langley asked impatiently. "The scare Courtney gave them last night may have been just the ticket Lucian needed to break down her resistance completely. If that did occur, Lucian should be occupied with his new trinket for some time to come. We won't have to worry about any suspicions he may or may not have, at least for while."

Langley and Charles met Courtney on the narrow street behind Royale searching for signs of life in the apartment and the antique Shoppe. There were no signs of Lucian or Alex, but a number of workmen were folding up for the day. A construction work crew was finishing its repair/cleanup, while a furniture company was pulling out after replacing the apartment furniture and incidentals. Another service van pulled up the rear of the exiting work trucks. The security people had not lettered their truck to avoid advertising the total and complete changes done to the building. "Hey Langley, what was that last truck that followed the other two trucks out of the side gate? Charles inquired curiously. "Probably changing the locks or something like that, nothing important," Langley threw back at Charles. "Let's see what repairs and changes Lucian authorized for the apartment!" Charles and Courtney hissed in unison. The three made their way over to the garden gate behind the antique Shoppe. The exterior looked the same, but no amount of scheming and finagling allowed them back into the gardens and rear stairs. "We will have to wait until tonight to work on the bedroom patio doors". Courtney said harshly. Or maybe we could outsmart Genevieve to go take a look, but that would leave a witness, a loose end!" she said angrily. "Now what?" Langley spoke inquisitively. "First, we go see if we can run a minor con on Genevieve to gain access," Charles answered confident of his ability to outsmart the shop proprietor. "Let's try the door and find out," The three stepped back from the rear gate, and walked down the street to the shop door. The shop door was locked. The lock was supplemented by anew deadbolt. Trying the door handle, a small wire broke almost imperceptibly. "We have to get out of here in a hurry! I think we just triggered a police alarm! Keep moving, not too fast. Do not attract any undue attention.

"What is all this new security?" Charles fumed. "Are you sure you have not heard anything around the dinner table, Langley?" "You should know Charles, you had dinner with us last night. Lucian has become quite secretive since his return from Washington State, hasn't he?" he asked Langley. "Courtney do not even talk to me! Whatever were you thinking? I know you have better sense than you been exhibiting tonight. You could, and probably did jeopardize all our plans already!" Charles ranted under his breath, trying not to draw attention to himself. The trio moved stealthily along the back streets inside the Vieux Carre, trying to reach the safety of the Royale and Charles pre-registered suite. The clandestine suite had two key cards Charles fingered in his jacket pocket. He let them all in the back door to the hotel, avoiding the Hotel's housekeeping, desk, and audit staffs. The staff was too busy, engrossed in their own tasks not noticing the arrival of Charles and his guests. The trio made their way upstairs to the second floor to take elevator up to their suite.

Langley sat back quietly, listening to the squabbling between Charles and Courtney, trying to remain calm -to determine their next move. "Stop arguing, the damage has already been done. We have figure out were we go next, what our next move will be, where we go from here!" he responded annoyed with the muddled plans made by this new situation. Charles and Courtney sat back into the living room sofa facing Langley seated in an opposing upholstered wing chair. "Since Courtney will be unable to gain access to Lucian's work schedule …and we must have that information…. and we must more information on this 'special project' too… and Alex Talbot may be our only source for the information we need to know." Courtney and Langley were sitting on the edge of their seats to pick up on his mumblings. Lifting his head, Charles looked back at the pair of them and began formulating a plan.

"I will have to undertake the responsibility of gaining the information myself since Lucian is poisoning Alex's mind against Langley, and Courtney certainly cannot get it now. I am sure

Lucian's glowing descriptions and warnings to Ms. Talbot, make the use of Langley's devastating charm useless to us!" Charles stated regretfully. "We cannot allow Ms. Talbot to become suspicious. It really is too bad she will not be staying here at the Royale for any revealing and unreserved chats. She is a remarkably open and candid young woman! That reminds me, Lucian telephoned earlier today and canceled Courtney's assignment to the Royale's staff next week. Do you know why?" Charles inquired Langley closed his eyes momentarily, thinking and mumbling; "Courtney, didn't you say Alex was going to be Lucian's hostess for this year's Mardi Gras Ball?" "From what I overheard, she will be. She's the only reason Lucian would fire me! I had him right where I wanted him before he left and found her! There must be an expedient means of disposing of Miss Alexis Talbot!" Courtney exploded. "Calm down, Courtney. I had the impression you might be overreacting to Alex's role in this fiasco. Yes, I think you might be right Charles. My brother rarely does anything he has not thought through carefully, if not actually planned outright," Langley mused thoughtfully. "Langley, I believe it would be a good idea if you go home tonight. Just inform Courtney here at the hotel if Lucian is already at home, or if he returns by morning. Try to pick up any information on this "Special Project' too. You may overhear your father and your brother discussing it accidentally. I will keep watch at Alex's apartment for ant developments there," Charles answered.

As they left, Courtney opened the overnight bag she had quickly thrown together at her apartment. Every minute spent packing, she half expected to see Lucian bursting through her door. Remembering the look on Lucian's face as he ran after her on the street, sent a shiver of fear down her spine. The thought of what he would have done to her had he caught her sent that sliver of fear through her heart.

CHAPTER ELEVEN

Alex and Lucian made their way down to the BMW in the parking garage and departed for the apartment to stash the Governor's file folder. "Where should we start our sightseeing tour? The Audubon Zoo?, the New Orleans Museum of Art?, Rivertown?, the Riverwalk Marketplace,? Or Blaine Kern's Mardi Gras World,? But first could we stop for lunch right after we drop this folder off in the apartment? I am famished after this morning's discoveries," Lucian inquired politely. "Sounds good to me," Alex answered. "This morning's events have taken their toll on all of us, especially the elderly security guards," Alex replied quietly. "The carnage was appalling, I told the remaining guards to lock up securely and set the alarms and take the rest of the day off! At least, we will all have a couple of days off on this long weekend before returning to work. We'll just stop in here to drop off the folder in the apartment and go someplace close by for lunch. Jimmy Buffett has a café close to the apartment; it's the Jimmy Buffett Margaritaville Café of New Orleans on Decatur Street." "Do you have your keycard, and remember the sequence we have to use to gain entrance to the grounds and the apartment? Alex asked.

"I have it right here in my breast pocket. I will run the folder up to the apartment, and then maybe visit the Aquarium of the Americas after our lunch at Jimmy Buffett's?" Lucian asked. "Sounds fun!" Alex answered. "Why don't I wait here in the car and wait for your return. That should go even faster, especially considering my somewhat shaky legs after this morning's occurrences. I will be fine, but I would appreciate a few minutes to regroup," Alex answered. "Fine, I will be back in a couple of minutes. Keep the doors locked. Sit back and relax awhile," Lucian explained. Sitting back, and snuggling into the seat, she locked the door, then closed her eyes, resting. She let out a breath and sighed. Waiting for Lucian's return, she tried to remember some of the brochures of New Orleans attractions to picture in her mind the Aquarium of the Americas. She started to doze, but was rapidly awakened by loud pounding outside her window. Her eyes shot open looking into the face of Charles Delacourt. Something in his manner, dissuaded her from unlocking the doors until she observed Lucian relocking the gate approaching the car. Lucian greeted Charles like the old fraternity brother he was. They joshed around a bit, before Lucian told him about finding a place to eat for Alex and himself. Then pantomiming rolling down the window, he reintroduced Charles Delacourt, his old friend. Then they were off to Jimmy Buffett's.

"We will begin sightseeing of one of our newer culinary delights. I think you will like Jimmy Buffett's Margaritaville Cafe, he serves fresh gulf coast cooking, with live music every day, served on the balcony or the main level. There is room for large groups and/or private parties. I think a private table near the rear will provide a nice quiet, private lunch before finding something a little more exciting. I thought we could start down here in the Vieux Carre right away, just a few more places than we could if we tried to see it all. There are a lot of sights to see for a newcomer. We can only do so much in our limited time constraints. We can start today, but tomorrow you can take a look at some of the others sights closer to the apartment. There are quite a few within walking distance of the apartment, and I must meet the Governor in Baton Rouge tomorrow, so you have a free day. Just be careful while you are out and about.

Lucian ordered his favorite Cajun prepared fish entrée while Alex mulled over the varied choices, stopping at choices that included lobster, crab, and crawfish. "I have never had lobster, but I do like crab and scallops. I will try the combo plate of crab and scallops," she instructed the waitperson, it sounds good. "Maybe, we should start at the Aquarium of the Americas, then move on to the Audubon Zoo? Blaine Kern's Mardi Gras World is another great place to visit," Lucian announced. They waited for their food, chatting quietly about nothing at all. Small talk was the only thing she could concentrate on at this time of the day. "What are your impressions of the people you have met here in New Orleans so far? Your views will be unbiased, unlike mine since most of those you have met are related to me," Lucian inquired just as their lunches arrived with a flourish. Lunch was served and both took their first forkfuls. "Delicious!" Alex announced.

"It has some of my favorite lunch specialties," Lucian declared hungrily and stabbed his first forkful with gusto. "Maybe we should start with the ones that are a little bit out of the way or on the exotic side?" Alex petitioned. "Then we will start at the Aquarium of the Americas, followed by Blaine Kern's Mardi Gras World as an introduction to Mardi Gras. Then we will follow that up with the Riverwalk Marketplace and the Haunted History Walking Tour if we have time. How does that sound to you," Lucian inquired. "Then we better hurry with lunch, and get started!" Lex responded enthusiastically "What is in the State Capital that demands your attention tomorrow? And please call me Lex, it is easier and less formal," she said.

"Well, as I started to tell you earlier today at Devereaux International, and it is still so hard for me to accept, the Governor has his own theory on drug running through the Port of New Orleans. That is why I asked your opinion on the other family members and friends at last night's dinner. Your opinion would be less flawed by familiar and warm feelings entrusted to our companions and confidants. I cannot trust my own feelings on these matters. "The Governor believes someone in a position of authority in the Port of New Orleans is involved in bringing drugs into the Port, and then distributing them throughout the Eastern Seaboard.! Someone must have cleared and approved the shipping manifests coming into the harbor, then assigned the suspect cargo to specific storage areas on the wharf. I have a difficult time believing anyone

I know could be involved in this. That is why we need to scrutinize all the Port Authority ledgers and all other records to trace the involvement of everyone related to this case, and to my friends and family," Lucian retorted. "We do complete accounting matches and verification. I hope you will accept this challenge!" he said thoughtfully. Lex watched his face carefully trying to discern his unsettled, edgy feelings. "If we only go to the sights you mentioned earlier, that would be fine. We have a lot of time to see the rest of *101* Louisiana, but the sooner we finish our sightseeing, the sooner we start tackling the ledgers and records involving receipt and storage of cargo in the port warehouses," Lex answered with reservation knowing she was foregoing some detailed and thorough sightseeing for a shorter and rapid walkthrough instead.

They were finishing their lunch when Charles and Langley walked into the restaurant. Lucian noticed them, first and stood to greet them. "We've just finished, but you can have our table. The table will be cleared shortly. We will be continuing our sightseeing excursions very soon now. We will be taking in most of the nearby attractions this afternoon and then maybe dinner at the Court of the Two Sisters this evening," Lucian told them calculatedly. With that he offered Alex his hand and helped her up, they turned and walked out the way Charles and Langley had just walked in. "Let's try a few of those attractions now. They shouldn't be able to tract us down for a little while. The Aquarium should be a fascinating and riveting experience for you, and the Riverwalk Marketplace should satisfy your shopping cravings. We will have to see how quickly we finish those attractions before moving on to the next," Lucian replied showing a bit of irritation, a bit rattled by the appearance of his brother and best friend The Aquarium of the Americas was a visual landmark. It was an educational exhibition.

Something she had not visited in Seattle. She enjoyed the sights, but regretted not having been able to see anything like this while still living in Washington State. The Seattle Aquarium was new and would have been a great comparison to estimate the value of both. Though this one was a vision, completely captivating on its own. They wandered through the exhibitions, strolling for several hours to take in the sights of everything offered. Casually exiting the Aquarium building, they missed an angry glare across the parking lot. "OK, so it's on to the Riverwalk Marketplace? Or will it be the Haunted History Walking Tour first?" Lucian inquired. "A brief visit to the Riverwalk Marketplace could be fun, but only briefly, my feet are wearing out, and I want more energy for the Haunted History Tour. It sounds like a lot of fun," Alex answered with interest. Alright, we'll set a time limit at the Riverwalk Marketplace. A half-hour, an hour? Will that be enough? We will have a limited time if we are going to catch the last Haunting Tour this afternoon!" he urged her on. "Then let's get going, a lot to do and a little time to do it in." They hurried to the car and drove out of the lot. The SUV followed at a discreet distance.

Parking outside the Riverwalk Marketplace, they left their car at the curb and walked toward closest stores. Out of the corner of his eye, Lucian picked up a large vehicle hurtling toward on a collision course. He tried lunging toward Alex, but only caught the edge of her shirt. He pulled her a little forward before the impact with the SUV came. This time it caught her hip, leg, and ankle. Alex was tossed to the ground just short of the raised sidewalk. The SUV sped away in a cloud of dust, leaving Lucian speeding to Alex's side. "Alex, Lex, Alex? Are you alright? Anything broken? Can you stand?" he asked, concern etched across his face. "I am a little worse for wear, but I think I am pretty much uninjured, at least not seriously injured. I think I would at least like to try to stand." Pulling her to her feet, she wobbled some relying on his solid presence to keep her steady. "I am going to be sore in the morning, but for now I am just shaky and teetering on the road. Can I hang on to your arm a while longer while we shop some. Only one or two shops, or three if I find something?" Alex responded meekly. "Sure, my arm is yours, "Lucian came back. They strolled into the first store on the Marketplace nearest the parking area. She picked up a number of knick-knacks and replaced them, looked around, then indicated her readiness to leave the store. "Can we check out a different type of store, not geared to the tourist industry?" she asked.

"Of course. I just know the one you might be interested in," he replied. "It's not very far from this store, do you want to give it a try? How are you feeling? Can you make it?" Lucian questioned solicitously. "Stiff, but otherwise ambulatory," Lex responded flippantly.

Arriving outside the second store, Lex rushed as quickly as she could into the shops racks. She reached into her back pocket to take out her wallet. She made her purchases and collected her packages. "And now a store catering to herb assortments?" Lex quizzed Lucian. "Last stop, one natural food store with natural herbs, coming up now on the left. We will have to cross the street again, so be watchful, very watchful while we cross," Lucian appealed. Looking both ways, they slowly stepped off the curb, watching intently for that speeding SUV. Reaching the natural food store, Lex purchased an odd assortment of herbs and spices. Collecting these new packages, Lucian reached out to help with her growing collection of packages. He carried them back to the car. Lex still hung onto Lucian's arm as they walked back to the car. Portions of the sidewalk, became an older boardwalk style commonly accustomed to the tourist industry also. But it was appealing, in an old-fashioned way. They covered the two blocks back to the BMW, slowly it seemed, but they made good time under the circumstances. Arriving at the end of the street, they looked directly into the car, and started looking up and down the street for moving vehicles. When the traffic was cleared they, as rapidly as possible, crossed to the other side and got into the car. Tossing the packages into the boot, Lucian was still on high alert. Squealing tires behind him gave him enough time to leap clear of the thundering SUV. The SUV clipped his driver's side back fender before speeding away again. This will take a call to the police, for both incidents now! Getting up, he brushed off his clothes and took out Lex' cell to dial 9-1-1.

Lucian then walked around the car and joined Lex in the car to wait for the police. "How are you? That was a fast move you made back there. You've got some small tears and scuff marks, but all-in-all you still look good! Did you get a look at the driver of that SUV?" she inquired anxiously. Police cars sounded The police cars came to a halt behind and facing the BMW. The precinct captain jumped from his squad saying "I heard your call come over the radio. What happened?" "Well, our mystery SUV has returned! It took two passes at us again. It barely ruffled my suit, but I did not get Alex completely out of the way. It looks like her hip, leg, and ankle took a hard hit. She did not think anything was broken, but the bruises and scrapes will take their toll tomorrow." "Give your statement to the other officer. I will get a statement from Ms. Talbot in the meantime," the captain answered. "By the way, did you get a look at the driver or the license plate? Can you identify this whacked-out geek?" he asked again. "I cannot in all honesty identify the driver, though I have my suspicions. I do know a person who drives a similar vehicle, but I cannot truthfully say this is the person attempting to kill us!" Lucian responded candidly. "After you finish statements, can we get out of here? I do not think we will be able to continue our sightseeing tour today, but getting a good dinner sounds good to me. Soaking in a hot tub for a half hour would do Alex some good too. Then some ice," Lucian mumbled. "Ice first to reduce swelling, then heat to get out the soreness," the commander informed Lucian. The officers finished taking statements and photographs of the BMW; Alex's leg, hip, and knee; Lucian's suit, the tears and scuffs; and headed back to their squad cars. Lucian walked forward and passed the damaged fender, running his fingers over the defaced vehicle.

Entering the car, he sat in the car and questioned Alex about more sightseeing or dinner at Brennan's Restaurant on the way back to the apartment. "We should have been putting some ice on those leg injuries on the first impact, I hope we can still do that. Then spend some time in that fancy Jacuzzi tub to work on the stiffness. I do not think you are in good enough shape at this minute to take on the Haunted History Walking tour," Lucian pleaded bluntly. "I am not feeling up to much more walking tonight. Dinner sounds good to me, but I do object to entering a fancy restaurant looking like this. Could we get take-out? I want to lock myself in my apartment and actually relax after today's excitement. "Alex truthfully stated. "No problem, will give a call to one of my private culinary chefs. They will deliver. I will meet them at the gate, and show them up. Sound good?" he inquired. "Certainly does, she agreed sincerely. He started the car, and headed back into the Vieux Carre. He made two calls on the throw away cell Alex had provided, one to a car-repair center, and another, friendlier call to his catering friend.

"We are on our way now, we should be back at the apartment in a few minutes. I will be parking in the garage behind the apartment away from prying eyes. We should have 20 to 30 minutes before the meals arrive. I will help you get up to the apartment, I know you are stiff and sore," Lucian stated openly. The new Lucite stairs and rails were nearly invisible to the eye. It made climbing the stairs an interesting adventure! It helped the stair tread placement was a standard height and depth to match conventional building methods. Reaching the balcony, Lucian pulled Alex up over the connecting wood and metal grate. This is a pretty site she commented overlooking the garden area. "But we did not take a left, instead we took a right along a small path into the garden behind some bamboo walls. In a way it is even nicer, more private than before! It was a longer walk back to the front door of the apartment now but it provided a wondrous view of the gardens. "These old stairs are only for show, many of the braces have been sawn threw as an exit ploy. Do not forget!" he spoke matter-of-factly. They found Genevieve waiting at the top of the stairs lounging on the balcony overlooking the gardens. "I have news! Genevieve responded excitedly. "Charles stopped in this afternoon, he wanted to gain access to the apartment, but I told him the Security changes to the building did not give me access anymore. He even came back here into the office to check if I was lying! So I showed him the new steel wall barricading the back door. He tried and tried to move the door, but it would not budge. He left the shop and I watched as he returned to his car. I waited until closing time and locked up. He was still out there watching down the street. You told me to watch out for suspicious behavior, and his was as suspicious as I have ever seen. It was so satisfying to press a button inside my desk drawer and have the false steel door pop open," Genevieve answered honestly, but with a measure of excitement too. "I have ordered food to be delivered to the apartment tonight, Alex is a little worse for wear from this afternoon's sightseeing tours. We had an encounter with a speeding SUV that turned out to be minor, but painful to Alex, less so for me. I have to get down to the gate to let in my Chef friend from inside the Historic French Market Inn on Rue Decatur. There should be enough for the three of us before you go home for the day. We do not want to inform any observant souls of your obvious deception of no access to this apartment. I do not care if any of our suspects see me answer the gate door. I will show them up and let them out again. Just say you were working on the monthly books, bringing them up to date," Lucian said, rapidly leaving the apartment to escort the food caterers up the stairs.

Genevieve and Alex went to the new door, and taking a key card from her back pocket and completing the retinol scan, the door audibly unlocked. "I am so glad I actually remembered the sequence to get into my new apartment. I do not think there is very much left in my apartment, but hopefully we can pull things together. Eating on the floor is something I have done before, it is like a picnic, really," Alex rambled on. "Not to worry, Alex. The new furniture has been delivered this morning, secretly through the garage entrance.

If anyone was watching, all they saw were trucks leaving the back entrance. I do love all this secret, hide-and-seek stuff. It is so James Bond! So intriguing. "Genevieve was saying as the door opened letting three white-clad deliverymen into the apartment followed by Lucian. Finding new coffee tables in the living room and a new kitchen counter in the kitchen, the food was placed on the available open spaces. Lucian led the waiters out and let them out the gate, ascending the stairs quickly on his return.

Entering the apartment a second time, he found plates and silverware assembled next to cups, glasses, and bowls waiting for them to dig in. He took one of the kitchen stools, and surveyed the bounty filling the Counter. He then went out to the living area to scan the availabilities out here. Picking up a plate and silverware, he began filling his plate inviting the women to join him. An assortment of Creole, French, and American delicacies. "Delicious", they all agreed, eating ravenously. They concentrated on cleaning up all the food laid out around the apartment. They even enjoyed a glass of an appropriate wine, chosen by the restaurant staff. Some Luscious deserts were also provided, but some were also set aside for tomorrow morning. "I am too stuffed to eat another bite," Alex admitted. "I am also ready to take that long, hot soak in that new Jacuzzi, too," Lex said quietly, rising on shaky legs, seeking a steadying handhold along the new furniture. Lex made her way toward the large bathroom outside her bedroom. She glanced into the open door and spotted towels, washcloths, and hand towels hanging from new towel racks. There was also a fresh nightgown and a thick, soft robe waiting for her. "Maddie sent some of your clothes down for you, too. They have been put into your bedroom. Not all of your things were destroyed by the vandals, just the items you had shipped through from Briscombe Bay! You have a new bedroom set in the bedroom now, too," Genevieve called out, taking her leave and heading down to the antique Shoppe books to continue the deception.

Lucian came behind her, turning on the spigots and filling the tub. Showing her how to operate the jets. "Have a relaxing soak, I will be cleaning up the spare bedroom so I can get a good night's sleep, too." "Alex? How are you doing in there?" Lucian called out, then rattled the door handle. "Wait a minute, I dozed off in the tub. Is there something important you wanted to go over with me?" Lex called back. "I will be driving up to Baton Rouge in the morning, but I have been sorting information from inside the boxes and trying to match shipments with manifests with authorizations and signatures. If you get back from your close-in sight-seeing tomorrow early, could you begin scrutinizing more of the records and looking for patterns?" Lucian inquired. "I am planning on getting an early start in the morning, but I will have coffee ready for you. Right now, I am going to bed in the second bedroom, it has been a long day! It's already past ten p.m.," he informed her, and walked back to the bedroom near the entry. Much of the information sorting had been going on in the living room. The dinner items had been cleared, tossed out, and replaced by open file folders on the coffee and end tables.

Alex glanced into the living room, pulled the big snuggly robe around herself and walked forward to the bedroom overlooking the street. Closing the blinds, she looked down on the street trying to see bogeymen in the dark. With the blinds totally closed it became dark and she sought out a light switch to crawl into bed. It was remarkably quiet in this bedroom given the proximity of the street and the activity going on below. It was dark and quiet and she drifted off to sleep quickly.

Opening her eyes slowly, Alex awoke to the smell of freshly brewing coffee and cinnamon wafting through the room. My bedroom is really beautiful and oh, so comfortable. She attempted to roll over, her aching body groaning in protest. Her bruises had grown since last night, and how she had stiffened. She clumsily got dressed, then walked in the direction of coffee and food. Lucian stood in the small kitchen with a cup of coffee in his hand, already dressed for his road trip. "Good Morning, here is coffee, and there is fresh juice and beignets from Café Du Monde out here in the kitchen too. The Café Du Monde is not far from here. There is also an assortment of fresh fruit in the refrigerator, too. Genevieve brought some things in with her this morning avoiding setting off any alarm bells in any of our spies! I am on my way out now, keep the security system on, do not go out if you are as sore and banged up as you look, I will be back before dark," he said before slipping out the door. Alex entered the living room on her way to the coffee, fruit, and beignets. Famished she pulled down one of Genevieve's pretty cups and saucers and a small plate for the beignet and a bowl for the fruit. She carried it all out to the sitting area.

Lex sat down pushing herself deep into the cushions of the new sofa. Her breakfast within reach on the top of a series of file folders, she took a bite of her beignet and took a sip of coffee. Whew! Strong stuff! Hot, too. Putting a fork into a large piece of fruit to cool off her tongue, she slurped it down greedily, wiping her dripping chin and cheek with a paper napkin left over from last night. Reaching for a ledger on the side end table, she began running her finger down a list of ships manifests for the Port of New Orleans. A lot comes into the Port every day! Each item merit's a line on one of the daily ledgers. Daily numbers are then totaled and recorded in weekly ledgers. Weekly numbers are then totaled and recorded in monthly ledgers. All of these figures had to be verified and matched from one ledger to the next. First verify totals then look for erasures and cross outs changing numbers. She knew the drill.

Lucian had been startled by her very colorful assortment of bruises this morning when he had left, wanting to forego his trip to the capital, instead hoping make her agree to visit her doctor, a clinic, or a hospital of her choice. Alex simply told him it looked worse than it really was. She was stiff and sore, but would take it easy today. She dragged herself back to the second bedroom seeking her old calculator and some long tabulating sheets to begin her work. She got them back to the sitting area to begin her work. She remembered Lucian's tormented, incredulous face trying to integrate Courtney's treacherous behavior, originally in betraying his trust by altering shipping records and now in attempting to run them down. It had been so hard to believe this woman had gained his trust so completely, he was loyal and honorable and expected the same qualities in his friends and employees. Alex was suitably impressed by the man and his work ethic!

She had to get him out of her head and get down to work. She undertook the verification of manifests and totals, beginning to notice a pattern of corrections and changes made from one ledger or tally sheet to another. Then she had tried to match the totals to the warehouse totals stored in the buildings along the wharf. Glancing at her watch, she was surprised to see how late it had gotten. Genevieve had popped in little earlier to drop off a sandwich purchased in the French Market. She left it on the kitchen counter, calling in her greetings. Alex finally stood and limped a little to the kitchen pulling out a stool facing the sandwich, turning back to the refrigerator seeking a cold drink, finding bottles of iced tea on a door shelve. She tore into her lunch and ate more ravenously than she would have thought, finishing every morsel on her plate.

Lex stood, stretched her arms and legs, cracked her knuckles and noticed the light streaming into the windows. She took a mid-afternoon shower, lathering up her tender arms, shoulders, and legs. The heat soothed her aching joints, and calmed a troubled mind. She picked up her shorts and tea shirt before putting them back on. Wandering slowly around the apartment, she found herself in her own bedroom looking down on Royale and the building crowds for Mardi Gras. It was almost two and many of the cars had already been banned from the narrow streets. The view from the balcony was going to be spectacular! Alex studied the many faces on the street, looking for familiar or suspicious characters walking along the street. Closing the patio doors tightly and securing the doors locks, she walked back to the living area and continued her auditing and verification duties.

Waiting for Lucian to return to New Orleans, she thought of her gown for the Mardi Gras Ball at the Devereaux mansion next Saturday. The costume was an antebellum concoction in green and gold done in satins, lace, and stiff brocades. It had looked absolutely stunning set against her long auburn hair and creamy complexion. She had not been thrilled with the low-cut and far too-revealing cut of the bodice, but Alex was never the less caught up in the Mardi Gras fever. She had felt daring, even a bit seductive and sexy in this new dress. An unexpected and disconcerting hot wave pulsed through her remembering Lucian's appreciative glean during that final fitting. Green, Gold, and Purple being the colors of Mardi Gras.

There is still another box of folders waiting to be examined, I must try to get through that box before Lucian returns. My next move will have to be verification and manual visible count in the warehouses on the wharf. And much as I mistrust him, I will have to stop and pick up more manifests from Charles on my way into the office on my way back to the Trade Center. She pulled the last box from the second bedroom and went to work again. She plodded along duplicating her earlier work until Lucian walked in the door and startled her. "How was your trip to Baton Rouge?" she inquired now fully spooked. "Did not mean to make you jump! No, not much new from the Governor's Task Force. We just re-examined most of the evidence we already had. But, I can now see the Governor's point of view," Lucian answered.

CHAPTER TWELVE

Sleeping later than usual, Lex hurried through her morning routine, then roused Lucian to prepare for work. Lex started brewing coffee and found the left over fruit and beignets and set them out on the counter. She could hear the shower running, followed by an electric shaver, then Lucian came around the corner into the small kitchenette. "Coffee smells good, but we could have gotten fresh fruit and beignets at the market this morning," he said. "I will need to stop at Charles office this morning to pick up the Port reports since Charles Delacourt is listed as second-in-command to you on the Port Board," Lex informed him. "I will meet you at the Trade Center with the reports when I finish my brisk walk this morning!" she continued. Leaving the apartment, she fingered the new keycards attached to the ring in her pocket and kept a quick pace toward the river. She found walking invigorating, especially when the weather was so beautiful. And the weather in New Orleans was beautiful this time of year.

Armed with the Port reports supplied by Charles Delacourt, Alex pondered a cryptic notation scrawled on Charles calendar: LD. 3 PM. #26. Pondering the message only briefly, Alex adjusted the portfolio under her arm thinking how she had wanted some excitement and adventure in her so-far boring life, but this was unreal! She wondered what the vandals had wanted in the first place. The officers said a Key had been used, Genevieve certainly had keys for the apartment, and the opportunity to make copies of them. But Genevieve had been so shocked, so at a loss. No one could be that good an actress. Looking around and getting her bearings, made a course adjustment, spotting the Trade Center Building and walked directly toward her office building.

She approached the reception desk at Devereaux International, identifying herself, asking for Mr. Lucian Devereaux office. She followed the receptionist down the center corridor toward Courtney Anderson's old office now hers and then Lucian's. Overhearing the conversation between Alex and the Receptionist, a young woman about Alex's age, came over and introduced herself. "Hi, I am Gail Wilson. I usually man the reception desk, but I understand Courtney is not in the office today and will not be coming back. How was your trip? How do like new Orleans? If I talk too much, or ask too many questions, Just tell to mind my own business. How does the weather in New Orleans compare to the weather in Washington State?" she inquired in rapid fashion. "It was Briscombe Bay, Washington. And the weather here in New Orleans is really quite pleasant New Orleans is really an exciting and beautiful city," Lex commented casually "And my name is Lex," Alex tried a more friendly approach, "All my friends call me Lex". "Follow me, Ms. Talbot," Gail Wilson said indicating a door up ahead and on the right. "What's all the commotion I've been hearing since I reached this floor," Lex questioned.

"There was a break-in over the weekend, and Mr. Devereaux office was damaged. The workmen are putting the finishing touches on your office now too," Gail Wilson informed her. "We had all heard about the beautiful, young, new assistant Mr. Devereaux hired up north. If we had known such a position was available, we would have assumed Courtney would fill it. Courtney is a very beautiful and ambitious woman. She has been getting very close and indispensable to Mr. Devereaux, and very powerful in the office. As Lucian Devereaux personal and private secretary, Courtney knows a great deal about Devereaux International and its business affairs, Mr. Devereaux schedule, and company clients and contracts. I want to warn you, Courtney was extremely angry when she learned about your being hired to fill this new position. You would be wise to be very careful concerning any dealings with Courtney Anderson," Gail forewarned.

"But I hadn't realized this was a newly created position. I certainly hadn't intended anyone be pushed aside when I accepted this position. The truth is, after my mother's death, I really needed a job. When this one was offered to me, I jumped at the chance. I needed a change, and I needed the money to pay for the hospital bills. Passing a door, Alex instinctively read the nameplate attached to it- Lucian Devereaux, President. Halting, she called Gail back. "I really would like to take a quick peak, I know Mr. Devereaux will not be in his office, at least for awhile, if it will not interrupt anything," Alex queried Gail. "I do not see why not. You will be able to pass through from Mr. Devereaux's office and into your own Through the connecting door, as soon as it is finished. Mr. Devereaux authorized the work as soon as you accepted the position! Listen Alex, I think I should tell you something. Because you were picked for this new position over Courtney, and because of the connecting doors and everything, just about everyone here will jump to the conclusion that you and Mr. Devereaux have more than just a business relationship. I know Courtney will not believe otherwise, or will not let anyone else believe it either. I know now that is not true, but Courtney still does not," Gail warned ominously.

Stepping through the connecting door, Lex approached Courtney's desk. She dropped the reports she picked up at Charles office on Courtney's desk noticing the remarkably similar reminder scrawled on Courtney's calendar: 3 P.M., #26, LD! Having second thoughts, Lex picked up the reports quickly explaining "I think I will take another look at these figures, just in case." That #26 again, she wondered silently. I seem to be surrounded by some very mysterious and devious people. "Ready Lex?" Gail interrupted her musings. "They do not seem to have gotten very far, this is just the way Courtney left it! "Your new office is right through this new door on the other side of Courtney's office. The new office was not yet completed, but the carpeting was partially unrolled and laid out on the floor. The dusty mauve was so quiet and peaceful. Her office was smaller than Lucian's but they would both be able to use this middle office as some kind of a library. A small bundle of trim sat beside the remainder of the carpet rolls, and still needed tacking. When Gail asked if she wanted to look over her new office furniture, Alex nodded enthusiastically in the affirmative.

Gail led her across the unfinished office into the corridor outside. This short corridor was obviously on an outside corner of the Trade Mart Building, the wall facing her office door, an unbroken wall of windows. Along the outside office wall Lex found her furniture lined up on both sides of her office door. Lex had believed her first position would find her behind a battered, gray-metal desk tucked into a cubbyhole of an office. What a surprise! A beautiful oak desk, a swivel chair, a pair of upholstered chairs, and in a darker, richer burgundy, a bookcase and several oak-grained filing cabinets lined the hall. The shelves were also stacked with boxes. "It looks like you will have your work cut out for you. You have a lot of reading and calculating material to get through out here already. "Gail commented already weary at the thought of reading all that material.

"I am just about ready to take a break. Would you like to join me for a cup of coffee," Gail invited. Saying she would indeed enjoy a cup of coffee, Lex followed Gail through countless winding passageways into a small employee cafeteria. Gail choose two coffee cups, picking a table away from the other employees enjoying a break. Pulling out her chair, Lex commented "You know, I never expected anything as extravagant as my new office, or even my new position." Sitting down beside Lex at the table, Gail commented "But Alex, you are Mr. Lucian Devereaux's Executive Administrative Assistant, and that is a very important position here in New Orleans. And I might add, it will relegate Courtney Anderson's duties to typing letters and filing correspondence. "But, "Gail warned "Courtney could become a serious threat to your success here at Devereaux International."

Reflecting on the latest warning, Lex quizzed "That is the third time you have warned me about about Courtney, Gail. I have never even met Courtney Anderson, and I certainly did not want to usurp Courtney's rights to this position intentionally. And just why are you telling me this? Courtney has been terminated already and will not be returning to the office any time soon. "I like you Alex, you are a friendly, unassuming person, and easy to work with. I think you will discover Courtney was not. She was difficult to work with and for, full of self-importance, arrogance, a hurtful, hateful person. Most people here were afraid of her, they tolerated her, but they did not like her," Gail advised her. Pushing her chair aside to stand, Gail apologized "I really have to get back to work. I have some typing to do for Mr. Dumont, one of our vice-presidents. Last week, Courtney seemed to have had all her calls routed to me at the switchboard downstairs, and I would hate facing the consequences should I miss an important call! Gail answered hurrying back to her desk, and her own switchboard. Alex made her own way back to her own office more slowly.

Lucian was in Courtney's old office waiting for Alex's return. "Coffee break already?" he asked glancing up at her flushed face upon her return. "Yes, I was meeting some of my new co-workers in the employee lounge. I did need a break when I finally reached the office building this morning," Lex responded to his query. Lex began calculating and collating information out of the file folder she had picked up from Charles Delacourt. Lucian went back into his own office to make some private business calls. Lex completed her work on this single file folder, making notes on and asking questions she developed on her own. She had questions for Lucian, too. She needed clarification.

Meandering back to the apartment, she needed time to digest all of this new information she had gained during the day. Gail's gossipy office anecdotes, the quizzical messages left by both Charles and Courtney on their desk calendars, the unexplained absence of

Lucian at the office all morning, left Alex pondering all the angles of these differing problems and predicaments and incidents. Gail had assumed Courtney would be Alex's secretary also! She was mildly surprised to hear Courtney had already been fired. A very interesting development!

Climbing the hidden stairs to her entry balcony, Alex heard her phone ring and inserted her keycard into the slot and peered through the peephole hearing the lock click. She hurried to the phone hanging on the kitchen wall, picking up the receiver and managing to close the door behind her. "Hello?" she implored breathlessly. "Hello, Miss Talbot?" a voice whispered. "This is Aimee' Devereaux," the women at the other end of the line advised. Startled, Lex gathered her wits and replied, "Good Afternoon, Mrs. Devereaux. How can I help you?" "It is not Mrs. Devereaux, Alex, just plain Ms. Aimee' Devereaux, sister to Jean-Claude Devereaux and aunt to Lucian Devereaux, remember?" the woman apprised Lex again. "I have some very important personal matters to discuss with you. Could I meet with you, perhaps send a car for you, have tea down in the Farmer's Market?" Aimee' inquired. "We could meet tonight, or maybe tomorrow after work," Aimee' argued persuasively. Alex was intrigued by the call. Feeling slightly apprehensive about the'important discussion' she would be having with Miss Aimee' Devereaux tomorrow, Lex was too restless to eat, so she changed into slacks and a blouse. Deciding to walk to Dixieland Hall, finding the combination of physical exertion and music soothing to her overtaxed nerves. She had seen the hall while touring the Vioux Carre' with Lucian, remembered the jazz playing there was out of this world.

Although alcoholic beverages were not served in Dixieland Hall, a large throng had collected out front to listen to the music when Alex arrived. Once inside, she found Gail Wilson and her husband Dick, who quickly invited her to join them for the evening. The jazz and the company were wonderful, and Alex was still excited about her evening when the cab arrived to whisk her back to the apartment after 12:00 a.m. She felt she had finally found a friend in Gail Wilson, and feeling better than she had in a long time, Alex rushed up to her apartment after clearing the security gate and finally the apartment locks She did not notice the second cab idling further down the block. Entering the apartment in a euphoric state, Lex ran into Lucian waiting for her in the second bedroom. "Where have you been? It is not safe to be wandering the streets at this time of night," Lucian stated anxiously. "I walked down to Dixieland Hall and met Gail Wilson and her husband. It was wonderful!"

Alex was surprised, amazed to find Lucian waiting for her. "Tomorrow is an important meeting With the Governor concerning drug smuggling in the Port of New Orleans, and will be meeting with state and federal agencies about massive smuggling within the port and disbursements to sights up and down the eastern seaboard. I must get on the road by seven to reach Baton Rouge by eight, the 91 miles will not leave any time for squandering on leisurely pursuits, so I will try to be back in the evening, as I understand you will be meeting with my aunt Aimee' in the early evening tomorrow," Lucian advised her. "You best get some sleep tonight, are you going into the office at all tomorrow? Why are you meeting with Aunt Aimee' anyway?" he inquired. "I do not really know exactly, she just wanted to talk about choices made in the past, and explain some things to me. I am very sure it has something to do with mom and dad, and Uncle Charles, though," she replied. "You are right though, I am heading for bed now!" Lex said turning toward the front bedroom and the fancy new bathroom. She heard "I will probably be gone when you get up, if not there will be coffee ready in the kitchen!" Lucian called out.

Slipping beneath her cool sheets following a brief but relaxing shower, her thoughts drifted to her day tomorrow. Her meeting with Aimee' Devereaux in the early evening, work at the trade center in the morning, and possibly Jackson Square and Pontalba

Buildings and The Cabildo since they are so close to the apartment in the early afternoon? Organize my time and stay on schedule, she thought burning it into her memory, but she needed to get her own home computer, and soon! She drifted into a heavy sleep. Meanwhile, in the car parked down the street, someone stared intently at the lights going on and off in the upper apartment. "I should have reached her before she got inside gate! I should have called her back to let me in the garden. Then she might question my appearance here at her apartment in the middle of the night. I will wait until tomorrow morning."

Lex woke to the smell of coffee wafting into her bedroom. A delicious smell pulling her out of bed and out toward the kitchen, for just a sip of that delectable aroma. It was still early, only 6:30 a.m. and she found Lucian in the kitchen brewing his own version of the dark, aromatic, hickory laced coffee made famous by the Café Du Monde in the French Market. He was also arranging fruit and beignets on a tray on the counter. "I could get used to this, it smells wonderful and looks so luscious!" Lex asserted noting her desire to taste the beignets and especially the coffee.

Alex was going to have a very busy day today. First, an appearance at the office to begin the verification of entries in the port records, pure accounting and auditing. Next, leave work early for a touristy look at the sights close to her apartment, Jackson Square, the Pontalba Buildings, the St. Louis Cathedral, and if I have time before my meeting with Aimee' Devereaux, even the Presbyter's and the Old French Market. I wonder what that meeting is all about, she asked herself. Finally get out to the family home in the Garden District. She laid out her plans for Lucian, who immediately put a set of keys in her hands. "There is a car in the garage for your use with a GPS locator in it. Here is the address for the house. Just enter the address of where you are going and the GPS will guide you there turn-by-turn," he informed her, before wishing her goodbye and good luck. "Wish me the same in my meetings with the governor, I should be back this evening, if not I will call," Lucian said leaving the apartment.

Checking the clock, the 7 a.m. time got her moving. Jump into the shower, wash and dry her hair, a dab of make-up, then check out the car. That will help me get around faster and easier and I just might have the time to get everything done, everything I want to accomplish in a single day, no walking, no busing, no public transportation of any kind at all. Hurry! Hurry! Get going! Alex was a blur in the bath, then back into the bedroom to pick out something nice to wear for her first real day at the office. The blow dryer whirred as her hair dried, combing and brushing her long, chestnut hair into easy, loose curls framing her face. Examining her appearance one more time, she slipped on her shoes, grabbed her new briefcase and set off for the day. Making her way out to the garage, she unlocked and opened the door, and was pleasantly surprised to find a cute, new VW bug in the garage. A little quirky, but I like it! No, I love it! It is a good thing I learned to drive a manual transmission, but this car is amazingly easy to drive, and vastly forgiving, she thought backing out of the garage. She located the GPS stationed between the front seats and entered the address listed on the stationary letterhead. She reached the Trade Center offices in minutes rather than the half-hour planned walking time. She pulled into the parking garage never noticing the SUV tailing her a block back.

She parked and locked the car, warily stepping out of the car, watching and listening for the sound of a running engine. She grasped her loaded briefcase and hurried toward the elevator. She pressed the button for the eighth floor, home of Devereaux International. She heard a shout of hold the elevator just as the elevator door closed tight. Gail and Candy were waiting as she stepped of the elevator. "Courtney and Langley are on their way up!" they exclaimed in unison. "We've sent for security, but I think they will circumvent the security desk downstairs. Mr. Devereaux left instructions to security to deal with Courtney Anderson. I did not know Mr. Devereaux's younger brother would accompany Courtney into the building," Gail responded excitedly. "Well, not to worry, we have strength in numbers! We just need to present a united front. Courtney does need to remove her personal items from her desk, but nothing more," Alex responded normally. "I will be in my office tabulating columns to match totals in these ledgers this morning," she said to her secretary and the office receptionist. Alex clocked in for 8:00 a.m. and had four good hours before checking out early to see of the attractions near her apartment before her meeting with Aimee' Devereaux at 4:00 p.m. this afternoon. Unfortunately, her insides were still quivering as she closed her door tightly, if a bit loudly.

There was quite a commotion in the front reception area when Courtney Anderson arrived with Langley. She objected to getting her personal things in a packed box and having to carry them downstairs subjugated by her own defeat. She insisted on looking around in case something was missed. But, Candy held her ground and the newly arrived security guards escorted Courtney back to the elevator. Langley Devereaux hung back and whispered conspiratorially to Courtney before she was led out, "Wait for me in the car, I am going on a fishing expedition. I will be right down, I just need to verify some information before we proceed with our other plans." He turned and asked the receptionist if Ms. Talbot was in, and could he speak to her for a moment? Gail picked up her telephone and dialed Alex's extension. Alex left her office and came out to greet Langley. "Hello Langley, I spent the night in my new apartment last night. Lucian's contractor's must have worked all night the night before and even installed some fancy new security items to make me feel safer,! I have some totals to check while Lucian is out of town, but I will be staying in the apartment from now on. I do have an appointment with your Aunt today at 4:00, though so I may see you later at the house," Alex rattled on. Alex tried to bow out of further discussion with Langley to get back to work verifying the port ledgers. "It was nice to see you again Langley, but I have auditing to finish up this afternoon. Maybe I will catch you again at the house this afternoon?" she asked before turning her back, retracing her steps back to her office. Inside her office, she let out an audible sigh of relief, and went back to work on the port ledgers.

At noon, Alex began packing up her ledgers, tidying up her desk and calculator roll tapes on her desk. She had found some anomalies and questionable entries in some of the books and ledgers. Things she did not understand or was afraid to find out. She was a little excited about the espionage aspects of this new position, a little thrilled and frightened about what had been happening around her lately, but looking forward to the new challenges facing her. She placed the anomalies in her briefcase along with notations on some of the questionable entries she found, hoping to ask Lucian about them later.

Lucian was such a complex and infuriating man. He had no intention of answering her questions family. He was so secretive, yet apparently so sincere; so cold and impersonal, yet so intense and impassioned, especially in reactions concerning his younger brother, Langley. Lucian Devereaux was definitely a man of conflict and contrast. She had only met Langley Devereaux once or twice now and only briefly. He was darker than his older brother, not swarthy, but good-looking like his brother, but shorter and stockier and more heavily built than Lucian. His appearance bordered on sinister in certain lighting.

She found her hew desk and office keys in the center top drawer of her desk. She attached the keys to the new key ring. She filled her new briefcase to bulging with port files and ledgers, the new calculator and anomalies she had discovered through the afternoon. Grateful for the expandability of her soft leather case, she took her keys into her hand and moved to the office door, unsure of locking the doors. Asking Gail and Candy to be certain, Alex was told to lock the doors. The cleaning crews and security forces had keys for the offices. Holding the keys tightly in her right hand and the bulging briefcase in her left Alex prepared to exit the Trade Center by way of the elevator down to the parking garage. Wishing her co-workers a good afternoon, she left for her afternoon in the downtown of the Vieux Carre. She really wanted to view the St Louis Cathedral and Jackson Square today before visiting Aimee' Devereaux this afternoon. She had attached one set of office keys to her key ring and had taken the other set and taped them to the underside of her desk drawer. She did not know why, maybe she had seen it in a late night movie or something. Courtney sat smoldering in her SUV for hours. Her anger toward Lucian had transferred to Ms Alexis Talbot. Her rage for Lucian was now directed toward to that little upstart that would not let her look around her office and Lucian's. Besides being removed, even temporarily, denied her access to the necessary information she had been supplying to the others. Information on Lucian's itinerary, the shipping schedules and deliveries, and the warehouse assignments. Her prestigious and powerful position with Devereaux International jeopardized her well-being and also arrangements with the others. She could not see Lucian's sleek little BMW in the lot, only a little bug on this level of the garage as she watched the elevator indicators descending to the garage level.. The bell rang and the doors opened. Taking the SUV out of park, she stomped on the accelerator aiming at eh elevator opening. The roar of the approaching engine, made Alex look up from her dropped briefcase only to see the distorted face of one unyielding and hysterical woman locking her sights on an unsuspecting Alex.

Alex scrambled back inside the elevator, reaching up to close the elevator doors. The doors closed tightly, just as the truck slammed into it. Bowled over and lying prone on the elevator floor, Alex lost consciousness momentarily. The sounds of screeching tires filled her ears, as she briefly blacked out. She awoke to a groggy acceptance her attacker had fled the scene. She began checking herself for injuries, only to find torn clothes, scrapes, and minor bruising. Then she grabbed her briefcase and popped open the locks, checking her files, notes, and electronic calculators and other auditing tools. Thank goodness for the sturdy, well-insulated and packed case. Everything was still working! Still a little dazed, she got to her feet. She brushed herself off, touched the bump on her forehead, and attempted to open the elevator doors. Shouting on the other side of the doors let her know maintenance and security were already trying to free her. After 20 minutes of hard and brutal wrenching, the doors finally squeaked and squealed open. Alex glanced out around and into the parking garage hesitantly, she made her way quickly to her bug and got the briefcase locked away in her trunk, hurrying back to get inside her bug. Rolling her window down, she thanked the maintenance and security teams for their assistance, and request a complete incident report be prepared for Lucian. Alex started her engine and made her way out toward the security desk on her way out of the parking garage slowly and oh so carefully. Watching intently, Courtney watched the little yellow bug leave the parking garage.

Alex readied herself for the walking tour of historical sites near her apartment. With Jackson Square to be the first of her adventures in downtown New Orleans. There were carriage rides around the square, maybe she would even catch sight of a trolley or streetcar. Of course she wanted to look inside the Saint Louis Cathedral, and other historical sites, the Presbyter' and the Cabildo. Not too much, she reminded herself, she had to get back into the Garden District for her meeting with Aimee' Devereaux. I wonder what that will be about? Having left instructions at the guard house, Alex carefully and slowly left the parking garage, scanning the moving and parked vehicles in the front and on the sides of her little bug looking for that suspicious SUV from the garage and the earlier trip to the River walk Center. She knew she could not spend too much time sightseeing, but still had to stay on guard for another possible attack! She kept checking her mirrors for that monstrous truck, but there were so many trucks and SUV's on the roads or streets as it were, she could not tell for sure. she hoped to park near a police car or two, just to be safe. She thought the square would be safe enough in the daylight, she would be able to see what was coming at her. She just had to stay on her toes and pay attention! She programmed her GPS for Jackson Square, and set off, still scanning the streets around her. She parked just outside the square, locked the car and approached the on-duty officer patrolling the square. She chatted briefly with the officer getting directions to visitor entrances and building hours for her historical sites and carefully extracted his patrol hours and change of shift information. Lucian would be so proud of her! Taking care of herself, seeing the sights, and being careful in protecting herself at the same time. She had not noticed the explorer pulling up on the other side of the square.

Alex hurriedly jogged across the square to join a number of other tourists entering the Cathedral for an impromptu tour. Her first look inside the old church was awe-inspiring. It was beautiful and decades old and still serving the City of New Orleans as a famous tourist attraction! The interior was beautifully and intricately detailed, with priests and brothers answering questions and showing tourists around the grounds. Alex then noticed the vaguely familiar woman entering the Cathedral, starting an uneasy feeling in the pit of her stomach. Alex immediately surrounded herself in the throng of other tourists following the tour. Moving up to the Alter, then examining the Sacristy, and looking inside the Confessionals, and then looking up to the Choir stand located over their heads. Staying very close to her fellow tourists, she kept an eye on that familiar/unfamiliar face trying to place it, and looking for a door exiting the Cathedral as quickly as possible. That uneasy feeling kept growing and Alex just wanted to escape! She just had to find a door, keeping the distance and the tourists between her and the mysterious woman, run out to the square intercepting the police officer patrolling the square. She just needed to get across the square to the little bug across the square and drive out to the Garden District and the relative safety of the Devereaux Mansion. Her early arrival for her tea with Aimee' would not cause that much of a stir and she could check on her Uncle Charles again before the tea. She spotted a door beside the main entrance door and made a sudden movement to get out, grasping the handle while crashing through the door startling her fellow tourists. Looking over her shoulder, she saw the baffled expression on her mystery woman's face. She ran hard and fast, bolting past the officer heading straight for her little yellow bug, pulling the keys from her jeans as she ran. Hitting the pre-programmed setting for the Garden District Mansion, the bug made exiting the parking space short work of getting out of the downtown area.

Alex drove around the streets near the mansion trying to calm herself and trying to recall a name to match the face that had make her so uneasy. It could have been Courtney, I have never had a really good look at her. But would Courtney go to all this trouble, what upsets her so much about me? And why does she want to kill me? Well, am I calm enough not to let fear and agitation show to Uncle Charles or even Aimee' Devereaux or even Jean-Clause? She turned another corner heading back to the house and spotted a black SUV creeping along up the street behind her. Instinctively, she hit the gas and the little bug leapt forward. The SUV also swung into action behind her and was barreling down the street after her. Alex began a zigzagging route back to the Mansion, relying on the GPS to help her find her way, hoping to lose the monstrous SUV in the winding route she was taking. The bug was nimble and took the corners well, but The SUV was powerful and tried to keep pace amidst scream-ing, squealing tires. The screaming, squealing tires alerted residents in this quiet residential area, and they dialed 9-1-1. Just as the sirens from the first squad sounded through the small residential com-munity, Alex's stalker broke off the chase and dropped out of the area. Alex followed the GPS instructions right to the front door of the Mansion.

Hands still shaking, she lowered her face into her hands, pulling herself together by sheer force of will. What would Aimee' and Joseph think if she arrived like this? Would Langley be in the house, waiting for her? Would they question her appearance, notice her frayed nerves? I need to speak with Lucian as soon as possible, show him what I have found.

The entire District was up in arms by the invasion of police cars. What was going on? Who was in charge? The questions and speculations were flying everywhere. Residents were out on the street trying to see what had brought the police out in such numbers. The only house with no one in the street, was the Devereaux Mansion! Unusual, to say the least, though a car was now parked out front of the mansion. Certainly, not one of the Devereaux automobiles, it was just a little bug, a little yellow bug! The Devereaux owned much nicer autos than this, BMW's, Austin Healey's, even a Rolls Silver Cloud for the senior Mr. Devereaux! She left her briefcase and ledgers locked in the trunk of her car. She did not want to be waving them around in front of everyone. Lucian had impressed on her the need for secrecy, he could no longer trust his closest friends and business associates, but his own family?

The little yellow bug, a new 2008 Volkswagen beetle, was a gift from heaven. It was wonderful to get around town so easily now, to save so much time and energy, and it parked on a dune! The GPS was a life saver, too, and on more than one occasion, too. Note to self: ask Lucian if I can use this vehicle on a more permanent basis! I like it and it is just my size. I have to keep so many secrets now, and my trunk is full of them! I hope Lucian returns to New Orleans soon! I do not know who else to talk to? One slip and we could all be in the soup, or worse.

Aimee' and Jean-Claude came out onto the veranda to see what was happening with a couple of the maids and even Joseph's nurse.

Exiting her car, Alex smiled and waved up to the second floor veranda. Trying to make light of the situation and her fears. Alex approached the front steps to the house, being admitted by the butler. Aimee' and Jean-Claude were hurrying down the stairs to greet her. It seemed they had been waiting for her. It seemed Charles had taken a turn for the worse and the doctor wished to speak to her as his last living relative. Forgetting her own latest brush with danger, she rushed up the stairs, hurrying past the butler walking arm-in-arm between Aimee' and Jean-Claude Devereaux. Her papers, calculations, reports, and port registers remained locked in her trunk Once inside the house, they were all met by the good doctor and Charles full-time nurse Anne Louise. Charles had fallen into a deep sleep, similar to a coma. His COPD and bronchitis had depressed his body's ability to fight for breath and he was now on a respirator. The doctor wanted to inquire about permanent and short-range arrangements for Charles long-term care. His care could or would be taking on a long and costly length of time, until his lungs might be cleared. Alex began mulling over the options almost immediately. When her mother became so sick, she did not have many options because of the late-term diagnosis in her mother's case along of scarce family finances and now her new much wealthier Uncle Charles. What a difference, now she truly had choices! She joined Dr. Ingram and Jean-Claude in the Jean-Claude's study to discuss possible healthcare options and costs, care requirements necessary for Charles Thorndyke's continuing medical supervision. Dr. Ingram favored a hospice care program or an assisted living complex at the edge of the garden district. Jean-Claude's take on the situation was that Charles was already ensconced in a guest bedroom upstairs and both Charles and I can easily afford the nursing care he will need during the duration of this newest illness. I think Charles should stay here, attended by a full-time nurse and a couple of part-time aides for the weekends. Ms. Talbot, in deference to Joseph Thorndyke's wishes you may want to consider a name change to Thorndyke yourself, should you be able to prove your lineage to the Thorndyke family. That will make your assumption of Power of Attorney duties in Joseph Thondyke's care a much simpler matter for you and your uncle both. "I do have a shoebox of items left to me by my mother, documents and birth and death certificates, but I have not had anything authenticated yet. I really do not know if Charles Thorndyke is my uncle or not, though from Charles himself and Miss Aimee' Devereaux, and what I read in the documents and certificates, I guess I may be Joseph's last living relative. Maybe we should invite Aimee' Devereaux in to help clarify things for us. We did have a meeting here later this afternoon anyway," Alex explained as best she could. With that Aimee' Devereaux was invited into the study. Aimee' Devereaux entered holding a familiar looking shoebox. "I am sorry Alex, but you left the shoebox in your upstairs room the other night. I kind of rescued it from prying eyes. There were a number of guests cruising the halls the last few days. I hope we can get things cleared up now," Aimee' said with concern. With that she opened and poured out the contents of the box on Jean-Claude's desk. They all began examining each document and certificate with care. They discussed and verified each certificate and document finally confirming Alex's identity as Alexis Rochelle Thorndyke. "You of course will have to legally reclaim your name, but it is certain," Jean-Claude admitted slowly.

"Well then, Ms. Thorndyke, let me be the first to congratulate you. But we do have a decision to make About Joseph's continuing care soon. Do you have any thoughts on your uncle's care?" Dr. Ingram asked. Alex spoke thoughtfully and carefully drawing on her own experiences with her mother. "If it really is all right for his to stay here amongst old friends and smiling faces, he may feel more at ease and actually recover more quickly here with just his nurses in attendance and old friends gathered around him," she said quietly. "Then it is decided!" Jean-Claude confirmed. He was justifiably elated over this minor victory in his care! "Thank you Alex, would you care to go up and take a quick peek at your uncle for a short time, maybe read to him for a couple of minutes?" Jean-Claude inquired. "Then, I believe Aimee' informed me that you two are to have tea and discuss old business," he said softly. Alex stepped toward the door uttering an affirmative to the meeting with Aimee' later in the evening, "But yes, I think I would like to read to him for a few minutes before my tea with Aimee'" Alex replied moving through the door and looking up the staircase in the foyer. Aimee' joined Alex near the stairs and walked up the staircase with her, taking her hand and leading her toward her uncle's sickroom.

"I will let you spend a little time with Charles, and then I will go down the kitchen and ask Maddie to prepare our tea and some light cakes, so as not to spoil our dinner," Aimee' acknowledged. "Now, go ahead and visit for awhile, I should have everything ready in an hour or so," Aimee' said whisking Alex into Joseph's room. His sickroom had now taken on the look of her mother's hospital room complete with IV's and oxygen breathing apparatus stationed around Charles new hospital bed. She was a little shocked to see Joseph in his oxygen mask with his slightly bluish skin. Anne Louise sat in the easy chair across the room and began filling Alex in on the doctor's orders and available treatments. Alex gratefully acknowledged her for her care and sensitivity in her uncle's care. "I will be reading to my uncle for the next half hour, does he have a book in here that he has been reading?" Alex inquired looking around the tabletops. "Yes, there is a book here on the footstool, and it is bookmarked where he left of before falling off into a coma earlier this morning. I grabbed the book before it slid off the bed to hit the floor," Anne Louise confirmed.

Anne Louise took a break, sliding out of the sickroom. Alex picked up Joseph's book and began reading in a low, soft voice. The book was a story covering Wall Street scandals through the years and she picked up hopefully where Joseph left off. Reading page after page she became quite interested in the stories she was reciting. Dr. Karl Ingram poked his head inside the room for one last look at his patient, reading the nurses notes and vital signs for the afternoon out of his patient file. He listened to Alex reading softly from her seat in the easy chair. Alex was really enjoying reading her uncle's book to him. she liked his reading material. So far it was very interesting, a real page-turner. "As you may or may not know, Joseph came to me about a year ago complaining of health problems, short-ness of breath, general fatigue and weakness. I ordered a full battery of tests, and found some quite serious concerns and anomalies," Dr. Ingram said quietly. "You have a very quiet and soothing voice, I am sure Joseph will be very happy having you here right now." Aimee' knocked on the door and informed Alex the tea was now ready downstairs on the sun deck. Alex hurried downstairs to the sundeck off the dining room.

CHAPTER THIRTEEN

Aimee' and Alex sat out on the settee on the deck sharing an afternoon tea. Maddie and the cooks had outdone themselves, an array of beignets, scones, light, lacy and delicate pastries were spread across some of the families silver plates and towers. Alex wondered about dinner with this feast before her, it won't be easy to eat dinner after all this. Aimee' began slowly laying the groundwork opening up the past for Alex. Aimee' reached for the teapot to begin pouring the tea, nodding to Alex to confirm her assent to a cup of tea. "Please," Alex answered her unspoken query. Choosing a half beignet, Lex transferred the pastry to one of the small dessert plates provided. Aimee' poured two cups of tea, placing one cup in front of Alex and one before herself on the small table. Choosing another pastry for herself, she sat down next to Alex on the settee.

"Many years ago, your mother and father ran from this house. Your mother had been briefly married to Judd Conklin over in St. Charles Parish. It was a marriage forced on her by her parents and arranged by his family. She found herself pregnant in a very short time, most likely by a forcible rape. She did not want the baby, but felt responsible for his care and safety. She had heard of your father's social work efforts in the Vieux Carre' where she had escaped. Jonathon hid her from her abusive, rapist husband Judd raged, seeking his missing wife, heaven only know what he would have done if he had found her. He searched high and low for Samantha, Jonathon keeping her just one step ahead of a crazed Judd Conklin For weeks, Jonathon kept Samantha safe, he worried about her, stayed with her through her pregnancy, even helped in the delivery room. They became very close by the time Judd, Jr. was born. By that time, Judd had moved on to a number of petty crimes at first, then more serious crimes later like bank robbery and assault. As you read in the news files, he was killed in a failed Bank Robbery in Baton Rouge just after little Judd was born. Samantha put the child up for adoption. She asked me to help place him in a good home with a good, upright family. I found an adoption agency that would take in the little fellow and keep him safe and anonymous. Samantha did not want the child to be found by either her family or Judd's family. It was important to her. I worked with the adoption agency for a few years before they found a home for the little boy with another family in the Garden District," Aimee' said taking a deep breath. "Then I do have a big brother!, Alex cried out confidently, hopefully. Aimee' searched her face for possible new facets of inner strength to face this new revelation. They both took a sip of tea, while eyeing their pastries. Setting their teacups aside, they both fingered their pastries idly. They both sat quietly, Alex digesting what she had heard and trying to face the possible implications, and Aimee' hoping her long-held secrets would finally free her. They chatted amiably for another hour, avoiding the new information entirely. She thought of letting Aimee' in on her own frightening adventures before her arrival at the house earlier, but thought better of it not quite trusting the rest of the family. She needed to talk things over with Lucian, to let him in on her suspicions. To let him know how truly frightened she had been, and she had to get back to the apartment tonight yet. Now she was frightened all over again.

She decided to visit Charles again before leaving for home, but could not quite easily call him Uncle Joseph yet. It really was hard to think of him as that already, mostly because she never knew of him at all. Jean-Claude met Alex on the stairs, informing her of a call he just received from Lucian saying he would not be home tonight, citing late night meetings with the Governor's cabinet. "I understand the apartment is finished again, I hope the new security features will help you get a good night's sleep. Or you could spend the night here?" Jean-Claude inquired. "I do want to spend time with Joseph tonight before heading back to the apartment. I hope the apartment is now safe. I want to get some work done tonight, verify some suspicions. Get things done for work tomorrow," Alex responded. Alex slipped into Joseph Thorndyke's room. He was quiet, seemingly at peace, breathing almost normally into his mask. She sat beside him a few more minutes, then leaving the house at a fast pace. Jumping into her little bug, she locked the doors and checked out the street before leaving the driveway. Turning on her GPS, she drove back to the apartment as fast as she could while keeping an eye out for the SUV. Pulling onto a side street, she made her way back to the garage unscathed. Once inside the garage, she locked the doors, then removed her ledgers and calculations from the trunk of the car. She lugged the briefcase out of the garage and up the staircase to the apartment.

She flopped down on the living room sofa opening the briefcase as she went down. Pulling the calculator out and setting it down in the coffee table, she re-checked her original figures.

Alex began double-checking each and every ship's manifest that had docked in the port today. Satisfied no suspected sugar shipments had actually come in today, she began tallying the totals for every other kind of shipment that had arrived in the port. She had to backtrack her totals, matching the figures to the ones in the in the port registrars and other support registers. But this was only today's manifests, she still had the last two weeks records to verify. She had begun the previous weeks books and records and had found some discrepancies and anomalies in several sugar totals in the earlier manifests. She wanted to make sure there were no other problems with other shipments. She rose from the sofa, intending to see what was in the refrigerator for dinner.

Alarm bells began going off in the shop down below. She carefully made her way to the apartment door and opened it a crack listening intently. Through the opening she heard Genevieve running up the stairs. Her words came rushing out as Genevieve burst nonstop from her mouth. "Charles Delacourt and Langley Devereaux just tried to break the security of both the shop and the garage for some unknown reason," she blurted out in what seemed to be fright. The little car appears to be alright in the garage, the new security features added in the garage seem to have frightened them off, and the police were called and notified immediately!" she finished. "I was just going to sit down and have a little dinner if I can find something in the fridge, would you like to join me and calm down a bit," Alex remarked hiding her own renewed fears. "If you cannot find anything in the'fridge', we could order out?" Genevieve suggested. "Then I will go down and open the door for the detectives," she remarked. "I was just working on some ledgers I brought home from the office this afternoon, would you like to join me for a little small talk?" Alex said growing a little apprehensive, but trying not to show it. "How about right after I take care of the police investigators," Genevieve responded.

Just down the street from the antique Shoppe and apartment, Charles and Langley slid into Courtney's SUV. She left the curb slowly so as not to bring attention to herself or her companions. Slipping the car into gear, she moved the already idling engine into drive, pulling into traffic. No police sirens screamed in the distance, so Courtney felt reasonably confident she had gone undetected, but she was disappointed, no serious injuries were reported over her CB radio.

Charles Delacourt, Courtney Anderson, and Langley Devereaux slowly made their way back to the Vieux Carre' hotel, Charles managed in the heart of the Old Quarter, intently noting the arrival of the police and the alarms set off in the neighborhood. Not to mention, the failure to gain admittance into the Antique Shoppe, left Charles especially in a foul mood. "Why couldn't we get into the shop to get up to the apartment this afternoon? he said irritably. "All we did was rattle the locked door handle, and all hell broke loose. It must be direct wired in to the precinct station all of a sudden! Well, now we know what one of the things Lucian and Alex were up to in the last couple of days. Lucian must have spent a bundle on this new security system, flaunting his money again, probably paying triple time to get the work done so fast!" Charles remarked, venom dripping from his words. "Hey, I thought you and my brother were old buddies?" Langley asked feigning mild surprise. "So what do we do now? Where can we get our inside information from now? She was quite civil with me, I think she may feel some sympathy for me because of Lucian's animosity for me over the dinner table. I can try to cultivate that sympathy into some kind of friendship," Langley mused aloud. "Well that would help a little, she certainly does not want anything to do me," Courtney answered defiantly. "Can you blame her? You have tried to run her down now, what? Three, Four times already and you have not even met her?" Charles and Langley spouted in unison. Pulling into the hotel parking space, Courtney cut the engine in silence, exited the SUV, stalking toward the hotel, then turning and pressing the button to lock her vehicle when her two passengers left the SUV. The two men caught up and joined Courtney at the side door of the hotel determined to enter the hotel unnoticed again this evening. Langley's uncut, and unabridged ramblings would need to be thoroughly examined later this evening in the suite, along with possible suggestions on getting around these new security features, Charles thought leading the way to the suite on the sixth floor.

Langley chose a seat in one of the suite's armchairs, leaving another armchair and the settee open for his companions. "So what do you both think of the situation as it stands right now?" he inquired thoughtfully. Courtney sat glumly on the settee, obviously irritated with both of her two comrades glaring at one or the other for the next five full minutes. She refused to join in on the discussion with her two co-conspirators. Langley and Charles huddled together in their armchairs facing away from Courtney's glare.

Courtney rose and walked purposefully to the farthest bedroom door in the suite. She gave a dismissive retort to Charles Delacourt and Langley Devereaux, her partners in this operation. Once the bedroom, her eyes narrowed and her brow furrowed in concentration, Courtney let her mind race through her options. *I will have to remove luke first of course, alex talbot is just incidental, not influential or prominent enough in new orleans society yet to be believed. By getting rid of luke, langley would take over devereaux international operations eliminating any threat posed by alex talbot or anyone else and ensuring acccess to information needed in the shipping times and records.* But she was worried. Why had Luke gone so far out of his way to hire this Alex Talbot and just who was she? Since Luke had not personally informed her of his travel plans or even his itinerary and then returned from some freezing place way up north with a brand new'Administrative Assistant' intent on some Special Projects! What Special Projects? Who is this Alex Talbot really? And why did Luke hire her in the first place? What was really going on here? She had been really upset to learn he had actually hired another Administrative Assistant, especially when she already knew there was no need for an assistant of any kind. Aside from her extracurricular activities, she felt she had been adept, even superb, and effective in running Devereaux International during his many extended absences.

Looking through the window out onto her balcony, Alex compared the narrow streets and her beautiful courtyard here in the old quarter to the expansive front lawns and gardens with the massive antebellum-type houses in the Garden District. Both were beautiful in different kinds of ways, but she decided she liked them both equally well. It was another world, only a few miles away complete beautiful spaces, beautiful homes, and gracious living. Alex closed her eyes imagining the pre-civil war era gone by. Genevieve spoke up about a restaurant she had heard of here in the Quarter. "I found a delightful new place near here, It's called the RioMar. It takes our local seafood and serves them with a Latin flavor. We could try the escabeche', it's a grilled gulf fish with peppers, olives, and caper relish. It has only 244 calories, but it is delicious, and its packed with nutrients. It is not far from here, at 800 South Peters Street. I snagged one of their business cards the last time I was there, so I can call in an order for two escabeche' for take out tonight. Should I give them a call?" Genevieve asked. "Go ahead, make the call. Find out if they will deliver in the first place. Otherwise, we may have to travel out for dinner," Alex remarked. "Oh no, we cannot leave this sanctuary now! They might still be out there waiting for us," Genevieve answered alarmed. "I am also reluctant to leave this safe place. I was also shaken up today and hurried home to feel safe and secure again. I just wanted to minimize my risk and try to relax again for a while. I can well understand your alarm. If they do deliver, maybe by the time we finish our dinner, our pursuers will have left the area. We can also call the police, so you can get home safely too!" Alex concluded. Genevieve made her call, verified their delivery policy, ordered the meals and waited for the delivery.

Alex began organizing and cleaning up her ledgers, notes, calculator tapes, books and registers, so that she and Genevieve could relax and enjoy a leisurely meal together. They shared an entertaining evening of relaxing girl talk, a wonderful dinner, a little get-to-know-you manager-tenant dialogue intensifying an already pleasurable and enjoyable relationship. It was nearly ten at night when Genevieve began putting together her things, readying herself for trip home. Genevieve was more relaxed, energized, and renewed as she made her way to the door of Alex's apartment. Alex touched her arm and called "Wait! let me call the police to see if they can give you an escort back to your bungalow/" She interjected. "I am feeling so much better after this refreshing evening, I had almost forgotten my earlier fright," Genevieve responded. "It has been fun, hasn't it? I really needed a good laugh today to let off some steam!" Alex answered. She let Genevieve out the apartment door, asking if Genevieve wanted Alex to accompany her downstairs into the Antique Shoppe to either wait for her police escort or make her way to her own car parked down the street and two blocks over. Genevieve put on a brave front, not wanting to bother the police for such a minor incident. But Alex convinced Genevieve to wait for the police escort just in case.

Due to the late hour, Alex began cleaning up the remainder of their dinners, eventually filling her kitchen garbage can before switching off the kitchen light to wipe down the living room coffee table. She also brought up her satchel containing her ledgers, registers, manifests, subsidiary registers, and even her calculator and calculator tapes. She began pulling out her register tapes and questions she had already found. The first thing she would have to do is finish matching manifests to port sub-registers and and then the formal Port Registers. She gave up, slipping everything back into the satchel behind the sofa.

CHAPTER FOURTEEN

In their suite inside the Hotel Provincial on the Rue Chartres, Charles and Langley went over their strategy over the Lucian and Alex problem. Courtney smoldered and paced in her room. The Rue Chartres was only a block south of Royal Street. They had easily made their way back to the hotel in the dark. An address of 1024 Rue Chartres from the 112 Royal Street were only 1 block over and 9 blocks down, for a total of roughly 10 blocks could be covered quickly by New Orleans natives. Alex sat quietly preparing for her bath contemplating the things she had learned, seen, heard, and come to understand in such a relatively short period of time. And she had not even called Janet Winslow yet! She had only seen Langley Devereaux briefly at the Hotel Provincial. He seemed to be in an intense conversation with Charles Delacourt. She still could not put her finger on why Lucian's old friend made her so uneasy. The rich, ne're-do-well image of Langley Devereaux did seem a little at odds with Alex's own first impressions. But then again he did seem to be in league, lock-step if you will with Courtney and Charles. Something to wonder at, she thought turning off the running water. She looked forward to a long soak to take out her kinks and than a good night's sleep.

Alex toweled herself off after her soak, and grabbed her bathrobe off the rack. She was tired and could not wait to fall into her new bed. She checked the new security features before slipping into her Shorty pajamas before drawing every drape tightly closed. She heard the sounds coming up from the street, deciding to slip out the French doors onto the balcony. Staying close to the exterior wall she tried to get more glimpses of Mardi Gras. She had left the lights off, and closed the door behind her in her attempt to observe her first parade below her balcony. She re-locked the French doors and re-actuated the security system before falling into her bed. She awoke to the smell of coffee wafting into her bedroom. It was a delicious smell that seemingly brought her to her feet magically, her feet barely touching the floor. She floated toward the living room and kitchen areas, finding Lucian busy in the kitchen area pouring fresh juice into two glasses beside two coffee cups and two desert plates of beignets.

"It looks and smells wonderful, again! You must have gotten here very early this morning. And just how did you actually get into the apartment this morning, anyway?" she asked blankly. "Still got my keycard, no problem!" Lucian replied.

"I found a few anomalies and questionable entries in the registers and journals. They will require further investigation. As it is, I am taking the little bug to the office today and continue working on the previous ledgers and journals to find out when all of this started. And thank you for the use of this bug.," Alex remarked before turning around making her way back to the bedroom. She checked the time on her alarm clock near her bed. Opening her closet door, she selected a crisp new business suit and chose a pair of low-heeled penny loafers for her feet. Dressing quickly, then applying her normal minimal make-up in the bathroom mirror, she stepped out of the bathroom looking almost radiant despite her bruised and mildly aching body in spite of last night's soak. Stooping slightly to pick up her briefcase, she grasped the handle firmly on her way to the kitchen. Snagging a beignet and a napkin, she brought her plate to the little counter in her kitchen. Fresh Squeezed orange juice and Lucian's own blend of hickory-laced coffee waited on the breakfast counter in separate cups and glasses.

Leisurely drinking their morning refreshments and nibbling on the beignets, they went over the entries Alex found in the ledgers and journals of the Port. "I will be taking one of my own cars to the office today, too, the BMW again. It is a heavier and nimble vehicle in case we are followed and attacked again. Be careful in that little bug of yours, and it is yours, by the way, watch for strange vehicles in front of you and behind you, coming at you from the sides. We have to be on guard all the time now, everywhere we go, until we get a handle on what is going on. You keep digging into the Port ledgers and journals, see how far back all of this goes, see if you can identify anyone involved in the Port's problems. I will be doing the same things, hopefully doubling our efforts and reducing our investigation time. I will be matching the people on duty, the storage facilities involved, and the types of shipments involved, even studying the ships manifests scrupulously," Lucian warned her. "Let's clean up our dishes before going in then," Alex responded carrying cups and glasses to the sink. "I will follow you in to the office, warding off further problems hopefully," Lucian apprised her.

Arriving at the office with little delay, Lucian smoothed her way into the parking garage, checking with the security guards about any recent strange activities, before driving ahead to find his parking space. Alex followed, parking her little yellow bug, just two spaces down from Lucian's BMW. Arriving at the elevator together, they rode up the lift to the offices of Devereaux International greeting their co-workers.

Alex and Lucian moved toward their own offices to begin their assignments, Gail sat at her temporary post at the reception desk in the front office. "Do you really think Gail likes her temporary appointment to the reception desk?" Lucian asked. "I have been studying Gail's employment file, she does lack a lot of formal education, but she does have some seniority here and most of the basic knowledge," he continued. "I am sure she will be absolutely thrilled to accept the new position, and the pay raise that goes with it!" Alex smiled at Lucian, then turned back to Gail and gave the thumbs up sign to her smiling broadly. "Good, I will be offering her the position this afternoon then," Lucian said softly, under his breath. "That's wonderful news for her. What she lacks in education, she will make up in enthusiasm, energy, and common sense!" Alex remarked wholeheartedly. Looking around, Alex found herself in unfamiliar territory. "Here we are," indicating a door marked ACCOUNTING.

Following Lucian between the work stations, they finally halted at the last desk in the corner of the department. He accepted a copy from Maggie, as noted on her desk nameplate. Glancing over this new piece of information, he took the paper from her hand, then placed it on the spindle on the edge of her desk. "As you can see this is the accounting department. You will be picking up your raw data here, verifying journal and register postings back in your office," Lucian said. And call me Luke here in the office, most everyone does. By the way, you will be getting a delivery this afternoon, a new office calculator for your desktop. No more hauling your own calculator back and forth to the office from home, leave it at home from now on," Luke instructed. He gathered up the daily sheets, logs, registers, and journals and ushered her out of the department. Trying to gather her wits about her to learn her way around the office, Alex watched with interest but simply followed Luke back to the offices. "Payroll records, Personnel files, as well as our Payable and Receivable files, and the Insurance departments are located in this office. You will need to come here to make your selections insurance coverage and payroll deductions as well as company 401K benefits. They will explain it all to you, even noting you new salary and current benefits," Luke spoke carrying all those files back to their offices, dividing them between Alex and himself almost equally.

Setting the first bunch down on Alex's desk, he continued on into his own office. "Remind me on Friday to leave the office early so you can familiarize yourself with the house and grounds before our Mardi Gras Ball on Saturday. I know it sounds rushed, but it cannot be helped. Let's get to work, now." She had the door swinging open, "I have a delivery for an Alexis Talbot," a young deliveryman announced. Standing in the doorway, a box announcing the new desk calculator held in front of him, he waited to be invited into her office. "I am Alex Talbot. My new desk calculator! You certainly offer fast delivery," Alex responded "now what do I need to know about this calculator?" she inquired. "All of the instructions and warranties should be in the box," came his reply. "If you will please sign this delivery receipt, I will be on my way," he requested. "Yes, of course, "she said taking the receipt book and scrawling her name on the line indicated. Taking the receipt book back, he turned on his heel to leave the office. Alex took the box and set it down on her desk. Opening the box, she carefully removed the warranty information, the operating instructions and the calculator from the box. She placed the reading items in the center of her desk on top of her assigned workload and the calculator on the right side of her desk. Going through the directions she recognized the calculator closely resembled the calculators she had used at the University, no learning time required.

Delivery copy in hand, Alex walked across her office space and knocked on Luke's adjoining door. Rapping lightly, she apologized for disturbing him asking "What would you like me with the delivery receipt for the new calculator?" Alex asked quietly. "Walk it over to the accounting department and drop it onto the payables desk," he answered. Taking a break from the mounds of paper covering his desk, Luke looked up, grateful for the respite. "Come on, I will walk you back to the accounting department," Luke volunteered. "Have you figured out exactly what we are looking for?" Alex asked. "I do not really know, but I have been entertaining an idea or two, especially after my first night's introduction to New Orleans," Alex answered ambiguously. Did the Governor mention the types of drugs he suspects are being smuggled into the Port?" she asked, seeking more detail. "As a matter of fact, he did. From the increased supply of street drugs, we should be looking for cocaine and other narcotic drugs, maybe some high-grade marijuana. But I do not know how that information will help you. If narcotics are being smuggled through the Port, our culprits have been very good at covering their tracks," Luke admitted.

"I have been cross-footing the ship's manifests, with the type and tonnage of storage facilities on the wharf. I believe I have found discrepancies in several types of commodity shipments; sugar, tea,cocao,etc.," Alex replied speculatively. "There are some other strange notations in outgoing shipments, too. Also in the storage assignments in the warehouses down by the river. This is going to require some hands-on inspection and physical counts," she said mulling over the implications of what she had just said. "You cannot travel the wharves and docks alone, especially for this kind of verification," Lucian warned her. "I will find another way to complete that phase of this investigation, understand?" he warned her more forcefully. "This is the beginning of a new week, we should think about getting a preliminary physical count at least! Check the storage sites along the canals against ship manifests and the records we have on file," Alex mused aloud. "Give me a few days to work out the logistics of this chore, with our safety in mind," Lucian commented.

She followed Lucian to the door, locked up and re-set the security measures succeeding Lucian down the stairs toward the garage. With bulging portfolios and briefcases they decided on separate cars for the drive into the office. She proceeded cautiously behind Lucian, keeping pace with his lead through the narrow city streets. Arriving at the Trade Center in a round-a-bout way, checking and double-checking their side-view mirrors making certain they eluded any pursuer's intent on causing harm. Pulling into the parking garage, they stopped at the guard station to inquire about any unusual happenings going on around the building today or yesterday, any future notices about upcoming events? Assuring the boss at Devereaux International and his new executive assistant that everything seemed to have settled down after yesterdays excitement. "Well, try to keep an eye on the incoming tenants, see if anyone you do not know enters the parking garage today," Lucian commented, still feeling a little uneasy. Parking on the third level, they again headed for the elevator.

Reaching the offices of Devereaux International, they greeted employees and friends and went straight to their own offices prepared for a long workday. Alex wanted to go over workday assignments with Candy and ask about all the ledgers and registers available on the Port, the Warehouses, Shipping Manifests, and transferring entries from one register to another. And so the day began. It was a very full and busy day for Alex but she was getting her feet wet in a big way. By afternoon, Alex started thinking about lunch. Candy and Gail Wilson popped into her office to invite her to lunch since she had already worked through her break.

Happy to join them, she followed the receptionist and her assistant out into the hallway. Because she had not yet familiarized herself with all the intricacies of the twisting and winding corridors, she followed Gail and Candy out the office door, stopping briefly at Lucian's door to inquire whether he needed anything for lunch or any of the books she had been working on. "Go ahead, I will be having lunch with my father and Charles Delacourt today," Lucian answered. Surprised, Alex backed out of the office and re-joined Gail and Candy in the hallway outside. To Candy and Gail she tossed out a seemingly innocuous question, "Does Charles Delacourt have an interest in the Port or Devereaux International?" Gail working the longest time for Devereaux International answered thoughtfully. "I don't think so to both questions, but he could have made arrangements with Lucian, or his father," she commented. Candy added, "New Orleans was made on private agreements and arrangements," Candy contributed. Alex held her tongue, pushing her misgivings from her mind with some effort determined to learn more about these private agreements and arrangements. Pushing the door open, exposing a busy, noisy cafeteria and break room, Gail and Candy ushered her into the real hub of Devereaux International.

Gossip was rampant, from the wildly unsupported, to the speculating grains of truth shared between old and new friends. Everyone wanted to see the new assistant to the boss.

They poured over the menu, deciding on the special for the day, tomato bisque with an entrée of seafood platters. Even more seafood, than Alex was aware of. Prawns, Shrimp, Scallops, Crawfish, even cut up pieces of Lobster with butter, garlic butter and various spicy & non-spicy sauces and dips for everyone around the table. The lunch turned out to be more than anyone expected and they in turn shared with the entire lunchroom. The gossip revolved around their table, and the chatting nearly became an uproar as the room converged on their table. The hands passed around in a whirl. They snacked and ate as quickly as they could hoping to get back to work with as little fuss as possible. Gail relieved her replacement at the reception desk, sneaking in just under the wire and Candy slid into her seat just outside Alex's office. "Fun lunch, hectic, but fun," Alex said as she breezed past her friend.

Gathering her ledgers and journals together, she continued her auditing efforts, noting any errors or inconsistencies' along the edge of the various journals and ledgers in pencil. She jotted down her questions on a notepad next to her ledgers and journals, especially on manifests and wharfs and dock assignments. She wanted to confirm some of her questions on the docking assignments and wharf storage assignments after unloading from the ships. What shipments were assigned to which docks and what particular wharves? She wanted a look at the entire area. She called Candy into her office and asked about the situations on the Port and how the locations of wharf assignments were made during the unloading process. How were shipments assigned to storage? Should she take a half hour and take a look at the docking facilities? Alex wondered and then asked Candy for directions to the closest of them, and then how far out they extended. She did not intend to visit all of them, but wanted to get a feel for the area itself. Alex left her office and walked to the elevator. Riding the elevator down to the parking garage, she went straight to the bug.

With the doors locked, she started programming her new GPS. She would start at this end of the wharf and watch the activities in the Port for fifteen or twenty minutes. She just needed to cement the feel of the place for herself. She watched from a side street slightly overlooking the area. She tried identifying the different workers and their level in the hierarchy. Some lowly field workers seemed to have much more authority than others. That created more questions for her than answers. She noticed workers pointing in her directions, but drove her car toward Gate in any case. She gave her Port credentials to the security guard and asked some general questions before backing out and leaving the area. The GPS took her back to the Trading Center where she returned her bug to its parking space. She locked and secured the bug before walking to the elevator.

She returned to her ledgers and journals and sub-journals and registers for the afternoon. Alex worked throughout the remaining afternoon hours. She kept returning to the two notes she had seen earlier. What did they mean, if anything. Why would Courtney have the same memorandum as Charles Delacourt jotted down on her office blotter? Then she tried to make sense of what that was about? She would have to consult with Lucian on the way home today.

CHAPTER FIFTEEN

Alex picked up her open work, tidied up her desk, then loaded her ledgers and journals into her briefcase, plopping her new calculator on top. Opening her office door, she stepped out into the corridor then made her way down to Lucien's office. Rapping on the door lightly she waited to hear Lucian's invitation to enter before popping in with her questions, some of the suppositions she was working on, even a few of the particulars she had discovered down at the dock that did not quite make a lot of sense to her. "Come on in, all done for the day? I am almost done myself," Lucian inquired. "Yes, I am finished, but there are items that I found at odds with the known facts included in the journals, ledgers, and registers!" Alex answered a little puzzled. "Do you have them all packed up in your briefcase already?" he asked. "I do" Alex replied. "I will be following you out of the building this evening. You took a trip down to the pier and warehouses' after lunch today! You cannot imagine how panicked I became when I learned you had taken such a big risk! I was on pins and needles until you returned. We will take the elevator down to the garage, but we will be a lot more careful from now on won't we? Lucian commented but Alex noted the crazed look in his eyes.

Leaving the office, Lucian locked his desk, the office, then turned to Gail at the receptionists desk to log out for the day. Gail knew something had frightened Alex on her outing to the jetty and warehouses' along the ships wharves into the port. The wharves serviced the many off-loading ships daily of their exports making them US imports! Imports were assigned to the warehouses by type and storage need. Imports covered a wide spectrum of merchandise and commodities, from automobiles to textiles to food grains and fruits to everyday staples like coffee and sugar and cocoa, etc. Though the wharves and docks were extremely busy during her visit, but it was the surly atmosphere on the docks that frightened Alex, and that fear followed her back to the Trade Center offices. Failing to explain her feelings to Lucian fully, Alex tagged along behind him into the elevator. She tried to explain her reasons for her abrupt decision to check out Port facilities and to familiarize herself with the Port's activities. She was still trying to explain when the elevator came to a thudding halt. Leaving the protection of the elevator with some trepidation she made her way to her little bug. The bug looked all right. The doors were still locked, the windows closed, as they should be.

Alex ran toward the bug, Lucian on her heels. Then he shouted a warning throwing a punch and ducking under an assailant intended blow. Alex jumped into action. Key in hand, she pushed it into the car door handle. Throwing her calculator and briefcase across the seat onto the passenger seat, she jumped in the bug, locking the door as she slammed it shut! Suddenly her bug was surrounded by viscous looking thug's intent on getting in the bug. The windows and windshield were being pummeled with fists, then sticks. Putting the little car into gear, she put it into reverse and floored it out of her parking space.

Thinking only of rescuing Lucian from their attackers, she was relieved to find him in his car coming up right behind her. Then she looked ahead, seeing a gauntlet of angry thugs brandishing fists, ball bats, and stones. Looking into her rear view mirror she saw Lucian signaling to ease over and follow him through. Not having enough room for that maneuver, she looked straight ahead and gunned the motor of her little bug! They came at her from the front, from the sides, she saw them in her rear view mirror, then heard one jump onto the roof of the bug. Refusing to slow down, she took her first corner to get out of the parking garage, throwing her unwelcome clinger off the roof of the car, and sliding him down its rounded sides as he desperately tried to gain a hold on the little car..

With Lucian now on her bumper, they fled for the gate. The attackers regrouped into a gauntlet again screaming, shouting insults and obscenities, grabbing whatever weapons they could find shaking and holding them in a menacing manner. The thugs had moved to the next level in the garage in order to slow their retreat. Intent on making their escape, Alex and Lucian flew toward the gate and it's guards. Lucian broke to a skidding stop, forcing Alex to slow and finally stop on the exit ramp leaving the garage. Lucian quickly explained their rapid escape from their assailants, put a call into the police, but do not try to detain them from leaving the parking garage. They were too dangerous! Try to take down license plate numbers but don't do it in an obvious manner, just readjust the garage cameras to record the plates, make and models and colors of cars leaving behind them. Leaving instructions for them to hurry, Lucian jumped back into his own damaged luxury sedan and pulled ahead of Alex on the exit ramp for the garage. Cautiously leaving the deceptive safety of the now quiet garage. Lucian vigilantly studied the street in front of him, then the side streets. With little hesitation he quickly merged with traffic Alex close on his rear bumper.

He took a left on Magazine then a right on Common passing St. Charles, then Carbondale and Barquine Avenues. Thinking gratefully how quickly they had left the antagonists behind. The two cars hurried past first the Public Library, followed closely by the Medical Center of Louisiana, and then signs for Vallere Avenue and Interstate Highway 10. Lucian decided quickly to swing right onto the entrance ramp of Hwy. 10 and then began circling the city. He knew he was south of Lake Ponchartrain, but he wanted to get around and pick up Hwy. 90, another Interstate, of course. He turned a left on business 90 waiting for a chance to get onto Interstate 90. But business 90 would take them back dangerously close to the docks were Alex had inexplicably wandered to start this tense situation. He felt secretly happy about her bringing this intrigue to a head, but now he worried after her safety. He saw signs for Highways 49, 55, and finally 10 looming large in his windshield. He needed Highway 10 to reach deep into Cajun country. Swerving quickly onto the 10 ramp, Alex followed his lead. Now they were back on the main interstate 10 highway. Weren't we just here? They glanced off St. Bernard's Parish, rocketing toward Plantation Country. Lucian did not start relaxing until he reached Lafayette. Lake Charles was on the horizon, then maybe things would calm down. But first maybe see a few sights along the way to see some sights, take in a bit of Louisiana history, it's culture and its heritage.

The tour of the African-American Museum of Art, Culture, and History illustrated the largest population of wealthy men of color in the Tree' district. Alex was surprised at the sight of the lovely Creole villa-style Villa Meilleur mansion. The mansion also housed a celebration of the African-American experience. Once inside, they strolled through a gallery of African art, illustrating the link between Louisiana folk culture and the Congo! When cotton was king and sugar was queen before the Civil War, New Orleans was the fourth richest city in America! Information Alex tucked away in her eager memory storage of New Orleans, something she had not read about in her visitor brochures. Lucian had passed up on the Chalmette Battlefield and Beauregard House in Chalmette. It was something he could pass up on, at least until the official anniversary of the battle every January.

Instead, Lucian passed the entrance ramp for Interstate 310, turned left on State 55 north to Interstate 12 and left again to Louisiana Indian Heritage Association in Robert, Louisiana. Alex was surprised to hear that Louisiana had more than 30 native American Indian Tribes who have lived in Louisiana! The Tribes had a distinct impact on the culture of the area. The Powwows held twice a year in Robert featured dance, flute, and drum, and craft exhibitions, as well as food, storytelling, and children's activities. Lucian hoped their pursuers would damper their qualms with their innocent diversions. Once again Lucian pointed his car west toward

Lafayette and the Creole Heritage Tour which wound through the Cajun Country. Lucian had visited most of these sites himself as a child or young man, but he wanted to introduce Alex to her new State culture. The diversity between Louisiana Cajun Country and a little fishing village in, Washington State, not to mention Big City New Orleans must have been a shock to Alex' system! A crash course in Louisiana culture around the state would not be harmful to her understanding of her duties in her new position at Devereaux International. He felt she would be impressed by the Longfellow-Evangeline State Historic Site along a self-guided tour named for the classic poem of an Acadian Exile and its circa 1815 Maison Oliver plantation house. The plantation house housed the Wannamuse Institute for Arts, Culture & Ethnic Studies in Washington. Washington, Louisiana that is. It suddenly struck him as funny, the comparison between the fishing village in Washington State and the Creole town of Washington, Louisiana, and he had to stifle a few chuckles under his breath. At the end of the tour they could rest under the Evangeline Oak, one of the most photographed trees in the world. The drive toward Lafayette was becoming more pleasant by the minute.

Lucian began humming and visibly relaxed behind the steering wheel. Alex noticed the new relaxed look and expression in Lucian's posture and facial expression when she pulled up alongside his Beamer. I wonder what that is all about?, she thought. She dropped back behind the Beamer again and resumed her place behind his lead. She studied the next sign, a sign noting the upcoming Lake Charles turnoff. Lucian took a small country road off US 49 toward Lake Charles.

Lucian was relieved to be coming up on the Imperial Calcasieu Museum in Lake Charles. The museum was housed in a quaint plantation-style home. It traced the cultural development of the area from Native Americans through colonial times and into the present. The museum acquired the white-and-orange old 1911

City Hall in Lake Charles recently. It had displays exploring the heritage of the area. It would be the last stop before heading into the Attakapas Coushatta Scenic Byway in Beauregard Parish. Beauregard Parish, the Neutral Strip or No Man's Land as it is sometimes called was not included in the Louisiana Purchase. A Spanish trading trail, the legendary Camino Real, became what is today the Attakapas Coushatta Scenic Byway. The Sportsman's Paradise area in the southeastern quadrant of the state was an old childhood haunt. He looked forward to exploring it again.

His youthful haunts beckoned, there were many spots in this wild area that were hidden, quiet, and very secluded. He prayed Alex would enjoy the experience after the earlier troubles leaving New Orleans. In his younger years he had spent many happy hours hunting and fishing, camping and exploring in the Sportsman's Paradise. This is an area with destinations like Shreveport, Bossier City, Ruston, and Lake Providence, Bastrop, and Monroe-East Monroe. He knew a number of destinations here to choose from. few others knew of these places or their meaning to him, his father, later his brother, and then also an old college brother, Charles Delacourt. He was beginning to realize those closest to him could be involved In drug importation and distribution. Maybe a couple of sites not shared with anyone else. He was now approaching Hwy.1 south to the Island, Plaquemine. The height of the crawfish season was February to May, it turned up in the bisque, etouffee, or best of all boiled with corn and potatoes. Not crayfish as pronounced in the rest of the country but crawfish down here. First timers should think of them as littler Lobsters, Separate the head from the body, twist to remove the first few sections of the tail to extract the meat. then suck the head for a blast of hot, spicy juice.

Shoot, I never thought to stop at the Manning Passing Academy at Nichols State University back in Thibodaux! Lucian thought unexpectedly. We have our own celebrities down here in the bayou. Patriarch Archie Manning, a former NFL Quarterback and his

two sons, New Orleans born Peyton and Eli Manning. Those
are names she should have heard even if she is not a football fan.
But we do have to find a place to sleep tonight, I have a couple
of ideas. Eunice or Opelousas, small towns between Lafayette and
St. Charles. Edgerly is a nice little town off the beaten track, as is
Sulpher or Beauregard. These small towns were quaint and pictur-
esque and followed the back roads, few knew of them. Out here,
every small town proclaimed to be the capital of something--like
Bridge City, the Gumbo Capital of the World or Crowley, the Rice
Capital, or Beaux Bridge, the Crawfish Capital, even Opelousas, the
Yam Capital. Fortunately, there would be other things to see tomorrow or the next day, depending on when they could get back to New
Orleans. He had been leaving messages for the State Police along
the way describing their flight and the reasons for their flight. I can
try to make this exile from New Orleans as painless and pleasant
as possible.

This entire area was Cajun Country, otherwise known as the
Crossroads, a nicely spiced melting pot of French, Spanish, and
English influences. He hoped to remember some nice Bed and
Breakfasts in tog for quiet and safe. Nothing in Edgerly, but one
in Sulpher. Alex came to a halt close to the BMW.s rear taillights,
then thought better of it and tried to find a place close by. She found
a space only a few spots over and brought the bug to a halt in the
flight from New Orleans. It felt good to stop, she did not like fleeing, she'd done nothing wrong, but having her life threatened was
another experience she could live without! What had happened?
What had started all of this? I did not see much of importance at
the docks along the port waterways, or did I? Let me think, did
anything stand out that pertained to my suspicions found in company records?.

Alex watched as Lucian descended the steps from the main door
of the Bed-and Breakfast. From his hand dangled two old-fashioned
keys, room keys. Alex relaxed a little knowing they had a place to

sleep tonight, it had been an eventful day. Realizing they had left New Orleans with only the clothes they wore and two cars full of ledgers, business records, and calculators, Alex suddenly felt crest-fallen. No clothes, No toothpaste, No toothbrush, No deodorant, the barest of toiletries. She felt like an orphan. Alone and Without. And there was Lucian, her new boss, beckoning for her to get out of her car, her bug. Getting the books, records, and calculators out of the car. He would get everything together and take them to the room. "We have some shopping to do yet tonight, and dinner to find!" Lucian spoke in a strangely upbeat manner, considering the day they had had. Lucian was already unloading his beamer, so Alex started unloading her bug setting the contents atop Lucian's pile of records, port ledgers, and miscellaneous notes, and other business records he had scavenged from his own office. He hurried back inside with his load, tossing Alex a key as he passed. "I will be right back, and then we can pick up a few things and go to find a place to eat," Lucian called out.

CHAPTER SIXTEEN

Lucian tossed the bags into his room, and turned to join Alex waiting below at the base of the stairs. "Let's go! Shopping and food are just around the corner," Lucian exclaimed, a little too enthusiastically, Alex thought. What is he not telling me?, Lex thought, but joined him as he stepped back onto the walkway. "A big shopping space right around the corner, huh?" Alex said with some hesitation, disbelief really. "Well, let's go check things out! We need some clothes, some personal stuff, some toiletries, and then finally some dinner," Lucian was saying as she caught up.

Lucian took her hand casually and slowly strolled toward the highway serving as the small towns main street. Reaching the highway /main street they moved left into a modest sixed parking lot serving a small number of shops featuring a variety of stores, a pharmacy, a dress Shoppe, boots, belts and other leather-tooled items, an assortment of tourist related shops, and even a few fast food places around more traditional local restaurants. "This looks like one-stop shopping, doesn't it?," Lucian remarked watching the flow of traffic on the main highway and the small side streets for any familiar vehicles. Lucian guided Alex into a pharmacy on the outside edge of the shopping complex. The hand on her back feeling a little insistent, a bit more insistent than she thought necessary. Alex stumbled a little at the slight push forward Into the Walgreens store. They both needed toothpaste, floss, and rinse. Maybe a little make-up, some band aids, a first-aid kit, deodorant, shavers and a small case to hold everything. Lucian paid cash for all the items at check out, collected his purchases, exited the store in the direction of the clothing stores. In the first clothing store, a dress Shoppe, he urged Alex to pick out a dress, some good jeans, some shirts, short-sleeved and ¾ sleeve blouses for comfort, a nice warm sweat shirt for the cool nights, and some comfortable shoes. While Alex selected her items carefully, trying to find pieces that could be worn together fashionably with reasonably matching colors, Lucian made his way over to the men's section for his own clothing choices. He chose two pairs of good quality jeans, comfortable t-shirts, a long-sleeved T, and a warn college sweat T-Shirt. He then returned to Alex, to see how she was doing. She was tarrying her selections toward check-out when he reminded her of undies he had nearly forgotten. She backtracked and joined him again at check-out. "this should do it," she said laying everything on the counter.

They left the Shoppe's loaded with their purchases, Lucian looking for a place to change their clothes. Glancing around the lot he quickly changed his mind and pushed Alex back inside the clothing store. "could we use a couple of changing booths for a minute?" He called out to the sales staff. "Go ahead" came he reply. At which time Lucian strode back to the men's changing area, telling Alex to slip into her jeans with a pretty shirt while he changed. too. He came back minutes later wearing his new jeans and a comfortable-looking sweater with Dr. Scholl's on his feet. He looked relaxed in his casual attire, but still very good looking. Alex came out a minute later in her own jeans with a light sweater and casual sandals on her feet. Lucian had tossed his old clothes into his bag, then told Alex to do the same. They walked out of the store looking like any other tourists after a day of shopping. "Let's find some dinner at that restaurant up ahead, I hope you like seafood,. It's a specialty down here," Lucian said. "Of course I do, we ate a lot of seafood in Briscombe Bay, too," Alex answered.

"I have been reading about some of the places we just passed through too. The old state house, renovated in the 1840's, is still standing despite capture by the Union, artillery fire, and abandonment during the Civil War. Even today, the old state house can be viewed everyday by visitors, like us, yesterday I also read about some things that surprised me a lot. I found it very interesting that

TABASCO is made right here on Avery Island! It is not really an island, just a bump on one side of one of the largest salt domes in the world! I thought the great Salt Lake and the Oceans of the world were our only sources of salt! I was also surprised to learn we are only 15 minutes to a half hour away from the oldest working rice mill in America. The Konriko Rice Mill in New Iberia and the TOBASCO Country Store & Factory on Avery Island! I was just wondering if we will be able to visit this 'Houmas House' I've been reading about? "Alex asked trying to keep up with Lucian. "The house is actually in Burnside, Louisiana," Lucian responded absent-mindedly. "The old Houmas Estate is one of the best examples of the good life a couple of centuries ago. The cool breezes just shake the pecans out of the tree above the finest grounds on the river. The exquisite house was the site of the film classic 'Hush…Hush, Sweet Charlotte' and a precious example of sugar-trade success.'"Lucian went on getting into the tour guide mode. "I think we will be able to take in the house and grounds before we move on," Lucian replied slowly.

Patriarch Archie Manning, may have been a NFL Quarterback before Alex was born, but his two sons New Orleans born Peyton and Eli Manning had made their own names famous in recent years, even if she were not a football fan!

Sulpher was a quiet and picturesque village, but Lucian had seen something back at the strip mall clothing store and pushed her back inside the Shoppe. But what exactly had he seen? He had become quite sullen and taciturn as he made his way to a small eatery resembling a bait shop in Briscombe Bay, Washington. It was sandwiched behind and between the more modern fast food equivalents of the day.

"Let's have some local gumbo, maybe a couple of Po'Boys to fill in the hollows?" Lucian inquired. reluctantly. "Sounds good to me!" Alex responded enthusiastically. The gumbo was served on a big plate on a bed of rice. Deciding to enjoy the gumbo right away, they also put in a delayed order for two shrimp Po'Boys to enjoy later.. Over the Gumbo, Lucian unwound slowly and began revealing the jolting recent worries that had changed his mood so abruptly. Leaving the café carrying their po'boys in bags with straps. The sandwiches could then be tucked among their other purchases, and carried back to the bed and breakfast.. They walked back leisurely to the Bed and Breakfast, casually repeating the day's events but still keeping a watchful eye out for any suspicious people or movement.. Arriving back at the Bed & Breakfast, they climbed the outer stars up to entrance, and took the stairs inside up to the room. A single room! A single room! Lucian shoved her into the room before she could cry out. "Calm down, Calm down. I had to tell the proprietors a small fib to get this room. It was the only room left. It's the bridal suite! Sorry, but I do not think we will be staying here long. But we did have to get clothes and a few supplies to continue on anyways. I am not going to force myself on you, let's look around and decide our sleeping arrangements, ok," Lucian pleaded softly. "We just pretend to be married, then?" Alex asked quietly. "We can do this, can't we Alex?" Lucian questioned. He pulled her into the room, depositing their purchases on a nearby chair while pulling her into his arms in a show of affection for their neighbors

CHAPTER SEVENTEEN

"What was that for?" Alex hissed in surprise. "I had to register as newlyweds to get this room! It is probably the last room available in this area. But this may be something to consider. It will definitely throw Our pursuers off balance. Consider this, I am past the age of 35, I abruptly cut off my last fiancé' and our engagement, then ran off with a new assistant no one's ever heard of. It does sound romantic and I must admit to growing feelings for you It's nothing I ever expected and has confused me too. I know you have growing feelings for me too," Lucian quavered. "Hold it, hold it, there is a small refrigerator in this room, isn't there? We need to go over the records we brought with us, it will give me time to take in all I have heard and seen today, and give me time to examine my feelings for you too," Alex responded tightly. "We also have to store these Po'Boys' inside something cold," she retorted.

"The refrigerator is right over there in the corner of the room, just under the microwave oven. I Just opened the door and dumped all the bags, files, and ledgers inside the room. We will sort through the files, organize their content, and examine the figures, then collate all of the information," Lucian spoke slowly. "You can keep absorbing these things while we start organizing and collating all this information. Afterward we can snack on our Po'Boys' and then begin sorting out our feelings for each other. Yes? Lucian inquired expectantly. The questions marred his handsome face, then "Maybe we should dig into All of these bags, files, and ledgers right away," Alex answered softly. "Let's get started. We still have a couple of hours to get some of the work done," Lucian said eagerly with guarded enthusiasm.

"I hope we will be able to draw some conclusions by the end of this evening, "Alex said sorting out individual detailed transactions, pulling copies for cross-checking. Grabbing her calculator she began the tedious process of collating and matching one ledgers entries to another registers entries and finally matching multiple products to Regression Analysis with reliable information on fixed and variable costs to making effective business decisions. I like the Eyeball Technique to verify the Contribution Analysis:

The break-even point and CPV (Cost-Profit-Volume) Analysis is used to determine the unit volume for given levels of profit. Let's get as deep as we can go" she commented quietly. I hate auditing all of this information over and over again. I trusted Courtney to keep all this information clean, accurate, and easily accessible for government and other interested parties scrutiny," Lucian replied in frustration.

They cross-checked and validated, verified each entry from start to finish noting errors, and possible discrepancies from one register to another. In the end, they found a notebook of errors, possible Discrepancies, deliberate and/or misleading, mistrusting changes of entries concealed in company records. Closing down the calculators for the night, they took the evidence they had accumulated, noted each in the extra blank ledgers they had brought with them. "I think it is time to call the Governor and the State Police to report our findings," Lucian began. His body sagged against the sofa behind him. "It has been a long night of double checking and cross referencing, but at least we have some answers to the suspicions that have plagued mine and the Governor's minds about what has been going on in the port. Give me a minute to make some calls....BOOM..." "What on earth was that? A sonic boom? "Alex and Lucian said together, whispering hoarsely. "It sounded like some kind of explosion outside, but being in here inside the B & B, I do know if it came from the parking lot or the street, Lucian started to say, but stopped short as the sound of doors opening and closing on the first floor reached their ears. Soon Police Sirens were coming closer and closer and the sound of feet pounding up the stairs was heard. "We are not safe here," Lucian said in clipped tones. Let's get all of these ledgers and notebooks packed up and stuffed into our shopping bags. Leave the calculators, just take the tapes. We have to lighten up now "Lucian spoke in great haste. Meanwhile, door banging was going on at the end of the hall. Doors opened, scuffling noises were heard, then thuds, and more door slamming. Lucian was alarmed and then the phone in his hand finally connected. Police sirens wailed to a stop in front of the B&B. Footsteps halted in front of their door, then raced back down the hall where they had come from "The police got here just in time, Alex. Now let's go down and see what all the excitement was about," Lucian remarked. He grabbed their sandwiches to heat in the microwave and eat down stairs, while they asked questions and gathered information on tonight's other entertainment. What was going on here? Many of the downstairs guests came out into the public areas looking a little worse for wear. The usual hubbub ensued, What happened? Are you ok? Was anyone hurt? Did you hear that explosion? Where did it come from. The police entered the lobby of the B & B with their own questions. Lucian strolled over to the lobby's microwave oven, sandwiches in hand and placed them inside the Oven, adjusted the dials, and started the oven. Once finished, he rejoined Alex at one of the small tables in the lobby. The police moved from one table to the next asking questions, jotting down answers and moving on to the next table. "I will be calling the State Police Headquarters and the Governor's Task Force to update them, on our findings tonight," Lucian informed her.

The police finally arrived at their small table just as the ding sounded from the microwave oven. Lucian stood solemnly look-ing at the oven before deciding to go fetch their lunches. He casu-ally strolled over to the micro, opened the door, and extracted both sandwiches onto hotel paper plates. He picked up both plates, judg-ing the temperatures of both sandwiches and brought back both to their small table. With both plates on the table before them, Lucian reached out to grab his sandwich, stating "I am sorry to be eating in front of you officers, but we have not only missed our lunch but what is left of our dinner," Lucian explained before taking a bite of his sandwich motioning Alex to do the same. Alex spoke up saying they would be needing something to drink. "Coffee would be fine, maybe with a hazelnut creamer? One of the officers standing around the table made his way over to the cabinet above the microwave, opened the door and examined its contents, then moved over to the small refrigerator Spotting a number of small plastic containers in a bowl. A number of different flavors were contained in the bowl.?He brought it over and splayed the contents over the table top. Lucian joined the officer at the coffee carafe next to the Microwave oven and poured two steaming hot cups of coffee for Alex and himself. Balancing the two cups on a small tray supplied by the B&B in the cabinet, he set then down on the table. A number of officers decided to join them.

The commanding officer sat back quietly until the commotion before came to an end. He watched silently as Lucian and Alex added creamer and stirred their coffees. "Now I checked on the owner of that BMW that was blown apart in the lot next to B&B here You wouldn't be the owner of that BMW, a Mr. Lucian Devereaux, now would you?" he inquired. Lucian walked briskly to the door and stared out the window to see what was left of his BMW. "Yes, that is my beamer. This is so disheartening. It was not even fully broken in yet. I guess I will have to inform the insurance company of the loss and file a claim" Lucian said quietly. I cannot fully comprehend the destructiveness of these people. Who are they Where did they come from? He had served in Kosovo and was not naïve, he had been around the world. But this destruction was nearly unfavathomable. "I have just received instructions from the home office in the state capitol, the Governor has ordered a full company of my men to protect you on your way back to New Orleans, we are your protection detail.. I suggest we leave as soon as possible before the saboteurs have time to regroup. Can you be packed and Have your things down here within the next hour? Depending on the danger involved, we will need at least one scout car leading the procession, one or two behind, and one alongside" the lead state trooper espoused to himself as well as his junior officers. "Looking at your auto out there, your beamer, I would say these people are very determined people. The Governor indicated your role in overseeing the operation of the Port of New Orleans. We have received some Intel about vast quantities of cocaine and other drugs being routed through the Port. If the Intel is true it could be quite a dangerous ride back to New Orleans. Remember to keep your heads down and your eyes open. Go get your things and store them in the trunks of the cruisers. We will leave as soon as you are ready.

Alex and Lucian scurried up the stairs to pack, get their things down to the desk, check out, and then Lucian had some other ideas to throw at Alex "what if we actually got there Governor to find us a minister and got married on the little escapade to Cajun country. It would throw everyone off! We have the new clothes and things. We could pull it off. Wear that new dress we picked up yesterday, the ¾ length Afternoon dress. I know it is not a wedding dress, but I do think it is quite beautiful on you. O will pick up a matching hat and/or veil for the finishing touch. I have a new suit with a weskit and new shoes. We could do this," Lucian coaxed. We do have complicated feelings for each other and you know I would never take advantage of you, while we were trying to untangle these feelings, and I think it would give us some cover, a reason for this unusual flight flight from New Orleans" he continued. "Do you really think so?" Alex asked. "Can we actually do this? Would the Governor really pull those strings for us and these things in a single afternoon?" Alex asked doubtfully. "I can only ask, let me dial and find out," Lucian answered.

From that moment on, things got a little out of hand. The State Patrol was ordered to sit tight temporarily, then pick up a marriage license from the courthouse in town, then pick up the minister on the way back to the B&B. Not dressed in elegant finery, but looking good in their Sunday casual best, Lucian and Alex were married before the B&B staff, the guests, and a full company of patrol officers and other passing folk.

"Now we had better get a move on. Thrown off our time schedule a bit by the nuptials, but I think we can work with it," the lead trooper was saying and Congratulations! "I knew this was not just an innocent jaunt through the countryside and backwoods for you two. Why don't we all get loaded up and be on our way now, It's a long ride back to New Orleans."

"We have to get back to the Big Easy. We have recievered reports on the seedy, scurrilous thugs you encountered back in New Orleans. We have been studying the available routes back to Orleans and decided on one or two lead cars in our security detail. We will also be providing several rear trailing cars and a side car to box you in, in this little procession. Your bags office ledgers, and equipment will be stashed into the trunks of various patrol cars. We will try by as inconspicuous as possible but a procession of security vehicles traveling together always attracts attention. Especially when we have to stop for meals and potty Breaks So why don't the two of you run back upstairs and bring all of your things back down here so wee can get everything squared away. "Lieutenant Briggs said.

Alex and Lucian hurried back up the stairs, double-checked everything to make sure they had everything. Placing a box in each of the first two patrol cars, Lucian carried down the two suitcases while Alex two large shopping bags, 1 in each hand.. Placing everything into the trunks of two squad cars. Lucian ran back up to make sure they had left no stragglers again and came down carrying I more large shopping bags, bulging shopping bags "Here's the last of it. I guess we're ready to get out of town now" Lucian reported.

What route did you finally decide on for the best way back to avoid what we've already been through. I would like to avoid any more problems with our rather unsavory pursuers, Lieutenant?" Lucian asked the squad leader. "Once we leave Sulpher, we'll take a more direct route to get back. "We came out on a very direct route, than the one you took to get here" Brigg's replied. "We came out on a very direct route, and just stopped at tourist spots along the way," Lucian explained.

"We came out on a very direct route and stopped at tourist sites along the way," Lucian explained. "We came out directly on US 10, with short sightseeing jaunts along the way. I had to introduce her to our local Football family's museum, the Manning's and of course our Jambalaya. It has been an educational trip for her. My old childhood haunts, the fishing, the hunting, the exploring and swimming. My family's vacation and special places we came to love and cherish. She needed to see them and learn their unique place in our History, before she becomes my queen of the families Mardi Gras Ball later this month"Lucian told Lieutenant Briggs. "Well US 10 is the shortest, most direct route back to New Orleans. We do have Bus 90 and State 1, but neither are the quickest or safest routes available. Well I think we will start back on US 10, if we encounter a lot of problems we can adjust our plans. I will notify the Governor of our plans," Briggs finished. "We are flexible, Lieutenant. You lead, we will follow "Briggs tempers flared. "Not follow, you'll be in the back seat"

Alex and Lucian settled into the back seat of the third car in the procession. Watching the road raptly as they pulled out of the parking area, they were intensely interested in their new security detail. They turned around quickly to see four more vehicles pulling in behind them. "That's so the last car can pull in alongside us on the highway," Brigg's explained briefly as they pulled into traffic. He was sitting in the front passenger seat of their safe car, the shotgun seat as some might call it," he finished saying. The cars picked up speed heading for the highway. They watched with interest as they headed back to St. Charles. Every car suddenly took on an ominous note. "Keep watching, Alex, let me know if you see anything or anyone you recognize along the way," Lucian told her. "I have seen so many confusing things already," Alex whispered almost to herself. Lucian leaned in closer to hear her words. "What things?" Lucian asked. "Well, I have seen signs for something called 'Mardi Gras Twelfth Night' at the Civic Center at Lake Charles, even a Mardi Gras Community Dance at the Lake Charles Civic Center. I Believed Mardi Gras was a strictly a New Orleans celebration.?" Alex asked seeking clarification.

Twirling the still unfamiliar ring on her third finger, she and Lucian relaxed a bit in the back seat of the patrol car., looking ahead at the two officers in the front seat, feeling quite safe for the first time in days. "That is really quite a common assumption, Lex. The Southwest Cajun celebrations can be quite Spectacular. Up until Krewes Night many celebrations are taking place all over Louisiana. There are at least 50 different Krewe Associations vying for King of the Krewe at Mardi Gras. The Krewe of Omega Parade kicks off at the Civic Center. That will be followed shortly by the Krewe of Barkus Parade, the Krewe of Cosmos Presentation bat the Sulpher High School Auditorium. The Krewe of Illusions at the Civic Center in Lake Charles, and the Mardi Gras Zydeco Dance at the Lake Charles Civic Center. There are many activities like the Mardi Gras Children's Parade in downtown Lake Charles or the Carlyss Mardi Gras Trail Ride at the West Cal Arena in Sulpher. Mardi Gras is a statewide celebration," Lucian continued.

I am glad we are going back this way to illustrate the expanse and importance of our greatest holiday celebration," Lucian said hoping she could see what her new role would encompass, Lucian thought hard about his destroyed BMW, Alex's battered bug and turned to face the front seat, "What happened to the little battered beetle in the parking lot?" he inquired. "The new 'Mrs. Devereaux's VW.?" Briff's responded. "Yes I was just wondering how we were going to get it back to New Orleans for servicing?" Lucian answered.. "Well right now one of my officers is attempting to drive it back at the end of this procession," Briggs told him. That is the way their little troop formed this unusual caravan. Alex had wanted to drive the first leg of this trip back to New Orleans, but had reluctantly surrendered her keys to the officer requesting them., when that idea was shot down by the Security detail.

Now Alex sat back and began to notice signs putting Mardi Gras happenings the day before Ash Wednesday. A Blaring sign announcing Krewe de Charles Sioux Mardi Gras Block Party in downtown Lake Charles. Alex was assembling the information and organizing it in her own mind.

Lucian broke into her solitary thoughts, "What will we be telling everyone back at the house when we get back? We had better get our stories straight. We can drop the bug off at a good repair shop along the way, and m trying to think of what I will be telling the insurance adjuster about my blown up Beamer! "Well, as close as we can get to the truth, would probably be for the best," Alex answered. "I know. We have not put a scratch either vehicle ourselves, but both are need of extensive repair and/or Complete replacement," Lucian acknowledged."We are almost back to Lafayette already," but was interrupted by a loud crash near the end of the caravan All heads swung around to see the reason for the commotion. The bug appeared to be holding its own, but two patrol cars were looking a little worse for wear. One squad was backward in the median and the other had been broadsided onto the other side of the road. Both officers reported back to Brigg's quickly. The patrol car in the median called in for roadside assistance from the home office. The cause of the accident were two sedate attack on the bug!

The on the side of the road continued limping along to the nearest service station/café. The officer they left behind waited for back-up and reinforcements while the rest of the caravan continued on to the café.

Each of her male companions had begun arguing about what had just happened to their quiet return to the Big Easy. How could these assassins have found them so easily and quickly? Were they under scrutiny? Ideas and theories flew from one officer to another, arguments and heated discussions were rampant. The officers called in to their superiors and described the attack on Volkswagen Beetle, and the ensuing melee on the highway. Lucian also contacted the Governor to explain the problems they had contacted on their flight from New Orleans, the reason for that flight, and the new and continuing problems that plagued them. As nil on cue, the phone calls ended and everyone made their way back to the vehicles. The officers reversed their roles and positions in the convoy and grew acutely aware of their Surroundings as they headed back to the city. It was here Lucian made his pitch to take over driving the Volkswagen with Alex. As he had expected, Brigg's objected. But after some jockeying for position, Brigg's made some changes to the security detail and Alex and Lucian were secluded in their battered VW Bug. With Lucian at the wheel, Alex took note of all the changes made to the security detail to Accommodate Lucian's request to drive Alex and himself back to the city. Seeing nothing that set off alarm bells yet, she let herself relax a bit, but only a little.. "We need a little privacy and quiet time to discuss a few things," Lucian began. "To begin with, what do we call each other : our full names, your new name, nick names, pet names well, my new name.?" Alex inquired quite uncharacteristically tentative. "Now that no one is listening what do we really feel about each other? About our unusually fast marriage? How and what do we tell our families about this marriage?" Alex pressed for an answer. Lucian drove the unfamiliar bug carefully sandwiching the little car amongst protective patrol cars as instructed. He followed his shield and blended into the bulwark of the security arrangement worked out with Brigg's. "I heard you call yourself Lex with your friends. Lex is your nickname and Luke has been my nickname since I was a kid.

That seems to solve the initial problem. I do not know if what I feel for you is'love' yet, but my feelings for you are very strong, and I suspect yours for me are the same, "Lucian was saying. "We have been closing in on home steadily, safely tucked away in the pocket of this security assignment. We will be approaching Acadia Park soon, then on to Houmas House, then Burnside. Doesn't going back seem so much shorter than going out?" Lucian mused. After reaching Vacherie, Kenner, and Metairie "I will have to begin contemplating what I will tell my father and Aunt," Lucian murmured vaguely. Then I had better start thinking about having that talk with my uncle," Alexis said pensively. "Then we can bring everyone together for a celebration? Then we can smile a lot, shake everyone's hand, drink champayne, etc., etc., etc.," she commented. Sure more good points, we are both exhausted by this trip,' our elopement', all this excitement, and we both just want to fall into bed!" Lucian laughed out loud seeing her expression.

"These seats are so uncomfortable to anyone with legs! I am glad this ride will be coming to an end soon. ....it is very cramped behind this wheel" Lucian remarked observed, smiling broadly ... Lucian wedged the bug in between two patrol cars, who managed to change their positions frequently avoiding both monotony and fatigue. All were keeping a watchful eye out for anything unusual, including Lucian and Alex.. Then outside Dhplessis, a truck came roaring up the ramp, burst onto the highway and shot the lanes of traffic ramming the first patrol car broadside, forcing it down into a manmade gully. Alex was amazed by the superb driving skills of the trooper. He kept the squad on its wheels and upright all the way down to the bottom of the gully, were it landed with the passenger door jammed against the bottom wall of the gully wall. Both officers scrambled out the driver's door, waving and signaling they were ok. With this latest threat behind them, a new semi-trailer trailer pulled in alongside the assorted patrol cars Protecting and surrounding the VW bug.

The driver in the pickup behind they patrol car following Lucian became extremely agitated, waving guns and gesturing wildly. It did not take long before a lone gunman was leaning out each of the club cab doors. The erupting gunfire, from the squads as well as the Club Cab scared off most of the traffic around them. The semi driver pulled his wheel a hard right, then a hard left forcing the club cab off the road and nearly slamming into the remaining rear squad car in the process! Lucian took the opening left by the tractor-trailer and shot past in the slingshot barely missing the returning tractor-trailer in the process.

"Hang on" he shouted to Lex. I know a few back ways into the Garden District."I hope to make it back to The house in one piece, while escaping these thugs," Lucian said between pursed lips. He stayed on 10 until He researched Reserve, then turned left on US 55, just before Laplace, then turning right onto State 61. He was heading for Kenner and Metairie. He kept on turning lefts and making rights before ending up in Carrolton near the I-90. "We are not far out now," Lucian told her. He took a right onto State 18, followed the river into Marreno, and then into Harvey, and then to the Ferry before reaching Gretna. The ferry would not take the car, so he headed further west to Bus. 90, with a crossing directly into the Garden District. He pulled directly onto St. Charles Avenue, then started making his way back to the house onto the Devereaux estate. But a few blocks out from the main house, he came face-to-face with that black SUV that nearly ran Alex down at the Lakeside Shopping Center. And driving that menacing vehicle was a familiar face. A face distorted by rage and a crazed malevolence. It was the nearly unrecognizable face of Courtney Anderson.! Lucian hit the brakes hard, Alex shrank back in horror, but Lucian was plotting hard to escape. He made as quick flick of the steering wheel, made the 90 degree turn he needed and accelerated away from the SUV. How long has she been waiting here? Her thought. She was not the attractive, self assured woman he had hired, even considered marrying. Good thing to know before things had gotten too serious, not that it felt the same way.

Alex looked hard into the hateful, spiteful, and vindictive face of her predecessor, Courtney Anderson.. I have never seen such hate consuming a person like that It really is ugly, isn't it. She asked. "Yes it is, but we have to get around her for the time being". Lucian responded. She really is angry with me Alex thought, Courtney thought she would be announcing her engagement at the Ball this year. Lucian momentarily forgot he was not behind the wheel of his BMW, instead of this VW Bug. Peering into the rearview mirror, and the confirming look into the side view mirror, he saw the SUV rolling up on them.

He used some quick thinking and unorthodox moves to lose her, but she stubbornly continued to hug his bumper! All he had to do was get to the estate and get away from Courtney in the next 1 or 2 blocks without being overtaken. Lucian spun the wheel of the bug attempting to both change direction and gain Some distance between their vehicles, shooting down an alleyway. The quick movement caught Courtney by surprise and it took her several seconds to correct. Those seconds gave Lucian and Alex a slight edge In this horse race Maybe they did have a chance. No one knew the back streets and alleyways of this neighborhood better than he did. Lucian sped down the alleyway he found himself on, took a right hand turn when he came to a recognized street. Another turn or two, then come up the back way into the garage! With luck Courtney will only see the garage b door coming down. But Lucian had forgotten he was not driving his BMW, but Alex's VW bug instead. How could he forget? It had to be the excitement, it has been an eventful couple of days, first we fight our way out of the parking garage in the Trade Center Building, fleeing the city, getting married, having his beamer blown up, escaping sinister forces to get back to New Orleans that must be it. Pay Attention! Pay Attention! His mind screamed at him. Have to get my mind back on the task at hand. Swing the car left, then pull it right again. "Alex, come across quickly, drive the bug into the garage when I hit the opener," Lucian spoke hurriedly. "Hurry up, Hurry up" he urged her Along. Scooting across and hopping into the driver's seat, she floored the bug through the doors, just as Lucian hit the button to bring the door down. Just then Courtney rounded that last corner and realized what had just happened! He opened Alex's door and helped her out of the car. The relief was palpable as they clung to each other in utter exhaustion and relief. Lucian wat6ched Courtney drive slowly by, pounding her fists on the steering wheel, through a small break in the corner of the garage window.

Alex and Lucian wcrc finally alone to talk and think things over. Lucian wrapped his arms loosely around Lex, looking around the garage interior Fixing his eyes on as door in the far corner of the space, he released Lex from his arms. "Follow me to this far door, there is a long corridor underground leading up to the main house", Lucian explained. "hope you are not too frightened of long underground tunnels," he said to her. "Is it dark? Creepy? Dark can be scary, Cobwebs? Any lighting at all?" Lex asked warily. There is some lighting, spaced every 10 to 15 feet," he responded. "Want to take a stroll?" Taking her hand, the other reaching for the doorknob, he pulled he pulled the door open, revealing a short set of steps leading down. These first few steps appeared dark, until another set of stairs were revealed at a sharper angle than the first set.

CHAPTER EIGHTEEN

The walk through the underground tunnel was mostly uneventful, despite a large cobweb or two, that tended to freak Lex out when they encountered one. They walked on down the dimly lit hall because of the unevenly spaced bare bulbs. They walked on down the hall until they encountered a new addition to the hallway. "What is this now?" Lucian exclaimed. He studied the box frame carefully. Finding the recessed button on the face of the box, Lucian pressed it opening a door to display the new modern elevator, just installed.. "Well wonder of wonders, where did this come from?" Lucian sputtered. "I heard father talking about replacing the old stairs with an elevator, because neither he or Aunt Aimee' were getting any younger.

But I am surprised to find it a fait accompli'" Lucian responded. "Well, should we go on up?" he said Placing his hand in the small of her back guiding her to the elevator and supplying her with his strength. "This will be even better than calling the main house from the garage. No big open spaces to cross No one shooting at us. Sounds good to me.! Lucian replied before pressing the button to the first floor.

Noticing large doors on either side f the elevator, she couldn't help but ask what they were for. "One side is the wine cellar for the house, and the other side opens into basement places with workshop spaces for the household., "Just like any normal house, right?" Alex mocked him, smiling broadly. "Not just like an ordinary house. Houses down here in Louisiana do not automatically come with a basement.

The water table is too high. Luckily this is an old house built long before water table ordinances and zoning commissions came along. Good thing this house is built on substantial ground, meaning it is built on a deep layer of heavy top soil. "Luke was explaining. "Shall we head up and face the family? It will be better than facing the gunmen and villains at the little rest stop back this side of Lafayette earlier today, remember?" Lucian urged here on. "Here we are," Lex said as the door opened. "It is not as fast as a commercial elevator, but not as slow or choppy as a normal household lift either," she said with some pride in her voice. "Yes, dad always seems to get the best available products for all of our needs," Lucian responded appreciatively. "But I wonder what brought on the necessity for the installation of this particular elevator, and have it done so quickly," Lucian pondered aloud.

Just outside what used to be the old cloakroom. Lucian and Alex made their way into ward his father, Jean-Claude and his Aunt Aimce'. In the ensuing hubbub, Jean-Claude shouted out, "Congratulations, my boy,"leaning over to embrace his son, and stretching his arms even further to include Alex in his embrace." I am overjoyed that you are home with us again my son. I have heard all about your exploits in the last few days. My friends and colleagues in the Governor's Office, as well As in Sulpher have let me in on the good news. I have already informed your Aunt, brother and sister, as well as Alex's uncle of this extraordinary news," Jean-Claude exclaimed. "Your Aunt is upstairs waiting with Joseph's for your return. No one has told him of your return or the marriage yet. Charles suffered a setback a couple of days ago just as you fled New Orleans. No one has mentioned the marriage, because of his condition. Dr Ingram waited nervously for the return of Joseph Thorndyke's niece. "So that is the reason for the new elevator," Lucian said giving his new bride a squeeze. "We had better go up another flight than, it sounds like the good doctor may start frothing from the mouth if we do not arrive soon," he remarked signaling the house staff to see to their things in the tunnel and garage.

"What were you doing with your fingers ass we got back on the elevator?" Alex asked "I did not ever realize you saw that signal, I just gave the staff instructions to pick up our things in the tunnel and garage. The tunnels here been here since the Civil War. They were made to get the people in the main house and into the countryside if the main house were vest ablaze by Union Forces.! Courtney knew nothing of this old tunnel, but Charles Delacourt may remember this tunnel to his old house. It was his his family home before it was lost in that card game all those years ago. We had better get upstairs now, It's as if Dr. Ingram may start frothing at the mouth if you do not arrive soon.! Lucian emphasized. Pressing the button to rise to the next floor. The elevator stopped and the door opened onto an extremely overwrought Dr. Ingram pacing the hall floor outside Joseph's room. "Dr. Ingram, I am Alex Rochelle Talbot or Thorndyke, I am not all sure of the rest," Alex said. Just before Lucian interrupted, "It is Mrs. Devereux, now, Mrs. Lucian Devereux. "There was a lot of information and changes for Lex to digest since she arrived in New Orleans. Alex, I realize so many frightful changes to your equilibrium," Lucian whispered into her ear. "Good morning Dr. Ingram, I wondered how my uncle was feeling this morning?" Alex inquired. "He is responding unexpectedly well to his latest therapy and the new medications," Dr. Ingram answered her first question. He then dispensed his rather pleasant directive. "I am very pleased with his progress since his original attack two days ago," he responded. "How would you like me to address you?; Ms. Talbot, or Ms. Thorndike, or some other salutatory greeting?".the doctor asked. "It is Mrs. Alexis Devereaux, actually, as of yesterday, doctor," she answered decisively. "I had heard some rumors around here all morning, "Dr. Ingram answered truthfully. "But I am very pleased you have returned to the house at this time. I know you do not completely believe all you have learned about your background yet, or the good fortune it has brought you since coming to New Orleans. But I can tell you, it is all true. I have confirmed all the details and information with both Joseph Thorndike, and also surprisingly Aimee' Devereaux. You should have a long talk with her in a short time. It will help straighten everything out for you. It really Helped me understand this convoluted mess," Dr Ingram explained.

Watching Lucian pull out of the driveway in Jean-Claude's Mercedes, Courtney flipped on her running lights and slipped her SUV into gear, hanging back a little so as not to be recognized. Pulling in to traffic, she followed Luke at a safe distance. She was disappointed no sirens sounded announcing serious injuries, forgetting about the police inquiries taking place already. She was reasonably reassured she had gone unidentified by the police. But she remembered the look of horror on Alex's face in her Short pursuit of them, and also the look on Lucian's face. The anger and hate in Luke's facial expressions. She was determined to try again for one or the other, at the first opportunity. Her eyes narrowed and her brows furrowed in spiteful concentration. Courtney let her mind race through her options. I will have to remove Luke first, of course, she thought Alex is just coincidental, not influential or prominent enough, in

New Orleans yet to be believed. By getting Luke out of the way first, Langley can take over Lucian's responsibilities at Devereaux, eliminating ant threat from Alex or anyone else and ensuring access they needed to the shipping records. But she was still worried Why had Luke gone so far out of his way to hire Alex in the first place? Was he suspicious? He hired her right out of college! For Pete's sake. Joseph was propped up in his bed, still, still a bit pale from his most recent health trials.

As Alex entered his room, the twinkle in his eyes told her he was feeling better. "Good morning, Alex, he said pushing himself a little higher onto his pillows. "I am pleased you came back this afternoon," he said indulgently. "I looked forward to your visit the other day, before my minor misadventure," he said not without some anxiety. "Lucian called late last night while you slept, Jean-Claude took the call in here," he was watching over me." "He said Luke would be back here in New Orleans this afternoon. He sounded quite excited, I think it may have something to do with you. Does it?" He spoke barely containing his own excitement. Yes he most likely was quite excited, Alex thought to herself.. "We were married yesterday, Lucian and I," Alex blurted out into the almost empty room. "And Just how are you feeling this afternoon, Uncle Joseph? "Lex asked the man propped up in the bed to her right. "I knew it, I just knew it," he exclaimed. "I just knew you would bring me explosive news today," he replied scarcely containing his exhilaration. "Congratulations, my dear, Congratulations. We must Have a celebration to announce your joyous news! Where is your new husband now, my dear?" her uncle asked with interest. "Well we arrived together, he was just outside the door, but he wanted to make an appearance at the police station, the State Police Office, specifically, "Alex answered her Uncle. He Interrupted her reverie, "Are you all right Alex? You were so far away just now. I wanted to get your attention! "I am sorry, Uncle," Alex answered back. "I am truly sorry uncle, but it is still so strange to call you Uncle Joseph. I just never knew. As a matter of fact, I was thinking about Lucian just now. But how are you feeling this afternoon, Mr. Thorndyke? You are certainly looking more chipper this afternoon, according to Dr. Ingram. Lucian wanted to speak to our State Patrol Escort, we lost them When we got close to New Orleans, earlier today, now I am worried about Lucian's safety. Courtney was lying in wait for us, she must be around here somewhere around here? She was mumbling.

Courtney followed Lucian toward the center of the city. "Now where is he going? Give me a chance, any chance. Come on Lucian, what are you doing now? Where are you going? Step out of that car, give me a chance at you now. Lucian pulled the Mercedes into a vacant parking lot, with Courtney hot on his tail. He noticed the Black SUV following him into the parking lot, he immediately starting dialing the number Of his State Patrol security detail head, Lieutenant Briggs… "I have a problem out here in your parking lot. Come out and join us now, ok. It is Lucian Devereux, It looks like

I may be trouble out here, bring reinforcements!" Seeing Lucian speaking into his cell phone, Courtney was in a conundrum.-who is he talking to., should I just ram him, and keep ramming him until there is nothing left And then a group of uniformed officers came running out of the State Patrol safety building in front of them. So he called the cops did he, really?. Well I had better make myself scarce or Langley and Charles will be so angry with me if I get caught. Things are going bad! With that she peeled out of the parking lot, hoping no one got her plate number or vehicle information in the darkening light..

"Who was that Lucian?" Briggs asked, coming to a stop beside Lucian's car window. "I think it was Courtney Anderson. She has a similar SUV that tried to run Alex and myself down at the Mall Shopping Center at the north end of town earlier in the week. I saw her face, and I could hardly believe this was the same girl I seriously thought of marrying before I found Alex!. Unbelievable!

"Let's see if one of my guys caught the license plate number. We can compare notes on everything that happened out here in the.lot, we may even have something on the video cameras out here in the lot.:" the lieutenant revealed. "Let's go n in then, I want to call Alex anyway," Lucian replied. "I kind of left her in the lurch with her uncle, when I left for your office. I left her alone to break the news of our marriage to him. He has not been entirely well since his setback earlier this week. I wanted to be there with her for this important occasion It is quite an announcement, I am sure her uncle will want to have a ball to announce our marriage, just as my father and my Aunt have been talking about, too" Lucian explained to Briggs. But it is so close to Mardi Gras, I think both Alex and myself both want to wait until the Mardi Gras season is over "I don't think it will be the most appropriate timing though," Lucian finished.

After calling Alex, the men compared notes, getting an APB out on the SUV and it's driver, Courtney Anderson. Then he headed back to the Garden District and home. Leaving the parking lot,

Lucian noted two officers pulling in behind him. He wanted to get to Alex and the house. He worried About Alex, his father, his Aunt, the entire family, really. Charles was in a precarious position, ill, weak, Bedridden, waiting for a visit from a newly discovered niece.

Leaving the central city, Lucian made his way back to the Garden District, deciding to take a side road into the French Quarter. He wanted to quickly check on the progress made on the company apartment. The apartment needed extensive repairs after Alex's arrival in New Orleans. What a ride she's been on, non-stop action and unbelievable intrigue with some very scary suspense, too. He stopped in front of Genevieve's antique shop, just to scan the outside progress made to the building and then on to the apartment upstairs.. From the outside, it was beginning to look like it always had. Genevieve hurried out to greet Lucian before he stepped out of his car. "Lucian, Lucian it is so good to see you. The repairs are going so quickly now, the apartment looks stunning again. I even have new keys and security codes for you and Ms. Talbot, too!" Genevieve gushed. "Genevieve, I was just stopping by to see the progress already made to the building itself and to the apartment alone," Lucian answered. "There is much I have to tell you though. Miss Talbot is now Mrs. Lucian Devereaux. We were married this morning in western Louisiana, in Sulpher the other side of Lafayette. We came back in a police escort. Mrs. Devereaux is visiting her uncle at my family's main house. I do hope the apartment will be ready for use very soon. I was just Thinking it make a wonderful honeymoon hideaway for Alex and myself. It is close to work, and right down here at ground zero! Alex is beginning to learn the ins and outs of the Mardi Gras season, more than a season, an annual event.! "Lucian filled her in on the changes that had taken place over the past few days.

"That is wonderful news Lucian, I've been saying for a long time you need to take a wife. It will be a beautiful place for a honeymoon. It is quiet, secluded, and private and the views are spectacular.. Shall we on up and inspect the changes and updates already finished in the apartment. I believe you will be pleased with everything. Just come back to the rear of the shop, I will get everything we will need before we go on Up," Genevieve expounded excitedly moving to unlock the shop's door. This is convenient for you to check on the apartment, it is also convenient for reaching the garages. "Lex will be so surprised with the And thrilled with the repairs thus far!" Lucian remarked to Genevieve as he strolled through the apartment. "It is light, airy, and modern. Just right for a honeymooning couple!" Lucian said, pleased with himself and the remarkable remodeling project thus far Lucian walked the railing of the balcony overlooking the street. He inspected the railing for some design modifications to prevent anyone from breaking into the apartment from the street below. His fingers stroked the railing looking for the in-corporation of some of his ideas to help secure the apartment and the entire building itself. After the break-in he decided to up the security for all residents of the building. He was pleased the new security measures were almost imperceptible to the naked eye, but he hoped they would prove themselves invaluable-able in the protection of the building's occupants. He made a mental note to speak with the crew the new security boss about the changes made and the active measures to deter and/or hinder any further break-ins in the building. Next he walked back to the garage to see the new modifications made back there. The walls had been fortified and the windows darkened so as to block viewing from outside the garage.

Genevieve handed him a small package of keys and cards for the building and the apartment, "I will feel so much better if you had these keys and cards for the building and the apartment", she said fretfully with a worried expression on her face. Her eyes darted from side to side, trying an assailant in the growing darkness. I have already had some not-too-friendly inquiries from not-so-friendly family and so called friends.. I do not know who to trust anymore, "Genevieve explained furtively. Taking the small package into his larger hand, he patted his jacket and pant pockets for a place to transfer the contents to. "When I was up inspecting the balcony I noticed a black SUV parked a ways down the block.. If I am not mistaken, it is the same sinister black SUV that tried to kill Lexi and myself several times in the last couple of days," Lucian responded. "Are you sure? You could be mistaken, there are many black SUV's around, especially in Louisiana," Genevieve replied quite logically, she thought. "I am going inside to notify the State police, Better to be safe than sorry," Lucian told her. While they waited for the arrival of a squad car, Lucian plotted his escape from the apartment. "If we can scare the driver off now, maybe I can get back to the house tonight yet" he spoke thoughtfully. Briggs came on the line momentarily and Lucian explained his dilemma to the officer. "Lexi? That is her nickname? I like it! Genevieve exclaimed. "So much more informal, less stiff and standoffish!" she proclaimed. She next took him toward the street entrance gate.

Gone was the big black gate giving entrance to the building and apartment, instead sat a replica perfect in every detail, but with modern up-to-date security details. "It is growing dark again, and we will be back in the morning to get these final updates looked over in daylight," he muttered.

Walking back up to the apartment, he strode out onto the balcony again to survey the situation. Yes the black SUV was still there. He gazed down the street and watched a New Orleans city officer approaching the SUV from the rear. The approach seemed to have an adverse effect on Courtney inside the SUV. She panicked watching the approach., then bolted down the street under Lucian's balcony. She took off fast squealing her tires and bringing the unwelcome attention of the city officer. It prompted the city officer to turn on his siren and pursue the SUV. Waiting for the State Patrol officer to arrive, Lucian walked around the balcony toward the stairs located near the back of the Antique Shoppe. Saying goodbye to Genevieve, he went out door of the store.. He waved at Briggs while getting into his car. Lucian exchanged some news, views, and explanations with Lieutenant Briggs. Briggs followed Lucian out toward the Garden District, at a safe distance He did not want to alert the driver of the black SUV or any of her confederates. Briggs followed Lucian loosely right up the drive to the house. Both men greeted Jean-Claude at the vestibule of the front entryway. Providing the patriarch with the basic details of the trials of the past week or two, and they adjourned to Jean-Claude's private study off the living area. Mean-While, noticing the commotion at the front door, Aimee' stationed herself outside the closed door of the study. The door was slightly ajar, so she strained to hear the hushed voices. Papers began shuffling and heads put together making plans, adjustments to plans, and momentarily the voices raised, just as the door slammed shut! "How rude!," Aimee' exclaimed jumping back instinctively. "I will take Jean-Claude to task for this! I have every right to hear what is happening in that room, in this family. I carry the history Of this family in my notes and diaries for the last five generations! How dare he shut me out! I do not want an edited version of what is happening, I want everything," Aimee' stomped for emphasis. Alex left Joseph's bedroom, closing the door softly, and made her way down the stairs moving toward Aimee' deter-Mindedly. "What is going on down there?" she asked Aimee' softly. Jean-Claude, Lucian, and a State Police Officer have locked themselves in Jean-Claude's study and have shut me out!" Aimee' responded. angrily.

"Then Lucian has returned from precinct headquarters in downtown New Orleans I am sure they won't be too long "Alex said soothingly to calm Aimee. Within 15 to 20 minutes, all three men exited the study somberly, clasping hands, punching arms, and pounding backs. Alex looked across the living space to watch their childish antics. Within 15 to 20 minutes, all three men exited the study somberly, then clasping hands, punching arms, and pounding backs they showed sudden changes in their behavior and facial expressions. "I need to park the Mercedes back in the garage tonight yet.," Lucian told his father. "Do not concern yourself about the car tonight son. I will get the car into the garage myself tonight. No bother," Jean-Claude advised his oldest son. "Well then, I will take my leave. Be careful, we do not know who the next target will be in this debacle. Tipping his hat, he said "Good night ladies, gentlemen," Lieutenant Briggs spoke boisterously. Tipping her head slightly, Aimee"let the officer out the front door. Her hand still on the door knob, Jean-Claude made his way out brushing past his sister, heading for the parked Mercedes. Stepping out onto the porch and into the walkway lights, he opened the car door and slid inside.

Courtney, waiting in the dark, watching the figure move down the walkway sprightly. Now, is this Lucian or his father, or perhaps one of the household staff?. Well, no matter, It will cause grief to the house at an y rate, an d put everyone on notice.. She watched and calculated, calculated and watched. A steely expression fixed on her face. The Mercedes ignited and within minutes it made its way into the street. Courtney sat and waited while the lone figure, shrouded by the descending fog and darkness, made it's way into the street. A easing her SUV into gear, she crept around the corner. Accelerating viciously and suddenly, pouncing on and towering over the much smaller Mercedes. She slammed into the rear bumper of the vehicle in front of her. Jean-Claude took the jarring hit almost expecting it in stride. The Mercedes took the hit, wrapping Jean-Claude in safety while he accelerated out of reach of the blackness behind him. Jean-Claude, displaying the skills of a much younger man, swung the car around getting out of the way of maniac in the SUV. Dialing Lieutenant Briggs, Jean-Claude informed the officer of this latest attack and threat occurring this evening by the driver of the black SUV.

Briggs had not gotten very far from the Devereaux Estate when he took the call from Jean-Claude in the Mercedes. He turned his squad car around, turned on the lights, sounded the siren, and raced back to the Devereaux estate. The sirens and lights distracted Courtney and she decided to depart the scene quickly, and escaped the area as fast as she could, noticing residents coming out on their porches to see what had happened in her rear view mirror.

Lucian, Aimee', Alex, even Dr. Ingram hurried out onto the porch to investigate the disturbance too. They only caught the aftermath. Lieutenant Briggs lights ablaze and sirens screaming tore around the corner, as Jean-Claude came slinking back into the drive. Jean-Claude wanted to see the damage to his rear bumper from the unexpected rear fender he had just received. He parked in the circular drive in front of the house, got out, walked around the Mercedes to eye the rear end of his car and inspect the damage done.

Lucian skipped nimbly down the stairs to join his father, leaving Alex, Aimee', and even Dr. Ingram to follow at a more casual pace. His father animatedly explained the reason for his abrupt return. Then, Lt. Briggs returned to the drive himself. Dr. Ingram came over and asked Jean-Claude rapid fire about his health, any injuries, neck stiffness, bumps, bruises or abrasions. Declining all efforts to assay her condition by Dr. Ingram, "No, No, I am all right. I sped up when that driver tried to rear end me, I am perfectly fine,"Jean-Claude spoke brushing aside any comments from the others. "Your not just saying that for my benefit are you Mr. Devereaux?" Briggs inquired skeptically regarding the man's age and fitness. "I made some accelerating turns and had you on my speed dial. I listened intently to you and Lucian earlier this evening Lieutenant and I thought I was ready for anything. But on that first threat, Isa that big black thing coming up behind me and I instinctively hit the gas and dialed 1 on my cell calling for help,"Jean-Claude said sheepishly. "Well I am glad you did!" Aimee' and Lucian said in unison.

"We must have matched speeds early on, see here there is the faintest scratch in the paint finishing in the rear quarter panel?" Jean-Claude spoke vigorously pointing out the offending mark. "It is a minor, almost scratch on your ear bumper, hardly anything at all," Alex responded, "I can hardly see it honest" she said. "That's not the point Alex, I just know it is there and that is the rub," Jean-Claude came back. Aimee' explained the situation to Alex. "Jean-Claude has always been so particular about his vehicles." "Yes I am more than a little particular, even vain about my vehicles," Jean-Claude said directly to Aimee', Alex, and Lucian. "I will say you are, I was surprised as heck when you gave the keys to keys to the Mercedes this time," Lucian said in surprise. "You never let me drive your cars, without sufficient begging and pleading," Lucian remarked with a smile. "We had better go inside, we are attracting quite a large crowd now," Alex and Aimee' responded again in unison noticing the people gathering on their front porches. "Look at all our neighbors coming out to see our little epigrammatic scene!" Aimee' espoused, pointing at the houses facing their own and the people now peering from their porches. "It is quite a site! Probably the m most excitement this neighborhood has seen in this century! Jean-Claude agreed. Lucian and his father waved and nodded to several of their closest neighbors. The Lieutenant again joined the entire family on their retreat into the family mansion. There were questions for all the members of the household before he could close his incident report. Briggs was amiable police officer, but also quite capable and thorough in the completion of his official reports. And these had to be official reports because he Governor had an expressed interest in this case. His superiors back at the station needed to be satisfied, at the precinct, before it was forwarded on to the Governor. It took nearly an hour to complete the interviews and statements from everyone in the study.

Alex and Aimee' drifted off toward the staircase and the second floor bedroom were Charles lay trying to hear what the commotion was all about. He called Dr. Ingram, but got no answer. His day nurse responded almost immediately, but had no clue to what had transpired downstairs or outside for that matter. With the arrival of

Amie' and Alex, Joseph got the opportunity to assay his witnesses and assemble the information he wanted. Both women recounted the events leading up to the ruckus downstairs in the first place, including the meeting with Lucian, Jean-Claude, and Briggs the first time. The first break in the meeting, then Jean-Claude's determination to park his own car in the garage, the attack of the black SUV, the return of Briggs brought back by a distress call from Jean-Claude, and the fast departure of the black SUV at the first sounds of screaming sirens in the distance. Just some interviews and statements before Lieutenant Briggs could wrap up the investigation and head back to the precinct station, nothing much they giggled.. Dr. Ingram was furious hearing that final bit of the conversation. "What have you two been doing? This is a very ill man. He does not need this kind of excitement!" he roared at them. "Mrs. Devereaux, I believed you had much more common sense about these things. I feel quite sure Joseph had questions about the doings downstairs, but you should have broken it up into smaller digestible pieces. Mr. Thorndyke is still in a precarious situation, and needs to remain calm and unexcited! "he finished. Both women were taken aback by the scolding. "Dr. Ingram, my uncle was already agitated by not knowing what was going on, and he did call for you to inquire, finally getting his nurse who had no answers either.!" Alex started explaining. "We just kind of rushed our answers together making it seem like a lark," Aimee' continued. "It does not sound like nothing much to me," he commented calmly in deference to Dr. Ingram. "Where did this black SUV come from, and why did it attack Jean-Claude, and is my old friend all right?" Joseph inquired hesitantly, fearing the worst for his best friend. "Jean-Claude is perfectly all right," Lucian said in unison with Dr. Ingram. He remembered a few of the moves we explained to him in our earlier meeting this afternoon. "I explained the moves I made to escape the same black SUV. And even better, he had finished putting Lt. Briggs on his speed dial!" Lucian said. "Everything has worked out well, Alex explained to him with Aimee's help. "The whole family is just fine!" Aimee' reiterated. Alex felt Lucian's presence behind her and felt a sudden calmness overtake her. He was back in the house and that was all that mattered.' That was fast, I never expected to feel this amity, this unity between the two of us so quickly. Especially after all we have been through, this marriage too. It seems to have made me stronger and more accepting.' At this point Lucian slid in behind her pulled her close and hugged her. He greeted Aimee' and Joseph, with a nod to Dr. Ingram.

"Changing the subject, we do not have a lot of time before Mardi Gras arrives in full force now. Shrove Tuesday is only two days away now. Ash Wednesday is here this week. Our Krewe is Having the ball this Saturday! Tomorrow night! I stopped by the apartment after leaving precinct headquarters earlier today. Heading home was were the excitement started. Had to call Briggs in again. "The apartment has had some new security features installed by my security team. It looks new and fresh and sparkling clean. I think it will be the perfect place for the two of us to hide away. Do not be surprised, we have to get you decked out tonight and in your party clothes. You have a lot of notes to take! You will need to memorize the names of all our Krewe members, and other Krewe's in the area. Many of them, will be at our Signature Ball on Saturday night. You will need the gown at the dress shop. Only time for one fitting, I'm afraid. "As my bride, you will be my new hostess of this ball., A big assignment so soon. After r our marriage, if only for convenience. You will need the gown of the season, be the bell of the ball so to speak"Lucian mumbled, thinking out loud. "It is this Saturday, isn't it? This past Wednesday was Ash Wednesday, so this Saturday will have to be one of the biggest balls of the season.? The day after tomorrow? So tonight what is it that I will need to memorize? We had better get started. We did cover much of this in our escape from New Orleans, just days Ago. I have a fairly good memory, and if I run into a problem, I can try to wing it," Alex spoke up. I will just have you brush up on my Krewe and the names of its members. Much is handed down from one generation to the next, and the importance and position of each member of the organization.," Lucian said calmly. "We will have to pick up your gown, I hope the ladies I have had time to finish it.," he said in an afterthought. "I can barely wait to see what Patti and Simone' have come up with, I hope it's not too racy or should I say, too revealing.!" And we will have to start out immediately," Alex said breathlessly in anticipation. "We need to call Simone' right away, run over for one last fitting. I am sure Maddie or one of the other girls upstairs can help you get dressed for the ball Saturday.

I will talk to dad again and see if I can borrow his car again to get over to the dress shop. I did call the insurance company and filed a claim on the beamer. The agent told me just to hear down to the dealership pick out a new car and get the customizations I want. So we can stop at the dealership on the way to the dress shop, before we get to the dress shop.," Lucian said firmly and decisively. "It has come up so quickly, it stuns me!," she stated. "Now I am really frightened. I am scared to death, shivering in my shoes, scared!" Alex said through chattering teeth. "Then we had better get going, before you chicken out completely," Lucian said tugging her along. The apartment is ready for us too. We can stop at the apartment after leaving the dress shop. Lucian said this aloud for the benefit of the complete assemblage: Jean-Claude, Aimee', sister Lucie, even younger brother Langley.

CHAPTER NINETEEN

"We must contact Simone' and Patricia about the ball gown today. It should be done and ready For fitting, wearing, etc., etc. now. Your suggestions should already be incorporated into the gown now, and I know you will be beautiful, Mrs. Devereaux. "I have already spoken to my father about using his car to reach the dress shop, and talked to my insurance agent about the beamer, I hope to receive a check for the replacement in the mail soon, but we can stop in to check on options on the way home. I do have a couple of other options to get a vehicle soon. I cannot keep using my father's car, I think I will need to get a rental until things are straightened out. The bug, on the other hand, will be picked up by the service garage. It will be repaired as good as new," Lucian explained to Alex. They left the mansion quietly heading for the dress shop, avoiding unwanted queries as to their whereabouts, past present, and future..

Though everyone knew instinctively what they were up to, considering the day and time. They followed side street down toward the river and the river district where the dress shop was located. Would they find Simone' and Patricia waiting with open arms and a completely finished ball gown waiting for Alex? And would Alex approve of the dress in the first place? Lucian hoped the minor modesty panel he had requested for the dress had been added. They had made it only 2 ½ blocks before they picked up a tail. Lucian mentioned it checking both the rear view and side view mirrors. "I see they were waiting for us, apprehending our every move, as it were," Lucian responded before making an evasive maneuver. "I do not know how long we can evade pursuers, but I will try to find us a large car park where we can tuck this car away. "Then we will have to proceed on foot to the Dress Shop only a few blocks from here," Lucian whispered hoarsely, pulling into a rear corner lot. "Keep your eyes open. You know what to look for. We will move fast to avoid anything they throw at us now," Lucian muttered determinedly. They hurried through the lunchtime pedestrian traffic, grasping hands so as not to be separated. They weeded their way *190* through two blocks of pedestrians, until they were within a half a block of the shop. They came up on the Black SUV.. It was empty, and they both began looking around for the driver. Courtney Anderson sauntered out of the shop at that moment looking very pleased with herself.. Alex an d Lucian scattered before being spotted, ducking down behind available parked vehicles along the street. "Stay down, are Are any others with her? I would like to know just who our enemies are," Lucian said gruffly.

"I do not see anyone. She definitely has a lilt in her, step though, I wonder why? What was she doing in the dress shop? I do not believe she has seen us, she's just too proud of herself right now. I want to get inside the shop as soon as it is safe, though," Lex hurriedly whispered back. As soon as Courtney jumped into her SUV she pulled into traffic almost immediately, forcing her way into an disrupting the normal flow of traffic. Accelerating down the street, she was soon losing site of the dress shop. Lucian and Alex stood up quickly and stepped back onto the sidewalk moving as fast as they could to the front entrance of the shop. They found Patricia and later Simone' lying prone on the dress shop floor.

Rushing toward the unconscious women, arriving simultaneously they ministered to the prostrate seamstresses. Patting hands, shaking them gently, they spoke to each as they gradually came around. "Oh my, Miss Courtney was so aggressive, violent even in her entrance to the dress shop, "Simone' wailed softly. "Did she do any damage here? We had better notify th4e police. Of this latest incident," Lucian stated ferociously. Simone' helped revive Patricia. "We must see if any damage has been done to the gowns hanging in the back. of the shop. They all hurried to the rear of the dress shop. What they found was disastrous. The carnage spilled out of the back dressing room! Every single dress was slashed and and/or damaged in some hideous fashion, flung from the viewing carts! "Just look at this willful destruction! These beautiful gowns viscously and diabolically destroyed, then heaped in the center of the floor. "Why would Miss Courtney do such a monstrous thing?" Patricia screamed, coming to and inspecting the carnage for herself. "We do have some gowns we moved upstairs to the second floor for completion. Miss Alex's dress is up there," Patricia responded helpfully. "Then my dress was spared this horror?" Alex said excited.

"Yes your dress is upstairs being fitted for the modesty bodice. There is also one other gown up there being adjusted for Saturday night ball," Simone' said introspectively. "Now we call the police to report this damage," Simone' said struggling back tears. "First we must clear away these destroyed gowns, then we can proceed with the fitting of your gown'" Patricia was chattering. "You will be beautiful, I Guarantee!" Simone gushed "Thank you, I have no doubts!" Alex responded in kind. "Shall we try on your new gown and see how it looks?" Patricia inquired. "The modesty bodice has been added and may suit you better now. Give it a try! Ok, show it to me now. Let me try it on and see how it looks now" Alex demanded. They all looked to the stairs to see the gown being taken down from the dress rack, a beautiful gown in a brilliant emerald green that contrasted with her own dark auburn locks. It is striking! Luscious auburn curls fell over creamy ivory skin highlighting the emerald green dress. "It is so beautiful", Alex exclaimed. Simone' and Patricia sprang into action. They picked up the dress flourishing it before Lex. It shimmered and shined in the light streaming through the windows, the folds draped over their arms as they led Alex toward the dressing rooms below. The color is so rich, so opulent, so luxurious, I have never seen anything like it before!. A the two women gathered up the underpinnings, putting the gown aside temporarily They began the process of getting ready for the ball. Soon it was time to fit the dress. It cascaded down from her shoulders, across her breasts, skimming her hips, flowing down to her feet.. The Ivory colored eyelet modesty piece above her bodice contrasted perfectly with the shiny emerald silken taffeta.. "I have no jewelry that will do this gown justice!" Alex fretted. She slipped into a dressing room, and with Simone' and Patricia's assistance, pulled the gown over her head, and let it skim down her body. It was soft and silky, and swathed her body in such unbelievable and impressive indulgence, she could not help hugging herself. Stepping out into the showroom, Lucian came forward with an impressive assortment of gorgeous emeralds displayed on a silver tray. The tray of jewels included a necklace, exquisite matching earrings, a bracelet, with marching tiara. An ivory colored mask was added to to the entire package. She looked stunning! Lucian wide eyes said it all. "I think I should have hired an Armed guard or an armored car to get you to the ball," he sputtered., holding her at arm's length to take in the splendor of her "How much do I owe you Simone', you have outdone yourself!" Lucian was both asking and exclaiming..

"Alex, we need to get you out of here discretely as possible.. Simone', do you have any other alterations that need to be made?" Lucian inquired. "There are a few minor alterations I need to complete before the gown is completely finished., I will have finished the gown by noon tomorrow," Simone' answered trying to clarify her position. "When the gown is finished, do we come back here to pick it up?" he asked. Or do you mail it to the house? He inquired again. "No there will be no time to deliver it by mail, I will send it by courier. "Simone' answered. "She is the most beautiful woman I have ever seen., So extraordinarily gorgeous. Unbelievable," Lucian finished again. "I cannot say how beautiful Alex is. she takes my breath away. I will go out and bring the car around, and we can go around and look at the apartment, maybe even stop at the dealership and go over the options. "The gown is spectacular Simone. Send it to the house just as you wish." We have help to get Lex ready for the ball' Lucian said with finality'Then are going into the Vieux Carre today then" Alex inquired. "I am grateful for all your hard work," Alex said to Simone' and Patricia.. "You will like what you see when we get there" Lucian said to Lex. Walking out the door Alex turned around and said "Nothing is more beautiful. It is exquisite, so stunningly gorgeous, no other way to describe it!" Lucian pulled up in the car at that point. Alex jumped in the Mercedes, A short stop at the dealership, choosing the options and color for the new beamer only took Minimal time as Lucian had been pleased with the original vehicle.. "Now on to the Vieux Carre. You will so surprised by what you see there. The builder, remodeler and I have put in our own thoughts as to for the improved security for the building and the apartment. You will be pleased with the improvements, I hope. I wanted to suggest we stay here in the apartment, it is our honeymoon, after all. I should have informed my father of these changes in my, our living arrangements. I should have but did not. So even though we cannot stay here tonight, I will inform my family of our intended change of address, and we can move out here right after the ball. I should have my rental, or heaven forbid my new beamer by the end of this week. Parking in front of the Antique Shoppe, Lucian got out of the Mercedes to open the door for Lex They left the car, walking toward the shop. "Here are the new keys and key cards to get in the apartment. We should go around and try the new street gate and try the new entrance". Taking her arm, he pulled her in the other direction toward the gated street entrance. He checked the keys and cards in the small envelope Genevieve had handed him. He separated the duplicates, kept one set for himself, and put one set on another small key ring. "Let's try these, and see if we can get in to the back yard of the apartment. You will like the new garage too, as we pass by. Turning the new key, and installing the new key card, the latch released and allowed them into the building's garden. Pushing the gates aside, he watched the gate clang shut and relock. "I am going back to park the car in the garage, keep it under wraps for safe keeping. I will meet you on the stairs to the apartment," Lucian waved to her.

Opening the garage service door into the backyard garden, Lucian moved fast toward the stairs to the apartment, joining Lex at the base of the base of the stairs "Let's go on up and check things out. I am reasonably sure you will love the renovations, "Lucian slipped an arm comfortingly around her "We'll see It together, no shocks this time," he told her. Putting a key in the door lock, he turned the key in the lock, and it sprung open at his touch. He showed her the entire apartment, starting in the kitchen, moving on into the breakfast room, a sitting room, the once destroyed bathroom, and into the recovered bedroom. He showed her the new sliding glass doors onto the balcony, and all the improved safety measures. She could not say enough about the new king size bed taking up space facing the windows onto the balcony. "You are so right, Luke. This is the perfect place for a honeymoon. I love it," Alex evoked her complete admiration. "I am so pleased you find this apartment so appealing, Lex" Luke commented.

"Take a look outside, this time of the day we'll have avoid turning on a light, or standing in front of the windows in any state of undress.!" he said pointing to the darkening sky. "It is beautiful, but I guess it is about time we head back to the mansion," Alex muttered, looking around the apartment one last time. "Yes I guess it is about that time, now," Luke responded in agreement. They left the apartment, locked up, and began walking across the balcony and down the stairs. He led her across the garden area, through a small seating area like a patio. A little further on they reached the garage area. He opened the door in to the garage, the Mercedes parked in the center of the space. We can head back to the estate now, and we've had quite an interesting day. "You like your dress, and love the remodeled apartment, you've helped me pick out the options and color schemes for my new car, and we've made arrangements for the pickup of you little bug. We have accomplished a lot, even spied on Courtney doing even more illegal things. Assault, Destruction of Private Property, and any number of other chargeable offenses.

"Well. Here we are, back at the estate, I need to have that talk with my father, and I know you want to check on your uncle. Let's meet again at my room, down the hall. We will be spending our first night together here, I am looking forward to this. "Lucian whispered in her ear. He made his way back to the entryway of the big house to see his father. The bug would be picked up by the service garage overnight, and a new beamer should be delivered tomorrow. There would be no necessity for borrowing Meeting back at Lucian's room, he held the door open to her. "Welcome!" he said grandly, whisking her into his lair. "I need a shower, do you want one too? Or maybe we can combine the two and save some water. Are you game?" Lucian winked at her. "I am not a prude, but this will be a first!" Alex stammered. Lucian opened closet doors, removed a large bath robe from the bar. Then he moved over to one of the dressers and removed a folded robe from the bottom drawer. He placed his robe on a hook outside the shower and tossed the folded robe to Alex. "Join me?" he wheedled her. "I am tempted, really, but I have never done anything like this before. But yes I am game, and we are married, so I will have to take that final step won't I? she answered. "You go on out into the bedroom, unwrap your robe to hang on a hook in here. I will undress and get into the shower to make this easier for you., you undress, and when you are ready you can join me in the shower, ok?" he cajoled. Lex began following his instructions to the letter until she stood naked outside the shower door. She could not believe she was actually standing here in the nude, ready to rap lightly on the shower door to enter and join a naked man in the shower! Instead of knocking, she grasped the shower door and slid it open, joining him in the spraying water. The water was hotter than her usual shower temp, but Luke was already lathering a net scrubby with a scented body wash.

He enticed her to come in further, using his fully lathered scrubby, to caress her body. While he lathered her body, he got a full view of her beautiful body. Alex in the meanwhile was also getting a full view of what he had to offer her. This frightened her a bit, but as he pressed his body into hers she began to have faint stirrings of what? Want, desire, lust? She could not identify, but here body was also having its effects on him. Embarrassing effects! He was pulling her into him, flattening her body into his, grasping her buttocks and pressing his manhood into the triangle, below her belly. He leaned down kissing her with a pent up desire he had been holding back. He urged her legs around his middle, and stood holding her tightly against him. He let her down gently as his manhood entered her fully opened and spread womanhood. It was tight, she did not scream, but only moaned as he entered her to take possession of her entirely. They started moving in that age old rhythm, kissing, hugging, touching awestruck in the beauty of each other. The shower took much longer than a normal shower. They grasped each other tightly as they released in unison. Spent, Lucian reached around Lex to turn off the water. Letting Alex slide down his body and setting her on the floor of the shower. Opening the shower door, he grabbed a couple of towels for the two of them. Toweling off, they both pulled the thick terry bath robes around their shoulders.

They dried each other's hair, and parts that were hard to reach. Fully dried off now, he led her back into the bedroom. Fully aroused once again, he wanted to take Alex to bed again, and maybe again and again. But he knew he might have to wait until she was ready. Lex walked up to the big bed smoothing the spread with both hands. Coming up behind her he untied her robe belt, easing the robe off her body. He lifted her onto the king sized bed, letting her know of his need. He opened his own robe dropping it to the floor and joining her on the bed. He playfully pulled, and tickled her beyond reason, growing more excited by the minute. They came together more tepidly than their shower encounter. He was amazed by their first union, Lex was looking at him with such amazement, he knew she felt the same thing.. He was ready again now and hoped she was too. Joining her on the bed, he started stroking and massaging every part of her body.

It raised both their temperatures and enticed amorous feelings. The hugging and kissing became breathtaking, they could not get enough of each other. The lovemaking became more and more aggressive, leaving them both breathless They came together over and over throughout the night Around dawn Lucian collapsed on the bed, exhausted. "Give me an hour to sleep, you wear me out woman, in a great way, don't get me wrong. But you wear me out. I love it, I love you Alex Devereaux. Hard to get enough of you!" Lucian declared. "Remember we must be up and around by six a.m.! There is only an hour or two before we meet and greet my family again. They will be able to guess our night's activities, believe me. It shows on our faces, and in our bodies Let's grab whatever time we can to sleep," Lucian replied, his eyes closing as his head hit the pillow. Lex closed her eyes too, snuggling tight against her new husband, putting a hand on his chest Lucian and Alex slept later than usual, only getting up when traffic in the hall picked up. They rose slowly, a little chagrined by her earlier demeanor, and a bit stiff too. Luke looked a little worse for wear too.Lucian did not have far to go to chose something to wear, this was his bedroom! Alex had only the clothes she had on yesterday. She had her things in the guest bedroom. All she had to do was sneak down to the guest bedroom, find a new set of clothes for today, and wait for her gown to arrive. Alex let the bed, picked up the robe Lucian had lent her and wrapped it around herself. She turned back to Luke saying "I am going back to the guest bedroom and get a change of clothes how long will you be here?" she inquired innocently., Looking at table clock at the bedside, he nearly launched himself from the bed, "Look at the time, I cannot believe I slept so late this morning, then blushed, oh yes I can! You kept me awake nearly all night!. And I am particularly wore out," Lucian said in affectionate amusement. Lucian strode over to his closet, pulling open the two double-doors and going inside, switching on the closet light.

"How formal should I dress today, my little minx?" he asked mischievously, winking as pulled out a top drawer in the dresser. "How about business casual today? Not too formal, but not jeans either. We'll have to go down and see if they saved us anything for breakfast? I wonder if the dress will be delivered today? he asked "Simone' agreed the dress would be here in time for the ball tonight," she responded to his query.. Luke retired to the back of his closet and came out in whit khaki's and a light weight short sleeve club shirt.The mint green striped club shirt hugged his body snuggly. It was a size or two too small, and was obviously one of his older wardrobe holdovers. "You look very impressive, for an old fart that was oh so tired this morning," she teased. "Oh fine, get out of here, find your clothes, and move them back here. Then we will have everything together tonight to take to the apartment when the ball breaks up, probably early tomorrow morning! Have one of the girl's help you get all of your things back into my room. Now go get dressed, while I consult with my father on the vehicle situation. I will meet you in Charles bedroom a little later. The dress will most likely show up before noon today. We can try and get some sleep this after noon," he chuckled. She hugged the wall all the way to the guest bedroom.

Maddie came into the room with a tray of breakfast treats. She bustled around the guest bedroom collecting and straightening things in the room. "I brought in some of the items off our dining table downstairs. I thought you might like a bite to eat before the dressing starts to get you ready for the ball tonight. I noticed you did not sleep in here last night, I hope you found a comfortable place to sleep," she commented slyly. "Yes, I did. Has my dress arrived already? Simone' was going to send it to me," Alex answered.. "Well it has arrived, it a big box, with everything you will need for the

ball tonight, at least according to the note she sent along with it."
"Great! Who will help me get dressed, I do not think I can get this done alone," Alex questioned. "Don't you worry yourself about that, I'll have one of the kitchen girls come on up at the right time to help me get you all gussied up," Maddie told her "What time is it now, Maddie? Would I have time to take a nap before getting dressed for the ball tonight?" she pleaded. "It is only coming on to 12:00 noon, We will need to start getting you ready by 3:00 pm., so yes you do have time for a nap, I will let Mr. Lucian know when I see him again," Maddie explained to her. "I need a little more sleep today, could you wake me in an hour or two? Alex asked. "You will need that rest to shine for the ball tonight!" Maddie giggled.

Alex climbed up on the bed, pulled the pillows down around her and started drifting off. Half an hour later, Lucian slipped into the room. He locked the door behind him, then looked at Alex in her shorts hugging a pillow. He joined her on the bed, replacing several pillows with his body. He pulled her close, kissing her forehead, fumbling with the snap of her shorts, She moaned turning to him inviting his kiss to her lips, and more while he pushed up the light top covering her breasts. The embrace became complete, He cradled her in his embrace, encircling her with his love, with his passion. She was very open to his touch. She welcomed it, pulling him even closer, pulling off her shirt and bra offering him full access to her body. They lapsed into their earlier lovemaking, as if nothing else mattered to them, and as if they had never stopped earlier," We do have a few more hours to fill before we go down to the ball, but I know how to spend this time filling it"Lucian said mirthfully They rolled around the bed, playfully teasing each other, kissing and caressing, hugging and touching. They enjoyed each other for an hour, before Maddie was again knocking on the door. Jumping out of bed, picking up his clothes and starting to dress, he and Alex behaved like school children caught in an indiscretion. He handed Lex her clothes to help her dress quickly, then. went to open the door for Maddie. Maddie exclaimed "Oh La La, Mr. Lucian., Miss Alex did not get her nap now? You really should be ashamed! "It is time to begin getting Miss Alex dressed now," She is getting ready to come out, now,"Lucian responded unapologetically leaving the bedroom in a hurry. Lex felt deliciously sinful, after their afternoon delight! She entered the outer sitting room to greet Maddie, putting the dress up on the closet door to admire. "It is so mesmerizing! I can barely take my eyes off of it. Maddie stood back to get the full view of it. I just need a minute to call down to the kitchen. One f the kitchen girls can assist us," Maddie told her. Maddie made her call, and one of the younger girls from the kitchen joined them almost immediately. The two women took the beautiful gown down from the closet door. Had Alex strip down before putting the gown over her head and pulling it into place. Lex then strode over to the Loveseat in the sitting room, picking up her under things. Wriggling into her under things, with the younger girl pulling everything into place from the top. "There is more! Maddie exclaimed. Little bags had been attached to the inside of the dress. A shoe box was also delivered with the dress. Next Alex had to get her stockings on. She pulled the pantyhose on gingerly so as not to tear them. In the meantime, Maddie was sorting out out the little bags attached to the waistline of Alex's gown. Also in the shoebox, Lex found the tiara she would wear with her gown. She set her shoes aside on the loveseat, then Maddie walked up behind her, zipped and closed the back of her dress. The dress was still long for the 5 foot 7 inch chestnut beauty.

She held the matching shoes to the gown, hand dyed to match. Looked them over once again hoping they would stay on her feet. A barrow strap came from her heal and crossed her foot to the front of the shoe. Will it hold? She gave the shoe a doubtful look. Removing the shoes from the box, she slipped them on. So far so good. They felt comfortable while she sat on the loveseat, but how would they feel standing? Or walking? Well here goes, as she attempted to stand. She got her feet back standing with the support of the door for assistance. She reveled in the soft silkiness of her under things. The ecru lace was a nice touch from the bodice to her wrists to the accents at her waist and at the hemline of her dress. Lex tightened up the straps on her shoes, hoping to keep them from sliding off. "We will keep you in your shoes missy" Maddie was saying. But we have a few other things to get on you, she continued. Standing behind Alex, Maddie slipped the emerald necklace around her neck. She also placed the tiara on Alex's head., handing her the matching mask. Lex started to put the mask on her head, when the younger kitchen girl came to her assistance. Though her shoulders were bare, there were long fitted gloves matching the long, lustrous emerald dress. Next comes the gorgeous, slightly tipsy shoes with the 4-inch heels. Lucian walked into the room carrying a small jeweler's box. The emeralds in the box, a bracelet &* matching earrings were a Perfect match to the necklace Maddie had already encircled her neck with. Determinedly, Alex took her first step in the new shoes, surprised at how comfortable the felt! She took a few more steps, actually turned and pivoted and walked back to the door. "Mrs. Devereaux, you are so beautiful!" Maddie interjected. "I want to go down the hall and show my Uncle Charles," Alex told them all. "I have to practice a bit moving in this dress and these shoes too!" she emphasized. You look so elegant, dear, you move with such grace, dignity, and poise," Lucian was awestruck "Beautiful, Magnificent!". the help agreed. "I do not want to spoil the effect before I show Charles and Aimee'" Lex sniffed. The 4-inch stilettos were perched precariously on her feet. She stepped lightly into the hall, carefully mimicking sedate dance steps she learned in junior high. Aimee' clapped leaving Charles room, opening the door wide enough to give Charles a glimpse of Alex's dance reverie It looked so surreal. Charles was suitably wowed by her entrance into his room. "Spectacular, Alex!" he expounded. "Lovely, my dear, just lovely," Aimee' agreed.. "Should I be thinking of getting a bite for dinner, or just waiting for the goodies to be served at tonight's soiree? She asked. "You can snack on all the goodies prepared by the kitchen staff this afternoon and evening," Aimee' responded. You are exquisite, beautiful, so lovely," Aimee' complimented her again.

Waiting outside the door for her to finish, Lucian extended his arm to guide her downstairs. Slowing slightly before Charles room, she turned facing the room saying "I feel like a fairy princess Uncle!" "You look fabulous my dear, enjoy your first ball tonight," Charles Thorndyke called after her. Lucian approached from the rear again preferring his arm. He marshaled her away from the sick room, he spoke softly. "You are so incredibly beautiful, I can hardly wait to make our appearance downstairs, let alone the Ballroom. I can hardly wait for you to take my father's breath away," Lucian said proudly. "Shall we take the elevator down, or grandly descend down the staircase?" he inquired. "I would enjoy using the stairs, It's like a secret wish of mine, like a fairytale. Do you remember Cinderella's descent down the staircase?" Lex inquired with some amusement in her voice, teasing and tantalizing Lucian with a twinkle in her eyes. Jean-Claude and Aimee' now watched from the bottom of the staircase. "What an amazing site!" they both exclaimed. "so beautiful! So perfect, so incredibly lovely!" Everyone in the vestibule looked up and awed out loud. Lucian carefully tucked her arm into the crook of his arm, proudly lead her down toward the ballroom.

Lucian and Lex glanced around the ballroom and surrounding garden area looking for familiar, t painted faces in the growing crowd. At first, glance, only family and some close friends could be seen. Lex and Lucian visibly relaxed walking into the ballroom. They made their way around the room., keeping in touch with some seldom seen family and old friends, before moving out into the garden. Lex admired the decorations that spilled out of the ballroom and continued into the tiled garden area. Alex cooed, the servants had done a superb job with all the decorations and flowers. They chatted softly, as the other guests began to arrive and fill up the available dance space.

Then Langley appeared at the ballroom entrance escorting a radiant Lucinda. He left Lucinda for their father's perusal. Jean-Claude then moved to the podium and tapped it to make sure it was on. "As some of you may already know, I do have a couple of family announcements to make at this time. First, My oldest son has brought home a wife this past week. I also have a beautiful daughter coming out for the first time tonight. This will be a particularly joyous Mardi Gras Ball! Three times the celebration!" Jean-Claude proudly announced. Privately regaling old friends of his with his personal good fortune recently. First, my lovely daughter Lucinda and most recently, my beautiful daughter-in-law, Alexis Rochelle. I have been truly blessed with great good fortune." Jean-Claude was resplendent. Most joyous of all, Lucian's exquisitely beautiful new wife is actually the niece of old family friend, Charles Thorndyke. It is a blessing for both Charles and myself. Both families united!" Jean-Claude proudly finished. "Alexis takes my breath away, my lovely little Lucy is so grown up. I feel flushed.! I am bursting at the seams!

Just then, a commotion was heard emanating from the vestibule, Jean-Claude turned back to face the vestibule area. Lucian, Alex, even Aimee' all turned back to see what the noise and excitement was all about. At the center of the fracas stood Courtney Anderson alongside Charles Henry Delacourt.. Courtney attached her arm to Charles Delacourt's elbow slithering into the ballroom. She was not sullen, but boastful and proud. Charles on the other hand behaved almost furtively, evasive. He seemed ready for flight, to escape the entire situation. It was very interesting watching Lucian's reaction to Langley's visible anxiety with these latest arrivals. It seemed all three were somehow connected. Courtney strolled and strutted into the ballroom, stopping directly in front of Lucian. She hissed malevolently. She was malicious and spiteful hissing into Lucian's face."What you did not expect me? The old hostess for this shindig? You replaced me with this slip of a thing? And just where was this gown hidden in the dress shop? It looked like everything in the shop had been trashed the last time I was there. This new replacement has usurped my duties, taken over an office much larger than mine, even locked me out of my own office. Yes, I hate her! This little college grad has taken everything away from me, including it seems even you!" she spat at him. She cast a disdainful look at Alex, then shoved her way out of the ballroom...

The ballroom silenced as she way out of the ballroom and into the vestibule. Charles Delacourt followed her departure meekly out of the room. Moving sprightly across the vestibule they moved swiftly to his waiting Mercedes. Surprisingly, to Jean-Claude, Langley shouted out to their fleeing figures. So stunned were the guests in the ballroom, no one attempted to bar their escape. Langley slowed at the front door only to watch Courtney and Charles drive away. He turned back to the ballroom and continued the presentment of Lucinda to their father's arm. Langley maintained what composure he had to the very end, even asking Alex for a dance.. He had to portray himself as a calm and composed man in this situation knowing he suffered under Lucian's watchful gaze. Lucian felt oddly jealous handing Alex over to his younger brother. He felt curiously protective, he was unaccustomed to this feeling, and it was totally new to him. He was confused. He did not like the feeling.

Alex spent the early part of the evening dancing with and getting to know Lucian's Krewe members. The heels turned out to be much more comfortable than she would have thought. She was enjoying herself, when Lucian broke in to reclaim his wife. "Well, Mrs. Belle of the ball, you certainly look like you have been enjoying yourself. You have danced with every member of my Krewe, but there are family members that would like a chance for a dance, including me. Then we can sneak out of here and head over to the apartment. It is only 9 or 10 at night, but we have had quite a lot of excitement the last few days,. So we can call it a night sooner than later. These Balls can go on until the middle of the night, or even until the next morning. I am exhausted, and with all the twirling you have been doing out here on the dance floor, you must be exhausted, too!" Lucian commiserated with her. "I am constantly surprised at how good my feet still feel in these stilettos! I feel like I have been dancing on air, and all of your Krewe member buddies were so very interesting and spoke well of you. The evening has gone so quickly, I cannot think of we're the time has gone. I have felt like a princess all night long. Dancing on the clouds!" Lexii responded dreamily.

"I could dance all night!" she replied. "Do you think I could tear you free in another half hour to an hour?"

Lucian inquired sounding burned out, weary. "I will have another dance with your father, then Langley, and look who's just entered the ballroom? Maybe I will have a dance with my uncle Charles first, he cannot be staying up too late either!" Alex said thrilled with his appearance in the ballroom. "All right, you dance, I will sit these next few dances out," Lucian responded wearily. "Oh and do not mention anything about our sneaking off early to get to the apartment tonight to anyone, especially family., ok?," he said as an afterthought "Mums the word, I'll get these last few dances done as fast as I can," she answered sympathetically. She greeted her new uncle, pleased with how much better he looked. Sending him back up to bed after their dance, hoping their twirl around the dance floor would not have an adverse effect on her new uncle. Next, she singled out Lucian's father for another dance around the floor. One last dance with Langley before she could get away. Langley was a charming dance partner, and they swept around the dance floor effortlessly. Though Lucian was weary, he watched intently as Lexii danced with his younger brother. He was attempting to decipher what had passed between Langley and Courtney and Charles Delacourt. He continued to ponder the questions swirling around Langley, and now Charles and Courtney, too. He ached to hear what Langley was saying to Alex. He ached to hold Alex again, too. How do I get the two of us out of here tonight? Alex welcomed one last dance with Lucian, Alex closed her arms around him and gave him an ardent and impassioned squeeze. When he said "ready?" She said "let's go!"

CHAPTER TWENTY

L ucian's new BMW had been delivered before Ball began. It sat out front among all the other vehicles of the guests inside. Saying they were headed to the bathrooms, they snuck out of the ballroom and out a side door. Charles took Courtney out for dinner, a little dancing, and some libations. He was soothing, calming Courtney after the explosive appearance at the Devereaux mansion. Charles became demanding and harsh and quite abusive with Courtney. "What were you thinking, Oh that's right, you weren't thinking were you? Your silly jealousy has nearly compromised our schemes to profit our wallets!" Charles rasped in her ear. You had no promises from Lucian. He merely asked you to be a hostess to the Mardi Gras Ball. It was not a promise, he did not ask you to marry him either, though I am sure you were hoping for that too. I have a greater grievance against the Devereaux's than you do! They live in my home! I cannot believe my grandfather actually lost the house on a turn of the cards! I think he must have been cheated! I remember playing and exploring that house as a child. And Lucian has held that against me all these years. He pretended we were best friends all through high school and college. It was so humiliating relying on his generosity at camp, on holidays, even for my position with the hotel. Hotel Manager! By the grace of his appointment! Charles railed at everything Devereaux. "But what about Langley?" Courtney spoke up. That was quite a coup wasn't it? Lucian has nothing to complain about there, he has always mistrusted Langley and let him know it too. Langley has been valuable to us, and there is no love lost between those two brothers.

Lucian and Alex left the party, slinking away into the night. The celebration of Krewe's Knight with a Mardi Gras ball at the Devereaux mansion. These were taking place all over Louisiana, in many of the cities, town's villages, and hamlets. The revelry has always been a state-wide celebration. A one - day celebration beginning the Lenten season the day after on Fat Tuesday. Ash Wednesday to Easter Sunday. A time of penance, of sorrow for past offenses. The church has a powerful influence over the people Louisiana from the Acadians to the French, to the Spanish, even black entrants into the mix What a wonderful time to celebrate ! Up north the cold winds are blowing, the days are dismal and wet, snow, sleet,, and rain!

Sprinting toward the car, Lucian and Alex jumped into the new navy blue metallic beamer. The appointments were lush, expensive, pricey, but not ostentatious. The heated leather seats were nice, but the air conditioning was even nicer. Alex sat back resting her head against the cushioned headrest. Lucian went through his driving checklist, then put the car in gear. And steered the beamer toward the Vioux Carre. It did not take long to bring the apartment into view. Instead of parking out front at Genevieve's Antique Shoppe, he pulled behind the shop and parked in the new garage. This garage had been rebuilt to match the original garage, but had been made blast-proof by the remodelers and builders. He swung into the new garage, opening the door electronically. "This is really nice!" Lucian responded. "We should take the side door and jog across the back yard. We can admire the flowers on the way over. The backyard gardens really are quite lovely," Lucian was informing her. "Are you sure we can cross this open space without being shot at, or blown up or whatever? Alex inquired remembering the problems they had encountered just days ago now. Was it just days ago, the memories were so vivid. "I think we can get across safely, there are few places for a sniper to find sanctuary in this neighborhood ", Lucian answered. Alex turned slightly to look up the stairs. "I am anxious to see my apartment now. Is it as comfortable-looking as before the carnage left behind by the vandals? I am so looking forward to seeing the apartment again. This is my first apartment, my first job, my first post- college assignment," Alex replied in amazement.

"Well then, we had better get you into the apartment as quick as possible" Lucian stated taking a key from his pocket Turning it, he popped the door wide open for her to see inside. It was bright and airy. She liked the natural soft color combinations, ands peaked into the kitchen and countertop area. "Nice" she commented. Looking right, she spied the second bedroom to the apartment. Glancing around the bedroom corner, she found the second bathroom. Changing direction, she looked into the into the dining, sitting, and living areas of the apartment. She glanced further down the hall to the bathroom, and beyond that to the master bedroom. The bedroom was gust scrumptious, it was even nicer than the original look destroyed by the vandals. It is just gorgeous! Beautiful. And look out over the street from those windows, I cannot even describe the luxury, the signification of what I am looking at. She walked over to a balcony door and opened it. She glanced at the floor on the deck, the balcony, and stepped out onto it testing its strength. In the darkness, she looked down each side of the balcony, noting the corner on the left heading back to the entry door of the apartment. Looking down at the street below she was fascinated by the street scene below. Looking up and down the street, she noticed few vehicles on the street below. She did not notice two characters in a truck on the opposite side of the street, a few slots down. He did not move and she did not see. He gave no intimation of his surveillance. Lucian called her back into the bedroom. "Well what do you think? The balcony has some new security features. No one will be able to climb up here from the street now. Did you notice the windows? They look black from the outside, but we can see out clearly. The windows are also bulletproof. So no one will be able to use a brick or some other projectile to gain access to the apartment either. Now even when the lights are on, we will still be invisible! Do you like it?" Lucian pressed.

"Yes, I love it! I is superlative! This is a great honeymoon hideaway. I was skeptical at first, but I've changed my mind. This is a perfect place to get to know and understand each other," Alex commented standing in the doorway, Lucian reach out and turned the lights down low. "Come over here, and let me help you undress. Turn around and let me undo you. He unhooked the top hook, then unzipped it down to the hips. That beautiful dress fell to the floor. Walking to the closet, he pulled a padded hanger from that dark space Scooping her dress from the floor, Lucian hung her dress from the hanger and placed it in the closet. Down to her skivvies, Alex moved to the bed, removing her nylons and shoes, she just luxuriated in the feel of that underwear on her skin. Rolling her nylons into a ball, she placed them in a shoe, placing the shoes under a side chair on the side of the bed. "Are you going to leave that on?" He asked. "It feels so wonderful on my skin," she cooed. Turning back to him, she watched him undress, neatly placing his things on the other side of the closet. Lucian joined her on the bed, saying, "I have been waiting all day for this moment. Drawing her close, They embraced, holding each other tightly. Falling back onto the bed together "You're right it does feel good against the skin, but what would feel even better is nothing at all," he told her gathering the camisole up and pulling it over her head. Unhooking the flimsy bra, he whisked the panties from her bottom. Embracing, exploring, and discovering surprising things they had missed this morning, reveling in each new discovery. Despite his earlier fatigue, Lucian astounded her with his passionate recovery.

Their lovemaking was impassioned, yet thoughtful and compassionate. After the long day and excitement of the ball, they fell solidly asleep in each other's arms. Sleeping late, Lucian woke to the feel of Lex in his arms. Sliding out of bed, he pulled the bedclothes up around Lex to substitute for his missing body. Making his way to the shower again, he needed a quick shower to clear his head and refresh his thoughts. Toweling himself off, he rejoined Alex in the bedroom. Walking straight to the closet, he found some clean casual clothes, lightweight khakis', a summer striped polo shirt, and loafers. He was finishing his morning ritual when Lexii began stirring. Opening her eyes, she squinted through the light pouring into the bedroom through the wall of windows facing the bed. "Morning already? She asked. "Yes it is as I can see myself. What are we getting dressed for? Work, Play, and Vacation?" she inquired. "Well, I have taken time off for our honeymoon. We can go anywhere you choose. Well, no not really. As soon as we get a hold on this mess in the port, we can finally take some time off. Just something light and comfortable, good serviceable walking shoes. We have a few casual days all to ourselves," Lucian answered talking to himself as much as to anyone. "OK, shorts, Capri's, slacks, jeans, dress, skirts?" Alex pleaded. "Just something casual, not too fancy, just like the tourists," Luke replied. "Of course, after we go get something for breakfast, could just stay here all day. Or we can just in bed all day and forget eating all together, at least until we pass out from exhaustion or lack of food. Our ravenous bodies lying here on the bed for lack of nutrition, emancipated, hungry and starving.," he joked with her Going to her closet, Alex chose a pair of light colored Capri's with a colorful tank top and skinny low heeled sandals. Grabbing a light weight shrug to cover her shoulders in case the air proved chilly. "Where are we going, Mr. Devereaux? Alex inquired mirthfully. "We have a choice of available options to us. From New Orleans long time favorites to the newer availabilities, modern fruits, etc, etc., etc. What would you like?" he answered, making the choice hers. "Well my normal breakfast is usually some seasonal fresh fruit and a cup of coffee or tea, but I think I would like to try the New Orleans favorite, beignets. It seems everyone here starts their day with them," she responded. Let us go see what is in our neighborhood. There will be much to see in this neighborhood. This will be our new neighborhood," Lucian explained.

"We can start our exploration of the neighborhood with a walk down to the farmer's market, pick up some fresh fruits, maybe some eggs, whatever you like for breakfast maybe stop in at DuMonds', there are also churches down here in the Vieux Carre. So many wonderful things to see here. We have to eat breakfast anyway, we might as well see the sights together on this first full day of our married life. I get to show you off a little too," Lucian started rattling off a list of things just like a tour guide. "Let's walk! Show me more of this Vieux Carre. Show me what I did not see!" Lex responded. "Lieutenant Briggs wants us to draw our pursuers out. We just need to act like the carefree happy couple we are. Sitting ducks, but with police protection. We will not always see our protection, but it will be there. Maybe then we can put all of this behind us. Briggs thinks he will be able to trap and capture the drug dealers here in the Port," Lucian whispered confidentially leaning down to her ear. Now we can go out and display our carefree affection and growing devotion to one another. We will be the prey that draws out the villains. We will move slowly and carefully, holding hands and laughing, deceiving our stalkers," Briggs has a plan, we will see how it works out. Briggs has incorporated the Governor's ideas into his own.

Now on to the Farmer's Market and look at some breakfast! Arm in Arm they skipped on down the block seeking the Farmer's Market. Alex could not keep from glancing over her shoulder for a possible attack. "Cut that out now, we have to be inconspicuous," he commented quietly. Strolling down the street they browsed unhurriedly, picking up one item after another. "Did you see anything that interested you?" he inquired. "The apartment is well stocked, but there are always things to pick up to make it your own" She answered. "I guess I like the old traditional things to surround myself with. A stole to ward off the cold, A few treasures to place in the rooms that provide special meaning to us. This will be all that I require. I do love you, and I hope your love for me is just as strong." Lex snuggled close to him. "We will have to stop at one of the restaurants along our way, and there are many to choose from," Lucian said tenderly. "I have to take my best girl out and show her off, don't I," he inquired. "Let's see the sights, but I am already getting tired! This past week has been quite intense for both of us," Lex responded. "You will feel much better when I get some food into you. We are getting close to the market now, it was not that far in the first place. We cannot spend all of our time in the apartment, and the sooner we draw our enemies out into the open, the sooner we can really begin our real life," Lucian muttered under his breath.

A nibble or two of the fruit at a market stand perked them right up. A couple of cups filled with fresh cut pineapple, a granny smith, a peach, and a handful of grapes, and cherries in separate bags led them to a small bench and sideboard. Here they could snack on their fruit, and get a cup of coffee. They also indulged on some of New Orleans famous Pastries. With pineapple juice still dribbling down their chins, they escaped the market area with their leftover feast remaining in their bags. Lucian led her on to Jackson Square, pointing out several attractions, the Pontalbo Apartments, the Cathedral, the oldest church in the US. They found a zoo and then later a marine biology unit situated between the Vieux Carre and the Harbor The Zoo was closer to the Garden District and fancier restaurants. They picked a restaurant for dinner and settled in for dinner of lobster, and fish, and crawfish. The walk back to the apartment was leisurely and further than they thought. They still strolled hand in hand, picking up the pace, back to the apartment.

Approaching the apartment, a blue pick-up not the black SUV squealed around the corner and a shot rang out. Pulling Alex down beside him, he hugged her tight and covered her head and body with his own They had dropped down behind one of those concrete trash cans placed all over the French Quarter. Lucian began scouting the area almost immediately for any further threats. The blue pick-up was squealing around the next corner. A half block from the apartment gate, Luke pulled Lex to her feet after looking up and down the street checking for any possible threats. Taking her hand again, he hurriedly headed for the safety of the apartment. The gate was still locked though it had tell tale marks of someone trying to

Jimmie the lock. Unlocking the gate, they rapidly closed it behind them, walking toward the now half hidden staircase, realizing a bullet could come anytime from the street, they quickly climbed the stairs to open the apartment door. Tossing the now soggy fruit bags into the garbage, they moved further into the security provided by the new apartment. Alex and Lucian collapsed on the new sofa in the sitting room. Well, we made it through our first full day playing possum. We are the perfect loving couple for all the world to see. "I am going to take a long shower, care to join me again?" Lucian asked wickedly. "I rather enjoyed our first shower together, yes I think I would greatly enjoy another," Lex said sensuously sliding a hand down his chest. "I will accept that invitation!" Lucian said pulling her with him to the bathroom. They took great joy in lathering up their loofahs, and washing each other upland down…

Another night of rollicking fun for the newlyweds left them to fall into an exhausted sleep by 2 a.m., sleeping soundly till after 9 a.m., Lex woke to a half empty bed. Panicky, she slipped out of bed and made her way to the closet. Getting walking shorts out along with a skinny strap t-shirt and tennis She made her way back to the small kitchen and dining counter. Pulling out a counter stool, just as Lucian burst through the apartment door, loaded with several bags of breakfast goodies. "Good, you're up. I have some fresh squeezed juice for the two of us, some fresh fruits, even coffee to have with our pastries later," Lucian articulating his absence from their bed this morning. "I also had to make quick calls to Briggs and the Governor this morning. I did not want to waken you. We were both pretty worn out last night" he commented. "Come and get it." They settled down on the sofa with all his purchases on the coffee table. Grabbing glasses and bread plates from the cupboard, Lex brought them over to the table. Staying in the safety of their apartment, they snuggled into the sofa before spooning out fruit and the like onto the bread plates. Pouring juice into the glassware on the table, she set out a glass for each of them. Enjoying their light repast and looking deep into each other's eyes. "What do we do now?" they both asked before exploding into laughter.

Teasing and playfully stripping down the hall, they arrived at the bed simultaneously. Diving onto the bed naked, their arms and bodies sought and found each other. They did not need the shower foreplay to begin their lovemaking, but it was more fun and even more amorous. They yielded to each other, were enamored of each other. The passion sizzled for the rest of the afternoon.

During the afternoon Alex and Lucian managed to take two more showers, then managed to get dressed for dinner out of the neighborhood. An upscale place featuring a live show with the meal. A French restaurant featuring the best of French cuisine. Beef Bourginoine, a nice red wine with a pleasant bouquet and French pastries for desert. They held hands through the dinner show and savored their meal before gathering up their things before reaching the new BMW. So far, so good. No threats to speak of this evening. "We can make plans tomorrow to see more sights around town, but we WILL get out of the apartment," Lucian responded sympathetically. Opening the car door, he held it open for Alex to step in. Let's hope there are no more incidents tonight.

Spending another frisky night in the apartment, neither one noticed anyone following them Finally relaxing, they fell asleep in each other's arms. "How about taking a ride up to the Plantation District? It is Old World New Orleans. Some haunted, some not. I will let you decide which is which!" he explained to her. "I am game. But there is another walking tour down here in the quarter that is also supposed to be haunted! Maybe we can keep them right down here in the French Quarter?" Alex queried. "We can draw off the first bunch down here, then they will have to regroup to follow us out to the Plantation District!" Lucian agreed. "It just could be a good divide and conquer strategy for us!" he again agreed.

"We ca n go West-North-West to explore Laura House Plantation, or Oak Ally Plantation, a little farther out we also have

Parlange Plantation and Nottoway Plantation. But then we could have a whole lot of fun at Dixie Landin' & Blue Bayou Waterpark.! Your choice," Lucia inquired mirthfully. "Ok, we can start with the walking tour here in the French Quarter and gradually work our way out, though your water park idea sure sounds good," Lex answered. "Excellent, we can pick up breakfast along the way and still make our tour. I have to warn you there are some spooky revelations along this tour., ready?" Lucian asked playfully. Let's go, but do not forget the water park," her eyes dancing in her impish way. Eyes open, notice everything. We are still on target detail. We still have to lure them out and I will inform Briggs of our plans," he said quietly, opening the door out into the garden. Out on the front street, they made their moves toward Jackson Square, the Pontalbo Apartments and the Ursiline convent Picking up a couple of bites from local street venders, they carried their breakfasts along with the tour. Though innocently appearing to enjoy the tour, Lucian tensed periodically with changing scenes passing by. Scuffling and pushing outside St. James Cathedral brought a number of officers scrambling, and four shady characters where taken in for questioning. Briggs was not impressed by the arrests, no high ranking miscreants, just local thugs. Alex and Lucian continued through the walking tour finishing in just over the allotted hour, then decided on a bit of fun at the water park. "I always feel as if I will be quizzed after going through all of the plantations, I just want to relax and have fun. A break if you will," Alex responded. "Fun first, Plantations next?" he asked.

They took I-10 north until passing through Gonzales, continuing north west to Baton Rouge they turned right onto state 42, seeing the signs for the new Dixie Landin' & Blue Bayou Water Park. and hearing the screams of joy along with the laughter outside the gates. It wetted their anticipation and excitement for adventure. Concerned with a number of vehicles behind them, Lucian put in a call to Briggs and called out the make, model license numbers and colors of the cars and trucks following them. Selecting an empty space near the center of the parking lot, he parked tightly in the space, leaving just enough room to open the doors. Keeping an eye on the suspicious vehicles following the beamer, he pulled Alex through the parked cars staying away the occupants of the pursuing vehicles. They reached the skew leading into the park. The vehicle occupants were further back in line, making it easier for him to avoid them. But coming toward him at a steep angle to intercept them was Charles Delacourt. Now Charles was an old friend and college buddy of Lucian's', but for some reason Lucian was on alert. Why would he be here? The thought screeched through his head. "Imagine finding you here!" Charles said in feint surprise. "We are here taking a break in our tours of the great plantations of the South," Lucian commented. Noticing several of the suspicious vehicle occupants converging on them, he pushed Lex into the line gaining a bit of time in the line. Waving a hand to Charles in dismissal, Lucian heard the sound of sirens in the distance. They moved ahead in their excursion into the first water park ride. From the corner of his eye he watched as Briggs and a whole battalion of officers looking to surround all the suspicious characters in the water park. Charles Delacourt however disappeared in the crowds. Some of the lower level minions panicked and scattered, only to be gathered up by the officers already on alert. Alex and Lucian went ahead on the ride, not making a fuss to bring attention to themselves. Lucian met with Briggs for a short time while Lex made her way midway style concessions'. Noticeably wedged between state patrol officers, she stayed as safe as she could. Lucian met with Briggs for longer than he originally planned. He gave Briggs the lowdown on their plans for the rest of the honeymoon. Briggs was hoping they would be able to mop this entire episode up quickly, hopefully without any injuries. Lucian gave him an affirmative nod. "We will try to have some fun on this honeymoon, and still try to bring all of these investigations to a conclusion. "I do not want to keep all of your officers at my beck and call indefinitely, it just has to end," he ended.

Lieutenant Briggs left a half dozen armed officers at the water park before he departed for Precinct Headquarters. He left stringent instructions for his officers, and very specific instructions before leaving for headquarters. Lucian decided to continue with their fun day. With the half dozen officers staged around the park, they moved down the midway, stopping to buy some cotton candy from a vendor. Enjoying another ride in the park, welcoming the cool splash of the water when they splashed down. A lot of screaming and laughing much later in the day after taking in all the rides and amenities in the park, the young couple were ready to exit the park. Walking arm-in-arm for the front gate, Lucian and Alex made future plans for the rest of the day, and then tomorrow too.

The shadows were growing deeper, Lex decided to postpone any inspection and examination of Plantation Houses. The Tours can be so informative, even illuminating. "ok, we can go take a look at the two closest Plantation Houses tomorrow, Laura Plantation House and Plantation and the Madewood Plantation House and there is one other thing in the neighborhood you might like to see. The Wetlands Acadian Cultural Center, a part of the Jean Lafitte N.H.P. The national historical park is near the Laurel Valley Village, too. Something a little different to see. No questions, I promise. You will be enthralled," Lucian advised her. "Can we go home now?" Alex inquired. "I will let our protection detail know we are headed for home so that they can go home as well" Lucian explained to her.

Stopping at yet another fancy looking restaurant Lucian offered his arm to escort his beautiful bride in for dinner. Leaving the car in the parking lot, he opened Lex's door offering his hand to steady her exit. Enjoying a dinner of French and Cajun food. They also liked the music playing before, during and after dinner. Slow romantic, and amorous music. Ready to go home, they left the restaurant quickly heading for the privacy of own apartment. The beamer eased out of the restaurant parking lot, maneuvering toward the royal street apartment. Checking the rear view mirrors for likely suspicious characters out and about on the roads and streets tonight. Despite everything, he still hurried home. Their security detail did not leave until they were securely locked in for the night. Lucian closed and locked the garage for the night before using the side door opening onto the back yard garden. Opening the side door of the garage, Lucian led Alex in to the garden. Up the stairs and into the new apartment. This really our apartment and I love it! She yelled wrapping her arms around his neck. This is great.

Genevieve was waiting for the newlyweds to arrive back at the apartment. She could not wait to give her congratulation to the young couple. Lucian and Lex were overwhelmed to be back in their own apartment. Hugging and squeezing, their intentions amorous they stopped in surprise at the chiming of the doorbell. Turning back to the door they had just entered, gazing through the peephole, Lucian swung the door open wide to greet Genevieve. Accepting her good wishes and congratulations, Lex and Lucian offered her a toast of champagne. Accepting the glass of champagne she made her toast of congratulations for a long and happy marriage. "I do not want to interrupt your evening, so I will be on my way. Well I will be on my way and get out of your hair. Go back to doing what you were doing," Genevieve said as she left. Alone again at last, they found themselves moving toward the front of the apartment overlooking the front street Disrobing at the bathroom door, they chucked their dirty clothes into the hamper inside the bathroom. This is becoming quite a habit, don't you think?" Lucian smirked smiling wickedly. With one arm wrapped around her waist, he ushered her into the shower. They were really starting to enjoy their evening showers. Of course the hugging and squeezing led to much more intimate behavior they continued in the bedroom. Instead of the frantic groping of their earlier couplings, they settled into a more amorous and intimate, more deliberate and less frantic lovemaking.

All night they giggled, laughed, loved, slept a little, and then loved some more. They repeated this routine all through the night. "Good thing we got a little sleep during the night. Remember to dress appropriately for our Louisiana heat. We will be touring some of our closest Plantation Houses today. If we get through the homes quickly there are a couple more homes in the northwest corner of the state. Just offhand we have the Parlange Plantation West Northwest of Baton Rouge. But I have other ideas. To the Northeast we have Zamurrey Gardens or the Global Wildlife Center. That would give us a break between Plantation House Tours. I have not been to all of the old Plantations myself. What can I say, I am a guy. I did not have any interest in the old Plantations. I know they are here, but I always had more interest in guy things like football, sports, and hunting, and fishing Good break for both of us, we will see History unfold and return us to the past centuries. Plus we will tour the gardens and the Wildlife Center. That's a no brainer," Lucian boasted of his new plans. Now just fill in Briggs about our plans.

With Brigg's on board with the new daily plans, Lex and Lucian grabbed breakfast at the Farmer's Market before setting off on the latest adventure. Lucian picked up a tail on the way to the market, but did not say a word to Lex. Not wanting to worry her needlessly, he simply pick up his pace back to the relative safety of his car. Tucking Lex into the beamer, he w2ent back to the driver's door. "Well, should we take in the two local Plantation tours first?" Lucian inquired with some apprehension. Glancing around at the crowds lining the sidewalks, he thought he picked out an undercover officer in the crowd. Feeling in more control now since noticing the thugs following them, he pulled out of his parking space heading for the first Plantation House for their tour. He got on State Highway 3127 heading out to Laura Plantation. "Now, we can get our first look at one of the most famous Plantations in

Louisiana," Lucian explained. It will be better to explore this one together, don't you think? At the door, they picked up some tour paraphernalia and a tour guide. They spent an enjoyable 45 minutes to 2 hours on the tour depending on the questions asked and how deeply they wanted to explore. Stopping at the gift shop on their way out, Lex picked up a sample of apple butter along with a loaf of Walnut-Apple bread. Asking for the loaf to be sliced, she took a butter knife off the counter and spread a little apple butter on the bread. "Wonderful" she exclaimed. Spreading another for her new husband, and offering the slice up to his lips. "It is good!" he replied. "I needed a snack for mid morning," Lucian admitted after their trek through the plantation. Studying his map of Louisiana, he looked over at Lex saying" What will it be Nottoway Plantation or Zemurray Gardens?" Which is closer?" Lex asked curiously. "Well depending on the direction we plan to travel, Nottoway Plantation is closer just off to the northwest. The Gardens are farther north on I55," he answered. Then, let's take in Nottoway Plantation first, before traveling on to the Gardens" she remarked to him. "OK, that's fine," clipping his response short to survey the parking lot. Standing as they were on the top step of the Plantation House, he had a bird's eye view of the lay of the land. He noticed one suspicious looking character in a corner of the outer lot, "let's start moving toward the beamer, before anyone else takes notice," Lucian told her. "Nottoway Plantation it is!" he said with verve, moxie to the rest of us. "I will let Lieutenant Briggs we are moving on to Nottoway next, and that we may be being shadowed on our way there,". Nottoway Plantation was next on their list, similar but not quite the same as Laura Plantation. They gave it a cursory look before heading to the Gardens.

The Zemurray Gardens were quite beautiful. A restful respite from the everyday. Because he knew where they were headed, Briggs was already placing his men along the way. He was giving his men undercover assignments to cut down on mistakes. Or maybe he was just trying to weed out possible turncoats in his squad. Money was the great betrayer. And Drugs were big money! I hope I don't have a Judas in the group! Briggs was worried, something was not quite right in the squad, but he could not put his finger on exactly what was wrong. But he had to keep the Devereaux's safe. That was his mandate from the Governor. Briggs gathered the half dozen trusted officers and gave them specific instruction in guarding the Devereaux's and about his uneasy feelings about this case. A half dozen eyes on the case was better than a single set of eyes. Lucian and Lex strolled through the gardens under Briggs watchful stare.

They spent two and a half hours seeing everything in the garden, and then stopping in the gift shop. But, the shadows were growing longer. The sun was setting, and they had quite a long ride home yet. Reaching their beamer in the parking lot, they dallied in their restive mood. Temporarily dropping their guard. Inside the beamer, the newlyweds, turned their car toward home. Leaving the lot, a truck pulled in behind them. Lucian was not trying to set any land speed records and was driving along at a comfortable pace. The truck behind them was urging them to speed up, at first honking his horn, then bumping the back fender. That first bump was Lucian's wake-up call. Donning a ferocious façade on his face, he stepped on the gas using the beamer's speed and agility to beat this challenge. He made some smart moves and put some distance between him and this latest pursuer, then saw the unmarked squad car pulling in behind the pick-up following them.

Lucian was doing better than 10 miles over the limit to escape the latest threat He slowed a little, bringing his speed down to legal limits. Now the pick-up was sandwiched between him and what he hoped was one of Briggs undercover officers. On the next bump and run from the pick-up truck, the pick-up truck was treated to his own bump and run from the car behind him Then, the officer in that car made his own moves, bumping his rear right bumper and sending him into a spin. Lucian seeing what was happening behind him, accelerated slightly to avoid the trucks uncontrolled skids, slides, and turns. When the pick-up left the highway in the last skid, Lucian tipped his hat to the driver coming up behind him. "Let's go home," a relieved Lucian expounded.

Driving into the night, Lucian relaxed a little, but still kept an eye on the vehicles around him. No new incidents occurred the rest of the way back to the apartment. Parking the beamer in the garage behind the apartment, He locked the garage down like a fortress., then walked around the car to open Lex's door. Offering Lex his hand, he helped her exit the beamer. Going through side door of the garage, they found Genevieve waiting for them. Visibly overwrought, she went directly to Lucian's side. "There was some trouble here at the Antique Shoppe today. Your brother Langley was here with you friend, Mr. Delacourt. They wanted to see the newly completed renovations done on the apartment. I explained I had given the only keys to the apartment to you, but it would be unethical of me to provide a passkey to someone else's apart- ment" she hurriedly explained. "But they were angry anyway, and Mr. Delacourt actually became very abusive. I hope I did the cor- rect thing," Lucian assured her she had. "They just wanted to get inside, but could not with the new security features we installed! I wonder what my little brother was up to this time, and with Charlie Delacourt too? "Lucian asked himself. "I had to call the police, Mr. Delacourt frightened me so badly" Genevieve revealed to him. "What has Langley gotten himself into this time?" he asked himself. It's not as if he hasn't gotten into a lot of scrapes off and on through the years. Trouble with the law and not. His rambling explanations, revealed his troubling feelings about his younger brother. Alex tried to reconcile his revelations with the happy-go- lucky youth she had just met at the big house. What could be his connection with what was going on all around them now? I cannot for the life of me figure out what the connection would be. Let me think about this a little longer. Langley followed Charles Delacourt and Courtney Anderson out of the wedding reception at the Mardi Gras Ball over the weekend, and he was supposedly with Charles Delacourt when Charles Delacourt frightened Genevieve so much, yesterday. Charles Delacourt's father had supposedly lost the mansion to Lucian Devereaux's father or grandfather. How many years ago was all of this? And just how close were they really? And where does Courtney Anderson fit in this tight little menage' e touts. No Courtney expected to be Lucian's hostess for the Mardi Gras Ball, maybe even an announcement of her engagement to Lucian? This was all so confusing for a small town girl from Briscomb Bay, Washington! "Good morning sunshine, where were you a minute ago? You looked a million miles away," Lucian queried. "Just thinking, piecing things together, that's all," Lex responded.

Calming Genevieve down, then sending her home, Luke joined Lex on the steps to their apartment. It was finally quiet time. "Have you enjoyed all the things you've seen today?" he asked her. The Plantation Houses were gorgeous, and I have never been in one before. The Gardens were beautiful too. The day was absolutely wonderful Even the stalking wasn't so bad, you handled everything perfectly!" Lex answered. Your composure helped me maintain my own cool," Lex replied. "Would you like to try your new keys tonight?" Luke asked, keycards in hand. Accepting the keycard, she gently placed it into the slot on the door. The light turned green and she pushed the door open. "Just like fancy hotel rooms!" she exclaimed. "And like fancy hotel rooms, they are much harder to break into," Luke responded. "Snack before bed tonight?" he asked "I don't know about that, the only snacks I might like are just chips or popcorn and a cold soda," Lex pleaded. "Just sit back and relax, you got it," Luke said plopping Lex and himself down on the sofa. Slipping his arm around her shoulder, he clicked on the stereo behind the sofa. The CD's he had loaded into the deck were slow and romantic, working that arm into a hug took no time at all. They settled back into the sofa, grasping and holding each other.

"I really hate to say this, but it is shower time! This is becoming quite a habit with us isn't it?" "Yes it is, but it sure feels good, doesn't it?" she rejoined. Their antics in the shower sated the sexual energy between them until they fell into bed. Now he could proceed slowly and tenderly as he examined and delved into her erogenous zones, his hands giving him and her continuous pleasure at the same time. The stroking was loving and gentle as they drifted into sleep.

Waking in the morning, the sexual attraction was still evident, but it was beginning to feel a bit different, more accepting, more relaxed, always there. Alex was becoming more relaxed in dressing before Lucian, silently enjoying the look of his naked body while he dressed. It was wonderful to be able to appreciate each other sexually and emotionally. They were more relaxed with each other and it was only coming on midweek. "What should we begin to do to get us back to a more normal time.? We could make an appearance in the office today, make sure everything is running on time, and not falling apart?" Lucian broached a more normal aspect of their lives. You can check in with your new secretary and I will check in with the new office manager, you enlisted to keep us on track," he responded. "Sure, let's poke our heads in and see what's going on. It could be a little awkward at first for me, but I'll get over it!" she said.

Office dress would be much more laid back, and leisurely for this trip into the office today. Lucian opted for natural wheat colored soft linen trousers with a matching ;sport coat, Alex went for a soft peach halter dress leather huaraches sandals. It was promising to be a warm day, and they went for comfort. Leaving by the front door, they walked casually toward the staircase. Genevieve waited by the back door of the Antique Shoppe, holding two cups of coffee and two beignets for their breakfasts. Thanking Genevieve for her thoughtfulness, they went on to the garage. Climbing into the new beamer, clasping hands, Lucian finally put the car into gear and pressed the button on the door opener. Looking up and down the street for any possible threats, he finally pulled out into traffic.

Pointing the car to the Trade Center, he blended into morning traffic. Turning into the underground parking structure, Lucian tensed slightly as he entered thinking of the last time he had been here. Glancing to both sides of the parking garage, he made the effort to prepare for the worst. Finding his parking space across from the elevator, he parked, let Lex out, then locked the doors.

Taking the elevator up to the fourth floor, they exited the elevator coming into the front foyer of the company offices. Meeting Candy at the reception desk talking to Gail, the new desk receptionist, she was clearing up details in Alex's schedule for the new week. This also aided Lucian's schedule. Walking in they created quite a stir due to the recent marriage, not much of a honeymoon, and checking in back at the office so soon. Of course everyone wanted to see the ring! Didn't all women want to see the ring? Of course they did. Laying her hand on the corner of the desk, the girl's gathered around each trying to pull the hand toward themselves for a better look. Ohs, Ahs, beautiful, and gorgeous were common adjectives regarding the ring. Basking in this adoration, Lucian and Alex finally pulled themselves free to get into their offices. Surprised to find most of their books, ledgers, record, and calculators sitting at the desk.

Luke explained the appearances as an organizational from the staff at the mansion and most of all his father. Sitting down at her desk, she immediately began organizing the data she had taken along. Re-filing the records, ledgers and other paraphernalia, she felt a little overwhelmed by the work and the physical demands in the warm office It felt good being back at work.

Lex spent most of the remaining morning re-filing account files, ledgers, records and other audit materials in the file cabinets behind her desk. She even had had time to visit with her newly made friends, Candy and Gail. It felt good to have friends here now, too Not fast friends like Janet Winslow and herself, bud budding friendships made out of isolation from her old world. She should give Janet a calk tonight before bed. I have so much news to share with her, Lex thought to herself. Who would have thought I would be marrying Lucian Devereaux when I graduated from college and buried mom? Certainly not I! Yes he is so good-looking., sexy as all get out, and very capable with his hands. How much can I really tell her? I need to think about this even more. My life has changed so much since leaving Briscombe Bay! I wonder if Jan has found a position since graduating too? What a world we have been foisted into. We really need to catch up!

A knock at her door revealed Candy and Gail waiting for admittance. "So how is married life treating you?", they asked in unison. "Can you take a break now?" Candy asked. "Sure, I really need a break now," Lex answered. "A cup of coffee or a cup of soup would really be appreciated, right now," Gail spoke up. "Let's make a run down to the cafeteria f or a few minutes and do some catching up," they giggled. Sitting across from each other at a table in the cafeteria, their hands wrapped around cups of coffee, or soup broth. The aromas assailed their nostrils. Holding hands, they pulled each other close into the table. They whispered fast and furiously about the changes in their lives in the last week. Only a week, the thought brought them all up short. "Wow, you have made some very important changes in your life, in a single week," her friends were astounded.

Sipping the hot coffee and soup, the friends kept their heads down sharing, giggling and laughing at each new comment made. It was not long before Lucian followed them down for another cup of coffee. "Well, Lex we should be getting back to our apartment. I have already had a full day here at the office, and we may still have a few more hours for our honeymoon. I wish we could take a more formal honeymoon in another week or month or so. We must bring some things to a close first. Briggs wants us to force our assailants hands as soon as we can," Luke explained to her. "Now we just have to decide on the best reason to draw them out?" Les inquired as her friends left the table. We need to devise a good ruse, Lucan thought out loud. What could we use for this ruse, Lucian racked his brain.

Signing out at the office. Alex and Lucian took the elevator down to the new beamer in the parking garage. "Briggs tells me we have to devise a plan that will draw out the leaders in Port drug case. I cannot think of anything that will draw out the leader's drug operation," Luke told her in the privacy of the locked beamer. "I drove down to the docks myself just last week before last. Scary but I got a chance to roam around pretty much unimpeded. I could try something similar to that first exclusionary trip?" Lex volunteered. "No I do not think that would be a very good idea for you personally. And I do not believe Lt. Briggs would approve you putting your life in danger again either. There must be another way, maybe using myself as bait," Luke ruminated. I guess all we can do is go over all of this with Briggs," Luke responded. Making it down to the 4th sublevel, the elevator doors opened wide. All seemed quiet at first, until they stepped out of the safety of the lift. Approaching the beamer with determined steps, the roar of a racing engine soon filled the parking level. "It just cannot be" Lex said spotting the Black SUV tearing out of the dark recesses of the parking level. She is very resolute isn't she? Why is she so obsessed with me? Lex asked herself. It's not as if I took her job away willingly or even knowingly. It was just something Luke failed to mention to me.

Ruminating was not a good way to spend the afternoon, especially when she had so many of her own questions that needed answering. Lucian wants to get in touch with Briggs and I need to talk again with Aimee'. Luke suddenly grasped her hand firmly and jerked her toward the beamer unceremoniously "Stay down!" he ordered. "We just have to stay out of the way of that 3 ton behemoth. I have put in a call to Briggs at the State Patrol office here in the Vieux Carre," Luke whispered hoarsely. They spent the next what seemed like an eternity, ducking down and dodging the squealing tires of the SUV. Finally, the sirens of the emerging squad cars were heard entering at the guard gate at the street level. They only had to descend four more levels t reach them. They only had a few more moments to duck and dodge this very tenacious and unwavering adversary. The squads were descending one flight at a time getting closer and closer with every7 tick of the clock on Luke's wrist. The squads descended another level when Courtney decided to put some distance between her and the oncoming squad cars. She lit out, moving quietly and quickly up the parking ramp. Lucian noted the departure, and pulled Lex up to her feet. Squad cars were racing up the tiers, sirens blaring, ands lights flashing. In all the commotion Courtney managed to evade arrest again! Alex could no0t believe each squad car had missed the escaping Courtney! It was a gaffe, ersatz phony sighting, each officer overlooked in their efforts to trap this miscreant. What was Courtney anyway; an offender, a criminal offender, an outlaw, but not a convict? She acted like a stalker, a thug, a hoodlum, or a felon, but she had appeared so professional, so competent, and so caring and thoughtful in previous years to Lucian. It seems she was a good actress too But what about his brother Langley, or his friend Charles Delacourt? And if Uncle Charles whole name is really Joseph Charles Thorndyke, why is he Uncle Charles? Did her father, Joe Talbot, unconsciously take on the first name of his brother? Was he truly in hiding, or waiting for his family to come for him? It was a lot to think about, but even more important was the allusion to an older brother. She had dreamt of a sibling in her younger days, but had forgotten it with the death of her father. She could make so many suppositions, but what was the truth? It would be necessary to have a long talk with Uncle Charles! She thought making that notation in her head.

The squad cars had stopped and the officers were walking toward them briskly. "Are you all right? We came as quickly as we could" Briggs shouted in the parking structure, his voice echoing off the walls around them. "Didn't you see Courtney sneaking down the ramp as you came up?, Lucian was shouting back. "She was here just now? She is surprisingly brazen. And she was still driving the black SUV? We all missed it again? Unbelievable!" Briggs shouted back in exasperation. "Yes, just look at the dents in some of the vehicles down here, where she tried again to eliminate us!" Luke yelled back. Several lower ranked officers scrambled back to their squads to resume the chase, but left at a much more leisurely pace. Briggs put out an all points bulletin, then called officers back. "And What were you doing back here at your offices? You are supposed to be honeymooning, aren't you?" Briggs asked in an agitated manner. "Yes, but we have been thinking about how to set a trap for these thugs. I do not want to endanger Lex' anymore, so the plan can only include me. I think I can make a few innocuous comments to my younger brother that will get back to Courtney and Charles Delacourt and any others in this evil cartel. I do not know who is at the top of this plot, but these two must be involved. Now what is it I should mention to get this ball rolling?" Luke queried Lt. Briggs.

Judson Briggs thought ardently about the senior cartel leaders. "So you think your brother, your old college classmate, as well as your previous Administrative Assistant are all involved?" he inquired feverishly. "Yes, I am almost sure of it. I should have seen many things earlier, but I had such confidence in the people around me. My family, my friends, and even my office confidant, were all a part of the schemes. I felt so betrayed on my return home from Washington State. I felt things were just not right, but I could not put my finger on what was wrong. It was not until Alex arrived to take over the company apartment that things went overtly wrong. They showed their hand, but now we must bait the lure, encircle and ambush them," Luke said passionately. "But how can I keep Lex safe? I know she has more questions to ask Charles Thorndyke. If she stays in the big house surrounded by my father, the household staff, Aunt Aimee', even Lucy, she should be fine, don't you think?" Luke inquired of Judson Briggs. "With all the household staff in the house, and everyone's awareness of the situation, it should be all right. But with the close ties within the family of potential treach-ery within the group, I will put my private number on the houses speed dial. I will make sure your father and Aunt know of this," Judson explained.

"Now, we just present a ruse," Luke said with relish. "We already know anything concerning me will set off Courtney Anderson, but Charles Delacourt is something of another color. We were old friends right through college, but he could still be harboring ill feelings toward my family. Especially, if he still considers the fam-ily mansion as his own. His father lost the house and some more acreage in a card game to my Grandfather. Grandpa was a shrewd card game player, and Charles father was a bit of a drunk, pardon my French, but he was and a bad card player to boot. He has not mentioned it in more than twenty years, but it must wear on him," Luke spoke bringing out some of the dirty laundry."He could have been stewing on this for those twenty years,' Judson responded. "I had not thought so, but it is a definite possibility. I got him his present position as Hotel Manager downtown in the Vieux Carre'. He does not know I own the rather prominent old guesthouse downtown. He believes it is owned by a business consortium. But he has been making it on his own, though I have been hearing of some discrepancies in the hotel books. I have not wanted to press him on the matter. That could be his trigger. Now I am going to use Langley as a conduit between me and Charles and Courtney," Lucian ruminated again. "We will smooth it all out as we proceed," Judson answered him.

Alex was on the other side of the drive lane from Luke and Briggs. What could they be talking about? She wandered over toward one of the vehicles damaged by Courtney rampage. She will not be happy when she sees the damage inflicted on her own SUV. Black paint chips, crushed fenders and crumpled doors. It was quite evident it was Courtney's SUV or one just like it. Now they had some concrete evidence for Briggs and his squad. Luke was turning back to her. "Ready to head home? What would you think of spending a few days at the mansion with your Uncle and my Aunt Aimee? I know you had some questions for them. You can have my old room, you will be very comfortable there. Briggs gave me some ideas I want to put past my father too," Luke informed her. With that Squad cars began filing out of the parking ramp. Lucian pointed the beamer toward the Garden District. Reaching the Devereaux mansion without further incident, Lucian and Alex climbed the stairs to the front door hand in hand. He watched Alex start climbing the staircase taking two steps up to give her a quick squeeze before leaving to find his father in his study. In the meantime, Alex went straight to Charles sickroom. "Hi you two, recognizing Aimee' as Charles guest in the room. I do have a few questions for you. I would really like to know about a so-called brother or half-brother mentioned in mother's shoebox? I feel so guilty not having inquired sooner. But I will be staying here in the big house for a couple of days so I can work some things out," Alex commented.

With Alex upstairs, Lucian made his way to his father's study, knocked briefly before entering, then joined his father over the desk. He settled into a large brown leather armchair, before beginning his recitation of Briggs new security suggestions. He spoke of the necessity for stronger security measures for the entire family as well as Alex. He explained the reasoning behind his and Briggs concerns for the family as well as Joseph Thorndyke upstairs and Alex. Leaving the study, he took the stairs two at a time to say goodnight to Alex. Alex realized this was a ruse designed to keep her at bay and out of harm's way. She begged him to be careful in whatever plan was worked out between Briggs and himself. Call me? "If you do not call me, you can be sure I will be on the phone calling you!, Lucian said determinedly. "Stay safe till we are together again," Alex hugged him. "And you stay safe too! I will check in with you when I get back to the apartment. I will be thinking of you every minute," Lucian said moving reluctantly toward the staircase.

Alex joined her Uncle and Lucian's Aunt Aimee' in her Uncle's sick room. She had questions about a so-called brother her mother gave birth to before her marriage to her father Charles Thorndyke was fuzzy on that subject, but Aimee' fidgeted in her seat, looking like she knew more that she wanted to say. "What is it you know Aimee'? Can it be so terrible? I know that my mother was very secretive with this information, liked she was so horribly ashamed. Thousands of women find themselves in similar conditions every day, why did she feel this disgrace so acutely? And what did she do with the baby?" Alex's questions spewed out of her lips. Aimee' made some tiny sounds clearing her throat, even coughing a bit. "That was twenty-five or more years ago! I met your mother many years ago at a home for unwed mothers. She had just lost her young husband in a bank robbery. He had tried to fight off the entire police force in Baton Rouge. She gave her young son his father's name, Judd Conklin, Jr. She worried about attaching his father's name to such a perfect little boy, would it stigmatize him as he got older, etc., etc., etc. She gave the baby up for adoption and let the adopting parents rename him. At the time, I has been donating my time to the foundling home. Jean-Claude's wife, Marguerite, had recently lost her baby boy. She was devastated. One afternoon, she decided to accompany me to the foundling home. Your mother had just dropped her son off at the foundling home, amid tears and hugs and kisses. He was already 18 months old, so it was really quite heartbreaking, for both mother and child. Marguerite was drawn to that little boy immediately. He was close in both size and age to her boy she had just lost. She wanted to take that little boy home and keep him. The little boy was totally lost and crying for his mommy, and Marguerite just held him and rocked him until he dropped off to sleep. She sang to him, read him stories, and bought him toys. She actually demanded Jean-Claude adopt that little boy and make him a part of her family. Jean-Claude finally capitulated, adopting the boy and renaming him, Langley Allan Devereaux,"

Aimee' explained. "Do you mean Langley is my older brother?" Alex responded perplexed. "Yes, I guess that would make him your half-brother, would it not?" Aimee answered slightly flustered. I guess I did know that subliminally but he is still our family. Your brother, half-brother, whatever is still my nephew. I have always felt that way about Langley. He is the little boy Marguerite chose to be part of her family. I have never even mentioned this to Jean-Claude either. All he knows is that Marguerite found a little boy at the foundling home that she wanted to adopt. They raised him as their own and loved him all these years," Aimee' said, wiping a tear from her eye.

"I will be sleeping in Lucian's bedroom tonight. He will be sleeping at the apartment. I will be calling him with the news! It is exciting news to me. I cannot believe I have a brother! I wonder what Luke will say to this piece of information?" Alex said skipping out of the sickroom. Once inside Lucian's old bedroom, she closed the door noticing the deadbolts attached to the inside of the door. Deciding to forego locking the door, she crossed to the king bed and the telephone on the bedside table. Sitting on the bed, she quickly dialed Luke's number. Dialing on these new push button dials, is so much faster than dialing on the old rotary phones. No Answer. Checking the number on the telephone in the apartment, she dialed again. Still no answer. Where was Lucian? Was he delayed by Briggs? Or was something more sinister going on? Hearing scuffling outside in the hallway, she was moving toward the door automatically. She was tempted to open the door to see who was out there. Turning back to the bed, she hit the re-dial on the phone handset. Again no answer. Now she started to worry. Should she call Briggs at State Patrol headquarters or just wait to hear from Lucian. She paced the room for several minutes, before deciding to take a shower before putting her call through to Lucian again. Pulling the telephone closer to the bathroom door, she kept an ear trained on the telephone for a call from Luke. Finishing her shower in record time, she stepped back into the bedroom still drying and fluffing her hair with a thick and thirsty towel from Luke's linen closet. Sitting down on the footstool at the foot of the bed, she brought the phone up onto the footstool beside her. Her worry made her a bit frenzied in her frantic dialing of the telephone. Pushing the phone away after making yet another mistake in dialing, she began forcing herself to calm down. She was holding the telephone in her lap, when it started to ring. Picking up the phone excitedly, she nearly shouted hello into her receiver. "Lex, calm down! What has you so upset?" Luke was saying soothingly into her ear. "Oh Luke, I have been trying to call you most of this afternoon! Where have you been? Did something go wrong on your way back to the apartment? Can you tell me what you and Lt. Briggs have decided to do about our situation?" Lex inquired breathlessly. "I also learned something important from your Aunt Aimee' earlier today also. Did you know I have a brother, or more precisely a half- brother? I think it is incredible. You will never guess who it is. Go ahead Try? You will never guess!" she kept chuckling. "Ok, I give up. What's the big news your holding over my head today? Lucian asked lightheartedly. "My brother is none other than your brother Langley! He is my Half-brother. Yours too, it seems," Alex spoke hurriedly. "What? You got this from my Aunt Aimee"? Does she know who his father was he? His mother would then be your mother too? I cannot believe it," he said rubbing his jaw. Now, I will need to have those questions answered. "What questions?" Alex inquired skeptically. "Oh, you know, who is Langley's father? If your mother is Langley's mother, too, what happened? How did she end up married to Charles Thorndyke's brother? How does my Aunt Aimee' know these things? How did my mother become involved with finding a foundling?" Lucian ran through his own list of questions. "Well from what Aimee' told us, your mother Marguerite had been feeling the loss of her own little boy, when Aimee' invited her along on a visit to the foundling house she volunteered at. Aimee' had been trying to counsel my mother on her options in raising her 18 month old baby. The baby's father had died in a shoot out with police after a bank robbery. She had given the baby his father's name, and was afraid it would haunt him his entire life. My mother signed the papers to have him adopted, giving him a chance for a new name at adoption. Your mother fell in love with him the moment she saw him. Took him home with her and started adoption proceedings right away. Since the child she had lost was roughly the same age, she had no trouble convincing your father to file the adoption papers. Aimee' was her confidant in hiding the secret from your father and Charles Devereaux both," Lex finished hr monologue. "I knew it! I just knew it! His father was a felon. That's the only reason to get involved in criminal activities. He had a natural bent for it," Lucian shouted adamantly. "Now wait just a minute, Lucian. Why do you believe Langley in naturally inclined to criminal behavior?" Alex responded scathingly.

"Because it is in his genes! His father was a bank robber, for crying out loud," Lucian shouted back. "Please try to keep an open mind, Lucian. Wait until we get more information on all the players. Please? Lex appealed to his inner conscious, and sense of fairplay?" Lex pleaded. "I just remember all the problems and scrapes with the law he has already put the family through. I hope his upbringing has overridden his genetic make-up. I just have not seen any sign of it, as yet. I will keep an eye on him, with an open mind, for your sake," Luke told her. "I will watch too, and maybe try to mitigate, or mediate any problems that turn up might be a better choice of words. Thank you, Luke, I appreciate your fair-mindedness, your sense of fairplay. Thank you for giving our half-brother a fair chance," Alex responded. I have always wanted a brother or sister, and now I have one! "And just how are you settling into my bed all alone?" Lucian teased. Oh, I am way ahead of schedule. I have my shower in and Maddie dropped off a plate of fresh fruit when I got out of the shower. When did you install all of the hardware on the door? And Why? Who don't you trust here? Should I be careful of anyone?" Lex implored. "No one in particular, but I had noticed some strange events taking place after I returned from Briscombe Bay. Just unexplained, that's all. So I added some dead bolts to the Inside of my door. I would put them on if I were you! There are a lot of people in my house now, but I have this feeling something else is moving around in the house now. My suspicions have been fully aroused now. Just make sure you lock yourself into the bedroom tonight. I miss you already! The only keys to the dead bolts are in my pocket, so no one else is getting in unless you let them in. Be careful. I cannot bear the thought of losing you. Do not just open the door simply because someone knocked on it. Be careful with your uncle, father, Aunt Aimee', Lucinda and the rest of the family. Do not mention anything to them, except father, tell him to begin 'stealth'. This is Briggs code for the family lockdown. Father will then alert specific staff members to maintain security. I will be seeing to the new security features in the apartment for next few days. I am going to sleep on your side of the bed so I can drink in your scent. I am getting ready to take my shower now, I am sitting down on the chair next to the bed, removing my clothes. Did you put on anything at all after your shower? Can you feel me? My memory of you will not let me sleep easily" Lucian sighed heavily. "Stop Lucian, you are making me crazy. I feel like sneaking over and sliding in beside you!" Alex sputtered aghast at his blatant suggestions. "Go to sleep now, I will talk to you tomorrow morning," Alex whispered into her receiver.

Lexii pulled out Luke's pajama top and pulled it on. She smelled his top hugging it to herself. She hugged it to herself, She lowered her head to the pillow, reaching out to turn off the switch on the bedside light. She lay back quietly on the bed listening to thaw house breath. The door handle rattled, in the calm darkness. The noise brought Lex to full attention. Controlling her breathing, cautiously and heedfully. She Gathered the quilts around her. No one called out! Do not open the door! ?Her mind screamed out. Gazing down at the floor, she a pair of feet shadow the bottom of the door.

Again the handle rattled. She slowed her breathing again sinking lower into the pillows, Do I dare call Lucian? If I cannot even open the door to see out, how can I get out to Joseph's room? Where is Aimee'? Who is all in the house?

Snaking an arm out from under the covers, she stretched until she felt the phone at her finger tips. Pulling the receiver off of its base, she drew it in next to her ear. In the glow of the dial she picked out Lucian's number at the apartment, one ring two, then three, four, and five rings, Where is he? Her cranium screamed in fright. The ringing continued, six, seven, eight, nine rings, getting ready to hang it up, to disconnect the call, Luke finally answered "Hello?" "Luke, Luke, someone just turned the door knob on the door!. What should I do?" her fear letting her voice rise. "Quiet, quiet, Lex, you don't want him to know you know he has been there. Can you see the shadow of his feet under the door? Hang on I will get there as fast as I can" Lucian said rapidly. "Yes I can see the shadow of someone's feet under the door. You told me not to open the door, so I did not. I will stay right here with my head under the covers until you arrive," Lex whispered hoarsely.

Lucian hurriedly pulled his clothes back on as he sprinted down the stairway. He sped to the garage, threw open the entry door in the back yard and made his way to the car. Hitting the button to the garage door, he pulled out accelerating rapidly, not taking notice of the vehicles on the street. He covered the few blocks from the apartment to the Garden District mansion in four minutes flat. He bounded up the stairs to main entrance placing his own key into the lock he was surprised when the butler opened it so fast, rushing past, he took the front staircase by twos, not stopping until he faced the door to his old room. "Lex, Lex, I got here as fast as I could. Open up, I left my keys in the apartment," Lucian responded in an anxious tone. Relieved at the sound of his voice, she scrambled off the side of the bed, leaving the bed covers on the floor beside the bed. She opened the dead bolts, flinging the door open, then rushing into his arms." Wrapping her arms around his neck, they embraced as if separated for days, or even weeks or months. "I would really like to check on Uncle Charles and your Aunt Aimee'. It could have been one of them, or perhaps your father even. I was too frightened to go out and check. Who all is in this house tonight? Is there anyone I should be scared of?" she inquired through chattering teeth. "Aimee's bedroom is two doors down from Charles room. We have probably wakened the entire house at this time of night. Let's see if we can soothe some flustered, crabby people this morning," Lucian answered pacifying the situation. Slipping down to Aimee's room, Luke knocked softly on the door. The door opened slightly revealing a fully dressed and robed Aimee, saying she had just left a fully sedated Joseph in his sickroom.

Escorting Aimee' from her room, the little procession made their way down two doors to. Joseph's sickroom. Alex stepped past Aimee' to get a firsthand view of her uncle still sleeping under the watchful eye of his night duty nurse. Everything seemed right as rain with all house members. Lucian decided to check on his father, first in his bedroom, and if not there then down in his study. Finishing a more thorough check of the house, he returned to Alex in his bedroom. Lucian could not resist her obvious unrest. Deciding not to return to the apartment tonight again he drew Lex into his arms, laying back into the bed. "Where did all the blankets go?" he whispered in her ear. "I think I left them all on the floor when I got up after hearing your voice on the other side of the door," Lex whispered back. "Well, I have to get up again to lock the door, I will pick them up on my way back to the bed," he responded resolutely. Approaching the door, he heard noises in the hallway and sprung the door open quickly revealing two maids and one of the night duty nurses conversing just a single door down from Luke's bedroom. Apologizing for his abrupt manner, Luke closed and dead bolted his door. Joining Lex in bed again, he postponed his return to the Vieux Carre' indefinitely. It seemed like an eternity since she had left him to return to the big house, and he wanted to show her just how much he missed her. Reaching for her and pulling her back into his arms again he nuzzled her neck telling her how much he loved her. "It is already 1:00 a.m., so we cannot continue this loving all night long again. After all, I am a 36 year old man, though in good shape, I am not an 18 year old buck. "You're not, you could have fooled me!" Lex laughed light heartedly. "More compliments, more, more," he elicited "Surely you do not need any more self confidence? She inquired. "You are so daunting, so self assured, so fearless," Lex entreated. "Oh come on up here you wily wench!" Luke teased locking her beneath him. Luke kept checking his wristwatch so he would not be overexerting for the entire night or what was left of the night. They both needed sleep, no matter how much loving they got. Holding, squeezing, fondling, hugging, and kissing they interspersed their lovemaking until nearly 3:00 a.m. Holding Lex tight to his side, they both fell into a sound sleep.

The house started humming around 7:00 a.m. Luke registered the noise, but was lulled back into slumber land by the still soundly sleeping Lex in his arms. Laying back, he slept until man incessant knocking on his door tore into his groggy consciousness. Nudging Lex, they both unwillingly tried waking. "Shower, then dressed, then downstairs, ok?" Right!

"I have to inform Judson Briggs about where I am. I think I lost the security team guarding me in my rush to get back here. I think I have solved the mystery of the turning doorknob, and even the spooky noises and brattling sounds coming from the hallway," Lucian responded. It was just a couple of housemaids and one of Charles night nurses making that commotion you heard. It was probably one of the housemaids rattling the doorknob," Luke happily concluded. "There was no other person in the house last night according to any of the servants or family members in the house." Alex relaxed a little, but only a little. Some things just did not make any sense. Like, why did the feet come back a second tine to try the door again. And if it was a housemaid, why did she not call out to identify herself? That worried frown fixed on her face again. It did not escape Luke's notice. He was holding the telephone in his hand waiting for a response from Briggs. Lucian was explaining his rapid return to the mansion last night and the reason for it. Briggs did not really share in Luke's optimistic relief in last night's high jinks. Luke could hear the skepticism in Judson Briggs voice. "This morning we actually found one of your menservants lying dead on one of the backstreets here in the Garden District," he announced. "What! Who, Was he dressed for coming in or going home from work?" Luke inquired seriously. "Well, he was carrying his lunch box. I did not think you had any servants who brought their own lunches from home," Briggs answered. "We do have a couple of new men in the man servant area. Father added a couple of positions when all this nastiness started. His trusted friend, Charles Thorndyke is in a precarious state of health inspiring the need for the added staffing," Lucian answered. "Someone in your home knows about the added staffing," Briggs repeated thoughtfully. Is your brother privy to these changes, your sister, members of the staff, etc., etc, etc. Who knows of these security changes?" Briggs grilled. "Just about everyone in the house knows something about the changes, maybe not all of the changes, just what they need to know right now," Luke returned. Most only have part of the reason for the added security, some very little, others more because of their status and responsibilities in the family," he responded. "Father and I are the only ones who are fully briefed in all aspects of the security changes," Luke refuted the implied allegations. We need more information about all allegations. Briggs thought carefully rubbing his temples searching for answers. "Can you leave the house without being followed?" he inquired.

We have to assume our adversaries are now privy to the security corrections we have already made maybe if we just proceed as if nothing were wrong, it would throw them off temporarily so we could take them by surprise! "And maybe you can all be killed too! Murdered in your own beds!" Luke and Briggs answered themselves. "So what do we do?" Luke pleaded, "You are supposed to have all the answers." "Let me think. It looks like we may need another plan," Briggs resolved. I will recon fur with the Governor and the new drug task force. We will come up with something.," Briggs responded adamantly. "Wait, do not leave your compound yet. I will get you an answer and fill in the plan as fast as I can. Wait for my call!" he shot back. Luke immediately went to find his father and notify him of the death and change in plans. Then he went to find Lex. Luke found Lex and his Aunt Aimee' in Joseph Thorndyke's sickroom. Charles appeared to be having a good day. Aimee' and his day nurse, Anne Louise were conferring with Dr. Ingram about Joseph 'scare and condition. His treatment for the day and his seeming resilience. Alex and Aimee' set up some chess and checkers on a couple of tables near his bedside. A deck of cards and a cribbage board were set on the end table in front of the window. QUIET GAMES, NOT TOO EXCITING OR STRESSFUL as per the Doctor's orders. Luke checked in periodically to see what progress was being made and if there was any more news pertaining to last night's goings on. Charles had been too heavily sedated to hear or see anything. But Aimee' had heard something on her way into her room after leaving a sleeping Charles in his sickroom, but could not say what is was. "I thought I was Langley wandering around the corner up there "she said pointing down the hall to her right. "But I am not positive. It was the only odd thing I saw last night," Aimee' commented. "Langley was here in the hall? Before I got here around 11:30 or after? Lucian inquired. "It was definitely before that. Maybe an hour or two. It was not long after Alex returned to your room to shower and turn in," Aimee' answered thoughtfully. So, Why did Langley return to the house tonight. He has not slept at the house in days. Chalk that one up in his debit column. Could he have let someone even more sinister into the house? Who else is there that is not already in custody? Delacourt? Courtney? That's all there are isn't it? Lucian's mind was moving at warp speed now. Do we know who the main culprit really is? I find it hard to believe Charles and Courtney would have dreamt all of this up on their own. WHY? The mastermind must be someone else! WHO?

Alex and Lucian sat back in a funk. Had any of the three of them been caught in a compromising situation with any other person down here on the docks? Alex and Luke were trying to put their heads together to form a clearer picture. "I thought I spotted Langley at the airport when I got back from Briscombe Bay. I did not think about it too much, but he did appear to be waiting for someone to arrive in New Orleans. I wish I had been paying more attention! Out of the corner of my eye, I thought I saw him connect with a man in a camel coat, average height, average weight, average everything!" Luke said in disgust. "Well that is a place to start! A camel coat. A warm coat, a coat for a cooler climate. It is a place to start," Lex responded hopefully. "We do have a date, and all the plane arrivals, and their departures, "Lex was mumbling trying to connect the dots, but there were not enough dots to work with! "Maybe Briggs will be able to get us more information, flight manifests, security camera film, a name would be good," Lucian ruminated aloud. I have to know who it was that Langley met at the airport. Maybe I will recognize a name, or maybe Briggs will.

"Briggs wanted you here were you be protected. Father hired a couple of new man servants to keep you safe here. But one of them was murdered on his walk home last night. So it is very possible, a murderer was stalking through the house last night that in itself is hard to fathom," Luke responded deep in thought. "Let me call Judson, and give him everything we have. Maybe he can come up with something," he rambled on.

Lex ambled up the stairs, ready to pack up their things. Halfway up the front staircase she met Langley coming down. After hearing Aimee' say she thought she saw Langley hurrying down the far end of the hall late last night, Lex had that queasy feeling in the pit of her stomach, but Langley was her brother. She passed him a bit warily. Langley cheerfully greeted her with a "how do?' tipping an imaginary hat to her. Smiling briefly, she nearly ran up the rest of the stairs, in her undecided state. Whistling, Langley took the remaining steps two at a time on his way out the front door.

She packed up all of last evenings clothing waiting for Luke's return. Aimee' joined her in Luke's bedroom, unsettled over the issue of last night's romp by Langley. What was Alex thinking about that episode? She had no answers that she could give. Aimee' was just as stumped for an answer. Did you visit your Uncle. You look like you are taking off again. Let him know you are leaving and will be back again."

"Yes, I believe we are returning to the apartment. Lt. Briggs has been looking into a couple of areas Luke remembered on his return from Briscombe Bay, Washington. I believe the apartment security has been fully upgraded and should offer us adequate safety. I do not want to endanger anyone here in the big house, especially my Uncle Charles. He is still in a weakened condition. You, Jean-Claude, Lucinda, and even Langley are all still largely unprotected here. Though Jean-Claude has hired new security for the house in the form of man servants, brawny man servants. Unfortunately, one of those man servants was killed yesterday afternoon when he left work here. I think someone gained access to the house last night. It may be safer for all of you if we are not in this house. I will try to explain all of this to Uncle Charles before we head back," Alex clarified her position. "Aimee' was more than a little put off by a few of Alex' comments. An intruder? In the house, you say? There is nothing disturbed, no injuries here, no broken windows or locks. The doors are quite substantial. All the windows have also been fitted with burglar alarms. I believe we should be safe and secure in our beds now," Aimee' contradicted. "I am sure you are right, so can we head down to Charles room quickly, so I can get this task finished. I know Lucian will want to lend his assurances also," Alex responded.

Locking up the bedroom door, Alex and Aimee' strolled down the hall to Joseph's sickroom. Tapping softly, they entered Charles room quietly, checking to see if he was resting or fit to see them. They found him half sitting propped up against his pillows, his book slipping out of his fingers onto the bed covers. Rousing himself awake, he sat up taller turning to face them as they entered. "It is wonderful to see both of you here today What have you two been up to cause such guilty looks on your faces?" he inquired. "Nothing guilty, but we did have some news to discuss with you. Last night, did you hear Aimee" say she thought she saw Langley floating around the hallway? What if it was not Langley? How could anyone gain access to the house without notice? We have just been discussing the possibilities. I just wanted to let you know Lucian and I will probably head back to the apartment later this afternoon. I just wanted to check on you before I left. I will return again as soon as I can, I won't be abandoning you. This will be a short separation. Lucian will most likely be in before we leave tonight too, just to reassure you," Alex replied trying to keep him calm. Just then Lucian poked his head in the door to see what the commotion was in this supposed sick room," Lucian remarked in an upbeat manner. "How is everything going with you?" Lucian asked Josephs. Alex dropped back a little to slip her arm in Lucian's needing his supporting strength. "So you want to whisk my niece away to your den of iniquity?"he chuckled. What has she been telling you? Is she questioning my integrity? My morals, my veracity?. Such a sassy woman!" Luke responded mirthfully. Sealed with a wink, Luke clasped Charles hand again and pumped it. Laughter and chuckles erupted all around the room. It brought Jean-Claude inquisitively into the sickroom. "What is going on in here, this is a sickroom after all" he inquired, joining the light hearted banter of the band of merrymakers." "I needed to let you know. Alex and I will be heading back to our apartment this afternoon. Because of last night's intrigues and yesterdays mishaps, it is probably better for us to stay away from here temporarily. We just have to wait until things fall into place for Lt. Briggs. We will not be away long," Luke informed his family. They both settled back to undertake 1 or two of the card and board games scattered throughout the room.

Sneaking out of the very busy sick room quietly, Lucian an Alex lightly tread the sound cushioned floor out toward the staircase. Leaving the front entrance of the mansion in the Garden District, the couple jumped into the front seats of the beamer parked in the drive. Unknown to them, other antagonists were keeping watch on the mansion. Exiting the drive leisurely, Lucian was feeling very confident in his security measures provided by Lt. Briggs. "We can make a stop at the trade center for an hour or so before getting on to the apartment," Lucian surprised her. "Really? Lex inquired mischievously "Really!, We do have police escorts roaming around us front, back and on both sides of us. We are both perfectly safe," Luke answered. Reaching the edge of the Garden District limits, they were suddenly cut off and surrounded by four malevolent looking pick-ups. Stopping the beamer, Lucian raised both hands in a sign of surrender. Nudging Lex, and motioning her to do the same. The occupants of two side trucks jumped out of the vehicles, guns trained on the couple. Grabbing the door handles, the doors were yanked open and Lex and Luke pulled out of the beamer Both were stuffed into the back of the truck facing them, and hog-tied. Covered with a tarp, rapping on the side of the cab to take off. The pick-up immediately shifted into gear leading the escorts on a merry chase. Lex and Luke had both been completely surprised by this latest move. They wiggled and squirmed trying to release their ties. Those little plastic cuffs were impossible to get off! Lucian was working a small pen knife out of his pocket, if Lex could just get it open and cut his ties?

"The ride twisted and turned, occasionally a passing siren. The pick-up sped and lurched along sporadically. Lucian was trying decipher some landmarks ass they sped away. A set of train tracks, The sound of a jet engine, a bridge? It was hard to feel the direction of the turns when you being thrown from side to side with each and every turn. Lex latched onto a side under wall and held tight. Luke tried to catch something to hold him fast, but missed any protrusion. Calling out to Lex, he attempted to wedge himself between an unidentified heavy object and the wall of pick-up. Getting tossed from side to side in the bed of a pick-up truck was a bruising experience. Lex asked if could tell where they were by the erratic movements made by the driver. Trying to articulate her question through the tape covering her mouth, made it an unintelligible mouthful. Behind his own taped mouth, Lucian made grunting and other sounds trying to bring her attention to the small penknife in his front pocket. Grunts, nods, hip rises, and every other kind of non-verbal communication.

More than an hour passed before the truck started slowing on what sounded like a gravel road. It rocked to a stop. The pair were unceremoniously dumped on the ground. The bags were removed from their heads, and the tape ripped off their mouths. Seeing the light of day finally, they were stunned by the brightness of the afternoon sun. Luke's eyes adjusted faster than Lex's, He identified Charles, and Courtney, then surprisingly Langley, and one other unidentified man driving a Suburban. Charles stepped forward and cut Luke's bindings. Langley came forward at the same time and cut Alex's bindings. straightening his legs, Luke tried to work the blood back into his limbs. Alex pushed her legs out in front of her working legs, her wrists, and her elbows to get the circulation flowing again. Alex attempted to stand but her legs gave out on her and she landed back on her bottom amid howling laughter among their adversaries. The lethal look she received from Courtney made her realize how serious their situation really was. It was a wicked look and then Alex saw the gun. It was an automatic. It looked sort of like a rifle, but she was unversed in firearms, so she was not exactly sure. Luke was moving in front of her, shielding her. "Move over there, inside the warehouse!" The man in the suburban snarled. "So you are the head of this cartel? What is your name, and where do you come from?" Lucian quizzed him. "Don't you recognize me? Charles and I have known each other since college. We have put together more profitable ventures in recent years, but you wound me sir. Take a good look. Are you sure you don't recognize me?" Pulling Alex to her feet, another adversary gave her a shove and another gave Lucian a shove. Stumbling Alex nearly fell to her face on the dirt packed roadway, with a smirk delivered by her masked assailant. Lucian, on the other hand recognized the smirk as one he had heard before. He knew Alex was in real trouble now, but who was this guy he was supposed to recognize? He tried signaling Lex to be careful when dealing with all of these antagonists. He recognized Courtney as one of them, one particularly opposed to Alex Thorndyke Devereaux. Luke was being shoved forward into the cavernous stowage.

A gun butt clipped him just above his ear and he slumped to his knees. Alex muffled a scream wanting to get back to Luke, but forced to keep moving.

Several squad cars circled the abandoned BMW, taking the owners ID from the glove box. Reading the name typed on the owner's line, they put in a call to Lt. Briggs. Briggs arrived at the scene within minutes. He wanted to know how this could have happened. Where was the security detail? How long were they out of sight? Soon the welcomed the arrival of the FBI. John Wager introduced himself as the Bureau chief for the New Orleans office of the FBI. "What has been going on here, Lt.," he inquired accusatorily. "I could ask you the same thing Agent Wagner. How is the FBI involved in a simple abduction?" Briggs retorted. "I believe our operations may have crossed each other, here. We have an undercover agent infiltrating a drug smuggling operation down here." "We have a pair of witnesses in protective custody that have disappeared, I am trying to understand how they could have disappeared inside the security derail?" Briggs recriminated. "Your witnesses may be in the same company as our missing undercover agent. Who are your missing witnesses?" Wagner inquired. Our missing couple are Lucian Devereaux and his new bride, Alexis Thorndyke Devereaux," Briggs worriedly spat back.

Our undercover agent is Langley Devereaux, a new graduate of the Academy at Langley. It seems it is all in the family!" Wagner responded in a conciliatory tone. "No wonder Lucian has been so suspicious of his younger brother in the past months," Briggs responded almost apologetically. "Do you have any way to track Langley at all? Maybe we could track our missing witnesses through Langley?" Briggs inquired. "Langley has been wearing a GPS tracking locator in his shoe to avoid detection," Wagner continued. Calling on his second in command, he asked for coordinates indicated by Langley Devereaux's GPS locator. "The locator is reading down here in the dock area only a few block away!" was the answer.

"We can all leave from here, but we do have to proceed carefully from here. We do not want our perps knocking off the witnesses or our new agent prematurely. Let's get to the scene and scope it out right away!" Briggs shouted back. Briggs and his men pulled in behind Wagner and his FBI associates. They were tracking Langley's GPS signal, and Briggs and his men were close on their tails.

The signal was leading down through the Vieux Carre', then down through to the docks. Not directly to the water, but leading into the warehouse sites. It was warehouse after warehouse, that lay before them. Briggs officers went into search mode, quietly racing to one warehouse after another. One warehouse after another was cleared in their search for the missing hostages. At the far end of this site were parked pick-ups, SUV's, even a new Chevy Suburban. License numbers were quickly gathered and matched names to faces on the driver's license. The name of Lucian's nemesis turned out to be Tristan Brooks, from Boston Massachusetts. He was a new investor and owner in an upscale restaurant on New Orleans west side. It was rumored to be a gambling operation as well. They began moving more quickly down to the other end of the lot. After inspecting the intervening warehouses, they began to hear sounds and blows coming from an approaching warehouse. Briggs and his men went into rescue mode backed up by the FBI team. Briggs and his second in command entered gaping open door leading into the dark center of the warehouse surrounded by aisle after aisle of stacked product. The bags, or many of them were stamped SUGAR. Briggs deployed the rest of his men to the back of the warehouse. They took several minutes assessing the situation and looking for the hostages. Sneaking further back into the warehouse they heard loud voices, then a gunshot. The gunshot kicked the team into high gear, and they moved at the ready in the direction of the shot. The joint operation of the State Police and the FBI was a large operation. It netted the arrest of the last instigators and those that provoked a drug induced world. The officers and agents had an acute interest in Tristan Brooks. Who was this Tristan Brooks? He was the only unknown factor in this group of malefactors. Mr. Brooks was a graduate of Charles Delacourt's alumni. Also Lucian's Old Alma Mater. So it is someone Lucian should remember, Briggs thought. But it has been almost twenty years, and people change. Did Lucian recognize him at all? Not so far, at least. Not that I can detect. Lucian is unconscious on the floor, where is Alex? Then began the frantic search. Lucian has been injured and was rendered unconscious, while Alex has gone missing. Courtney was here and is angry.

Taking the four of the biggest drug lords into custody, and packing them off to the State Patrol Precinct Headquarters. Briggs and his FBI protégé Wagner continued even further into the warehouse. Searching for another 25 or 30 feet, they finally came across Lucian's still body. They turned Luke's body to his side and checked his vitals. He was still alive, so they for an ambulance. Throwing a blanket over prone Lucian, they left an officer with Luke and moved on. They examined every aisle and the contents listed on each bag piled high in the warehouse. It took what Briggs thought to be forever before an officer shouted out he had found Alex. Alex also lay prone on the warehouse floor, but checking her vitals found she was merely unconscious. Alex was bruised, but did not appear to be hurt too much, why was she out so long? With all the jostling, Alex refused to be roused. Is she shot, poisoned, anything? Briggs shouted, calling for a second ambulance to transport both newlyweds to the hospital Wagner and his men were examining the contents of each bag in the warehouse. They were also field testing the contents of each bag in the warehouse.

Wagner was triumphantly bragging about taking down millions in cocaine. Brigg's was putting a call through to the Governor, updating him on the latest information involving the new Mr. and Mrs. Devereaux. Lucian was on his way to the hospital with Alex close behind him. Alex was subjected to an immediate CAT Scan, along with physical examinations to ascertain her well-being. Lucian on the other hand was discovered to have a bullet wound. The bullet was extracted and Lucian sent to a recovery room. He woke three hours later screaming for Alex. Forced to lie back by the male nurse at his bedside, Luke returned to his resting position.

Alex was slowly coming around face-to-face with the person in her mirror. "You are looking so much better this afternoon, Mrs. Devereaux. How are you feeling now? Still a bit groggy? Your CAT Scan looked pretty good. No permanent damage, just a hard knock to the head. Painful, but not debilitating, atleast not totally. Your husband has been through surgery and is now in recovery. He has been calling for you, so you can see him as soon as you are ready to get there. "How do I get there?" she demanded. "Can you stand on your own or do we use the old stand-bye. A wheelchair is on its way, and I will get you to his room" the candy striper explained with a bathetic expression covering her face. Alex just wanted to make sure Luke still lived. She was not sure after the beating they both took and the shot she heard.

The candy-striper bundled Lex up, led her to the wheelchair provided by the hospital and took her out of her emergency care room also provided by the hospital. They made a quick left turn then steered for the elevator. Going up two flight they arrived at the acute- care- unit for post surgical patients. Watching the room numbers go by, Lex tried to read the candy-stripers face if they were nearing their destination. Bringing the wheelchair around they entered Room 0312. Lucian was agitated, but looked in reasonably better health than the last time Lex had seen him. He was patched up, and the color had returned to his face. He looks much better since surgery, the candy striper commented. "You're right, he does look good!" Lex told her. "Lex, how are you, I worried so much when they told me they could not wake you," Luke gently took her hand folding his own over hers. "My CAT Scan showed I took a harder hit than I thought I did," Lex told him. "I will be filling a room here in the hospital for a night or two, also" she answered. "Do you think we can share a room?" Luke asked the candy-striper. "I believe the hospital is already trying to make that arrangement. Mrs. Devereaux does not yet have a room assigned for her stay here" was the answer. A nurse entered the room then bringing more news of their coming stay at the hospital. "I just came in to ask if you wish to share this room, or we do have a larger suite down the hall?" the nurse inquired. Briggs and Wagner invaded the room then with vital news. "Mr. Tristan Brooks and Ms. Courtney Anderson have escaped our custody!" they blurted out simultaneously "We are blanketing the entire area around your apartment, Mr. Brooks's restaurant, even this hospital," Briggs explained. "How could they have gotten away?" Luke wanted to know. "Apparently one of their henchmen was inadvertly released from the State Patrol custody yesterday, and managed to corral one the cars delivering the two suspects. The driver sustained minor injuries but was otherwise not hurt. A dragnet has been launched all around the city, but so far they have escaped capture," Wagner continued. "Have you checked out the hotel Delacourt manages, or Courtney's apartment, or even the many levels of Brooks holdings?" Lucian insisted. "We have guards on all the homes, apartments and businesses, but so far nothing.," Briggs explained. The Lieutenant and the agent sat down with their never-ending cups of coffee to take stock of the situation and regroup. "Let's roust the men and wake them up a bit," Briggs told Wagner, standing to leave.

With Briggs and Wagner exiting their room, they were energized to re-examine areas they thought were already cleared. Possibilities presented themselves at every turn. The FBI canvassed Brooks holdings, then were on their way to Courtney's apartment. Two hours into the operation, the reports were all negative. Briggs men were taking on Delacourt's hotel and home. Tristan Brooks and Courtney Anderson still in the company of their rogue cohort released from the district hoose gow. The patrol officers were not so difficult to break away from. Their first choice was to reach Brooks restaurant and other holdings, but changed their minds at the police presence barricades. Next, they turned to Courtney's address, only to find a similar situation around her residence too. "Where to from here?" she asked Tristan. "All we have left is Delacourt's place and the hotel downtown. Shall we eliminate them one -by-one, or... ? Brooks was inquiring. Courtney cut him off, "Charles installed some fancier suites in the sublevel of the hotel. And I have the key to a side door leading to an elevator that will get us there," she said proudly. "Let's get there. Which side street?" Brooks said losing what little patience he had left. "It is on Dauphine Street a couple of blocks from St. Anne's Street coming up here next,"

Courtney was elucidated. We have a couple of suspicious vehicles circling around here, too. They could be unmarked cruisers. Or Fed cars. We wait till the last one goes around the corner, then we make our way back to the hotel. We just need a few minutes to plan our next moves. We'll leave the tuck on the next street over and walk back. With that the driver dropped them off Dauphine Street near the employees only side entrance. "I will come back and let you in, in 15 minutes," Courtney told their rescuer.

Lucian and Alex were beginning to feel safe again, temporarily at least. Taking advantage of the lull in activities, they fell into deep sleep with the nurses monitoring their sleep. Other than the temperature and blood pressure checks, and injections for Lucian, they had great rest. The nurses drew the blinds in the room, darkening the room for them. The nurses left the room as quietly as they had come in.

As Tristan and Courtney relaxed in the suite, put their legs up, and poured a couple of stiff drinks, Tristan's mind was racing along. "You know that hospital they took our two informants to, is not far from here We could maybe get inside the hospital rooms and eliminate our problems in one fell swoop," he ruminated. "Do you think we should take that chance?" Courtney half heartedly inquired. She wanted one more chance at Alex Devereaux anyway!

Luke and Lex slept blissfully for a full seven hours, and woke feeling refreshed and much better, almost normal considering the recent mishaps in their lives. A new shift of nurses were there to greet them. The beds were not placed side-by-side like in a regular hospital room but foot-to head. They could see each other and talk to each other easily, without physical stress or discomfort. "You still seem wiped out, are you sure you are all right?" he asked. "I do feel as bit flagged out, but I guess the bonk on the head was harder than I thought. Why is Courtney so angry with me? It's not that I came here t make her lose her job or anything. I did not even know her or her position in the company?" Lex asked quizzically. The nurses were reappearing again. Another set of blood pressure tests, more thermometers, and for Luke another injection, and more pills. Alex was then taken down for another CAT Scan. Bringing Lex back to the hospital room, her evening nurse announced that the evening meal had been held and would be available to them as soon as they were ready. We will just pop them into the microwave to heat them up. Hearing that last part, Luke sat up saying he was ready.

Getting Lex back into her bed, the nurses raised both heads of the beds getting them ready to eat some dinner. Facing each other again, Lucian inquired how her tests went. "The tests went really well, and he showed define improvement," she answered. Dinner arrived, and was placed on their trays. Luke looked at his tray with disgust. "What is this stuff? It looks like baby food!" "You just left surgery not long ago' and this is the dinner for surgical patients," his nurse returned. Lex almost liked her selection of foods, A medium Chicken Caesar salad, with a glass of cranberry juice, and a small bowl of fruit. She started eating her dinner, daring Lucian to try his own.

Finishing their dinners, Lex felt refreshed, while Luke felt not sated but appeased. Asking Luke if he felt completely safe here in the hospital with Tristan and Courtney still on the loose. "I am sure Briggs and Agent Wagner have back up here at the hospital 24/7."'I guess I wonder if they can really protect us" she pondered. "The hospital is not that far from Courtney's apartment, Charles home, or even this Tristan Brooks's businesses and holdings," she answered. "I really think we will be quite safe here for the time being.," Lucian responded. "But considering what happened this morning, it would be a good idea to have a back-up plan beforehand," Luke answered. "Should I be scouting out our immediate vicinity?"Lex inquired. "I know I am a little under the weather, but I can gather your information to analyze., he said. I will go out and take a look around, and I will come back to report in a few minutes," Lex told him. "Look for exit doors., especially unsecured doors, windows, balconies, everything that looks unusual. But do not take any chances, get back here as soon as you can. We will have to make secondary plans, just in case our first plans do not work. If Courtney and Tristan do get into the hospital, we have to have all the escape routes identified. When you get back, we will sketch out possible escape routes out of the hospital," Luke remarked. With that Alex hurried out of the room, after slipping on her bath robe. Moving quickly up and down the hall, stopping occasionally to inspect anything unusual. She noted all exit and staircases moving through the hallways. There were many connecting hallways in the hospital and it did take long before she was completely turned around.

She was so turned around, she had to stop at the nearest nurse's station to get directions back to her own room. A nurse volunteered to walk with her part of the way back, then give her directions for the rest of the way. Lex was exhausted by the time she made it back to her room, but not so exhausted she did not notice some unusual things. Like masking tape placed over the locking mechanisms of four doors leading up from street level entrances. As she walked by each door, she pulled off the tape making sure the doors locked. When she finally walked back into her room, Luke was clearly unnerved, his body shuddered as he reached out for and pulled her close. At this point Lex explained all she had seen, how she had gotten lost. The tape she had removed from the four doors leading up from the street level and pulled them closed checking to make sure they were indeed locked.

"I do not know who would have or why the locks were taped open, but I am glad you did what you did. Though that's not to say there are no other doors taped open in the hospital. The hospital is very large, as you just found out in your rambling investigation It is not to say you found all of the taped doors. I think we should move rooms just to increase our rate of survival. It will give us a cushion of time," Luke answered, keeping the rest of his thoughts to himself. Lex tossed her cotton bathrobe over the chair at the end of the bed, and was climbing into bed. "No, No, don't do that. Call the nurse in here and tell her we need to change rooms," Luke told her. Then you might be able t a good night's sleep. Negotiations with the nursing staff gave them access to another room with numbers that seemed transposed. But they got a room at the end of the third corridor over. Moving all of their clothing, shoes, etc. the nurses loaded them into a pair of wheelchairs, they trundled off to a new room The new room took a series left and right turns until they arrived at the new room. The new room was comfortable, but more importantly it offered an extra margin of safety. "Now this room will not show up on any transfer medical charts, will it?" Luke was asking. "Considering your special circumstances, only the three shift nurses are aware of the room change. Only the shift nurses keep track of your whereabouts to keep your medications in order. Of course it does cause a bit of inconvenience to take blood pressure, temperature, and other vital statistics. Often, the nurses will be caring for you in this room last, because of its distance from the other rooms in the unit. I hope that does not inconvenience you, you should be getting out of here in a matter of days anyway. We have all sworn ourselves to secrecy, the word is mum! AND IN A DRAMATIC MOVE PUT A FINGER TO HER LIPS AND SLICED HER THROAT! You will be able to get a good night's sleep here," she explained. After finishing their vital statistics and medications, the nurse made her way to the door and lowered the lights. In the darkened room Lucian extended his hand in search for hers. "What do you think about our situation now? She queried. "I think we may be a bit safer than we were, but not entirely out of the woods yet. Courtney and Tristan both knew the name of the hospital they were taking us to. There are too many entrance doors in this hospital, Briggs and Wagner cannot keep them out entirely. Briggs and Wagner's men could split the difference in surveillance, but they cannot be watching every single minute, hence we take our own precautions. "I know you are exhausted, why don't you take the first two hour sleep. Then I will wake you to take my two hour sleep. We will continue this way all night, so we both get some sleep while the other keeps watch," Luke theorized. "All right, if you are sure you will make it?" she quizzed. "I am all right, stop wasting time, and get to sleep now," he urged. Needing no further encouragement, Alex dropped off into a fitful sleep, but sleep none the less. For Lex her two hour sleep went by in seconds instead of minutes, to Luke time just could not go fast enough. Groggily, Alex sat up, shook herself up sternly and encouraged Luke to get some sleep. It was past midnight now and Alex knew she had to get up and move around a bit or she would fall back to sleep. At two hours, she woke Luke again, and nodded off again for another two hours sleep.

Luke was beginning to feel better after surgery and some sleep. A nurse appeared in the room then to check his vitals and remove his IV. He was feeling more adventurous and through on his own cotton hospital bathrobe and ventured into the hall. Once in the hall, he looked left then right and proceeded to his right until the end of the hall. He was feeling all in after his brief excursion into the hall. Just then he caught a brief glimpse of Courtney entering the corridor at the other end of the hall and backed himself into a nurse's station out of sight. He tried to keep an eye on Courtney as she walked down one hall and entered another. At least she's moving away from us, he thought. He tried to follow inconspicuously, stepping into available alcoves as needed. Courtney was ambling around peeking in doors, and was even confronted by a nurse for visiting after hours. She apologized and feigned looking for the elevator to leave the hospital. But she had no intention of leaving the hospital without finding were the Devereaux' were hiding. She slid into a recess on the other side of the elevator doors were soda and juice machines were lined up. Waiting for a clear escape to present itself, slinking out of her shadowy recess she quickly moved along the hall toward him. Luke turned abruptly facing, surprisingly his old room. He ducked inside, looking for a place to hide. There are not many places to hide in a hospital room, except of course the bathroom or closets. He opened the closet door and rejected the small space. He went on to the bathroom, checked out the facilities. He noticed the shower. It was located behind a brick wall with a shower curtain. Well the brick wall would hide him if she only looked in. But then Courtney never did do anything haphazardly. Luke looked at his watch, noting it was past time to wake Alex. With Alex still sleeping soundly at the end of the hall one corridor over, she was a sitting duck for a vengeful Courtney. Luke had already searched for his cell phone only to discover he had left it in his room with a sleeping Alex. With that he heard the door to the hospital room door open. He listened intently for hushed footsteps on the carpet. He heard the click of closet doors being opened and closed. Then he heard the thump of her knees dropping to the floor. What was she doing, checking under the bed? Luke thought. Then the door handle of the bathroom started to turn. He waited silently, barely drawing a breadth. He pushed himself back further into the corner of the shower behind the brick wall. A hand reached in and flicked on the light. A head showed itself as it looked in. Seeing nothing, she backed herself out, closing the door silently behind her. Luke exhaled a breath he had not even realized he held. He waited until Courtney moved farther down the hall, before opening the door. Lucian had seen the fingers opening his bathroom door, but more importantly he had seen the gun she held in her other hand. He thought he could take her, but then where was Tristan? Gathering his thoughts and deciding the better part of valor...," his thoughts trailed off. Getting to the door of this original room, he cracked the door open just enough to peek out. He observed Courtney skulking back down the hall. She was trying to avoid detection by the nursing staff, as she encountered Tristan leaving the third corridor on this floor. Now they were preparing to follow this hallway back to Lex' room. Looking down at the watch on his wrist, he saw it was past time to wake her up. Now he had to devise a way to get past his two nemesis just up ahead of him, and then get Lex out of their room. Using the nursing staff to his advantage, He shadowed a pair of nurses making their 4 a.m. rounds. All their futzing around was bound to bring Lex around, at least partially. Lucian moved furtively as the nurses left the room, hurriedly making his way to Lex' hospital bed shaking her slightly to wake her fully. Whispering, he apprised her of the situation and extolled her to dress quickly. Moving quickly, they threw on some clothes and slipped out of the room and into a utility closet on the other side of the door. Just as they entered the utility closet, they heard the hospital room door reopen again. Instinctively, Lucian locked the utility room door. Luke and Lex hid behind the extra hospital supplies. Not too many moments later the door handle to the utility closet turned. The door was holding, but they hung back just to be safe. The handle turned again and still held, forcing their enemies to force the door open and bring attention to themselves or to move on. Their footsteps were heard trailing off down the hall. "If Briggs men and agent Wagner's men running surveillance on the hospital and the suspect's homes and businesses, why hadn't they intercepted these two on the way in?" Luke thought out loud. "I am going to give Judson Briggs a call to let him know our suspects have been prowling around the hospital tonight. It is a good thing I was up prowling around myself and caught a glimpse of Courtney sneaking around our old room here in the hospital. I used some of the nurses following their routines to make my way back here to spring you. But I had an interesting moment or two in our old room, I had to hide in our old bathroom in the shower! But besides, seeing her hand snake in pushing the door open, I saw the gun in her other hand," Luke replied. Making the call to Lieutenant Briggs, Luke made his revelations known to the proper authorities, requesting a pick up the suspects. He hoped they could be arrested leaving the hospital this morning.

"I hope they are caught leaving the hospital. They are two devious and calculating adversaries. Dangerous, too," Alex commented. "Very dangerous and ruthless, too," Luke ruminated. "Can we get out of this storage closet now?" she inquired. Luke unlocked the door just as the head nurse arrived with her key to the closet. Luke and Lex, totally chagrined, slunk back to their room. Arriving back in their room, they were shortly followed by Judson Briggs and then Agent Wagner. Luke recounted his overnight adventures and strolls into the halls to stay awake and then evade detection by Courtney Anderson.

"Anderson came right in this hospital undetected?" Wagner demanded. "Yes she did, and she was armed too!" Luke shot back. "Not just Courtney Anderson, but also Tristan Brooks roaming around the halls of this hospital, too. I saw the gun in Courtney's hand and I am positive Tristan had one too. I saw him at the end of this hall right here, this close to a sleeping Alex!" Luke's voice rose n his anxiety over the threat to his bride's wellbeing. "I never thought they would be so brazen!" Judson Briggs whistled through his teeth. "You are sure they were both here? They have to be hiding out close to this hospital. They are not in Courtney Anderson's apartment, nor in Delecourt's home. Agent Wagner's men are still going through Tristan Brooks holdings. Is it possible there are secret suites in the hotel in the French Quarter? I have heard a few rumors, not much else. "I really do not know about hidden suites in the hotel, but I do remember processing some very expensive remodeling invoices for the hotel recently," Luke reported rubbing his chin. I looked over the invoices quite thoroughly, and with some of the design notes the additions may be in the basement of the hotel. Maybe two or three sub floors under the hotel," explained Luke. "How do we get in this sub floor hideaway? We found nothing at the main desk in the lobby of the Hotel" Agent Wagner queried? "I looked over a portion of the plans that accompanied the bills and invoices for the remodeling expenses, I believe the entrance will be found on the south street of the hotel. In the center of the street, if my memory serves me," he expanded. "I am stationing my men around this hospital day and night until the escapees are back in our custody," Lt. Briggs was assuring them. "I will be stopping back at your offices to pick up a copy of that invoice and those attached plans and drawings. Then I will accompany my men in a search of each sub floor space. Just how many separate spaces are diagramed in those plans and drawings?" Wagner asked bluntly. "My memory tells me there are a total of six separate suites on each sub floor," Luke responded. Briggs and Wagner left to pursue their appointed duties. Alex and Luke settled back into their beds to sleep and heal, now that they could be safe, or could they? With the appearance of the nurse attached to his unit reporting to his bell summons, Luke requested a more frequent check of himself and Lex while they attempted to sleep. He also informed them of last night's adventures. The nurses were more than a little shocked by last night's shenanigans going on right under their noses. So instead of sleeping in their room, they were transferred to the prison ward one floor up. Now they could finally sleep!

CHAPTER TWENTY-ONE

When they woke up the next morning, the nurses already had the television screens turned on to the local news. The screen was filled with arrests in a joint operation by Louisiana State Police and the local FBI office. And right there was Judson Briggs ushering numbers of handcuffed miscreants into waiting police vans. Agent Wagner was announcing the arrests of a number gang members belonging to a gang called the Gotten Boys. These gang members not only terrorized local inhabitants, but spread drugs across the country. In the background, some familiar faces came on the screen. Courtney Anderson and Tristan Brooks were being led handcuffed out of the hotel.

For a wild few minutes there was rejoicing in that hospital prison ward. The nurses shared in their jubilation. A hearty breakfast was served, to Alex at least, Luke was still on his post surgical diet. He was not thrilled with his breakfast, but the bland food was nourishing if not tasty. By afternoon, early evening really, Briggs and Wagner were back to fill them in on the arrests Luke's information had made possible. It turned out to be a feather in both their caps, and both were expecting promotions in their careers. So all around it was a joyful encounter.

Lucian was released by the hospital the next afternoon. Lucian and Alex drove to their apartment In true peace and quiet. This was something of a letdown after their frantic weeks before and after the wedding. Now they had time to really get to know each other.

EPILOGUE

When Lucian and Alexis were released from the hospital they learned even more news. Langley was a secret FBI undercover officer sent to infiltrate the drug operation in the Port of New Orleans. His sneaky ways that had raised Lucian's dander were just his attempts to keep his cover through the end of the operation. Langley and Jean-Claude joined them at precinct headquarters after the newlyweds quiet return to the private apartment in the French Quarter. His mind relieved, Lucian embraced his younger brother, entreating for more forthcoming information on when he had had the time you complete FBI training at Quantico. Questions flew back and forth until all were answered. Lucian embraced his younger brother and both were embraced by a smiling Jan-Claude. "It is so good to see you two reconciled again," he gushed. Returning to the mansion, Aimee' greeted them on their arrival. "I have even more information for you, something that I believe you have been asking yourself Alex," Aimee' retorted. "It is that question you asked about a brother, remember? Well not even Jean-Claude is fully aware of this. That baby boy your mother gave up before you were born was adopted by a prominent family here in New Orleans. The woman was Marguerite Devereaux. After the loss of her child she was at a loss. She saw Judd Conklin, Jr. at the foundling home I visited weekly. She had to have that little boy so much like the little boy she had just lost, I kept that information to myself. That little boy is now Langley Allan Devereaux! So Langley is that adopted brother to Lucian, and the half-brother to Alex. So Langley is also the thread that joins the family together," Aimee' announced. SURPRISE!